The **VIRGIN** *of*
SOLITUDE

Middle East Literature in Translation

Michael Beard and Adnan Haydar, *Series Editors*

The VIRGIN of SOLITUDE

A NOVEL

◆ ◆ ◆

Taghi Modarressi

Translated from the Persian by Nasrin Rahimieh

SYRACUSE UNIVERSITY PRESS

Fic
Modarressi

English translation copyright © 2008 by Syracuse University Press
Syracuse, New York 13244-5160
All Rights Reserved

First Edition 2008
08 09 10 11 12 13   6 5 4 3 2 1

Originally written in Persian with the title *Azraye khalvatneshin*.

The paper used in this publication meets the minimum requirements of
American National Standard for Information Sciences—Permanence of
Paper for Printed Library Materials, ANSI Z39.48–1984.∞™

For a listing of books published and distributed by Syracuse University Press,
visit our Web site at SyracuseUniversityPress.syr.edu

ISBN-13: 978-0-8156-0933-9
ISBN-10: 0-8156-0933-7

Library of Congress Cataloging-in-Publication Data
Modarressi, Taghi.
['Azra-yi khalvat'nishin. English]
The virgin of solitude : a novel / Taghi Modarressi ; translated from the Persian
by Nasrin Rahimieh. —1st ed.
p. cm.—(Middle East literature in translation)
ISBN 978-0-8156-0933-9 (alk. paper)
I. Rahimieh, Nasrin. II. Title.
PK6561.M74A9713 2008
891'.5533—dc22
2008034027

Manufactured in the United States of America

◆ ◆ ◆

For Anne, who made it all possible

Born and educated as a physician in Iran, **Taghi Modarressi** won a literary prize for his first novel *Yakolia and Her Loneliness*. He continued his education in the United States and became a member of the Department of Psychiatry of the University of Maryland School of Medicine and director of the Center for Infant Study. He pursued his writing in Persian and translated two of his novels into English, *The Book of Absent People* and *The Pilgrim's Rules of Etiquette*. He lived in Baltimore with his wife, novelist Anne Tyler, and their two daughters until his death from lymphoma in 1997.

Nasrin Rahimieh is Maseeh Chair and director of the Dr. Samuel M. Jordan Center for Persian Studies and Culture at the University of California, Irvine, where she is also professor of comparative literature.

CONTENTS

TRANSLATOR'S PREFACE

The best literary translators, I have always thought, are those whose names we note hastily as we turn the page to begin reading a work of fiction. They fade into the background to let the writer speak to us in another language with apparent effortlessness. This preface contravenes my preference as a reader of translated texts in part because ideally in this case the author would have acted as his own translator. When after a hiatus of twenty-five years Taghi Modarressi resumed writing fiction in the 1980s, he translated his own novels from Persian to English. My intrusive presence here would not have been necessary had Modarressi lived to complete the translation of his last novel, *Azraye khalvatneshin (The Virgin of Solitude)*, but his untimely death in 1997 shortly after he had finished writing this novel gave me the bittersweet gift of becoming his translator.

Long before I took on the translation, I had the privilege of getting to know Modarressi's work, his views on the position of the immigrant writer, and his approach to translating his fiction. The English translations he did of his own novels were not accompanied with glossaries, footnotes, or introductions to his concept of "writing with an accent." My translation of *The Virgin of Solitude* follows Modarressi's own practice and is shaped by my understanding of his insights into his art.

Instead of reviewing the particulars of Modarressi's biography, which can be readily accessed in the on-line version of *The Encyclopaedia Iranica* (http://www.iranica.com/newsite/), I devote this preface to shedding light on the spirit that informed his writing and what he imparted to me in the course of our decade-long dialogue.

This preface is also an homage to the man who taught me how to look for lightness and mirth in the depths of alienation and exile. To Taghi Modarressi I owe my recovery from a profound sense of loss I mistakenly equated with being a transplanted Iranian. He enabled me to see the unfathomable depths of estrangement that frequently predate the experience of migration. In the course of our conversations, in letters, on the phone, and in person, Taghi showed me the path out of what appeared to be a forbidding underworld. The light he shone for me transformed frightening shadows into intelligible and occasionally likeable images.

I had known Taghi Modarressi for ten years when he succumbed to cancer in 1997. He had already begun translating the Persian text of *The Virgin of Solitude* into English, but his illness did not give him a chance to get beyond a few pages of the first chapter. At a time when I was lost in grief, Anne Tyler, his wife, came to my rescue with the proposal that I translate the novel into English. This invaluable gift reconnected me to Taghi's voice and assuaged the pain of loss. I had not anticipated that translating would become the work of grieving, reimmersing me in the creative vision that had encouraged me to delve deeper into the unsettling aspects of exile.

Translating the novel put me closely in touch with the unique blend of psychological anguish and humor that marks Modarressi's representation of the distances that separate languages and cultures. My experience became even more enriching because I had the benefit of having my work overseen by Anne Tyler. Her careful reading, editorial suggestions, and guidance taught me how to burrow into the characters' minds and hear them speak. We worked together on each chapter, and more than once when she read aloud from the translation, we dissolved into giggles. For me, those moments resonated with memories of conversations with Taghi, his endearing laughter, and the path that led me to his work.

My first encounter with Modarressi's fiction was in the spring of 1986, when I was working on a doctoral dissertation in comparative literature in Canada and I came across a review of his novel *The Book of Absent People* in a Canadian daily. The review did not mention if the novel was translated from Persian or was originally written in English. Because of my interest in immigrant writers, I was intrigued by the novel and could not wait to read it. When I got my hands on a copy, I was amazed at its language. I could not read the sentences in English without immediately thinking of their equivalents in Persian. Throughout the novel, I found literal translations of Persian idiomatic expressions that made me smile with recognition. Phrases such as "In which grave were you lost since this afternoon?" (Modarressi 1986, 74), "What glory have you brought us that no one dares to say there are eyebrows over your eyes?" (91), and "In Paris, if you hit any dog on the head a hundred painters will fall off" (116) were compelling reminders that the characters who spoke these words had emerged from a linguistic and cultural sphere very different from the one in which I now found myself.

The ease with which I sank into the language of *The Book of Absent People* made me wonder how readers unfamiliar with Persian would experience the novel and what had motivated the writer to present them with an English text so interlaced with patterns of Persian idiom. This style was particularly remarkable because in the wake of the Iranian Revolution and the hostage crisis, many Iranians living in the United States were at pains to conceal their heritage, fearing discrimination and hostility.

My curiosity led me to write the author via his publisher. Months after I had sent off my letter, I received a reply from Modarressi in which he described the maze through which my letter had made its way to him. This communication initiated an exchange of letters in which he answered my questions and clarified for me that he wrote his fiction in Persian and then translated it into English, relying on his own accented voice. He had arrived at his personal philosophy through a discovery of a new voice as an immigrant writer.

Modarressi's first novel, *Yakolia and Her Loneliness,* was published in Iran in 1953 when he was a twenty-four-year-old medical student at Tehran University. After he left Iran in 1959 to continue his studies in the United States, he wrote one other novel, *Sharif Jan, Sharif Jan,* in 1961. His professional work as a psychiatrist and his new life took him in new directions, however, and it was not until 1986 that his next novel, *The Book of Absent People,* was published in Iran and the United States. It was followed by *The Pilgrim's Rules of Etiquette* in 1989.

Modarressi attributed his return to writing to the arrival of Iranians in the United States in the wake of the revolution. In his essay "Writing with an Accent," he describes how finding himself surrounded by newly arrived Iranians and listening to their conversations excited his senses:

"The excitement was almost unbearable. My feelings were so intense that I began to wake up every morning between four and five A.M., at which time I would drive to my office and work on a story that was actually an invented memoir" (Modarressi 1992, 8). As he points out in this same essay, the urge and the need to write were inextricably bound to the cadences of Persian and their accompanying evocations:

> To write this story, I had to rely on a device that I called "my internal voice," [which] I discovered ... unexpectedly, while listening to the sound of Persian in the streets of Los Angeles and Washington. It was the sound of the Iranian refugees, bargaining in American shopping malls. My new voice did not have any content. It was more like a rhythmic humming, perhaps a ghost of a Persian accent. It was like the humming we do when we are alone or when we are intrigued by an idea. At times, my mind was silent and the writing came to an unexpected halt. Then I hummed with my internal voice. That melodious Persian sound that could sometimes throw light on forgotten scenes, bringing them out of total darkness and allowing me to invent memories of a time when I wasn't even born. (8–9)

The emphasis Modarressi places on Persian, its tones and inflections, is equally prominent in his renderings of his work into English. In a letter dated August 4, 1987, in response to my question whether *The Book of Absent People* could have been composed in English, he wrote: "It would have been impossible to transplant the atmosphere of the novel into an English-language form." Following this creative impulse, his English translation of the novel was infused with deliberate literal translations, requiring readers to be alert to the nuances of different rhetorical patterns.

To submit English to Persian turns of phrase was integral to Modarressi's vision of the immigrant writer: "The new language of any immigrant writer is obviously accented and, at least initially, inarticulate. I consider this 'artifact' language expressive in its own right. Writing with an accented voice is organic to the mind of the writer. It is not something we can invent. It is frequently buried beneath personal inhibitions and doubts. The accented voice is loaded with hidden messages from our cultural heritage, messages that often reach beyond the capacity of the ordinary words of any language" (Modarressi 1992, 9). What Modarressi's accented voice conveys is the very untranslatability of speech patterns from one language into another. This experience of translation is the opposite of his first forays into English when he arrived in the United States as a medical student. Remembering his initial transition from Persian into English, Modarressi wrote: "If I wanted to say something, I compared Persian and English words, as dictionaries do. Persian and English words arranged themselves in two parallel lines like dancers in a nineteenth century ballroom, bowing to each other and trying to find a mate" (Modarressi 1992, 8). This analogy lays bare the artificiality and the performance involved in transferring one cultural ethos into another. It also hints at the difficulty of finding a perfect match. The protagonist of *The Pilgrim's Rules of Etiquette* explains to an American colleague his belief in the impossibility of transplanting his Iranian self into an American setting: "'To be sure, there are common features between the Easterner and the Westerner, and in certain respects each can benefit the other. But in the end their encounters remain barren. It's like the quince-orange tree, which is a graft between a quince and an orange, or the mule, which is the result of the horse-and-donkey copulation. Of course each has some use. But they themselves are barren and fruitless'" (Modarressi 1989, 8).

Relating this maxim to the plane of language, we cannot expect Modarressi's fictional characters to speak seamless, idiomatic English. To experience them in their own native setting, we have to hear close approximations of the expressions they would use naturally in conversations in Persian. Finding idiomatic English equivalents would thus rob their speech of intensity and spontaneity. Equally jarring would be the insertion of explanatory notes or glossaries to provide the reader with historical or cultural context. We are meant to stumble on unfamiliar names, unrecognizable cultural practices, and unknown literary allusions, and to wonder whether they are real or made up. In Modarressi's novels, we encounter poets, politicians, and men of the cloth whose speech is at odds with their purported passions and convictions. We are taken in by their highly wrought phrases before we realize that they are hiding behind linguistic subterfuge. We glimpse lost souls lurking behind the mask, struggling to reveal themselves in an uncertain world. Their rhetorical acrobatics are part and parcel of an alienation they struggle to keep at bay.

What Modarressi conveys through his use of an accented voice in English translation was already apparent in his first novel, *Yakolia and Her Loneliness*, which drew on the archaic language of the Persian translation of the Bible to depict the paradoxes of the human condition. Like a golden thread, the theme of estrangement and the endearing human effort invested in glossing over the feeling of being a stranger to oneself run through Modarressi's works.

The Virgin of Solitude takes us into the lives of protagonists whose estrangement is inscribed in their looks, their language, and their demeanor. Set around the time of the revolution, the novel follows the parallel lives of a transplanted Austrian woman, known in the family as Madame, who has made Iran her home and her grandson, Nuri, who desperately misses his emigrant mother but hides his longing behind the veneer of teenage bravado. As the turmoil of the revolution envelops the country, grandmother and grandson distantly observe the dissolution of social, class, and political order, while all along searching for an elusive sense of belonging.

Through their eyes, we glimpse the eccentricities of the Iranian society of the time and its self-image vis-à-vis other cultures. In the gaps between image and reality are captured idiosyncratic speech and dialogue that open vistas on a changing society that Modarressi viewed from a distance with the keen eye of an immigrant writer. Conscious of his own position as an outsider, he celebrates the possibilities inherent in his position. The insight he experienced on a flight out of Iran encapsulates his vision of a writer straddling two worlds: "On the plane returning from Iran to the U.S., a strange idea kept occurring to me. I thought that most immigrants, regardless of the familial, social, or political circumstances causing their exile, have been cultural refugees all their lives. They leave because they feel like outsiders. Perhaps it is their personal language that can build a bridge between what is familiar and what is strange" (Modarressi 1992, 9). Taghi Modarressi's personal language—like the language of the twelfth-century Persian mystical poet Jalal al-din Farid, from whose *Conference of the Birds* the epigraph to *The Books of Absent People* is derived—initiates us into new ways of seeing and speaking about the arduous yet pleasurable journey of self-discovery:

Oh, may your journey to the border of Sheba be happy.

May your speaking the language of birds with Solomon be happy.

Hold back the demon in chains and in prison

So you will be the keeper of the secret like Solomon.

WORKS CITED

Modarressi, Taghi. 1986. *The Book of Absent People*. New York: Doubleday.

———. 1989. *The Pilgrim's Rules of Etiquette*. New York: Doubleday.

———. 1992. "Writing with an Accent." *Chanteh* 1, no. 1: 7–9.

The VIRGIN *of* SOLITUDE

Late in March 1980, when people were still exchanging the customary New Year visits, Madame lay stretched out on her bronze bed in a deep coma, snoring intermittently. The setting sun's blurred shadows slowly extending onto the furniture, the walls, and the half-open windows made Madame's dull and waxen fingernails seem peculiarly elongated. The fading sunlight gave her face the alert and watchful look of someone who even in a coma could see everything: the vigilant countenance of a dead or transfigured person no longer needing to connect with the external world. The face of a fairytale princess under the spell of a monster, awaiting the arrival of her Prince Charming to break open the bottle containing the monster's life—although in waking life she looked more like a shriveled old woman, especially since her gray hair was so thin that light passed through it and reflected off her pinkish scalp.

Most amazing was the way in which she suddenly came out of her coma. She raised her head unexpectedly, picked up the book sitting on the bedside table, and muttered a few lines of it to herself. She squinted into the mirror, as if struggling to recognize herself, and mumbled something in German. She mistook Badri Khanom, Dr. Jannati's wife, for her old friend Princess Bertha and asked about people with foreign names. Then she got out of bed and, standing in front of her vanity mirror, smeared on a great deal of rouge, giving her cheeks the appearance of two round, rosy radishes and making her face look like a Dutch doll's. She combed her hair in a boyish style, pressing down the white curls on her forehead with two fingers. After this, she donned a narrow-brimmed, red, broadcloth hat appointed with an ostrich feather. The hat was so small that it perched on her head like a tiny cardboard box. She put on her cotton slippers, picked up the cane her husband, Senator Zargham, had brought back for her from Berlin, and got on her way. She curled her spidery fingers around the banister and at each step tapped the mosaic tiles hard with the tip of her cane, as if announcing her arrival at a lavish ball. Pounding her cane on the floor, she passed by her framed embroidery, checked on her tropical plants, and, raising her braidlike eyebrows, which she had painted over where she herself had shaved, stared out into the distance. In that state, she looked no different from a normal, healthy person. Even if in midsentence she fell back into her coma, it would be put down to absentmindedness or to a momentary pause caused by searching for a word just on the tip of her tongue.

From the middle of April, when her condition worsened, ladies dressed in black began to drop in to visit her. Their dresses and skirts were so tight they had to use their hips to help themselves walk. Some of them brought along a change of clothes and slippers. They changed in the bathroom on the third floor, sat in a circle in the middle of the hallway, and, speaking in whispers so as not to disturb Madame, talked about politics, the dollar's rate of exchange, and new treatments for cancer. They mentioned names of doctors who could cure cancer, even the most malignant and tumor-ridden variety. They argued over the results of Madame's blood and urine tests, the X rays of her pelvic bone, and the biopsy of the tumor in her bladder. After this, they tiptoed to the bedroom and through its half-open door threw a sad glance at Madame lying on her bronze bed. They slapped the backs of their hands, bit their lips, averted their eyes, and said, "Oh my, why has Madame changed like this?"

From the moment Madame's grandchildren, Nuri and Ladan Hushiar, had moved to this house six years ago, Nuri had expected a path to open up before him. Some nights he got so excited he couldn't sleep until dawn. In the mornings, he strolled alone through the rooms, and as soon as no one was around, he would go into the storage room Madame had shown him once before his father's death and his mother's departure for America. Madame had let him open the closet holding her opera dresses and had watched him mimic Fred Astaire in front of the oval mirror. Nuri didn't know why on this silent afternoon, just as in the days of his childhood, he had this desire to go again into the storage room and gaze at Madame's strange postcards for half an hour, making their designs reflect on a silver cylinder until they transformed into images of people dressed in the sumptuous medieval garments of Europe. He wanted to walk between the rows of Madame's opera dresses and search the drawers of the old desk for something; he was not sure what.

He thought of the first day after they had moved to the Dezashibi house. Madame took him to the third-floor balcony and sang an aria from Wagner. She did not believe a thirteen-year-old child could be so moved by a foreign song. She promised to introduce him to a world that would lend him strength in the absence of loved ones and help him obtain whatever his heart desired. Nuri blinked, but he did not take his eyes off her face. Madame went on in her bookish Persian. "A true dream is in fact a death that appears to you in the form of silence."

Not only then, but even now Nuri had trouble connecting those words with the idea of dying, with funeral rites and memorial ceremonies. Whenever he thought of the ambulance sent by the coroner, he imagined Madame's body, wrapped in a funeral shawl, being carried by a few young men from the neighborhood and placed in the back of the ambulance. The ladies gathered around would be dressed in black, with puffy red eyes and faces bare of makeup, white as chalk. The men would not talk to each other, or if they did, their exchanges would be private and limited to groups of two. Nuri and his sister, Ladan, one on each side, would hold their grandfather, Senator Zargham, and accompany the body up Mostowfi Alley.

Nuri preferred to remember Madame the way she looked the year she still wore her black mourning dress for his father, Papa Javad. It was a satiny black dress that fell loosely across her breasts, and its skirt, as simple as a high school girl's, sprawled over her bare legs and made her appear almost naked. She wore casual net shoes with thick straps that crisscrossed her fair, freckled skin. From her fit body, prominent cheeks, and blue eyes there emanated a stubborn frankness that Badri Khanom called "donkey-headedness." The women in the family paid Badri Khanom no mind. Most of what she said they put to jealousy and envy. Instead, they themselves followed the latest European fashions, wore heavy makeup like movie stars, and tried their best to attract Madame's attention. Yet even before her illness, Madame had showed no interest in such matters.

When she sat on the rattan chair, her long arms and legs wrapped around each other like the branches of a tree in a jungle. She displayed her bony body with abandon, as if she were alone and had no concern for others' gaze. Even when she wanted to cut someone off, she would not utter an outright rejection. She would simply rub her fingers together and after a deliberate pause say, "Pardon me, I have to excuse myself."

A week later, when Madame's condition temporarily improved, the relatives began to grumble: "Can't Nuri think about anything other than going to America again? Why hasn't Madame's kindness had the least influence on him?" Madame looked after everyone. Anybody with a problem went to Madame first. Her enemies, even those who made fun of her German accent, spoke highly of her good nature and love for others. But Nuri talked, dreamed, and thought only about returning to America. In the evenings, when he came home exhausted and weary, he sat on the rattan chair waiting and hoping that his mother, Maman Zuzu, would call from New York. He placed his chin on his palm, watching the sparrows in the garden. He did not let anyone know what was on his mind. "What was the use of Madame's bringing him up?" the relatives asked. "If the outcome of an Austrian upbringing is this gutlessness, then a hundred thanks to our own child-rearing methods. At the age of nineteen-plus, Nuri is proud of nothing but his European looks. Oh, dear Father, sometimes it's not bad to have some shame."

One day Badri Khanom put aside all ceremony and, taking on the grim demeanor of a widow, declared with dignity and deliberation: "Being Austrian is not just about having blue eyes and blond hair. It also has something to do with good manners and kindness, with consideration and caring for others. Not like a good-for-nothing from Chaleh Maidun, who from the moment he steps out of bed thinks and talks about nothing but dumbbells and weights and shows his muscles to anybody passing through the garden door and lets weeks go by without ever asking about his sick grandmother's condition. Or asking his poor sister how late she stayed up the night before, how many times she had to put the bedpan under Madame, and whether she needed any help."

Nuri feigned ignorance. He stood up for the ladies who came to visit Madame, said a few polite words, and asked about their health. With a bow, he paid his respects to the gentlemen. When he noticed that everybody was distracted, he slipped out of the house and spent hours waiting for an exit visa at the Division of Fingerprinting, the Offices of Notary Public and Foreign Documents, and the Department of Student Affairs. He relayed a few facts about his family and educational background to office clerks and troubleshooters. He listened to the other petitioners' footsteps echo on the gray tile floor, which made the hallways seem wider and emptier. Every few minutes he sorted through his documents inside the glossy yellow folder he always brought along and glanced out of the corner of his eye at the bureaucrats who did not want to issue his passport and exit visa—this he knew from their brooding eyes and impatient looks. As soon as they saw him from a distance, they turned their heads away and locked their hands together under their chins. They reasoned that a student should first get his high school diploma, then think about going abroad.

Nuri knocked on so many doors that he finally found a smuggler named Ali the Mechanic who agreed to take him across the border into Turkey. And without a criminal background certificate from the Office of Fingerprinting, the required six photos, or a tip for the clerks at the Passport Office. Nuri simply placed two hundred thousand tumans in an unmarked envelope on which he wrote, "For the kids' cookie expenses" and took it to the Kazerun Tea House on a Thursday evening. As Ali the Mechanic put the money in his breast pocket, he lowered his head and whispered to Nuri that up to the time of his departure he should act natural and follow his daily routines. "Nobody . . . do you understand what I'm saying? . . . nobody should become suspicious of you! Not even the people at your house. Do you understand?"

Nuri followed these instructions so closely that he finally aroused Badri Khanom's suspicions. She extended her hand to him like a man and said, "Goodness me." She looked at him inquisitively and said, "If you want to get a visa to America, well, go to Turkey. Why go to Cyprus, which nobody knows anything about? Up to now we haven't heard of anything in Cyprus but donkeys and the Archbishop Makarios."

Nuri frowned and said nothing.

As long as Madame was still conscious, Badri Khanom had not dared to bring her blind father, Amiz Abbas, to the Dezashibi house on the pretext of inquiring about Madame's health. But now they visited the house at least every other day. When they arrived in the front hall, the other guests stopped talking. A chair was put outside Madame's bedroom door for Amiz Abbas, who would place his tall, lean figure in it. He always wore the same brown serge suit and dark glasses held on with a piece of black elastic, his hairless head shining in profile like an oily egg. He would cross one leg over another and wait a little, while Badri Khanom raised her black scarf over her head and curtsied to the guests. As soon as Badri Khanom knew the relatives were not watching her, she would squint her eyes and, with the curiosity of a tinware peddler, estimate the price of the various ornaments in the room. One early evening in the middle of April, she secretly went up to the third floor, where she examined the furniture and the decorative objects, lifted the corner of the quilt to read its label, and then, with the same stealth, rejoined the other guests. She folded up her scarf and put it away in her leather purse, turned to Ladan, who had caught her in the act, and asked in an undertone about Madame's condition. "How is she? Does she still recognize you?"

Amiz Abbas, seated in his chair outside Madame's bedroom, perked up at the sound of Badri Khanom's voice and asked why Madame, in her delirium, did not inquire about him. Delirium was no different from drunkenness. There was a saying from the olden days: drunkenness is truthfulness. Finally he swallowed and said, "Madame has grown so important she doesn't recognize the little people anymore."

Amiz Abbas claimed that had he not gone blind, the Senator and Madame would never have been united. Before the Second World War, when he had just become familiar with Dr. Arani, the famous Communist, Amiz Abbas lost half his eyesight within a mere four months. In those days, Dr. MacDowell was the head of surgery at the American hospital. After one look at Amiz Abbas's swollen eyes, he recognized that the infection in his gums had spread to his head. He ordered Amiz Abbas to brush his teeth twice a day with Schnaup dental powder and immediately consult the world's most renowned eye specialist, Professor Fritz Ziegler, to prevent losing the rest of his sight. Amiz Abbas's father, the late Fattali Khan, had never been abroad and did not speak German, so he asked his brother, the present-day Senator, to take Amiz Abbas to

Vienna immediately. The Senator, who in those days was simply known as Agh'Ali, spoke German like a native and knew troubleshooters at the Foreign Ministry who could expedite matters. However, Amiz Abbas did not trust him. He knew a thousand experienced people who spoke German and would have been honored to take him to Vienna. And they would not have added to his father's expenses, God rest his soul, with visits to cabarets and dance halls. "How expensive can it be just to set foot in Vienna? All this money is being wasted."

Moreover, in Vienna they had to wait a month for an appointment with Professor Ziegler. The professor had gone to the Karlsbad baths for rest and recreation. He postponed his return for so long that Amiz Abbas lost his eyesight completely. Amiz Abbas grew so depressed that Agh'Ali, using Fattali Khan's money, was forced to take him out every night and keep him occupied until midnight at the Café Imperial listening to Madame's singing. In those days, she was known by the name "Fräulein Frieda." Of course, Amiz Abbas could not see anything, and it was impossible for him to watch the dances and the acrobatic parts of the program, but from the very first time he heard the song "Chapeau," he was smitten with Fräulein Frieda's singing. Even now, after all these years, the name "Fräulein Frieda" could make him smile. "You have never heard such a voice in all your life. Don't judge Madame by her present condition."

The song "Chapeau" apparently had a special charm not only for him, but for all the Viennese. There was a rumor that Hitler, disguised with a fake beard and mustache, would come to the Café Imperial to listen for a while to Fräulein Frieda and Princess Bertha sing. Then he would return home clandestinely through the café's back door. In addition, Fräulein Frieda had developed a strange liking for Amiz Abbas. Now, why and wherefore even Amiz Abbas could not figure out. Certainly the favor of such a lady could not have anything to do with his misty eyes because Professor Ziegler's assistants had cut off his velvety lashes with their special electric scissors. Perhaps the reason was his wavy, thick, black hair that not a single Viennese barber would cut short. The barber next to the Raso Bar had said, "If you could see, you wouldn't dream of cutting such precious hair."

Wherever Amiz Abbas went, Fräulein Frieda followed. She would take his arm, cuddle up to him, and talk constantly about Iran. She did not leave him alone a minute in the room he shared with his uncle at the Hotel Excelsior. After the show at the Café Imperial, she brought champagne to their room and stayed with them until late. She would pour so much champagne for Amiz Abbas that the poor young man would get drunk and pass out on the floor. Only when he woke up in the middle of the night to go to the bathroom would he realize that Fräulein Frieda was still there, whispering German gibberish to Uncle Ali. Pretending to be asleep, he would stretch his arms stiffly in front of him to avoid obstacles and grope his way to the bathroom. He wondered why sometimes they mentioned his name. Why did they praise him so much? Why did they suddenly burst into laughter and, instead of chuckling, pant? Perhaps they were being considerate and feared that their bursts of laughter would disturb Amiz Abbas's sleep. Little did they know that Amiz Abbas stayed awake for hours, listening to every mysterious sound, especially the creaking of the rickety old bed that sometimes made it difficult for them to breathe normally. Like asthmatics, they wheezed so loudly that Amiz Abbas worried about their health.

Amiz Abbas's reminiscences were not, of course, appropriate in view of Madame's illness and the discussions about placing the Senator in an old-age home. Nevertheless, they gave Nuri a sense of anticipation, not unlike the feeling that comes with the approach of spring and the thought of green fields and the scent of blossoms. In his imagination, he would travel to a European city and drink Alsatian wine in an Austrian bar. He would listen to German songs, and his stomach would clench with desire. Once, when he reported Amiz Abbas's memories to the Senator, the Senator laughed so much that his mouth opened wide, exposing his decaying teeth. But his eyes quickly grew weary, and he smirked and excused himself.

If Amiz Abbas's voice did not reach Nuri on the third floor, he would entertain himself by listening to the workers cementing the stone pool, to the footsteps of Puran, their servant's adopted daughter, or to their chauffeur, Vaziri, who whistled as he shined the Senator's greenish yellow Mercedes Benz with a dirty rag. Nuri would travel back before his time, to the years before the Second World War. In his mind, he would board a ship with Agh'Ali and Amiz Abbas. In Baku, he would buy a train ticket to Vienna; he would get a room at the Hotel Excelsior for a couple of weeks; and, like Agh'Ali and Amiz Abbas, he would go to the Raso Bar every Saturday morning, drink a few glasses of Alsatian wine, and whet his appetite for lunch. The owner of the bar was Mr. Raso, originally a Hungarian Gypsy, whom he knew from the Senator's descriptions and could imagine even without ever having met him in person. He just closed his eyes and Mr. Raso's features took shape in his mind. A man of around fifty with big, dark eyes that always glittered with devilish joy at the sight of customers. Mr. Raso positioned a few strands of his hair like a row of leeches on his bald head. As he passed a table, he wiped his sweaty forehead with his starched but dirty cuff and smiled, showing his gold teeth. Nuri could feel the bar's dim ambiance and cool dampness, and he could see the green palms planted in gunmetal vases. The sheen from the beverage bottles, the wine flasks wrapped with Italian straw, and the pickle demijohns brightened the dark room. Just thinking about the velvety green wallpaper, the paintings of a foxhunt in an English village and of ducks in a pond in the middle of reeds, he imagined he had returned to his childhood home after many years. He remembered the swept and tidy space that, despite its strangeness, seemed familiar to him. Just like a lithograph of Paris before the First World War, which appears unreal when seen through a magnifying glass. Like the children's Ferris wheel at the Luxembourg Gardens, with fathers and mothers who from a distance appear frozen in their curtsies to each other.

Listening to memories of the past forced him to be in two different places at once, overcoming limitations of time and space. Any time he peeked at Madame through the crack of the bedroom door, he was taken aback. Looking like a folded piece of cardboard wrapped in muslin and placed on a bronze bed, her body had none of its old fullness. Nuri compared this image to what she looked like the day he and his sister had first arrived at the Dezashibi house—that is, the Thursday afternoon six years ago when they went to the Senator's study. For two hours, they had played the organ, sung, and built houses of cards. Madame had talked about a trip she had taken to Prague in 1939 with her friend Princess Bertha. She did not explain where or how Princess Bertha had become a princess. With vague allusions and broad hints, Madame made Princess Bertha into an imaginary creature for Nuri. She had been born somewhere, perhaps in Odessa, to a Russian nobleman's family. She had many tutors and nannies who taught her English, French, German, piano, ballet, and singing. In the heat of the Russian Revolution, her family put all their belongings in a basement storeroom, stashed their fur coats in a gap between two walls, and with a thousand hardships made their way to Vienna. Madame related all this very fast, fluttering her fingers to indicate she wished to pass over these unimportant events and reach the passionate love story between Princess Bertha and a young Austrian named Siegfried von Friedhoff. Then she lowered her voice, gazed around the room, and placed her hand on her breast. She seemed to be barely aware of Nuri. When he stirred and prepared to leave the room, she grabbed his sleeve and forced him back into his seat. Nuri imagined himself in a very large and empty opera house in Prague, with the chandeliers dimming and the red velvet curtains gradually parting. Madame, Princess Bertha, and Siegfried von Friedhoff, like three ghosts summoned from the world of the dead, appeared on the stage and sang together as though they were echoing an ominous message from an invisible world. Nuri poured a shot of Monk's Syrup in a glass and set it before Madame without any tray or chaser. In order to tempt her, he said, "Yum, yum!"

Madame, stretching like a cat aroused from sleep, ducked her round and delicate chin, and took the glass eagerly from Nuri's hand. She winked and said, "Oh, Nuri, what a bad boy you are!"

She took a few quick sips and recited her memories of Princess Bertha more flamboyantly and in a more excited tone of voice, explaining that the Gestapo had invited Princess Bertha to Prague to play the role of Elizabeth in *Tannhäuser*. In her letters to Madame, Princess Bertha had written, "How much fun can it be to travel by yourself? Why don't the two of us go to Prague so if something bad happens to Siegfried, we will be close to him and take care of him?" Perhaps this trip would be their last together, and they would never see each other again.

Then all of a sudden Madame's face took on the same tired expression as when she felt unobserved, the look of a person who has seen both the cold and the warmth of the world. She stood in front of the half-meter statue of the Virgin Mary, praying for Siegfried and making the sign of the cross and genuflecting quickly.

Madame had bought the statue from a Polish priest at St. Bartholomew's Church the first year she arrived in Iran, and in the same church she had had it baptized as the Virgin of Solitude. When she knelt before it, bit by bit she would become transformed into one of those strange creatures Nuri and Ladan had seen only in the movies about the supernatural. Sometimes they imagined the Virgin of Solitude as a living person who was closely related to Madame herself. The language in which she spoke to Madame was different from ordinary languages such as Persian and German, and no one could decipher it. To a certain extent, it was like the private code Nuri and Ladan had shared as children. In front of the relatives, Ladan would call Nuri "Mamakh," and Nuri would call Ladan "Khormalu." This was their secret, and no one else understood what they were talking about. They would look at each other in a funny way and suck on their cheeks so as to imitate the young adults' romantic gestures in front of them. Ladan would say, "Ghagh!" and Nuri would immediately answer, "Gheegh!" signaling that the two of them were in league.

In Madame's absence, Nuri and Ladan would twist her rosary between their fingers and become so absorbed in the Virgin of Solitude's calm face and chalky, opaque, and inward-looking gaze that sometimes they thought they had established a connection with her mysterious world. They forgot about themselves and imagined that the Virgin spoke to them in the special language she used to communicate with Madame. But she did not speak. Instead, little by little, they would start talking to each other in their own invented language, which made their relatives laugh and say, "Why are you talking like this?"

In front of the mirror on that first day, Madame patted her cheeks with the palms of her hands, pinched the corners of her lips, and stretched her skin so that its wrinkles disappeared. She sat down on the couch and after a few nervous, dry coughs showed Nuri the picture of Siegfried and Princess Bertha in a double oval frame placed next to the statue. Siegfried, in his Nazi uniform, resembled a pale shadow of a Teutonic idol whose golden hair shone even in the black-and-white photograph. A trace of a smile faded into the controlled lines around his mouth, and he drew Nuri to him.

Madame was slowly sipping the Monk's Syrup when she began to cough and in her bookish Persian apologized to Nuri, young as he was. She gazed wistfully at the sky and gradually her face took on a blank expression. Nuri's feet barely reached the organ pedals, but he sat down at the organ and tried to play a tune. He slid off the stool so many times that Madame burst into laughter. She took his place at the organ, moved her pear-shaped bottom rhythmically and encouraged Nuri to sing along with her in German:

" . . . O, Hall so very dear, I salute you."

Her stare reminded Nuri of the beetle shells that remain stuck to tree trunks at the end of spring as though they are still alive. She talked about 1932, when she had predicted her own papa's death. She lowered her head and peered at Nuri over her spectacles as though he knew all the details of Papa's life. She regretted that she had not been with "poor Papa" in his last moments. She had picked up the receiver hesitantly and heard a breathing similar to Papa's. It was so calm and regular that she had anxiously repeated, "Hello! Hello! Hello!"

Instead of an answer, there was the metallic and grating sound of the telephone being hung up. She suddenly realized that Papa had said good-bye to her for the last time. He had always called her before leaving on long trips. Imitating the Gestapo officers, he had spoken politely and formally. "Frieda, auf wiedersehen. Take care of yourself."

Madame rounded her mouth into the shape of a rosebud as if she were saying "ouch." She smoothed Nuri's blond hair with the tip of her painted fingernails and said, "Papa, poor Papa!"

Nuri didn't say anything, and Madame went on. "You Easterners only pretend to feel emotions. Why don't you show real emotions?"

Nuri shrugged, "I don't know why."

"My dear, Your Honor, please sit at the organ and play a piece by Wagner for your humble servant. 'Of all that you play, the one by our beloved is the sweetest.'"

She had learned from books to refer to herself as "your humble servant" and to others as "Your Honor" or "Your Excellency." Even in ordinary speech, she used the old bureaucratic style.

Nuri said, "I'll play another time. I have to do my homework now."

Madame threw her head back and laughed out loud. She drank up the Monk's Syrup and greedily licked the bottom of the glass.

Since Madame had fallen ill, the once clean corridors were now musty and smelled like unmade beds. Puran, Black Najmeh's adopted daughter, had been brought from Tafresh to take care of Madame, but she lasted only half a day. She had screamed "Aiee!" and fled the bath in a flash and never mentioned Madame's name again. Instead, she called her "this one." "Phew! Phew! How awful this one smells! What is this one? How one shudders just touching its body."

Now Aunt Moluk gave Madame a bath every Wednesday morning. For an hour she would rub Madame's frail body with a special glove and wrap the washcloth tight around her own index finger and turn it around various orifices till its froglike sound echoed in the bath. Madame's loose, pale skin reminded her of her older sister Bibi Ghezi's corpse at the cemetery where the dead are washed before burial. At night, Aunt Moluk woke up in a terror, wondering if Bibi Ghezi were sitting in the dark on a wooden chair, pouring handfuls of ginger down her throat to cure her chill.

Every day, however, Madame painted her fingernails and toenails with orange polish and assumed a sort of impervious European neatness that made one shudder after touching her bare skin. Badri Khanom, who had just become a dervish, believed Madame's cheery mood had nothing to do with her cold-blooded constitution, her Teutonic Aryan origins, or her prayers in front of the Virgin of Solitude. It was the raw meat she ate on Sundays. Before noon every Sunday, before her prayers and organ practice, Madame pounded raw meat in a small mortar and made meatballs out of it. She put them next to each other on a silver platter and sprinkled them generously with salt. She went to the third-floor balcony, and, like a dog who has found a bone, she ate them all away from everyone's eyes. She chased them down with a bracing glass of Monk's Syrup, which was rumored to be mostly raisin vodka and cognac.

The Senator himself believed that the real reason for Madame's cheerful mood was the arrival of spring. When buds started appearing on branches, Madame could not be contained. She always wanted to busy herself with something. She would summon Ladan in the early evening to the second-floor balcony to see the slopes of the Alborz Mountains and breathe in the delicate late-April air. In her enthusiasm for the green fields, Madame pretended that there was nothing wrong with her and that, as when she first came to Iran, her voice could still reach high C. She closed her eyes in the soft breeze and, taking deep breaths, seemed to be swooning from the smell of honeysuckle. She gazed intensely at her own framed embroidery as if seeing these images for the first time: wild animals, wild bird hunts, and broadleafed tropical plants hung with a calculated disorder on the walls.

An hour after sunset in the middle of June, Ladan handed over Madame's care to Aunt Moluk and was about to go to her own room when suddenly she heard Madame screaming. Madame wanted to send for the clergy—the *akhund*—Shariat, at that very instant so that he could prepare her for her journey to the next world. Convinced she had little time left, she was afraid she would leave "this world's abode" before Shariat's arrival. Badri Khanom guessed that Madame had had a vision in her sleep and had imagined the Prophet and his four holy descendants coming to help her on her journey. She deduced this from Madame's eyes, wide open and frozen in an apprehensive gaze directed toward a corner of the room. Madame did not answer any of Aunt Moluk's questions. Instead, she muttered under her breath that she trusted no one but Mr. Shariat to prepare her for dying.

The relatives were busy talking when Shariat, dressed in a turban and cloak, appeared in the darkness of the stairs. He wrapped the tail of his cloak tightly around himself and took wide, ungainly steps so as not to touch anyone else. As soon as he entered the bedroom, he made everyone leave, shut the door, and set to reciting the story of the five holy figures in a monotonous voice. When he got to the part about seeking absolution, Madame's weak voice could also be heard, reciting Goethe's "Song of the Nightwanderer" in Persian with her German accent.

The ceremony was not yet completed when the ladies rushed into the bedroom bareheaded. They paraded before Shariat in their broad-shouldered jackets and narrow black skirts that made their bodies look like upside-down trapezoids. They lined up beside the bronze bed and offered Madame the bouquet of flowers they had bought from the Jordan Flower Shop. Madame closed her eyes in gratitude. She called Nuri's name. Her puffy eyes examined his face not with the blame Nuri would have expected, but rather with greed, as though she could not get her fill of seeing him. Then she motioned for the ladies to leave the room. She wanted to speak to Nuri alone. "Nuri-jan, look after the household a little more carefully. Why don't you buy me embroidery patterns and oil for my sewing machine? Nuri-jan, your humble servant cannot remain idle. Hurry up, maybe I can arrange my affairs."

She did not utter a word about Nuri's studies at Saint Joseph's School, Maman Zuzu's life in New York, or the performance of a Wagner piece. Even if she had said something, it would have most certainly been in a language he could not understand. Nuri was no longer a child. He could not sit at the organ in the study all the time and for the sake of his grandmother's happiness listen to her talk or practice one Wagner piece after another.

Maman Zuzu called constantly from New York, pleading with Nuri to bring Madame to New York immediately for treatment—even though in the heat of mass arrests and "desert tribunals" Nuri's leaving for New York would be pure folly.

♦ ♦ ♦ In the old days, the family had spent the two months of their summer vacation in Damavand or Ramsar. During their absence, weeds would grow in the flowerpots and the cracks between the bricks, giving the apartment an unused look. Early mornings when Nuri had opened his eyes, he was alone in his bed in their summer house. Through the window, he would watch the sky become pale. The ticktock of the clock on the wall had lent the entrance hall the tidy air of a washroom's white tiles, and Papa Javad had appeared like a ghost wrapped in folds of cloudlike linen. On the radio, a little girl prayed for the health and longevity of the Shah of Shahs, the light of Aryans. Maman Zuzu would call from the kitchen, "Ladann! Nuriii!" urging them to get out of bed.

Then, it was the beginning of spring in 1974, the Iranian New Year, not quite a week since Papa Javad's fatal car accident. The only thing Nuri remembered from that accident was the picture of the Volkswagen and its bent fender printed in the daily paper *Ettela'at*. He also remembered Papa Javad's face and his thin and gradually receding hair. The drooping Turcoman mustache he stroked as he spoke, the thin and sprouty eyebrows, and the daggerlike lashes that made his face look freshly washed. The glint in his eyes implied a sort of grogginess and a tendency to forgive and make friends.

The legal announcements and estate claims had not yet been published in the papers. Maman Zuzu was already busy preparing for her trip to New York, where she planned to get a certificate in therapeutic massage. She no longer had her former enthusiasm. She had wanted to send Nuri and Ladan to the Dezashibi house for the duration of the funeral and memorial services, but Madame and the Senator did not approve. So instead she sent them to Dr. Jannati and Badri Khanom's house. With no explanation, the children's lives were suddenly upset. The relatives talked ceaselessly about Nuri's thin and bony frame; they fretted over why Maman Zuzu did not give him liver extract to strengthen him. They brought up the subject of his eaglelike blue eyes. They thought of strange remedies for his nervous condition, which, for fear of offending Maman Zuzu, they mentioned in secret and only to insiders.

The night Nuri and Ladan arrived in Dr. Jannati's courtyard, Nuri felt completely lost, and, uncharacteristically, he followed Ladan's lead on everything, especially when Badri Khanom's gaze fell on him. She squinted and, without addressing anyone in particular, asked why his manelike hair was longer on the left side. Why didn't he part his hair so his face would lose that bland, half-baked look of a boy not yet out of puberty?

Although it was a quarter past ten, he could still hear the hushed voices of a few children and the noise of passing cars in the street. He was so distraught he hugged his own arms like a naked man in the cold. He hunched his shoulders and did not budge until Badri Khanom took both of them to a very clean and simple room on the second floor. She spread out two beds next to each other, showed them the bathroom, and then went downstairs so quietly that Nuri grew scared all over again. The devil was once more getting under his skin. He had no doubt that soon he would do something he would later regret. But he could not stop himself. He put his head close to Ladan's ear and said excitedly, "If I tell you something, you promise not to tell anyone else?"

"I promise."

"Maman Zuzu is planning to leave you in Tehran and secretly take me with her to America."

Now, what made him tease poor Ladan like this? He had no idea himself. But his heart was jumping with joy at the sight of Ladan's wide eyes and horrified look. Ladan asked, "Why?"

"Because Maman likes me more than you."

Ladan, who had listened intently to him up to then, sat up straight on her bed and protested, "Why? What have I done?"

"Nothing. Sometimes somebody loves one person and not another."

"You're lying. My Maman loves me very much."

"I didn't say she doesn't love you. Certainly she loves you, but because you are an orphan, she doesn't love you as much as she loves me."

Ladan jumped up. "What are you saying? I was found abandoned on the road? Is it me, or is it you, with your body washed by corpse washers, who is an orphan? You think you're talking to an idiot, that I believe what you say? Why are you telling me this nonsense?"

"Because you are my sister. I thought you should know now. One night, Maman Zuzu will wrap you up in a blanket and take you to Naser Khosrow Street in a cab and drop you off outside the Jewish orphanage. If you don't believe me, say so."

"Obviously I don't believe you. You always lie like a dog. Wait till I tell my *maman*."

She raised her hand, and Nuri drew back so she couldn't hit him. "Do you think you have a *maman* you can go report to?"

"Just let me tell her, and you'll see how she pays you back."

"Didn't you promise not to tell anybody?"

"I will if I feel like it."

"Shall I tell you why? Because only orphans break their promises."

"You want to make me mad so I'll get nasty with you. I should hit you on the head with both hands, but I'm not mean like you. Instead, I'll tell Maman tomorrow."

"Don't you know how much Maman dislikes tattletales? She gives tattletales to the Jews so they can pour their blood in a bottle and make special breads with it on their Sabbath."

Nuri assumed a horrifying expression and exaggerated his gestures to imitate someone stealing Muslim children's blood. He did it so realistically that he scared himself. He screamed, "Ladan! Hide under the quilt! Boris Karloff is under the window, and he's coming after you!"

Both of them hid under the quilt.

The sun had risen very high when the sound of footsteps came from the corridor. Badri Khanom brought them a tray of toast, butter, jam, cream, and tea. With a deliberately cheerful expression, she shouted, "You little devils, get up! If you have wet your beds, it's no shame. Just remove the linen."

They all sat together around the breakfast spread. Nuri's mouth first came in touch with the roughness of the toast and then with the softness of the butter and jam, and it tasted wonderful. He felt such lassitude and serenity that whatever he saw in the room struck him as edible. He was tempted to rifle through the locked closets and find tastier meals. But during the mourning period, it didn't look right for him to be interested in food. Nazi, Badri Khanom's daughter, criticized her mother for giving Nuri so little cream. Badri Khanom poured more cream into Nuri's saucer, but with such haste that it was obvious she was angry. Then Shahrokh, Nazi's older brother, took them to the basement and taught them to dance like Fred Astaire. He bit his lip during his performance to concentrate on his balance. Around noon, Badri Khanom and Dr. Jannati returned from the memorial service. Dr. Jannati gave each of them a ten-tuman bill to buy whatever they wanted. Then he took them back to their own family's apartment so that they could attend the seventh-night ceremony at Papa Javad's grave.

In the apartment, the furniture was still in its old place, but nothing looked like before. The relatives surveyed the rooms, pointed out the electrical appliances to each other, and asked, "What is this thing?"

"What is this good for?"

"Have you ever seen a toaster like this before? And with such a long cord? At least they could have given it a shorter cord to make it easier to plug into the wall."

How Ladan had grown. Like a housewife, she received the guests with all the proper etiquette. Nuri, in contrast, drifted through the places to which he no longer felt an attachment and walked about among the guests. Even when he saw Maman Zuzu in the hallway, he did not recognize her. Her face was pale and bare of makeup, and she had not plucked her eyebrows for a week. A strange smile appeared on her lips, as if suggesting that, among all those gathered, she and Nuri alone were aware of an important secret. She pressed the tips of Nuri's fingers, kissed his cheeks, and said, "Are you all right, dear?"

The events of the past few days and the changes in Maman Zuzu's face made them strangers to each other. She took Nuri by the hand and walked among the guests until they found Ladan. She embraced Ladan as well and kissed her on the cheeks. She took both of them to the bedroom and shut the door. She held them close and in a muffled voice told them she was very happy with them. Tears welled up in her eyes. She lowered her chador over her face and cried noiselessly.

"Don't get upset. Sometimes you feel like crying and you cry. If you two feel like crying, go ahead. There is no shame."

Nuri said, "We don't feel like crying."

"OK. It's not necessary for you to cry. Crying is for grownups."

She stood up and, looking in the mirror, puffed her cheeks to make her face look healthier.

Nuri hated the thought of going to live in his grandparents' house in Dezashib, but he had no desire to go anywhere else either. Wherever he went, he felt lost, as if he were at the wedding of someone he didn't know. He would get all flustered about his appearance and what he was wearing. The day they were supposed to leave for the Dezashibi house, he paid a lot of attention to his clothes. He stood in front of the mirror, wet his blond hair at the sink, and slicked it back so tight that it stuck to his temples, straight and glistening. Instead of his normal clothes, he put on his Texas cowboy outfit. He put on such a large Mexican sombrero that its brim reached the bridge of his nose. He chose his narrow-tipped boots with brass spurs and the silver Indian necktie he wore to parties. Although Ladan was three years his senior, she took even longer getting dressed. Three times she changed in and out of a white blouse with an open collar and puffy sleeves. Twice she cleaned a spot from the blouse with a wet towel. The cab that had been called was waiting in the street, and if Ladan took any longer, it would leave without them. Maman Zuzu grew annoyed, and after shouting for Ladan, she took off running toward the cab.

In front of the garden gate at the Dezashibi house, Maman Zuzu did not get out of the taxi. Maybe she was anxious about arriving at the airport late. She just lowered the window and waved to them. She signaled to the driver to hurry up. "Agha, what are you waiting for? Let's get going."

Nuri asked, "When will you come back?"

Maman Zuzu wiped her lips with the corner of her handkerchief, knotted her eyebrows, and looked inside her purse for something. Nuri opened his arms wide and, stumbling about, imitated an airplane crashing. "Gowwhow! Don't let the plane crash, OK?"

Najmeh, his grandmother's servant, muttered, "Hey, Agha, why do you mention such unlucky things?"

Maman Zuzu grumbled, "How dumb you are! Do you think an airplane crashes so easily?"

Then Maman Zuzu wiped the tip of her nose distractedly with the handkerchief. She raised her eyebrows and looked at herself in her pocket mirror. Several streams of mascara spread around her eyes, making her bruised face look like a crumpled piece of paper. Ladan asked, "What's wrong with you, Maman?"

Maman Zuzu managed to say nothing but, "Why do you imagine there's anything wrong with me? I'm fine. When I get to New York, I'll call."

Nuri started feeling mischievous again. "What if your plane falls out of the sky?"

Najmeh scolded him. "God forbid that such a thing should happen. Agha-jun, don't you have anything else to say?"

To lighten things up, Maman Zuzu pretended to be angry, "That's enough now! How spoiled you two have become! Quit acting like this."

Ladan said, "This is all Nuri's fault. He really is a pest. At Dr. Jannati's place, he said you would leave me at the Jewish orphanage. He thinks I don't understand. How is it even possible to wrap someone as big as me in a blanket and leave me outside the Jewish orphanage? Do you see how nasty he is? Amazing how evil his nature is and how much he lies! Am I right, Maman? Why don't you say something to him, so maybe he will become more normal?"

Ladan pursed her lips and threw a vengeful glance at Nuri. Maman Zuzu swallowed her smile. She pressed a tissue to her eyes and kept it there for a few moments. Then she said, "OK. Now go to your Mumzie-jun. She is waiting for you."

They wanted to bid Maman Zuzu farewell again after the taxi got on its way. Maman Zuzu clung to the window and stuck her head out so far that the wind blew her hair into her face. Years later, even after his own trip to America, Nuri remembered this image of Maman Zuzu in all its blurred and murky details: her worried eyes opening wide in the exhaust fumes emanating from the cab, and the same cloudy void swallowing up her face, soon leaving nothing but a brown whirling mass in the air.

They had sent the larger suitcases ahead, and now they had only their carry-ons to take into the Dezashibi house. They entered the garden, the two of them walking in front of Black Najmeh. Nuri limped like a cripple, and Ladan asked, "Why are you walking like that?"

"I am lame."

"You're crazy. You're loony."

This was Ladan's way of showing that she was no longer mad at Nuri. It was like her to forgive him so quickly. Black Najmeh grumbled, "A little slower. This is not your own house that you can mess up."

They were still laughing when they arrived at the entrance hall on the first floor. They immediately looked for the traditional New Year sweets—glazed almonds, *yokheh* cookies, and sugar-powdered biscuits—and they were amazed to find instead the customary offerings of the mourning period, mixed powder of nuts and sugar. They were reminded that they had not yet completed the period of mourning for Papa Javad. Ladan kept fiddling with the metal buttons on her blouse, pulling down the hem of her plaid skirt, folding over her short white socks, and spit polishing her shoes.

From the top of the stairs came the sound of an old record. A male singer was singing mournfully in German. His voice was nasal, as if he were suppressing a sneeze. The air smelled of a mixture of the water from the cistern, chopped leeks, and freshly brewed coffee. Sunlight shone through the windowpanes, and its gentle heat felt so pleasant that when Madame appeared on the landing, they wondered again why they were there and why Madame was dressed in black from head to toe. She glanced casually at the children. She lifted the hem of her skirt and gracefully descended the stairs. Her black garments were so at odds with her heavy makeup that she looked unreal, almost plastic. Nuri shuddered at the thought of giving her even a superficial kiss on the face. If their Maman Zuzu had been there, she would have hugged them and showered them with kisses, but Madame had a special ritual for kissing. First, she stretched out her "My dearrrs!" Then she lowered her face and held it steady so each in turn could kiss her on the cheek. She informed them that their grandfather, Senator Zargham, had gone to the royal court to offer his New Year greetings to His Majesty and would be back shortly. She put the palms of her hands together and motioned Ladan and Nuri to enter the reception hall. She brought out from the pantry a silver tray on which she had placed cream puffs for them and a measure of Monk's Syrup for herself. When Nuri reached out to take a cream puff, Madame pulled the tray back and held it above her head. She bit her lips in shock. "Eh, eh, what is the matter with Your Excellency? Gentlemen wait for ladies to be served first." She picked up the glass of Monk's Syrup from the tray, "Salud!" The children sat quietly as before and did not touch the food. Madame frowned. "Why do you not desire to eat anything?" They still could not bring themselves to touch the cream puffs. Madame bowed in jest. "I beg you, do me the honor of tasting a little of these trifling cream puffs."

Ladan ate her cream puff with utmost elegance, taking dainty bites. "Mumzie, see how neatly I am eating my cream puff?"

Madame nodded and smiled in admiration, "God bless you. God protect you. What a polite girl!"

A circle of cloudlike steam came out of the brass chimney of the locomotive that Madame had brought for Maman Zuzu from her trip to Prague. Its monotonous click-clacking gave Nuri a headache. It went quickly over a metal bridge, passed matchbox houses and spotted cows and sheep in a green field, entered a tunnel, came out the other end behind a stony mountain, and blew its whistle, which echoed in the reception hall. But Nuri was not a child to be given a toy or to be placated by Madame for the loss of Maman Zuzu. Anyway, according to Badri Khanom, he was, God willing, almost like a "grown-up gentleman" who no longer enjoyed such juvenile activities. Even if he did keep some habits from his early days, he was no more childish than his classmates. Like them, sometimes before going to sleep he saw the furniture take on strange shapes in the darkness. The shadows on the windowpanes would grow legs, like desert monsters, and begin moving toward his bed. His insides would churn with fear.

The sky that New Year's Day shone a pleasant bright blue through the glass door, but Nuri felt helplessly angry instead of excited and happy. If he could, he would take a felt-tip marker and blacken the glass. An inexplicable fury engulfed him. He was being uprooted and could not sit still. He wanted to kick the toy train. No doubt Maman Zuzu was sitting back comfortably in her seat on the plane, happy to be alone and not bothered by anyone else as she approached the frontiers of Europe. Nuri pitied Ladan for her lethargy and passivity. The way she held her naked and goose-pimpled elbows away from her body, like a plucked chicken. She folded together the hem of her skirt and meticulously rearranged herself on the sofa. She put her limp hands in her lap as if she were pleading her innocence. Her eyelids gradually drooped, and she fell asleep in that same position. Nuri thought about waking her up, but Madame reached from behind and placed her hands on his shoulders, as if she had read his thoughts.

If Nuri needed comforting, it was from Maman Zuzu, not anyone else. When he thought of the distance separating him from Maman Zuzu, his head began to spin. He did not belong here. The scratching of the German record tempted him to run away, to go to his family's old apartment in Shahreza Street; to the alley behind the university where he and his friend Buki Tahmasbi had gone cycling all during his childhood; to the Tahmasbis' apartment in Amirabad Avenue, where he used to hang out at all times like a member of their family. When he walked through the door, Mrs. Tahmasbi would bring him tea and almond cookies. Soraya,

Buki's sister, who was ten years his senior, would give him money to go to the Shadman Stationery Store and buy pictures of her favorite movie stars and borrow a few old novels she had already read two or three times. Cyrus, Buki's older brother, would gather up the children in front of Cinema Diana and under the streetlamps show them pictures he had taken of his prostitutes in Naser Khosrow Street motel rooms, with their walls of peeled plaster and rickety foldout beds. Sometimes even Colonel Tahmasbi and his friend Mr. Ra'oof played a game of backgammon with him, betting a pair of socks. If Nuri won, they would go back on their word, laughing. "What socks?" He liked this teasing. They treated him like one of their own, cheated at backgammon, and made no fuss when he arrived at their apartment.

The easiest thing would be to excuse himself to go to the bathroom and walk out of the house. But he did not know why he suddenly lost his courage in Madame's presence. By the time he understood what he was doing, it was too late. He had kicked the table laden with traditional mourning offerings so hard that everything fell to the floor with a clatter.

Tall and imposing like the statue of Justice, Madame stood in front of him. She asked: "Do you feel better?" When Nuri did not answer, she pointed a finger toward the carpet. "Do you see that dish? Please pick it up."

Nuri had to obey Madame's orders, but as soon as he heard her accented voice, he saw red. Bending down in front of a foreign woman was beneath him. He put his hands in his armpits and stared downward, pouting. He did not budge an inch. With her handkerchief, Madame pretended to blow her nose in polite European fashion. She arched her eyebrows to show Nuri how fed up she was with his silly antics. "So? Your Excellency's Eastern pride prevents you from treating your grandmother in a civilized manner. Now anger has got the better of you. You are not controlling your anger."

Nuri raised his voice so that she wouldn't imagine he was afraid of her: "Do you think I am your servant that I should follow every one of your orders?"

Madame half opened her mouth in jest and disbelief and then with a few fake coughs stared at the ceiling. "You, my servant? Really? God forbid.

Is it only servants who work? Gentlemen don't ever dirty their hands? I don't want to pick a fight with Your Excellency, but you don't understand my language. You interpret my words very, very, very poorly."

"What don't I understand? What do I misinterpret? Are you the only one who understands anything? You're damn wrong. I do understand, maybe even better than you."

"My dearrr. There is nothing wrong with not understanding. Great men have always been proud of limited understanding. 'He who does not know and does not know that he does not know will for eternity remain in quadruple ignorance.'"

She lifted the hem of her skirt, knelt down on the carpet, and picked up the dish. Then she turned her attention to the locomotive, which had fallen off the table. Its piston had become detached from the shaft and its red light was spinning around on the carpet. Nuri said mockingly: "This won't be worth anything anymore."

Madame shook her head: "What a pity, a hundred pities. Your servant is certain that Your Excellency will fix it himself."

Nuri pointed his finger to his chest: "Me?" When he noticed that Madame was not paying any attention to him, he said in a Rashti accent: "Mo?" Madame tried to fit the shaft back into the piston. Nuri could not stand the silence: "Buy a little whistle to replace it."

Madame raised the piston toward him: "Fix it, Your Excellency!"

Nuri backed off: "You fix it yourself. I don't like this place. I want to go to New York and be with my mother."

Madame aligned the groove in the piston with the shaft. "Put this back together. In the future, you will become a renowned engineer."

"I am already an engineer. If this were fixable, I would have fixed it in no time."

His brashness did not have the desired effect on Madame. On the contrary, it cheered her up. With a childish happiness, she took his hands and folded them around the piston and the shaft. She said, "Here is the ball, and here the field. If you are a man, you'll fix this."

Nuri had no idea what to do with the two pieces of the rickety train. Should he reassemble them? Or should he throw them in the air and let them fall to the ground and break? For this decision, he needed a signal from Madame, but Madame gave nothing away. He ended up fixing the engine, but quite by accident. His hands began moving and brought the shaft and the piston slowly together. Involuntarily, he shouted, "Mumzie, look! Look how it is fixed!"

"My dearrr!" She took the engine from Nuri and held it up. She twirled around happily and placed the locomotive on its tracks as if it were a plane landing. "Bravo! Well done! In the future, you will become a great engineer, and you will lead life's caravan happily to its appointed destiny. So allow your humble servant to invite Your Excellency to stay with us here." She rounded her eyes. "I promise to teach you secrets to lighten the burden of your mother's absence. Would you like to stay here with us?"

Nuri hid his hands behind his back. "No, I wouldn't like to."

Najmeh's voice came up from the first-floor hallway. "Nuri, have some shame. You are not supposed to talk to your grandmother this way."

"Sure I can talk this way. What business is it of yours? I want to go back to our own place."

In the mere second he had turned his face, Madame vanished. Most probably to punish him for his pigheadedness. He followed the scent of her sweat to the stairs and climbed them on the tips of his toes. He had seen the cupboards full of antique objects, the big china vases, and the framed embroidery, but now he was looking at them as his own possessions. The dervish's begging bowl and dagger, the needlework with a velvet background in a bronze frame, the water pitcher and the china hookah lid from Naser al-din Shah's era, the agate rosary with beads as large as plums—all neatly arranged on the glass shelves, reminders of a cozy corner in a room with plaster moldings and paisley rugs, with floor cushions and old-style korsis from the Qajar era, matching silver candleholders and mirrors, old-fashioned lamps, and long-stemmed, tulip-shaped lights placed among European furniture for display. He entered an enclosed space he did not recognize. A storage room filled with strange shelves, old furniture, and a thousand knickknacks covered with dust. He heard Madame's voice from outside. "Don't go in there. I am here on the balcony."

Nuri pretended not to hear. He picked up an old guitar painted with paisley patterns in bright yellow and red. He passed his fingers over the strings, and as soon as they produced a sound, he stopped it with the palm of his hand. He came to a writing table with a little ledge in front, a thousand tiny drawers the size of matchboxes, and a wooden cover that rolled down over it. As he reached to open one of the drawers, Madame's head appeared in the doorway. She beckoned for him to follow her. He left the storage room and spotted Madame through the open door of the study. She sat at her organ, facing the breeze from the Alborz Mountains and waiting for him. As soon as she saw him enter, she narrowed her eyes and asked, "Which song should I sing for you?"

"None."

With her mouth open in the shape of a shoehorn, Madame began singing. She held up her hands in midair as if halting an invisible creature's advance. The song was strangely mesmerizing. Nuri's eyes hurt from the bright uniform blue of the sky. He had been tricked, but he had no idea how.

Madame's song came to an end. Her voice was still echoing in the room when she opened her arms wide for Nuri. "Nuri-jan, don't be shy."

"Do you always sing alone?"

"Singing is beautiful. Wherever you go, you take a beautiful voice with you. Even in prison you can sing and keep yourself busy. Why do American blacks have such nice voices? Because they sing in prison and keep themselves happy."

"Where did you learn to sing?"

Madame pursed her lips. "Would you like to sing?"

"I don't know."

"If you stay with me, you'll learn."

"I don't like studying."

"Oh, I'll teach you in such a way it will be pure pleasure. In your country, pleasure is hated. People here think suffering is good for your soul. But 'without pleasure and wine, life is not possible.'" She took Nuri's hand and walked elegantly toward the parrot's cage. She put a fingertip between the bars of the cage and said, "Hellooo, Asali!"

Asali puffed up the feathers around his neck and answered in a nasal tone, "Hellooo, Asali!"

"Give us a kiss"

"Give us a kiss."

"Hurry up, give us a kiss!

"Hurry up, give us a kiss."

Madame turned a self-satisfied gaze toward the ceiling as if she had just accomplished something important. She lowered her face so Nuri, standing on his toes, could kiss her. She said bashfully, "Thank you. I am very grateful."

In front of the hall mirror, she ran her hands over her hair, lifted the hem of her black skirt to her knees, and then dropped it again. The silk furled around and settled over the curves of her thighs. She seemed to enjoy this sensation. She narrowed her eyes at Nuri with exaggerated pride, as if saying, "Is there anyone else like me?" Nuri got a whiff of a perfume like apple blossoms, subtle but moist and refreshing. Madame put her fingers under Nuri's chin. In a German accent she said, "Dearrr, I am most eager to take your mother's place, but I see your heart must stay empty for your mother." She gave him a hug. "I can't fill that empty space, but I can familiarize you with a world you would enjoy and find your wishes fulfilled. It is said . . . " She smiled and recited a poem Nuri had heard before: "'Because there was no aloe wood, I brought willow wood. I brought a black face and white hair. You told me loss of hope is anathema, I followed your promise and brought hope.'"

Nuri corrected all her mistakes. "It's not black, it's white."

Madame nodded in agreement. "Correct . . . correct . . . 'black hair and white face. You told me loss of hope is anathema, I followed your promise and . . . '"

"'I took your advice . . . '"

"Correct . . . correct . . . "

Nuri threw his arms around his grandmother's neck and hugged her. He remembered the German lullaby "Sleep, My Child," which Madame had sung for him during his childhood, long before he came to the Dezashibi house. Madame repeatedly said, "How nice! How nice!" She put one hand on her chest, leaned back, and surveyed Nuri's face. "Your blue eyes are German, but Your Excellency looks at the world like Easterners do."

"What does that mean?"

She shrugged and pursed her lips. "How do I know? Easterners have a dreamy gaze. It's hungry. A hungry person's life is dreamy."

Nothing in the Austrian woman's smile and blue eyes was Eastern, not even the softness with which she delicately put her fingers on Nuri's shoulders and directed him toward the organ in the corner of the study. Nuri was gradually drawn to distant and forgotten places. Fatigue relaxed his muscles. He remembered Ladan, who was probably still snoring on the old sofa. Maman Zuzu's plane had probably by now flown over Beirut. He fell asleep on the rug in the study.

. . . 2 . . .

Nuri's only contact with Maman Zuzu was through the brief letters she wrote to him on prestamped airmail envelopes twice a month and deposited in a mailbox on her way to the Beauty Institute in the mornings. She filled the letters with phrases such as "you all," as if addressing a group of relatives. About Nuri himself, she always implied that he was becoming terribly sensitive. Had he taken after his Papa Javad, who exploded at anything and chanted slogans until everyone grew quiet?

Nuri wrote to her in the tone of a grownup. He never said a word about the pain the corn on his left foot's pinkie was causing him or about the new pimples he was getting on his face. Imitating Papa Javad's modern poetry, Nuri sometimes started his sentences at the end or the middle. With poetic turns such as "You too are a memory of the sky," "I am filled with the green of the loneliness of the woods," "You are a vista on the mirage of the imagination," and a handful of other sayings that showed off his talents, Nuri indicated to her that he was not all that naïve. Either Maman Zuzu did not catch on or did not admit to catching on. In her joking tone, she wrote to him: "How quickly you become emotional in that Tehran of yours!"

She spoke mostly about the Beauty Institute. She talked about shopping centers and Sunday picnics with Princess Bertha on Staten Island, her heavy workload, her financial difficulties, and the fact that she had to study day and night and devote herself to learning English. Despite all this, she made him long to join her for a stroll through the streets of New York, to eat lunch at a restaurant whose off-white linoleum sparkled, whose air smelled of the gentle dampness of old basements, whose waiters, dressed in black pants and white aprons, brought them dishes they had not tasted until then. After lunch, they would go to a movie and watch a film advertised on a large color poster in which a man and a woman stared into each other's eyes and a space shuttle carried them along a silvery trajectory to the most remote stars, or in which a man with startled eyes was frozen in the act of jumping out of a burning car, arms lifted up in the air, a boy clutching his blue jacket from behind and pulling him in the opposite direction. Scenes indicative of time having come to a standstill at a dangerous and sensitive moment.

Nuri remembered going to movies on Friday afternoons with Ladan, Maman Zuzu, and Papa Javad. As soon as they entered the theater, he got a whiff of some peculiar chemical like gasoline or shoe polish. In the dusty and dark theater, the actors' movements blended with the spectators' moonlit faces, and a low and terrifying music slowly amplified the flitting light on the curtain. Nuri stood on tiptoe, clinging to Maman Zuzu's wrist, and excitedly smacked his lower lip.

Most nights now, he picked on Black Najmeh and even found fault with Madame, asking why their bread was not as crusty and delicious as before. When he stretched out on his bed, he complained that it was not firm enough. His mattress curved and did not let him sleep properly. Even when he fell asleep, he was afraid of opening his eyes later and failing to recognize the second-floor room Madame had given him. Between sleep and wakefulness, he saw images that had some connection with Black Najmeh and the strange stories she told from the South. Thirteen years ago, when Maman Zuzu was traveling in the South, she went into labor with Nuri. They searched everywhere but could not find an obstetrician or midwife. Black Najmeh finally found an Indian doctor by the name of M. G. Singh in the Central Police Station, which also housed the trade office of a shipping company. How she managed to convince Dr. Singh to attend the delivery was a long and adventurous story that Black Najmeh changed periodically. Sometimes she talked about peculiar rituals a few Malaysian orderlies performed in order to persuade Dr. Singh to examine Maman Zuzu. The only segment of the story she never changed was the part when Dr. Singh looks at Nuri and says, "This child's eyes are not normal."

Black Najmeh is dumbfounded. "Why? What's wrong with such a beautiful child?"

Dr. Singh throws Najmeh such a strange glance that she gets scared. She lowers her kerchief to the tattoo above her eyes, grabs the baby out of Dr. Singh's arms and screams at him, "There is nothing wrong with this baby. He is just thirsty."

She was right. Nobody questioned Nuri's beauty. As Aunt Moluk said, "This is not just a baby! He is a houri, an angel!" He had such blue, mesmerizing eyes that Madame sat for hours in a corner and stared at them. She could not take her gaze off them—as if from behind those eyes a hopeful and deprived soul were trying to draw her in with its magnetic force. Sometimes she begged Black Najmeh not to leave her alone in the house for fear she might be entrapped by Nuri's eyes. Maman Zuzu frequently got into fights with Madame when she talked like this and then would not visit Madame for a long time. No matter how many messages Madame sent to her that she liked Nuri only as a grandson, Maman Zuzu would not leave the baby with her. Instead, Maman Zuzu grumbled that were it not for Nuri's blue eyes and blond hair, Madame would not be so attached to this small baby. She mentioned the twelve plaques Madame Julie had given to Madame in 1935—especially the oil paintings depicting an Austrian boy and girl with golden locks, exactly like those of the angels painted inside churches, and blue eyes that automatically drew one toward them. Up to the day the news of Maman Zuzu's pregnancy reached the relatives, nobody knew that these paintings even existed. But as soon as Madame heard the news, she screamed joyously that her second grandchild would be a boy, and she hung on the wall of their Shahreza Street apartment one of the plaster plaques for Maman Zuzu to see several times a day so that the baby she carried would be born with a face as beautiful as the ones in the paintings. Another instance of this connection was the German lullaby "Sleep, My Child," which Madame murmured to Nuri some nights. This song brought such tears to the child's eyes it was as if he belonged to some other place and desperately longed for it. All the older women who saw Nuri during those years believed this kind of extreme sensitivity was abnormal in an infant. As young as Nuri was, he responded to cooing and smiles with huge waves of laughter. When he got tired, he sat in his cradle and sucked his thumb and sighed deeply, as if he missed someone.

Even now, at the age of thirteen, every morning when he woke up early and stood by the window of his new room, he felt the green and damp of the garden so vibrantly on his skin that he feared he would embarrass himself in front of Madame and the Senator. The sky was reflected as the color of quicksilver on the surface of the stone pool, and in Nuri's imagination it appeared to be bubbling like a spring full of tinsel stars. He saw his grandparents' house as an enchanted and mysterious palace. He got an urge to roam through the rooms and look into every nook and cranny. The house had been built in the European style by a Swiss architect during the reign of Reza Shah. It had brick walls, windows with awnings, a green copper roof, a large mirrored hall, portals in the shape of the sun's rays, columned hallways, and plaster moldings representing baskets of fruit and flowers that still showed an influence from the architecture of the end of the Qajar era. Yet the main building, in the northern corner of the garden, had been erected with turrets in the style of a nineteenth-century eastern European city such as Prague. A city unlike Tehran, one with overcast skies, winding and cobblestoned streets, misshapen buildings, pointy turrets with rusty surfaces, slanted roofs, and inhabitants who lead a busy but utterly quiet and melancholic life behind windows framed by stone walls. Exactly like the old lithographs that depict people—a few burned-out matches—wearing multicolored hats, carrying canes, standing in the distance on an iron bridge, and looking at a sky that could represent only the calm and quiet of a European city and the void of a rainy, cold place. Whatever Nuri saw appealed to him and spurred him to move about the house and discover a secret he thought was being kept from him.

His loneliness stemmed not only from Maman Zuzu's absence, but from his own depths, and it eventually led him to do things that he recognized as illogical. At night, any little stirring in the house woke him up. The sound of the toilet tank emptying when the Senator went to the bathroom several times a night because of his prostate problems. The sound of Black Najmeh's coughs, which she still tried to control by chain-smoking despite the chest pains and bronchitis that had enlarged her heart like a pumpkin. The sound of Ladan tossing and turning in her bed, which after a few minutes ended in her snoring—sometimes until morning if she did not turn onto her left side.

One night toward the end of spring, Nuri finally fell asleep but awoke with a start at two in the morning. He realized he was not in his own bed and that he had fallen asleep on the carpet in Ladan's room. He could not figure out how he had gotten to Ladan's room and where he had found the sheet he had pulled over himself. He lifted his head from the pillow and stared into the darkness with his sleepy eyes. The early-morning breeze reminded him of the brittleness of mountain air. He heard a moan that echoed like a bow letting loose an arrow. He rose and tiptoed into the hallway, which was neither dark nor bright. The intermingled shadows made the walls look like the square windows of old basements. Along the length of the hallway, he distinguished the shapes of flowerpots and antiques in clusters. Nuri climbed the stairs, as if his going up to the third-floor balcony were being directed by a force outside his control. He first saw the light in the bathroom, which stretched like sharp scissor blades from the crack of the door almost to the edge of the wooden floor. But the light was turned off in the Senator and Madame's bedroom, and nothing could be heard from the study. Nuri's heart beat so fast he could hear it pounding in his ears, and he realized that he had gone up there for the express purpose of visiting the storage room. The best thing would have been to file the whole idea away and return to his own room. But it was already too late. He had to proceed.

With great trepidation, he opened the storage-room door and turned on the light. The room looked very different from a few years ago. Worse than the backstage of a provincial theater, filled with knickknacks that, aside from their connection to Madame's past, had no function. He started out from the old ice chest whose missing lock had left a mark on its door. He found a beaded soiree purse wrapped inside an Iranian prayer shawl. The name "Frieda" was embroidered on it in the Latin alphabet with imitation pearls. He looked at two cloth paintings from the time of the First World War, a yellow cage, and a guitar that Madame and the Senator had bought from a mental asylum in Prague during their honeymoon. He got to the headless and armless mannequin, dressed in a gray felt uniform, which up to a few years ago Madame had still used for her dress fittings. Then he saw his own reflection in the tall mirror framed with inlaid woodwork. The longer he looked, the more bizarre it appeared. He imagined someone spying on him from the hallway. He left in such a hurry that he forgot to switch the light off.

The next morning he tidied his room with unusual care. He took a bath and was putting on his navy blue New Year suit when he suddenly remembered he had left the storage-room light on. If Madame noticed, her suspicions would be directed toward no one but Nuri himself. Ladan would never have had the courage to do such a thing. Nuri hurried to the storage room and turned the light off, planning to return to his room before he was seen. But first he stood in front of Madame and the Senator's bedroom for a while and listened to the silence. If someone were to ask what he was looking for this early in the morning, he would trot out a whole array of unbelievable excuses.

He went down to the garden quietly and picked a few branches of honeysuckle near the stone pool. He hid the branches behind his back and once again climbed the stairs to the third floor. When he reached the balcony, he put his fingers between the metal rods of the parrot's cage and, imitating Madame, said, "Helloo, Asali!"

Asali answered, "Helloo, Asali!"

He didn't find any trace of the Senator. Most probably he was in the study making phone calls to unknown people in Gorgan about the sale of his Aghcheh properties. He hardly ever had time to come to the table for breakfast, lunch, or dinner. Whenever Nuri wanted to see him, he would run into the study with the insecticide pump, chasing down flies and bees, saying breathlessly, "Should I hit you? Should I destroy you? Should I send you into the other world?"

The Senator always pretended not to notice anything. He continued to hold the open newspaper in front of his face. But this early in the morning, playing that game would be crazy.

Nuri waited until Madame came out of her bedroom. He offered her the honeysuckle branches with two fingers in the operatic pose he had learned from her. Madame's jaw dropped with happiness. She examined Nuri's round face with admiration. She buried her nose in the yellow and white flowers of the honeysuckle and drew a deep breath. She took on a playful look and said, "Why have these flowers turned yellow?"

"Being away from you has made them turn yellow."

Her eyes glittered. "What a clever child Your Excellency is!"

Nuri started laughing like a maniac. He had no idea why. Madame left for the balcony and, singing under her breath, began watering the plants. She believed that tropical plants, like humans, had souls. They enjoyed hearing songs and would grow faster. She seemed preoccupied with her chores, but she was looking at Nuri from the corner of her eye. She placed her key chain in a brass bowl on the antiques cupboard and said, "Your Excellency is well?"

Nuri shrugged. "I am quite happy. Today our school is closed."

"Oh, how excellent! I will teach you such tricks that your brain will fly rrright out of your head into the sky." She gestured with a fingertip flicking away from her temple. "Guaranteed, my darrling. A guarantee that you will never forget."

"What will I never forget?"

"I do not want to say."

"You have to say."

She weighed something in her mind. "Are you hungry?"

"I'm always hungry."

"Oh, how wonderful! A hungry person, like me, becomes jealous and sad. He wants more. He wants to have more, isn't that right?"

"So?"

"Your servant has devoted much love to your literature. I have breathed in much smoke from the burning lamp by which I had to read; my bright days became dark like night, and my dark nights became brightened until I memorized more than a thousand verses and Persian parables. I bet that I too, like Allameh Ghazvini, will someday glorify into print corrected handwritten manuscripts. From olden days, great Iranian men have said that the more we want, the more we expose ourselves to danger. But your servant believes that the more greedy I am, the more alive I feel. The more I enjoy myself. Right?"

"I don't understand what you mean."

"Your servant will teach you a trick so that you can have whatever you want, but under one condition."

She waited for Nuri to grow anxious. Nuri said, "Under what condition?"

"Under the condition that you never use it."

Nuri answered in total puzzlement, "Why are you teasing me?"

"Are you prepared to pass tests all your life?"

She put the watering can outside the bathroom door and left. Wherever she went, Nuri followed. In the storage room, she took from an old cupboard a rectangular box lined with blue satin. She crooked her fingers with the delicacy of a young girl and coyly opened the box. First, she asked, "Does Your Excellency know what we do with this?"

"No."

She shook her head. "Noch, noch, noch. Horse racing! Fine. Now tell me, what do we do with this box?" Instead of Nuri, she herself answered, "Horse racing."

"Oh?"

She took out of the box a piece of paper with a purple background, a paintbrush, and a small bottle of a phosphorus-looking liquid. She inserted the brush into the liquid and drew two parallel lines on the paper. "Does Your Excellency see these lines? Each one is a line for horse racing, OK? We have two excellent horses we have to give beautiful names to, right? Isn't a nameless horse useless?" She wrinkled her nose. "Phew, throw it away. So let's find a name for each horse, all right?"

"All right."

Absentmindedly, Madame stared at him. She began again, as if talking to a child. "What should we call the first horse?"

"A good name everyone will like."

"We'll call the first horse Rostam, after the legendary epic hero, OK?"

"OK."

"That's excellent. So we'll call the second horse Ashkabus, Rostam's adversary, OK?" She paused. "You don't like that?"

"Yes, yes, I like it very much."

"If you don't like Rostam and Ashkabus, we'll call them Laurel and Hardy."

She gave the piece of paper to Nuri. She held a cigarette lighter beneath it, and with green phosphorous sparks she lit the lines for Rostam and Ashkabus. Although Ashkabus's flame reached the end of his line faster, she declared Rostam the winner. She threw her hands up in the air. "No, Rostam will never lose."

She put the box back in the old cupboard. Next she brought out some round cards called "thaumatropes." Along their edges were two strings, and when you pulled the strings, the cards spun around. The pictures on the backs of the cards would superimpose themselves on the pictures on the fronts. One of them was a picture of an empty mousetrap. When she spun the card, a mouse appeared in the trap. When she spun the next card, a nineteenth-century Austrian calvaryman appeared on a horse that at first had not had a rider. Madame seemed to tire quickly of this game as well. She took a metal cylinder from a drawer and stood it vertically on a card. The card's abstract patterns were reflected on the cylinder as a village scene, with hills and a few cows and sheep. The pattern on the second card became the entrance hall of an Italian house. An imposing person stood by the staircase with his hands on his hips. At that point, Black Najmeh shouted for them to come down and eat breakfast. Madame shrugged as if she did not feel up to it. She murmured a song that apparently Princess Bertha had sung to Siegfried von Friedhoff in a Prague hospital—a song so sad and melancholic that Nuri stuttered, "How nicely you sing operas."

Madame smiled with appreciation. "I am most grateful."

She complained about Princess Bertha, who had constantly been ready for the worst calamities and had always met with a far worse fate than she had imagined for herself. In Prague, with one look at Siegfried's face, she had seen an image of death.

"Siegfried, the elegant and handsome prince, the white dove of Prague!"

Madame looked disturbed. She was restlessly looking here and there for something to occupy her. She took her handkerchief from her bosom and sighed, "Finita la commedia!" She held the handkerchief to her eyes and grew pensive. "Your servant notices that Siegfried in his hospital bed has one sock on and one off. I ask the head nurse to bring me some water so I can wash the blood from his face. The head nurse brings a bucket of water. I put my finger in it. It's cold as ice. I tell Her Majesty: 'Dear lady, this water is too cold. How can one wash a friend's face with cold water?'"

She stood up, brushed off her skirt, and took a camera from a cupboard drawer. "Would you like to have a picture taken to send to Maman Zuzu?" She showed him the camera up close. "Your servant offers you this measly gift so that you will never forget your servant. Be attentive to my requests. Never forget your servant, OK? I thank you. May God preserve Your Excellency for your mother."

Nuri said nothing. She placed the camera on a tripod, pressed the automatic button and, like an excited child, came over to Nuri and squeezed his shoulders, urging him to smile into the camera. Then she went to the pantry. On a silver platter she brought out three biscuits for Nuri and the Monk's Syrup for herself. She thanked Nuri excitedly. "I am grateful. May God keep you safe for your mother."

She took the old album from the shelf and showed him her engagement and honeymoon pictures near Lakes Como and Lugano. In these pictures, she was dressed all in white, in a cotton dress with a loose skirt, a broad-brimmed straw hat, silk stockings, net shoes with the heels placed close together and the toes wide apart. Neat, tidy, and freshly washed, exactly like a patch of cloud that has descended to a white beach. With the bashful smile of a proud virgin and a look that seemed faded in the sunlight, blond or auburn hair—it was difficult to tell in the old black-and-white photographs. A few strands of hair showed from under the brim of the hat; she was pushing them back with the tip of her fingers—a gesture that made Nuri aware of the gulf between them.

Madame stood up to go to the first-floor hall for breakfast. "You have not eaten your breakfast. You must." She blinked. "You will get thin. No one will like you."

They descended the stairs together.

Nuri was free to spend hours in the storage room, exploring each corner. He had to wait for everyone to fall asleep at night. Although he spent the time he would have normally been at school walking about the streets—buying himself a salami sandwich from the shop next to the Metropol Cinema, afterwards taking the bus home—the hours nevertheless passed very slowly. Around sundown, the relatives gathered together by the stone pool to discuss finding a wife for Amiz Hosein, Amiz Abbas's sixty-year-old bachelor brother. Nuri sat quietly in a corner and listened to the relatives until Badri Khanom arrived and reported Amiz Hosein's own plan, now evidently dropped, to marry a widow named Shuri Khanom Malayeri. Despite the relatives' uproar over this match, Nuri's mind was elsewhere. He listened to a prolonged silence he called "the sound of silence." Madame was right. Silence was merely a reflection of the passing of time.

He tried to call the Tahmasbis' apartment, but no one answered the phone. From his window, he listened to Amiz Abbas talk about a special magnetic pencil, like the Emperor Franz Joseph's unique fountain pen. The pencil's glass tube held a small replica of the Hotel Excelsior that moved up and down. Badri Khanom once again returned to the topic of Amiz Hosein's marriage, but this time in a joking manner to dispel his misgivings. "Uncle dear, why don't you think a little bit about marrying one of these pretty women? You are well over forty."

Amiz Hosein protested, "Why?"

"Well, you can't expect to have educated young women line up outside your house and wait for the next twenty years to have you choose one of them."

Overcome with indignation, Amiz Hosein stood straight as an arrow. Badri Khanom quietly mentioned Shuri Khanom's name and watched Amiz Hosein out of the corner of her eye to see what effect it had on him. First, she mentioned how Shuri Khanom had become a widow; then she slowly moved on to a description of her youth and beauty, the facts that Shuri Khanom did not have any children and that from the tip of every one of her fingers flowed a thousand arts. Despite being raised in Ardabil, she surpassed the Tehrani women in her beauty and her stylish manner of dressing. Since the year she had lost that young husband of hers, she had never stepped outside her house without a dark and appropriate dress. Whenever Mr. Malayeri's name was mentioned, she got tears in her eyes and told them about the year the bitter cold drove the wolves into the town of Ardabil and even into the government buildings. When she got to Mr. Malayeri's name, her innate modesty made her use only the pronoun *he* to refer to her late husband. Several hours after the offices had been closed, "he" was busy balancing the Post Office accounts when suddenly a wolf came into "his" office and tore "him" apart in the most appalling manner.

Shuri Khanom was not the kind of woman to lose her equanimity after such a calamity. She got a job as a typist at the National Bank. Praise be to God, she had a good income and perks including monthly rations of rice, sugar, oil, and tea, as well as life insurance, medical insurance, and a down payment toward a piece of land on which to build a small house for herself. Badri Khanom, who had just returned from a three-week tour she had taken with her husband, Dr. Jannati, to New York and Niagara Falls, suggested that Amiz Hosein and Shuri Khanom spend their honeymoon at Niagara Falls. After that, the voices faded away. Nuri overheard snatches of conversation and finally the relatives' customary good-byes, which, as always, took fifteen to twenty minutes.

Once the guests left, the restlessness Nuri had felt earlier in the evening returned. He had no appetite. He just played with the *kuku* that Black Najmeh brought him for dinner. He felt like a fish out of water. Wherever he was didn't feel as if it were his rightful place. He didn't even fight the old temptation to go to the storage room. He tiptoed to the stairs and climbed to the third floor. His heart was pounding, and, most strangely, he was more scared of himself than of any other creature. That is, scared of the persistent and irrepressible thoughts that tempted him to enter the storage room.

Only a weak lightbulb glimmered like a small candle down by the floor. The Senator plugged this light in before going to sleep to avoid bumping into things when he got up at night to go to the washroom. A dog barked in the distance, somewhere in the back alleys of Dezashib. Once again silence returned to the hallway. The Senator's raincoat was still hanging on its hook. Nuri recognized the Mutual Credit Bank's checkbook on the shelf by the side window. Ladan jokingly referred to the checks as "Muchul." He ran his fingers along the edge of the two panels of the storage-room door to prevent them from creaking when he opened them. He entered dexterously and shut the door behind him. Turning on the light would draw attention, but in the dark he could not see anything. He hit the light switch and immediately spotted Maman Zuzu and Papa Javad's wedding picture on a cupboard. They were standing in front of the ceremonial wedding spread, and their faces were so touched up that they looked expressionless and faded. The groom clutched the bride's arm with pride, and the bride, holding a bouquet of flowers to her chest, smiled with the intention to please. A white veil covered her hair, curled around one of her arms, and trailed behind her for a couple of meters. Nuri found another picture of Papa Javad that Maman Zuzu, unbeknownst to him, had taken of him. He was in the middle of the staircase that went up to their apartment, wearing a knapsack on his back and holding a canvas suitcase. His face was sunburned; there were two wet stains in his armpits; and the tail of his checkered cloth shirt had come untucked from his pants.

The more Nuri saw, the more his appetite grew. With great haste, he took Madame's special cards out of the drawers of a desk, reflected their patterns on the metal cylinder, and made pictures appear that depicted a modestly furnished room of the pre–Second World War era—an era in which women wore long dresses in Hollywood movies. Their skirts were loose, like the robes of Arab nomads, and descended to the tips of their shoes. A piece of cloth wrapped around their hats like Indian soldiers' turbans. In several scenes, Nuri saw a middle-aged man and woman performing various sex acts on a foldout bed. The woman had her head turned sideways. Her hair was loose and made her look like someone in an old postcard, sitting on a swing in the middle of spring blossoms. The man had a goatee and a shaved head like a person recently released from a hospital or a mental asylum. His lowered gaze seemed pensive and philosophical.

Nuri would definitely take these pictures to Buki Tahmasbi. Buki himself sometimes brought pictures of his older brother, Cyrus, and pretty Pari entangled naked in each other's arms on a bed. During school recess, Buki and Nuri would escape to the alley behind the university and look at the photos in a hurry. Nuri got so excited that he had to act clownish. He laughed and pointed to various parts of Cyrus and Pari's bodies until Buki himself was overcome with laughter. But deep inside Nuri felt moved by an instinctive urge he could never satisfy. Even that lack of fulfillment was enjoyable, though. He didn't know why the image of Madame's naked body suddenly floated into his head. He tried every trick he knew, but the image stuck with him. Finally, he threw the cards inside the cupboard drawer and shut it. He looked for something to distract him. From between Madame's opera dresses, he saw a replica of a series of buildings, the tallest of which was no higher than half a meter, in a European village that Madame herself had apparently arranged. Nuri sat down on the floor and grew so absorbed in looking at the stone walls, the ivy climbing the rain gutters, and the edges of the roofs that he temporarily forgot the image of Madame. The windmill, the well, and the pulley in the center of the village, the bakery, the grocery store, and the pharmacy, so delicate and real that Nuri did not know which to focus on.

He heard the creaking of the door behind him. When he turned, Ladan was standing in the doorway in her nightgown. Her hair fell straight down around her face and curled in a semicircle on her neck, making her look almost Japanese. Nuri was happy to see her and signaled to her to come in. Ladan was mesmerized, her mouth open in surprise, as she looked at the objects in the room. On tiptoe, she approached Nuri. "Mamakh, what are you doing here?"

Nuri showed her the replicas. "Come over here and have a look at these."

Ladan, her attention still riveted, kept staring around the room. "Mamakh, what are you doing here at midnight?"

"Why have you come here?"

"Why shouldn't I come? I came out of the bathroom, and I noticed the light was on. If it were you, wouldn't you have asked why the light was on? So I did the same. I realized it had to be you. No one but you has this disease of going into nooks and crannies. You're not like me, who won't go anywhere without permission."

"Oh, right. So who was it who wanted to go into Madame's room and try out her perfume?"

"I wasn't looking for her perfume. I was looking for her loofah."

"Looking for what?"

"The fruit of one of those plants by the stone pool. She takes their skin off and uses them to make washcloths for herself."

"What's wrong with fabric washcloths that you have to go into Madame's room for the sake of a washcloth made of some plant and risk your reputation?"

"You have obviously not smelled them, otherwise you wouldn't ask. When you wash with them, your body smells of jasmine for three days.

Madame brought the seeds from an Austrian village. Most of the villagers use these loofahs. When you enter the village, you get dizzy from the
smell of jasmine." She drew close to the rows of Madame's opera dresses.
She took one of the hangers that held a dress with a navy cloth ribbon
instead of a belt, and she rubbed its blue satin fabric between her fingers.
"How pretty this is."

Nuri wanted to show her the cards, but he worried that she would
report him to Madame. He changed his mind. He pointed to the dress and
said, "Try it on, let's see how you look in it."

"You want me to try it on? Mumzie won't like that."

"How pious you are! Try it on already. Then I'll show you a French
village you won't believe."

Doubtfully, Ladan pulled the dress over her nightgown. She raised
one side of the skirt in front of the mirror. She bent her knees in a gesture
of respect and smiled with satisfaction. Nuri covered his mouth to stop his
laughter. "At the service of Her Majesty, the Queen . . . "

Ladan frowned. "If you want to get silly, I won't go along."

"Your Majesty's servant, your servant would like to ask . . . ha, ha,
ha . . . "

Ladan took the dress off and left the storage room in a hurry. Nuri,
now alone, turned the light off and followed Ladan down the stairs. "Wait
for me."

Ladan didn't answer. She entered her room hurriedly and shut her
door. Nuri placed his mouth to the door and in a childlike tone cooed,
"Khormaloooo-jun. Khormaloooo-jun."

"Shut up, you spoiled brat! You'll wake everyone."

"Will you open the door, or shall I come in on my own?"

"Save your clowning for your good-for-nothing friends who like it. If
you don't leave, I'll scream and wake everyone up."

"But I'm not sleepy. Let's chat a little bit together."

"Not now. We'll talk tomorrow."

Disappointed, Nuri returned to his own room. The same image of
Madame in the nude came back to him. This time he tried to change it into
an innocent religious image, something like the Virgin of Solitude. He
didn't succeed. He thought about Maman Zuzu, who seemed to be going

sightseeing with Princess Bertha almost every day. Wherever they found something taller than themselves, they had their picture taken in front of it. Pictures that raised the relatives' eyebrows. Some of them asked the Senator and Madame on the sly about "Zuzu-jun." Others lowered their eyelids and exchanged smiles with each other, pretending to be happy about Maman Zuzu's life in New York. What did it matter if Maman Zuzu took Princess Bertha's arm and stood so carefree in front of Times Square, the United Nations Building, or other places and had her picture taken? The relatives themselves neither had the patience to go to New York nor understood anything from looking at Maman Zuzu's pictures. If they decided to go abroad, they would choose places no one else had visited, maybe Madagascar or the Horn of Africa. Otherwise, anybody with a few tumans of the government's money in his pockets could buy an excursion ticket to New York and a week later return to Mehrabad Airport with ten suitcases full of American junk.

They were flabbergasted that Maman Zuzu did not look like herself in these pictures. Something in her face had changed, but they could not quite put their finger on it. Americans probably also wondered what these meaningless smiles were all about. Don't Iranians know anything besides laughing? What did it mean that a recent widow who had just lost such a sweet husband should behave so superficially and embarrass all Iranians in front of the Americans? Why didn't she put on a mournful expression and a black dress at least to save the poor departed one's honor? For instance, they had their picture taken in front of Macy's, showing half of the twenty-story building; in front of the Empire Estate Building; in front of the statue in the middle of Times Square; and in front of a man dressed like Uncle Sam walking on stilts in the street. They raised themselves on tiptoe to look head-and-shoulder taller than the image behind them. It was as if they were locked in a battle with New York or were struggling not to let the glitter of the stores, the noise in the streets, and the clamor of its strange people make them lose their moorings. In only one picture did they have their profiles turned to the camera, standing by a lead railing that stretched along the seashore like a water pipe. The steely color of the sky blended with the clouds. The outline of the Statue of Liberty was a bluish and faded smudge, holding a flame and gazing beyond the watery horizon that belonged to another world. Maman Zuzu looked carefree as a schoolgirl, with half-closed eyes and a self-satisfied smile. The wind blew into her face, brushed her hair back, and disheveled it. Nuri didn't like seeing his mother so cheerful among a bunch of strangers. Why was it necessary for her to insist on proving she was having a good time? To go on picnics with large groups of people and make funny faces, while Princess Bertha appeared impatient in her yellow-striped dress and the large sunglasses that covered half of her face? When the princess waved in front of the camera, most frequently she raised her leather purse up in the air as if she were hailing a cab.

Badri Khanom was not one to wash someone's sin in public. She had recently become a dervish and spent all her Friday evenings in the Gonabadi House of Dervishes, counting her blessings and praying until morning. The one time she said something behind Maman Zuzu's back, she had good intentions, and, to some extent, her comments could be interpreted as praise. "God be praised, knock on wood, how chubby and pretty Zuzu looks in these pictures! She obviously no longer has any cares in her life. If she gets homesick, she just goes out to one of New York's pleasant parks, gets some fresh air, and feels as good as new again." Even if Badri Khanom mentioned "her sweet husband's" car accident, she meant it as a complaint against this world's instability. "Khanom-jun, there are no more than four steps ever separating us from our graves. Whosoever grows attached to this world has given his heart to the wind. No sooner has your head touched the ground and your burial shroud has dried out than everyone forgets you. As if nothing ever happened."

Among all the pictures, Nuri chose one of Maman Zuzu by herself taken at a regular portrait studio in New York. He propped it against the bedside lamp. Like a bride who has just plucked her eyebrows before her wedding, Maman Zuzu looked remotely and strangely like herself. She had her hair cut in the current fashion, and a blue line traced all her features in such a way that it seemed her eyes, eyebrows, and pointy tresses had been cut from a piece of paper and superimposed on her face. He felt a need to explain to Maman Zuzu that his running away from school was not simply a matter of laziness. Had he not skipped school, he would have gone crazy. He looked forward to Thursday afternoons, when he was finally rid of schoolwork, took the bus home, threw his schoolbag on his bed, and rushed right up to the third floor to practice the organ. Sitting on the stairs, he first peered at Madame through the crack of the open door, at the strange faces she made in the mirror, the way she ran the tip of her fingers cautiously over her hair and murmured the famous folk song "Wheat Flower, Beloved" to herself. Then a few minutes before three o'clock Nuri went to the study, poised his fingers on the keyboard, and in his mind reviewed the new tunes he had just learned. Madame could not believe that at the age of thirteen Nuri could play Bach and Schubert so well. She lowered the corners of her mouth in surprise. No longer did she take him to the storage room or ever utter a word about his going there at night. Perhaps she did not yet know about it. Her unnatural silence tormented Nuri more than anything else. He was prepared to do something rash to be caught by Madame and rid himself of this state of uncertainty.

◆ ◆ ◆ In the fall of 1978, the year Nuri turned seventeen, all was proceeding more or less normally at the Dezashibi house. Nuri and Ladan rarely fought over their turn at the weekly magazines, the choice of seats at the dining table, or who picked up the phone first. If Vaziri was not able to drive them in the Mercedes to their old school near the Shahreza apartment, they took the bus from Tajrish to the Pahlavi intersection and from there went on foot to Amirabad Avenue. Maman Zuzu was supposed to come to Iran for three weeks of her summer vacation, but she kept postponing her trip because of financial difficulties. Nuri wished they all could go to New York. Madame hinted that if they went to New York, she would sing from *Tannhäuser* with Princess Bertha beside the ocean.

One Friday afternoon, many of their relatives were supposed to come to the Dezashibi house. Nuri got an urge to go to their old apartment to see how he felt about his past now that more than four years had gone by. In the hullabaloo of the relatives' gathering, no one would notice his absence—especially since they were going to listen to Ladan recite one of her compositions on the radio program *Youth and the Radio*. For some time, Ladan had been writing compositions that all began with one question, "Fate . . . ?" in which she explained in the language of sewing machines, tractors, and catapults how they had been made and what service they offered people. The assistant principal of Shahyad High School, Mrs. Nokiani, knocked on so many doors that the radio network finally sent an invitation to Ladan to recite one of her compositions that night.

At 3:30 in the afternoon, when nobody was paying attention, Nuri put his money in his pocket and quietly left the house. No one expected that he would go to their old neighborhood on his own. It had been more than a year since he had last gone bike riding with Buki Tahmasbi. He used to spend most of his time at the Tahmasbis' apartment. He had talked to Mrs. Tahmasbi, borrowed books from the Shadman Stationery Store for Soraya, Buki's sister, and brought her pictures of her favorite movie stars, James Dean maybe, or Alain Delon. Buki had apparently told Soraya about the storage room because now Soraya kept sending Nuri messages to lend her one of Madame's opera dresses for a few days so that Mrs. Tahmasbi could make two like it for her and her friend Shuri Khanom. Nuri was dying to go to the Tahmasbi apartment and see all of them, but not to the point of leaving Madame's dress in the care of someone as irresponsible as Soraya. Not a day went by that Soraya didn't lose her purse, sunglasses, keys, or something else.

From the street, Nuri gave a two-fingered whistle so that if Buki was home, he would come out. After a few minutes, when Buki did not show up, he went down the slope of Amirabad Avenue and returned to the Parand Pastry Shop in Shahreza Street. As usual, Reza Shahabzadeh, Naser Shahandeh, and Buki were locked in an argument under a street-lamp. Buki shouted to Nuri from a distance, "Didn't you say you couldn't come on Friday afternoons?" Turning toward the others, he said, "They won't let him."

They laughed. With a frown, Nuri quieted them down and said, "I've come to go to the movies with you."

"I don't feel like it. I'm going with Cyrus to the American Club. He's supposed to arrive any minute now."

They waited for Cyrus to pick up pretty Pari in his Dodge and drive her slowly like a movie star on Oscar night from Amirabad Body Shop to the Parand Pastry Shop. Getting out of the car, they would link arms and wave to the kids from a distance. The owner of the pastry shop was a tall Armenian named Khachator who always had a thin strand of hair waving across his gaunt face. He would draw the tip of a pencil across his chubby fingers and, waiting for Cyrus and pretty Pari to place their order, stare at the ceiling fan. Cyrus would say, "What shall we eat today, Monsieur?"

Khachator always answered with a frown, "Whatever you wish."

"Whatever we wish, Monsieur?"

"Whatever."

Khachator would bring them freshly baked cookies and Turkish coffee. Cyrus would take from his pocket a big wad of banknotes and, without counting them, leave them on the table for Khachator's tip. Then he would drive pretty Pari home. Later, he would return alone to the pastry shop and reclaim the banknotes from Khachator.

After half an hour, the pink Dodge appeared at the head of the street. Cyrus revved the engine and hit the brakes suddenly. Sure enough, next to him sat pretty Pari, for whose benefit he was showing off his driving. Buki stretched his hand out, offered his palm, and laughed, "Hit it there. Didn't I say he would bring his *gheegh?* I swear to Imam Hosein, he has brought his *gheegh.*"

For Buki, *gheegh* meant "prostitute," but Nuri preferred *ghagh.* "His *ghagh!*"

"His *gheegh.*"

Dressed in army fatigues and polished boots, Cyrus stepped out of his pink Dodge in front of the Nahid Pharmacy. He leaned against the car. That was his way of recovering from all his running around. He needed to get some rest. Twirling a chain around his fingers, he spat in the gutter and turned his gaze toward the boys gathered in the street without focusing on any one of them. It was clear from his demeanor that he did not have any patience for them. He made it obvious they should not come near his car.

It was beginning to dawn on Nuri that all was not well between Cyrus and pretty Pari and that they all would probably not go to the movies. Pretty Pari did not emerge from the car. She tilted her head against her seat and pouted at the passing traffic. Right then Cyrus jumped into the car, revved the engine, and took off to drive pretty Pari home.

Cyrus did not take long to come back. The speed with which he drove made them realize he was still angry. In front of Cinema Diana, he hit the brakes so hard that the hood of the car bounced up and down several times like a spring. The smell of burned rubber permeated the air. Cyrus gave Reza Shahabzadeh a tuman to watch over his car. He pinched his trouser legs with two fingers and shook them to bring back their freshly ironed look. He put his hand in his pocket and brought out the new pictures he had taken of himself and pretty Pari in the motel room. He gave the pictures to Buki to show the other kids. He leaned against the car and, cleaning his teeth with a toothpick, leveled a cold and devil-may-care look into the distance.

After the boys had seen the pictures, none of them dared to laugh or make jokes. Without saying a word, they gave the pictures back, and Cyrus put them inside a pocket notebook. He lowered his shirt collar and showed them the bruise on his shoulder where pretty Pari had bitten him. The boys got excited, but just when they wanted to ask something, Cyrus lifted his shirt collar back up and covered the bruise. He seated Buki next to himself in the Dodge and took off for the American Club.

It was getting dark and too late for Nuri to go by their old apartment. He said good-bye to the other boys and set out for wherever he pleased. First, he wanted to buy a chicken sandwich, then he would walk by the electronic stores, the Saderat Bank, and Aram Restaurant. He would run into a stranger whose face was not clear in the fading light of day. The stranger would greet Nuri warmly and, like a long-lost relative, ask him about Papa Javad and Maman Zuzu. Nuri saw a rattle-box vendor who was carrying a tray on his head and three whirligigs in his hand. The whirligigs spun alongside one temple and made him look like a turbo plane getting ready to take off. Nuri followed the vendor. He passed a well-lit and busy street and turned into a quiet, dark alley that dead-ended at a house with an old-fashioned wooden door. He thought about how he was alone in that alley and how no one would recognize him anyway. If the vendor cut his throat, no one would come to his rescue. He decided to run away. In sudden retreat, he ran nonstop all the way to the Tajrish bus depot.

When Nuri got to the Dezashibi house, he walked behind the row of boxwoods up to the kitchen, which was quiet now. He sat on the steps leading to Black Najmeh's room and with a soup spoon slowly ate the piece of meat she brought for him. If one of the relatives showed up, Nuri would quickly leave, go to the first-floor hallway via the back door, and avoid the family greetings and grillings. The relatives were gathered around a transistor radio by the stone pool waiting to listen to Ladan recite her composition on the *Youth and the Radio* program. They waited a couple of minutes until the program *Unspeakable Secrets* ended. Then the ticktock of a clock could be heard, and an announcer with a fine voice announced the official time with poetic words such as *eventide* that Nuri had read only in Papa Javad's poetry. "Dear listeners, it is now eight o'clock of eventide in Tehran."

Madame rearranged herself on the sofa and said in a loud voice, "Ladan will win a prize. They will give her a prize."

Amiz Abbas snorted and said, "Frieda, dear, prizes are not given; they are bestowed."

Madame thanked him. "Thank you. The prize is a copy of Ferdowsi's *Shahnameh,* which will be bestowed upon Ladan at the end of the program."

The golden and fiery orange of the fall leaves traveled up from the garden to the space outside the windows and made the parlor look brighter. The sunset turned the sky a steely blue. The shimmering of the light drew Nuri out of himself, excited him, and made him feel as if a hundred-watt bulb had been turned on in his head. Grandpa Senator was busy with election reports in the study. Out of range of the relatives' gaze, Madame secretly smiled at Nuri and kept listening to the radio. She seemed to be somewhat worried about Ladan, hoping she would not stumble on words and embarrass herself in front of the relatives. First, they listened to a student from Razi High School play the violin. He was believed to be a prodigy. He could whistle all of the movements of Beethoven's Fifth Symphony from memory. To tune his violin, he played a piece Amiz Abbas recognized from the "great" Russian composer Rimsky Korsakov—the *Scheherzade Suite.* Amiz Abbas chose the word *great* to be more poetic. The main part of the program was a prelude from a Bayat-e Esfahan piece called *Love's Flower Offering,* which the student from Razi High School played twice in a row. The second time he got to the faster part, which required adept movements of the bow, one of the strings on his violin snapped, and Ladan was forced to recite her composition four minutes ahead of schedule. The title of her composition was "Fall's Yellow." It was the story of a fall leaf that in the cold of a remote land asked after friends and acquaintances. At the end of the program, the announcer said that Miss Ladan Hushiar would recite compositions on the subject of computers, calculators, and space ships over the course of the following weeks, and he wished Ladan great success in her future. The relatives clapped for Ladan and cheered, but Nuri was thinking about Shahreza Street and his visit to his friends on Amirabad.

It was not that he had not seen them over the past four years—only that this day's visit was different from other days'. He had seen Naser Shahandeh's gang, and nothing had happened to him or Buki. With them, he had entered a realm completely separate from the Dezashibi house and the relatives. That itself was a blessing because apart from practicing the organ with Madame, nothing about that house and neighborhood cheered him up. From now on, he would leave the house whenever he wanted without letting anyone know. Even if someone caught on, so what? Let Ladan sulk, "So, you monkey of the world, would your mouth have gotten too cold if you told us where you were going so that we wouldn't worry so much?"

"Worry about what?"

"Worry about what might happen to you."

Fearlessly he would go into the storage room, take the opera dress Soraya had asked for, and give it to her as a present. She would like that. If Mrs. Tahmasbi made dresses exactly like it for Soraya and Shuri Khanom, his standing would go up in their eyes.

... 3 ...

The bell rang. The students climbed over each other like a bunch of lizards and spilled into the twists and turns of the hallways. Nuri, unlike the others, was in no hurry to get to the school cafeteria to buy junk food like Kim ice cream bars, cheese puffs, and Laurel and Hardy lollipops. He lazily placed his books inside his bag and patted the inside of his desk, searching for his notebooks. It was a Thursday, and he had four hours before his organ practice with Madame. He thought about sneaking out through the octagonal foyer. He was nauseated by school, by the recitation of aphorisms and the assumption of artistic poses.

That day Madame was planning to perform once again the comic epilogue of Berg's theatrical piece in the storage room. At the end of each of her performances, she asked Nuri to stand in for her audience and applaud her. Using gestures unsuitable for her age, she would kneel in front of Nuri, place her palms together, and, with a supplicating and longing look, sing Mendelssohn's aria "O, to a Dove's Wing." Nuri was suddenly reminded of the pictures of the nude he had seen in the lovemaking scenes on the cards.

He checked his surroundings out of the corner of his eye. Everyone was busy. Their teacher, Mr. Daftari, with his long and horselike face, was still sitting behind his desk and correcting test papers. He shouted Nuri's name so gruffly that Nuri was scared. Since the end of September, Mr. Daftari had been warning Nuri that if he did not come to class regularly and do his schoolwork, he alone would be responsible for his actions. "Don't imagine we'll cut you any slack." This last sentence was a direct hint at Nuri's being related to Senator Zargham and to the fact that Mr. Daftari was not afraid of the Senator's position and power.

53

For a while, Mr. Daftari pretended not to notice Nuri. He quickly leafed through his books and arranged the test papers in piles on his desk. Finally, he handed Nuri a sealed envelope and in a surly tone ordered him to deliver it to Madame Zargham.

No doubt the letter concerned Nuri's absences from school and his failure to do his work. As soon as she got the letter, she would read every line. When she reached the end, her curiosity would change to worry. She would crumple the letter in her hands and look at Nuri beseechingly, as if asking, "Why?"

Maybe it was better for him to tear the letter into tiny pieces, throw it away, and not say anything to anyone. But he had second thoughts. After a few days, Mr. Daftari would call their home and fill Madame in. Even if he didn't call, she would certainly get the news from some other source.

Toward the beginning of the evening, he found Madame alone on the third-floor balcony watering her tropical plants. He took a deep breath and said, "Hello."

"Hello."

He showed her Mr. Daftari's letter. Madame threw half a glance at it, and the lines on her face disappeared. "For your servant?"

"It's from Mr. Daftari."

With even more surprise, she asked, "For your servant?"

She put down the watering can and opened the letter. When reading Persian, she had a habit of mouthing the words to herself like a first-grader, and it took her a long time. But she read Mr. Daftari's three pages of small print in under ten minutes. When she got to the end, she didn't speak. She went to the balcony and sat in the easy chair. She held her chin between her fingers, sighed, and smiled. Something occurred to her suddenly. She stood up and threw the letter in the wastepaper basket. Nuri sighed with relief. Madame waved her hand in dismissal. Then she rose and retrieved her watering can and went over to the plants. That was it! No questions, no interrogation, nothing.

The more Mr. Daftari issued warnings to him, the less effective they were. Nuri plotted with Buki to find Mr. Daftari alone in some alley, give him a few boxing punches, and hit him in the groin until the news of

His Holiness reached his father in the seventh heaven. Fortunately, Buki dissuaded him.

A couple of weeks went by after the letter episode, and Mr. Daftari still hadn't let on how he planned to punish Nuri, who continued to skip most of his classes. To annoy Mr. Daftari, he stood in the yard with his back to the window and posed like a movie star. That is, until the day Naser Shahandeh put a pair of scissors through the window bars and was about to cut Nuri's blond hair when Mr. Daftari caught him and said in English, "What is this, you mule?" Naser Shahandeh just stared at him with a hateful look as sharp as a dagger's blade. Nuri grumbled, "Why do you want to cut my hair? Are you itching for a fight?"

Then his tongue froze. He couldn't believe what he saw with his own eyes. Even in his dreams, he would never have imagined that Madame, without telling him and in her full regalia, would come to the school. First, she appeared in the octagonal foyer. She walked hesitantly, with the demeanor of a person out of her element, looking to spot someone familiar. For Nuri, school was an impenetrable fortress and belonged to him only. It didn't occur to him, especially since Madame was a foreigner, that she could enter it and walk right up the office steps in the middle of the day wearing a white muslin dress down to her knees, a black velvet hat whose narrow brim circled her head like a priest's cap, and beige high-heeled shoes with narrow toes in black. Precisely like a model in old-fashioned magazines who at the sound of music lowers her eyelids and drunkenly falls into the arms of her dance partner. Madame impatiently hit one white glove into the palm of her other hand and surveyed the classrooms out of the corner of her eye. Then she bowed to some passersby, placing her long fingers near one temple to keep her curls in place.

Nuri was not concerned about the teachers. He was afraid that the kids would write something about Madame on the bathroom wall or get together during recess in the school cafeteria and say things about her. His fear was not unfounded. Mr. Daftari was measuring the size of the earth with the help of a math formula when Naser Shahandeh wrote a few lines on a piece of paper and slipped the paper to Nuri: "Oh, sweetheart! I bought her for a hundred."

Nuri wrote his answer on the back of the same piece of paper and threw it to him: "Give your hundred to your pretty sister."

Nuri was afraid Madame would ask the others where he was and then come over and kiss him on the face. He would play dumb, pretend he had no idea who Madame was. He would even gang up with the other boys and say a few risqué things about Madame and make the others laugh.

As soon as Madame started walking toward the office, silence descended on the whole classroom as if the electricity had been cut off. In the hallway, there was no echo of the hurried footsteps or occasional coughs of the students who had arrived late. The humming of the electric meter, which usually didn't attract anyone's attention, could now be clearly heard. The older-looking, gangly students in the back row craned their necks and followed Madame's movements. She finally stopped in front of Nuri's classroom window. She waited a while for him to come and greet her. When he didn't, she climbed the stairs to the office with determined steps. She had not yet arrived when Mr. Raji came out to greet her. He gave such a deep bow that his head reached his knees. Nuri had never seen Mr. Raji bend up and down for someone, and for a few minutes he couldn't focus on Mr. Daftari's words. With his hands at his waist, Mr. Daftari angrily called Nuri's name several times. Nuri jumped up, startled, realizing that he had to go to the blackboard and measure the surface of the earth in front of the class. Listless and hesitant, he stood like a wind-up doll, put his hands in the pockets of his honey-colored corduroy pants, and took big clumsy steps to the board. When he drew close to the classroom door, he suddenly took off like the wind and fled from the school.

He knew only that he was running south down the slope of Amirabad Avenue. He was oblivious to the fact that Buki was behind him, screaming, "Slow down! Wait for me to catch up with you!"

When Nuri fled, Buki had left the classroom on the pretense of needing to go to the bathroom. He was an expert at every trick. At the age of seventeen, he was already running his own life. Three times a week he went to Amirabad to sell newspapers in Iran-e Novin Street by the Indiana Complex and the American Club. He had once agreed to take Nuri there. In the American Club's trash bin, he found things such as transistor radios, electric blankets, and steam irons, which he sold in the bazaar within two hours. Outside the club, he shouted the names of foreign newspapers for the benefit of the Americans passing by, and he spoke his halting English with them. He put his hand by his ear, kept his eyes half-open, and instead of "paper" called out "peeper."

"English peeper?" he would shout out. "Oh peeper, oh peeper. *New York Times* peeper, *Washington Post* peeper. Oh peeper, oh peeper!"

Near Shahreza Street, Nuri ran out of breath and waited for Buki to catch up. Buki ran his arm over his high forehead and thin hair and focused his black, cunning eyes on Nuri. "You are really crazy, Nuri. Daftari will put a stick up your sleeve."

"Let him."

They reached the Amirabad Body Shop. Cyrus was sitting behind a desk in the office, signing receipts. He waved to them. "Would you like tea? Should I order some?"

They were not interested. Buki had to go to the American Club. He had come to the shop just to pick up the ball bearing, cam shaft, iron spool, and wrench he had ordered and deliver them to his customers, who were mostly school kids. He grumbled at Nuri, "Nuri, are you crazy? Why do you run away from school like this?"

"Why do *you* run away?"

"I have to make a living for a whole family."

After Buki left, Nuri's excitement evaporated. It was as if he saw the buildings and screened windows in a dream. With great effort, he got himself to Cinema Diana. In the dim light of the Parand Pastry Shop, Khachator's figure, dressed in an apron with his sleeves rolled up, seemed to move imperceptibly. He wiped and shined the tables. A white cat sniffed the ground in front of Nuri's old house. The concrete steps leading to the first floor seemed shorter and narrower than Nuri remembered. The sight of the stairs, the tiled entrance, and the brick crescent over the door made him sad. He curled his fingers around the railing, hoisted himself up and got to the second floor. He didn't have the heart to ring the bell. Two rolled newspapers lay outside the apartment. Along the hallway, from behind other apartment doors, came the smell of fried onions and *abgusht*. In the place where the brass plaque with the name "Engineer Javad Hushiar" had hung, there remained a gray lozenge-shaped spot and two nail holes. Nuri leaned his weight against the iron railing, slid down, and returned to the street.

Nuri didn't feel like going back to the Dezashibi house. Wherever he looked, he knew everything here like the palm of his hand. During the summer holidays, in the afternoons, he used to wear his cowboy outfit, hide behind the university's iron fence, and, as soon as he spotted Buki, step out in front of him. Pressing two fingers like a revolver into Buki's stomach, Nuri would make him surrender: "Ken money yard!"

He said "Ken money yard!" just to sound as if he were speaking English like the American actors. Meaning: "Stand still! Drop your gun! Confess that you are the gang leader!" He would press gently on the imaginary trigger.

On the sidewalk, children had drawn a hopscotch game with chalk, but instead of playing, they were fighting. Exactly like the fight Nuri had had with Naser Shahandeh two years ago over a miserable fountain pen whose purple ink when dry turned a golden color. Nuri hopped down the squares, and when he got to the end, he saw an old man dressed in rags watching him. His auburn hair was shaded by a shawl. He had draped over his shoulders an officer's faded jacket, and his boots looked dusty and old. The man jumped onto the middle square and stumbled. He put a cigarette butt between his lips and handed a matchbox to Nuri. "Do you know how to light a cigarette?"

Nuri struck a match. The man drew a couple of times on his cigarette and rounded his eyes in pleasure. He pushed the shawl away from his wrinkled forehead. "May you be paid back for your good deed. May your hands not hurt. Thank you very much."

"Just because I lit this cigarette butt?"

"Just for this!"

Nuri laughed and said, "Ohh?"

"Appreciate your own kindness and generosity. Evil and pestilence are as abundant as the grains of sand in a desert. Good people like you are rare."

"How do you know I am a good person?"

"Your face screams it out. I had a son your age, kind and good-hearted. He was very, very good." He rubbed his palm over his chest, as if something pained him. "With your permission, I'll take my leave."

The man walked slowly along the sidewalk. He turned his head back only once. This time he looked at Nuri with the dazed expression of the beggars who hung out in the alleys by the Mihan Tour Bus terminal. They would pick bits of stale bread off the street and place a kiss on the bread so that it looked as if they were smelling it. People who, like a stray shoe, were bits of the forgotten parts of the city's poorer neighborhoods. Nobody knew where they spent the night, what they ate, what they thought about. The notion of not having to answer to anyone overwhelmed Nuri. He preferred the people he didn't know, who didn't belong anywhere and could be found everywhere. The kind of metamorphosed people who can be found in the paintings in butcher and coffee shops in the poor neighborhoods or in the Amir Arsalan and Hosein the Kurd story. Eyes eternally staring into another world, forlorn gazes reluctant to divulge a calamity.

Nuri suddenly got an urge to go to his aunt Moluk's old house. To its small yard that smelled of damp earth in the evenings and its alley lined with brick facades and dusty, dim streetlights. From behind the walls always came the sound of people's footsteps, clothes being washed, children crying—sounds that made everything appear distant.

Twenty-some years ago, when Papa Javad had come to Tehran from Yazd, he had rented the house in one of the winding alleys near the Hasanabad intersection and lived with his three sisters under the same roof—spinster sisters whose ages qualified them to be his mother. If their mother, God rest her soul, had not died, perhaps they would have stayed in Yazd and not come to Tehran. The middle sister, Bibi Safa, had contracted a strange disease that first year in Tehran. Every night her fever had gone higher than forty degrees centigrade; her coated tongue had gotten a bluish tinge like the veins of older people and swelled up so much it did not fit in her mouth anymore and almost choked her. It didn't take more than a week for her to become delirious and die. Then Bibi Ghezi, the older sister, had gotten a strange ache in her eyes from the cold of the winter. She put drops in her eyes constantly and wore dark glasses so that sunlight would not bother her. She also paid a lot of attention to her diet. Yet she still got welts, and the skin under her arms swelled up so much that she had to hold her elbows up like a clothes hanger. A few nights before Nuri was born, when Papa Javad had been exiled to Bushehr for his left-wing activities, Bibi Ghezi was still conscious. She swallowed ginger powder and made Aunt Moluk promise to make sure nothing happened to that "innocent child" in exile. She squatted in the corner of the room and said that she had to make the offerings to a white dove she had promised as part of her pledge for Papa Javad's freedom. At the Buzarjomehri intersection, they bought a white dove with wishes for Papa Javad and made their way to Karaj. Bibi Ghezi herself opened the dove's wings beside a creek in Karaj and freed it for Papa Javad. She got tears in her eyes and followed the dove's movements for a few minutes with a gaze that seemed not to believe what it was seeing. When they returned home, she put over her head the special shroud brought from Mecca and saved for her death, and she lay down in the hallway facing Mecca. She spoke with Aunt Moluk in a thick Yazdi accent. "Moluk, I think I am going to be freed. Someone is calling to me in my sleep. This person calls out my name, but does not say anything else."

Aunt Moluk offered her a few lackluster words of comfort. Reminded her not to eat heavy foods at night and not to sleep on her stomach to avoid bad dreams. Then Bibi Ghezi spoke in the monotonous and frightening tone of dead people who appear in dreams. She pointed to the corner of the room. "Moluk, Moluk, why don't you get up and offer something? His Holiness the Emir has honored us with his arrival."

Aunt Moluk saw no one. His Holiness the Emir appears to his disciples only at the time of their death, and this appearance indicated that Bibi Ghezi was preparing herself for her final journey. Their dear departed mother and some of the other deceased relatives also paid her a visit. She asked that her body be taken back to Tazarjan and be buried next to their mother. She rested her head on her pillow, and the minute she closed her eyes, you would have thought she had been asleep for thirty years.

After being released and returning to Tehran, Papa Javad took Nuri to that house a few times so that he would never forget his past. The two of them would sit on the floor with Aunt Moluk in front of a spread and eat noisily. On a platter, Hasani brought them tea, cotton candy, *ghotab,* and bakhlava. Aunt Moluk wrapped herself in her chador and silently watched them eat. Only when they were about to leave would she suddenly throw her arms around their necks and kiss their faces as if she would never see them again. After Papa Javad's accident, she became distant and haughty. She came to the Dezashibi house a couple of times, put on airs, and was overbearing with Madame. Her excuses were, first, that she had no blood relationship to the Zargham family and, second, that she had never been happy about her brother's marriage into a Tehrani family with all those pretensions. But she never talked about her real reason, a person by the name of Comrade Morteza Binesh. She did sometimes weave his name into the conversation and said, for instance, that Comrade Binesh had sent good tidings that the "Organization," meaning the Tudeh Party, would publish the French translation of Papa Javad's poems in Sweden and dis-tribute them for free to the initiated, the cultural connoisseurs, and the "progressive international classes." "Are Javad's poems any worse than others'? In this socialist world where prizes are given to beggars, why shouldn't one be given to that child? Why should all sorts of medals such as the Peace, Lenin, and Stalin prizes be bestowed on a bunch of foreign hooligans who don't understand anything? Then they have their pictures taken, snickering and showing off their gold teeth to the oppressed and colonized masses."

She would fix her excited stare on a spot, rub her bare knee with the palm of her hand, and swallow a smile. Ever since she had received her membership card for the Tudeh Party, she had grown so friendly with Comrade Binesh that she allowed him to come to the house as he pleased. Without asking permission, he went straight to the refrigerator and helped himself to anything he wanted—Russian vodka, white bread, chicken, olivier salad, salami, and bologna—so that he wouldn't have to go out to buy food and get himself unnecessarily tangled up with the secret police. Aunt Moluk kept an umbrella, fedora, and raincoat for Comrade Binesh in a closet so that if police agents suddenly came to the house, he could slip out incognito and get himself to a safe place. The Zarghams, especially the Senator and Amiz Abbas, ridiculed Aunt Moluk. Behind her back, they said she had lost her mind after Agha Javad's death. How could a devout person such as she who never missed a prayer join the Tudeh Party and get herself worked up over the oppressed? Aunt Moluk paid no attention to them. She looked dejectedly out of the window and said that the Hushiars had no attachment to material possessions and preferred to die of hunger and would never leave their studies half-finished. If she was pleasant to Madame and the Senator, it was simply out of respect for her beloved brother and his darling children. Whenever she saw Madame, she spoke in a heavy Yazdi accent to be one step ahead of Madame's accent. She said that Madame spoke Persian with an accent just to be fashionable. She was willing to bet that if you woke Madame up in the middle of the night, she would speak Persian in a Tehrani accent exactly like the old servants.

Aunt Moluk opened the courtyard door for Nuri, and the minute she saw him she said happily, "How wonderful, flowers and rose water! Oh, Nuri-jun, is that you? What a surprise! In which direction has the sun risen that you remembered your old aunt Moluk? Come near, let me look at your beautiful face that I have missed so much."

She illustrated the "so much" by pointing to one of her finger joints. She took hold of a corner of her chador and adjusted it on her head as if Nuri were a stranger. She asked about Maman Zuzu, Madame, and the Senator. "Why doesn't he ever ask about us? Has he forgotten his manners? We have to go out of our way for them to remember us. We had only a darling brother, and he passed away. These hardhearted people don't even once ask what has become of the poor, grieving sister. After all, there's a difference between relations and strangers, friends and enemies, hats off to all of you."

She seated Nuri on the carpet in the guest room that opened onto the courtyard. She called out to Hasani to bring them tea and something to eat. She was not sure where to begin. She ran her fingers over the floor cushions and said, "So, Nuri-jun, you are obviously doing well at school."

"Not bad."

"What's not bad? Why have you turned out so shy? There is no shame in being the head of the class. No need to be shy in front of your aunt."

"Who said I was the head of the class?"

"Your Papa Javad said you always got the highest marks in your class. He stood in this same doorway and said that this Nuri will finally become a genius and invent something."

"Aunt-jun, it's nothing like that. If I can pass my courses without having to repeat them in the summer, I'll throw my hat in the air."

She picked up the violin case sitting on the carpet in the corner of the room and took out the violin and placed it on her shoulder. "I'm learning to play the violin."

"But you never had such interests."

"Don't you play the organ? I am learning to play the violin. Everybody is learning to play the violin according to the Suzuki method, so why shouldn't I? The world is changing. We have to change with it."

"What about the neighbors? Don't they complain about the noise when you practice?"

"They want to complain? So let them. I'm not about to give up the violin for such conspiracies."

She put the violin under her chin and drew the bow across it and made a sound like a piece of cloth tearing. Hasani entered with a tray of tea and Yazdi treats. Aunt Moluk put the violin away in its case and unexpectedly introduced the topic of her brother's death. She talked as if he had not died of innocent causes. She could not believe her brother would take all those wishes to the grave with him. There was probably a plot behind the accident. Near the Jajrud River, she herself had heard from the driver of a sixteen-wheeler that in the whole of the Middle East there was not a driver as competent as her brother. He was no ordinary driver to have an accident so easily. Surely they had cut his brake lines. Aunt Moluk brought out her brother's collection of new poetry and anxiously asked, "Nuri-jun, what do you think I should do with these? A couple of publishers have called and asked to have them published clandestinely."

Deep down, Nuri liked what Aunt Moluk said. She said Papa Javad had saved a couple of thousand tumans for a rainy day, but now no one knew where he had hidden them or to whom he had given them for safekeeping. No doubt the Tehrani libertines had already swallowed up the money and were spending it in Switzerland. Aunt Moluk claimed that on Fridays her brother used to go to the neighborhood park and read his poetry aloud to a bunch of people he didn't know. He never talked about his secret work with anyone in order to avoid giving police agents any information and having them cancel his contracts with the government. "Nuri-jun, do you remember the big poster?"

She meant the big poster in Papa Javad's room. Nuri answered, "Of course I remember."

"The one that had a picture of a barbed-wire fence?"

"Yeah, right."

"Barbed wire is a symbol of struggle. As Papa Javad used to say, barbed wire means living at the point of a bayonet. In other words, a life of imprisonment. The truth is that we all are prisoners."

"But the barbed wire was pretty thin."

"So what? Did you want it to be thick so that they would figure it out with one look and tie up Papa Javad and send him to Bushehr again?" She grew pensive for a few moments and then asked, "Do you know what a symbol is?"

She spoke of roses as a symbol of the spilt blood of conscientious and self-sacrificing individuals such as Comrade Golesorkhi. A symbol of those who were not afraid of death and opened their chests to enemy fire. A symbol of trampled human emotions, humane values, and the suffocated song of those who prefer freedom to dying.

She left Nuri alone in the room and went to the hallway to answer the phone. It was clear the call was about Nuri. She said a few things and quickly returned to the room. She had her earlier abashed and secretive look. She sat on the edge of the carpet and drank up her tea. Nuri asked, "Who was it?"

"Madame is looking for you. She's anxious about you."

Nuri shrugged his shoulders, "Do they think I am a child?"

Aunt Moluk gave him an exasperated look. "Dear, you aren't all that old either. With what courage do you roam around this city? They'll kill you. Get up, dear, go on home. I'll put these treats into a handkerchief for you to take along. But don't eat all of them. Give a little bit to your poor sister as well."

Aunt Moluk accompanied him to the door and pressed his face to her chest. It was the first time he had said good-bye to Aunt Moluk without his

father. It was as if Papa Javad were standing in front of them and searching his pockets for change to give to the beggars in the alley. He would
turn his head away to avoid looking at the money he put in the beggars'
hands. Nuri kissed Aunt Moluk's cheek. "Do you like that?"

"Like what?"

"Do you remember how Papa Javad used to kiss you?"

Aunt Moluk came close to smiling. "If you want to kiss me like your
father, you have to put your arms around me and say you will sacrifice
yourself for me."

She opened her arms to Nuri. Nuri put his arms around her and
kissed her and, like Papa Javad, teasingly said, "May I sacrifice my life for
you, Sister-jun. I missed you so much."

She grabbed his wrists and looked at his face inquisitively. "Nuri-jun,
what kind of kissing is this?"

"Why do you say that? Was it bad?"

"You got spit on my face. You kiss like your father."

"No!!!"

"I swear to Imam Ali." She took Nuri's arm. "Do you remember how
he used to spread his arms wide before wrapping them around me? He
pressed his fists so tightly on my back I couldn't sleep for three nights
because of the pain."

With her finger, she pointed to a spot on her back. Nuri said, "No kidding! Really?"

"Yes, dear. You have to promise to come and visit me more often and
have lunch or dinner with me."

"When are you coming to visit *us*?"

"It's hard for me to come to Dezashib all alone. It's too far. You are
younger and should come here. I am past all that, dear."

Nuri wrapped his arms around Aunt Moluk and this time pressed
her back with his fists.

The first person he saw in Dezashib was Black Najmeh, who was cleaning a serving spoon with a damp dishcloth. Her shapeless cotton dress
reached down to her knees and easily covered her column-shaped legs—
in other words, she looked like she usually did, except a little disheveled,
grumpy, and impatient, which Nuri put down to the atmosphere of the

house. Even in the dusk, she recognized Nuri and grumbled something he couldn't hear from that distance. He walked up to the row of boxwoods and reached the large iron pail in which Vaziri kept the oil cans and water hose. If he hadn't fled from Mr. Daftari's class, he wouldn't be taking the silence seriously. He sensed that Madame herself had imposed this quiet to prevent the Senator from finding out about Nuri's running away from school. Otherwise, there would be pandemonium.

Once he was close to Black Najmeh, he heard what she grumbled. "Where have you been until now?"

"Where did you think I was? I went to the movies."

Black Najmeh didn't believe him. She raised her eyebrows first, then her shoulders in a gesture of hurt and went back to the kitchen. But she continued to grumble, and after a while Nuri heard her voice from the kitchen. "Madame has asked to have you sent to her room as soon as you get back. She wants to speak with you."

"Let's leave it till later."

Black Najmeh stuck her head out of the kitchen and shook the serving spoon in Nuri's direction. "You have to go right now. Haven't you caused enough trouble for yourself? Do you want to add to it? Go on, go on upstairs already!"

But Najmeh's grumbling made him more stubborn. "Do you have something for me to eat? I'm hungry."

"If you want rice *kufteh,* I'll bring it to you."

She put the *kufteh* inside some bread and handed it to him on a plate. Nuri sat on the edge of the stone pool and took a huge and angry bite because of his extreme hunger. Madame's voice came from the third floor. "Najmeh, where is Nuri?"

Nuri put a finger to his lips to stop Najmeh from speaking. She didn't pay any attention and answered, "Madame-jun, he is coming right away."

Nuri asked, "Where should I leave the plate?"

Najmeh took the plate and went back to the kitchen. "Agha-jun, do you hear me? You have to speak with Madame. If not, things will get worse."

He went up to the third floor and with one look through the study window realized all was normal. For the Fourth of Aban, the students of

Shahbaz High School were supposed to perform the *Goddess of Harvest Ballet* in the auditorium in the presence of Her Excellency Shahbanu the Queen. Ladan was rehearsing the role of the goddess. She wore a jersey ballet outfit whose puffy skirt spread out around her waist like a red carnation. She stood on tiptoe, twisted her arms above her head, arched back in a semicircle, and lifted her breasts heavenward like two nuns in prayer. The only thing that surprised him was Madame herself, who apparently was intent on having a chat with him at this particular moment. She usually talked about important matters only in private and in a soft, casual, and friendly tone so as not to embarrass him. She was leaning back and watching Ladan with a relaxed posture, as if she didn't have a care. She was also moving a baton to the rhythm of "Wheat Flower, Beloved" and tapping one foot on the carpet. Nuri didn't think that his arrival would cause Madame to make a fuss. Not that she was the kind to make a fuss anyway. Even when she was annoyed, she would proudly illustrate her point with sayings she had learned from Dehkhoda's *Parables and Fables*. In any case, Nuri had not committed such a crime that he should be afraid of anyone. He entered the room and stood in a corner. After a while, when they took no notice of him, he thought about slipping out again, but he hadn't even opened the door yet when Madame lifted the needle off the record and shouted, "Your servant has something to say. I have to speak to you in private."

With the tip of the baton, she motioned for him to sit down in a chair. Seeing the situation had taken a turn in her favor, Ladan quickly gathered up her clothes and said, "I'll leave now. Tomorrow I'll start practice at the same time."

As long as Ladan was there, Madame stood still and kept her eyes on Nuri. No sooner had Ladan left than she took a threatening step toward Nuri. "Your Excellency is very late."

"I went to the movies with my friends."

"Which movie?"

Nuri was preparing to answer when Madame raised a palm. "Stop! No answer is necessary. Your servant is not an interrogator and will not get a confession from you. I am a foreigner who, out of good intentions, wants to utter a few words to her grandson. Is that correct? Is it better for me to say 'to proffer'? What is the difference, my dearrr? Extracting a confession is one of the worst things a human being can do to another. It is much better for a confession to be made in solitude. Confessing in solitude is like communing with the One and Only God for the purpose of liberating the human soul from this world's prison. Nuri-jan, my heart burns for you. I am afraid of your carelessness and indifference. I am afraid you might forget yourself."

Nuri decided to make the first move and ask, "Did you come to our school today?"

"Yes. Your Excellency has fallen behind in his studies. You have to tell me how to help you."

"You have done all you can for me, and I am very thankful. Now I have to take care of my own affairs. Today Mr. Daftari said there are birds in the North Pole who migrate south every year. I want to be like one of those birds. Not that I want to migrate south. No, I just don't feel this place is mine. An outsider has no rights and always feels caged. No matter what you give me, it is like charity. I don't see it as my right. As long as a person cannot go where he pleases, speak and act as he wishes, he remains an outsider."

Madame lowered her head. "I'll tell you something. You must believe it."

"What?"

"Your Excellency has to stop being a stranger in his own heart. Otherwise, wherever you go, you'll be a stranger."

"How?"

"A stranger has high expectations of himself and takes himself very seriously. The higher his expectations, the more he waits for miracles. If you don't want to be a stranger, apologize to Mr. Daftari tomorrow."

"Why should I do that?"

"Because you are an ordinary student and no different from the others."

"But I haven't done anything that I need apologize to Mr. Daftari for."

"In my opinion, apologizing takes courage." She got up from her chair, sighing, "Oh, how quickly I get tired. I think it's anemia. Right? It could be this bad air I'm allergic to, right?"

She slipped her fingers into her pockets to search for something. Nuri asked, "Mumzie, do you feel all right?"

"Your servant? Of course, I'm better now. I think I'm fine. How are you? Do you feel well?"

"Not bad. But did you see how Mr. Raji harasses me?"

"I promise it will get easier for you. I remember you in your crib. You had just been born in Bushehr. You cried a lot and were hungry. You put your mouth to my face and wanted to suck on it. I said, 'Peekaboo, mousy!' Your Excellency cried. I would say, 'Peekaboo, mousy!' and Your Excellency would cry." In front of the mirror, she rubbed her cheeks with her fingers. She pulled at her skin, and her eyes grew wide. "But as soon as I sang for you, you would relax and smile."

She moved her fingers around her head like a butterfly, rearranging her curls.

Nuri was still uneasy. Perhaps Madame had caught on that he went into the storage room. Maybe from the way the cards had been strewn, the way the fake mustache and beard, ballet masks, and opera dresses had been moved, she had guessed that someone inside the house was responsible. Tomorrow he would get up early and return to his old house. He was anxious about confronting Mr. Daftari and his classmates. They would probably surround him and tease him. Mr. Daftari would call him in before the first period and meet with him alone in the classroom. Sometimes he got so angry with Nuri that he seemed to lose his head. "I keep talking gently to you, watching out for you, trying teach you a couple of things, and you play dumb, you donkey? Dumbhead! You think you have become some shit and are dealing with an ignoramus."

But the next morning Nuri realized he had no choice. Come what may, he had to go to school that day. He switched on the bathroom light. The damp air and the smell of toothpaste made him queasy. He held himself squinched up to keep his naked body from touching the cold tiles on the wall. He was startled by the image of the suddenly enlarged and misshapen figure in the mirror. He was looking at someone else.

The classroom had just been swept and washed, and the floor was still damp. To intimidate the students, Mr. Daftari stood in front of the class frowning and self-absorbed. He clasped his hands and began the lesson straightaway. He didn't ask anyone to come up to the board, to draw a diagram of a cell, or to explain vegetal protoplasm. Only when the class ended did he smile and beckon Nuri to his desk. Nuri turned around to see whether Mr. Daftari was pointing to another student, but all the others were leaving. Puzzled, he asked, "Did you mean me?"

Mr. Daftari shouted, "What is this, Agha-jan? What are you afraid of? Do you think I'm a monster about to eat you?"

Nuri noticed a shadow move about, but he didn't recognize whose it was. The other students had gathered around the barred classroom window and were looking in at him. Among them was Buki, with his arched eyebrows and lips that he constantly bit into. Nuri turned back and saw the old, yellow ruler on Mr. Daftari's desk. Mr. Daftari's smile meant he was not about to punish Nuri. He spoke in a soft tone. "Come a bit closer. It's getting late. I have to leave."

"What do you want?"

"Mr. Raji wants to have a word with you."

"With me?"

"Why don't you ever smile? Smiling is not work, like studying."

Mr. Daftari's own smile was probably meant to comfort Nuri, but Nuri felt nauseated by his expression, especially the way he puffed up his cheeks. Fortunately, he didn't keep Nuri very long.

Buki Tahmasbi was still standing behind the window, waving to him and jumping up and down. Nuri was too anxious about going to Mr. Raji's office, though. Mr. Raji had never called him to his office. What did he want from him, then? Nuri shooed Buki away. He bent down, undid his shoelaces, retied them, and with determined steps walked toward the office.

He entered without knocking and stood by the door alert and polite. His eyes grew accustomed to the dark interior of the office and slowly made out Mr. Raji's figure. Mr. Raji stood by his desk and watched Nuri from behind his tinted glasses. His skin had an unnatural pallor, as if from a chronic, hereditary disease. His gray suit smelled of a particular cologne and a mixture of sweat, tobacco, and burned rock candy reminiscent of funeral services and religious shrines. Maybe he had put on the cologne to mask the smell of opium. Nuri waited for the wall clock to ring out. He thought of scenes from gangster movies with fights and gunshots from behind a water cistern and the gang leader's taking aim from the top of a tall building. Mr. Raji spoke in the nasal tones and lisp of an opium addict. He asked Nuri, "How are you?"

"Not bad. Fine."

"I've heard you're good at sports."

"With your permission."

"You are apparently very interested in sports."

Nuri looked down and mumbled, "With your permission. You are kind."

"Oh, you speak so formally! 'With my permission'! I am kind? Ha, ha, ha. You have learned these things from Madame Zargham?"

"No, I learned them on my own."

"Good. Well done. You probably know other things as well. Football, and so on. What else do you like?"

"Gymnastics."

"Is that all?"

"Dumbbells as well."

"How about wrestling?"

"No, I have never wrestled yet."

"Wrestling is good. Try it. It is good for the figure." His face took on a satisfied expression; he held his lowered chin in his hand and thought. "You have probably heard that Her Majesty the Queen is going to visit the school."

"Our school?"

"Yes."

Nuri tried to speak in the respectful manner of radio announcers. "Does this mean Her Majesty is going to bless this place with her steps?"

Mr. Raji tossed a matchbox into the air and snickered meaningfully at Nuri. "Yes. Hadn't you heard?"

Nuri didn't trust Mr. Raji. His tossing the matchbox indicated that he still hadn't revealed the reason why he had called Nuri to his office. On the desk, he had put a Boy Scout uniform whose purpose Nuri did not know. He refrained from asking questions until Mr. Raji began to speak again with the same snicker that gave his face the appearance of an invalid.

Apparently, Nuri was to wear this uniform on the day of Her Majesty's visit, stand in front of the line of students, and welcome Her Majesty with a proper salute.

Nuri pointed to his chest and said, "Do you mean me?"

Startled, he looked at Mr. Raji, who was now showing him the uniform. "Take this and go see your physical education teacher. Mr. Minu will teach you the salute for Her Majesty's arrival."

Nuri picked up the green uniform with its golden quadrangle ribbons and headed out of the office. When he reached the door, he raised his hand and asked for permission to replace the Boy Scouts' two-fingered salute with a regular military one using four fingers. Contrary to his expectations, Mr. Raji closed his eyes in assent and with a gentle movement of his hand indicated that Nuri could leave the office.

Nuri had already seen Her Majesty on a television program. She listened to ordinary people's comments, always holding a bouquet of flowers and smiling unconsciously. He didn't know why he, from among all the studious and dedicated students, had been chosen to welcome Her Majesty. Perhaps because he looked different. Perhaps the queen liked blue eyes and blond hair. Maybe it was for this reason that she spent her annual holidays in St. Moritz, Switzerland. It wasn't likely that an average student would be picked out to greet the queen without some intervention, though—especially a student who rarely attended classes. No doubt Madame had a hand in this choice, but didn't want Nuri to know. He was slowly beginning to understand why Madame had come to the school and held secret discussions with Mr. Raji.

... 4 ...

It was not that Nuri was flattered to be asked to greet Her Majesty Shah-banu the Queen. That kind of rubbish was beneath him, and if Papa Javad had been asked to do this, Nuri was certain that he would never have given into such a shameful act. If Nuri didn't lock horns with Mr. Raji, it was only because he didn't want to create a scene for no reason. He wasn't afraid of Mr. Raji or of anyone else, for that matter.

From the few words they had exchanged, Nuri had figured out what an insecure and corruptible person Mr. Raji was. Even in his dreams, he had not imagined that he could reduce Mr. Raji to such an earthly being and haggle with him like an equal over how to greet Her Majesty Shahbanu.

Now Nuri felt entitled to spend more time hanging out in front of the Parand Pastry Shop with Buki Tahmasbi and the other neighborhood boys, razzing the schoolgirls, bugging the shop owners, and throwing rocks at the license plates of passing taxis. But all this was one thing; another was his animal longing to meet an unknown being. The more fearlessly he plunged himself into fire and water, the more he became enslaved by his inner cravings. The sense of rootlessness that had bothered him during the first couple of years of his life in the Dezashibi house used to make him fearful and cautious, but now it seemed to be making him into a daredevil.

In the evenings, when he ran a higher risk of getting caught, he went into the storage room and used the replicas of the French village to set the stage for the first Iranian opera, which he himself had composed. After Wagner's *Flying Dutchman,* he called his opera *The Flying Iranian.* For its performance, he set the different buildings side by side in a corner, creating a shoreline for the landing of a ship belonging to an Iranian sailor

73

named Sinbad. He had no idea what it was that Sinbad the Sailor searched for all across the seas and why he dropped anchor at the port Nuri had built. He simply imagined Sinbad as a mysterious person who would eventually reach a shore long familiar to him. Nuri got so excited sometimes that instead of directing the opera, he took on the role of a spectator. He squatted on the floor for a long time and, biting his fingernails, stared at the stage and waited for the next act. Exactly like a researcher who starts an experiment and forgets everything else while waiting for a foreseen result.

Nuri had become bored with anything repetitious or predictable. He was on the lookout for the unfamiliar and sought out change, anything that was strange and wonderful. He thought of change as vital, and he grew fearful in its absence.

A sticky sweat plastered his long hair uncomfortably to one side of his forehead. In the mirror, he saw himself as a haggard invalid whose fever had just broken, his fleshy lips like a ripe fruit about to spoil, hungry and so dry that he had to wet them constantly with the tip of his tongue. As soon as he spotted one of the schoolgirls, maybe Zhila Shabahang, on the way to school, he took off uncontrollably after her, after her naked white calves half-covered by a pair of short white socks. And so great was the longing, he thought his mind was falling apart. In the early mornings he stuck his arms and legs out from underneath the bedcovers. The cool morning air caressed his restless limbs and excited him. It was as if he were being eroded from within. He felt he was approaching infinity and the most distant stars, and yet never, ever reaching a goal.

In such a state, it was hard for him to get out of bed and go to school. He did not want to back down in front of a spoiled brat like Naser Shahandeh and be humiliated with a few inept jokes. Naser Shahandeh, who was from an elite family, bribed the school janitor, Hajji Mash Ghorban, to let him leave school during recess to buy himself a one-tuman salami sandwich. When Naser Shahandeh was in the right mood, he would sometimes bring back sour-cherry ice cream cookies in a nice purple color for his buddies, especially Reza Shahabzadeh. On the playground, the boys would surround Naser Shahandeh and, to please him, imitate Nuri greeting the queen. Nuri was in no mood to pick a fight with his schoolmates.

Moreover, he was not so out of it that he would give in and act like a sissy. Most days he wore his Texas cowboy outfit. He would strike a pose in front of the other boys, insert his hands in his pockets in the manner of movie stars, cross one leg in front of the other, and hunch his shoulders as if he did not take any of them seriously.

Nuri was standing in front of the third-form classroom window when Naser Shahandeh showed up among the boys in the playground. From his first glance, it was clear to Nuri that Naser had a pebble in his shoe and was looking for an excuse to pick a fight. Imitating Nuri, he rubbed the palm of his hand over his forehead and combed his hair with exaggerated meticulousness. He heaved a deep sigh, indicating his troubled mood. Nuri paid no attention to him. He leaned his elbows on the window ledge and narrowed his eyes. Naser Shahandeh rolled up a copy of *Roshanfekr* magazine and held it in his hands, pretending it was a bouquet of flowers to present to the queen. Taking theatrical and uneven steps like a dandy, he walked up to Nuri to be properly greeted by him. Reza Shahabzadeh put the bullhorn to his mouth and cursed the boys for not suitably applauding Her Majesty's arrival. He hoisted up his trouser legs to make it look as if Nuri were wearing short pants, stood at attention in front of Naser Shahandeh, and shouted, "We, your humble servants, scatter our greetings at Her Majesty's feet."

Wherever Nuri and Buki Tahmasbi went, the other boys followed with the even, threatening, and silent steps of an army not yet ready to attack. They started their march from the other side of Amirabad Avenue and continued to the rear of the university and up to the busy Pahlavi intersection. In front of the Tajrish bus depot, they got a whiff of pickles and salami from somewhere, maybe the corner deli. It didn't seem wise for Nuri and Buki to stand there alone, no matter what their strategy. They changed directions, walked along Pahlavi Avenue, down a few side streets, and got away from the busier spots. Now they could hear even the quietest steps taken by the boys behind them, like walking in tennis shoes on a cotton comforter, with deliberate pauses that made the alley seem more deserted and terrifying. The only thing that disrupted the silence of the alley was the tap-tap of the stick Buki ran across the brick walls.

Now the dustiness of the walls in the alley was replaced with a soft darkness that was moist, like late-spring air, and gradually enveloped the houses lining the alley. They could hear voices more clearly and distinctly from inside the courtyards. At the head of the alley, Naser Shahandeh and Reza Shahabzadeh whistled with two fingers. Their whispers had the cautious tone of secret meetings. Nuri thought things were taking a turn for the worse. He felt in his pocket for his brass knuckles, and the minute he touched the metal, he gestured to Buki for the two of them to get on their way. "Listen, Buki."

"Go ahead."

"If they attack us from behind, duck your head and roll on the ground as long as possible. Don't let Reza Shahabzadeh grab the scruff of your neck. Get a hold of his leg and hit him in the balls with the brass knuckles."

Buki listened to Nuri carefully. Zhila Shabahang and another schoolgirl, most probably Shohreh Farasat, both wearing blue smocks, walked along the street arm in arm, moving farther away from them. The sight of Zhila Shabahang calmed Nuri's fears. He mumbled to Buki, "Follow me and keep talking."

"Talking about what?"

"Whatever!"

They covered the distance between the alley and the street without any incident. Naser Shahandeh and his buddies were gathered on the other side of the street in front of the Shadman Stationery Store. It seemed they were waiting for Nuri and Buki to get there, probably to cut in front of them and start a fight. When Buki tugged at Nuri's shirt from behind, it was already too late, and Nuri couldn't turn around. He had imagined that most fights were started by boys who were not particularly close to each other or no longer on speaking terms—the type of boys who cannot satisfy themselves with talking to the other person. They are too embarrassed to acknowledge others openly and fearlessly. Now Nuri crossed over to Naser Shahandeh's clique. He proceeded as if nothing was the matter, or as if they had run into each other accidentally. First, he confronted Reza Shahabzadeh, who was stronger and very proud of it, too. "Reza, I know someone who has never been beaten in a fight with anybody. Do you want to wrestle with him?"

At first, Reza Shahabzadeh was too stunned to answer. He looked around a bit. He put on a mischievous expression and raised his eyebrows. "Why not?"

"For that you have to come to our house."

"OK, I'll come. Do you think I'm afraid of anyone?" He pointed to his biceps. "All because of these arms. If I were your friend, I would start saying my last prayers."

With a glance toward Naser Shahandeh and the other boys, Reza Shahabzadeh asked them to back him up. Nuri said, "We'll fix a time tomorrow." He turned to the others. "You are my witnesses. You saw that he promised. He says he is ready to wrestle with anyone I choose."

Nuri relaxed and dragged the heels of his cowboy boots across the asphalt. When he got a bit closer to Buki Tahmasbi, he pretended they were going to rent bikes and ride around the university. Together they walked slowly toward the Shadman Stationery Store. Nobody made a sound. A white limousine's horn echoed in the air like the metallic sound of a bugle, but the quiet of the alleys was quickly restored.

Naser Shahandeh's clique slowly dispersed among the crowd on the sidewalk. Buki suddenly stood still. He snorted. He had something to say. "Nuri?"

"Huh?"

"Do you want a revolver?"

"What revolver?"

Buki slowly drew a revolver handle from his pocket. Nuri turned his palm up, as if asking, What kind of trick is this? Buki took the whole revolver out of his pocket and laid it on Nuri's palm. Nuri felt its smooth metal. It was cold and creepy like a snake. He gave the revolver back to Buki. "This is not my kind of thing."

"Don't be an ass! If these boys find you alone, they won't leave you in one piece." He crooked Nuri's fingers around the revolver. "Keep this. We'll settle our account later."

"But I said I don't want it. How pushy you are!"

Buki laughed. "Take it. You were never so shy before."

Nuri asked haltingly, "How much are you asking for it?"

Buki smiled like a wheeler-dealer. "Consider it a gift."

"Meaning it's free?"

"OK, for you a hundred tumans."

"This?! A hundred tumans?!"

"What did you expect? It was made in Czechoslovakia." Nuri was trying the trigger when Buki clicked off the safety. "Nobody holds a revolver
with such long nails. It'll go off accidentally and kill someone. Why don't
you trim your nails?"

Nuri pointed the revolver at Buki and made a face. "Ken money yard!
Bang, bang, bang! Don't worry. If it goes off, it will kick up and won't
hit you."

"A Czechoslovakian gun has no kick. Whichever direction you aim it,
it will hit its target exactly."

Nuri shrugged and gave the revolver back to Buki. "It's not my kind
of thing."

"Why?" He slung his arm around Nuri's neck. "Why don't you
want it?"

"Just because."

"You worrying it'll land you in trouble? You're the type who can't stop
himself when he gets an urge." Nuri said nothing. "Fine. You don't have
to want it, but if you ever change your mind, I'm at your service. Call me
and I'll bring it around to your house."

Nuri lifted his arm and hailed a bus whose headlights could be seen
in the distance. Still miffed, Buki wrapped the revolver in a handkerchief
and put it back in his pocket. He sat down on the sidewalk and dangled
his legs in the empty water canal. He took a dozari coin out of his pocket
and spun it around on the sidewalk. "Do you know how to spin a dozari
like this?"

"No."

"My sis, Soraya, holds a dozari with her finger on the dining table and
spins it. She always asks about you. She wonders why Nuri doesn't come
to our house after the incident at her wedding ceremony with Shirzad. She
asks, 'Is he not speaking to us anymore?'"

"Give her my regards. Tell her I'll come visit her next week."

A biting breeze rose up from the direction of Shemiran. It chilled Nuri's skin even under his clothes and made him feel refreshed. Nuri pulled himself up onto the bus dexterously and waved to Buki from behind the bus's steamed windows. Buki was paying no attention. He walked along the edge of the sidewalk, holding out his arms like the wings of an airplane. Then he started hopping from the edge of the sidewalk onto the street and back again onto the sidewalk, heading away toward Amirabad Avenue. All alone, he was so absorbed in his own world that he reminded Nuri of their childhood.

Buki's father, Colonel Tahmasbi, with his bony and fragile figure, didn't look anything like an army officer. More than anyone, the Colonel made fun of his own body. He rarely went out without his blue uniform. Always, in their apartment and when he played backgammon with Mr. Ra'oof, he had his officer's hat on. The hat's leather band left a mark on his forehead. Mrs. Tahmasbi, in contrast, was relatively tall and had black hair and blue eyes. In front of strangers, she twisted herself around and talked with the nervous tics of someone who has fleas. Most of the time, she was either cooking in the kitchen or waiting in front of the door for someone to invite her for tea and pastry. Buki's brother, Cyrus, with his pouting expression and stout, athletic figure, sometimes did such strange things that smoke rose from Colonel Tahmasbi's head. Sometimes Cyrus would shave his hair off completely, lie buck naked next to pretty Pari, and take pictures of them. Like a spoiled brat, he dwelled on everything, and his feelings got hurt over simple little nothings. Once when he was not yet fifteen years old, he got into a fight over the bus fare he received every day from Colonel Tahmasbi to go to school. From that day, Cyrus neither touched the money nor glanced in its direction. He found a job at the Amirabad Body Shop and separated his expenses from those of the rest of the household.

But the Tahmasbis together were one thing, and the older sister Soraya something else. She was a movie all her own. For example, at her wedding to Mr. Shirzad, the *akhund* had barely started reciting the marriage vows when Soraya retrieved a wad of chewing gum that she had taken out of her mouth and stuck on the frame of the silver mirror, put it back in her

mouth, and, chewing noisily, stood up to leave. In front of the guests, she
took off her wedding dress and brought the ceremony to an abrupt halt.
Nuri's heart had beat so fast that had it been possible, he would have hidden himself in a corner, although he liked Soraya's role playing and always
spoke admiringly about her. Even as a child, he had followed Soraya like a
devoted dog wherever she went. Was it good luck or bad luck that Soraya
never turned him away? She didn't say anything to hurt him. Only during
the six months of her engagement to Mr. Shirzad, when he came to their
apartment to court her, did Soraya have no time to talk to Nuri as before
and no longer cared to send him to the Shadman Stationery Store to borrow novels or buy new pictures of her favorite movie stars.

She always spoke and acted in such a coquettish way that Nuri became
completely bewitched by her. She appeared hurt and even aggrieved, like
a delicate being asking him for help. She put her hands under her chin,
narrowed her eyes, and as soon as she had Nuri's attention, she said jokingly, "Nuri-jun, don't lie. On my own life, tell me how pretty I am. Who
do you know prettier than me?"

Nuri didn't answer. He grinned like a madman and offered her such
a smile that it embarrassed him and made him want to hide under a pile
of rubble for a few days to chase away the memory. As luck would have it,
Soraya's image stayed stuck in his mind like a tick. Even if he wanted to
forget her, he could not.

◆ ◆ ◆ That evening, Nuri got this nagging urge to telephone the Tahmasbis. He made his way quickly to the second-floor hall. He picked up
the receiver and had even dialed the number when he heard the garden
door. The smell of gasoline and tires made him realize the Mercedes was
approaching the house. The car's headlights created a band of light that
passed across the windowpanes and brought the leaves out of darkness
and made them appear a dusty shade of moonlight. Like the prow of a
floating ship, the car traveled up to the stone pool in the garden, and its
lights shone on the dark surface of the water.

Then a few unfamiliar people, the kind the Senator referred to as
his "private guests," came into the garden on foot. With deliberate steps,
Vaziri directed them toward the reception hall and indicated to them

with his own cautious gestures that they should be careful not to disturb the household. Nuri heard the relatives, who were gathered together in the first-floor hall, grow quiet as they watched the new arrivals file into the reception hall, half of which could be seen from where he stood. The guests bowed to each other a few times, repeating "Welcome." No doubt the reason for their gathering there was the future election, the exorbitant price of arable "Aghcheh" land in Gorgan, and the *bazaaris*' financial distress. The minute they sat down at the table, the phone began to ring noisily, like an ill-tempered infant. It was not free for even a minute so that Nuri could call the Tahmasbi apartment. Whenever he picked up the receiver, Mr. Shariat, Grandpa Senator's personal secretary, shouted to him from the reception area to hang up. "Agha-jan, the Senator has to call an important person."

The relatives tried to busy themselves with their own conversation. Only Badri Khanom occasionally raised herself up on her knees from where she was sitting on the floor to get a look at the "private guests." In the middle of all this, Amiz Abbas suddenly made a joke about the Senator. The sound of the relatives' sudden laughter disrupted the whole building for a few moments. After that, Amiz Abbas, imitating the Senator, addressed the relatives with a political speech. "My dear fellow countrymen, it is no longer possible to fool the masses. No longer can a handful of hired foreigners and mercenaries dupe you, the alert and heroic people of Iran, and paint sparrows for you. Remember. When you slide your ballot into the box, do not forget Ali Zargham."

Mr. Shariat shouted from the reception hall doorway, "Could you speak a bit more softly so that we can get on with our business?" Amiz Abbas stopped talking, but the trace of a smirk stayed on his face. Then Mr. Shariat came into the hall, and from the bottom of the stairs he motioned for Nuri to go to the reception hall. "The Senator wants to see you."

Nuri panicked. Up to now the Senator had never allowed him to participate in this kind of gathering. Only lately, the Senator called him "Mr. Nuri" instead of "Nuri," treated him like a grownup, and kept promising that soon he would involve Nuri in his private affairs. But maybe the Senator had heard of Mr. Daftari's complaints and now wanted to nail Nuri in front of a group of strangers.

The first person Nuri saw in the reception hall was Mr. Shariat. He placed special sheets of paper in front of the guests and started counting them, moving his lips slowly. He was a poised and corpulent person about thirty or thirty-five years old whose black mustache and beard made him look older. He walked straight as an arrow, and when he spoke, he looked down, never into a person's eyes. Before shutting the reception hall door, Mr. Shariat threw a meaningful glance in the direction of the ladies.

All around the Senator sat quiet and frowning men. With a smile, Mr. Shariat welcomed Nuri and pointed to a chair close to him, where Nuri sat down. Mr. Shariat watched Nuri's every move from behind a row of long, curling lashes and appeared to make mental notes to himself. His black suit lent his chocolaty eyes a certain depth and made him seem mysterious and conniving.

Then the representatives of the various guilds appeared in the entrance leading to the reception hall. Each one carried under his arm a black carton marked with occasional white stripes, which against the black resembled clouds. Mr. Shariat unwrapped the narrow ribbons around one of the cartons and ran his thumb across the ballots, shuffling them like a deck of cards. In front of each person, he placed a handful of ballots and showed how to write the Senator's name and those of the other candidates in a legible and careful handwriting. They began writing out the names. In the quiet of the room, the squeaking of the pens across the ballots could be heard clearly. Exactly like those classroom exercises where students copy down the teacher's carefully pronounced words, which appear distinct and come to life in the students' minds. Mr. Shariat kept walking around the table with his hands on his waist, and as soon as a ballot was filled out, he placed it in a pile with others in shoe boxes on which he marked the designated number with a thick felt-tip pen.

The last visitors to come in were a group of men wearing velvet fedoras. Each one carried a stack of documents. For some time, they stood hesitantly in front of the door, obviously wondering whether to take off their shoes, whose heels they had turned down according to their custom. The Senator's welcoming gestures persuaded them that they did not have to take off their shoes. They came forward hesitantly and put down the documents with a great show of respect. Mr. Shariat introduced Grandpa Senator. "No doubt you are already familiar with Senator Zargham. As you know, in reality he is a senator elected by the deceased—those whose names are on your documents—and his constituency is in the other world."

The newly arrived guests stared at each other in disbelief, uncertain whether to laugh or to ignore the remark. All the guests suddenly broke into laughter and made a great deal of noise. Taking advantage of the situation, Nuri gently tiptoed out to the first-floor hall.

The relatives had already left. A weak light emanating from a second-floor lamp reached down to the first floor and gave the furniture vague shapes. The scattering of the pastry, nut, and fruit dishes seemed familiar to Nuri and, for this very reason, dulled his appetite. He climbed the stairs to his own room, turned off the light, and without taking off his clothes lay down on the bed. Once again he saw himself as a frightened schoolboy facing danger, struggling in vain to jump over life's hurdles.

Buki at this very moment would be shouting out antishah slogans and distributing political pamphlets in the back alleys of the university. Fine! Everyone has to choose his own path. As Madame said, everyone's final destiny is the same. Madame had recited for Nuri the famous John Donne poem and assured him that true democracy happens only in death. Fairer than any judge, death deals with everyone the same way.

Vaziri's voice could be heard from the garden. "Farewell to all of you."

The next day, like all other days, Vaziri would get up at the crack of dawn. He would wear the same navy blue jacket, gray pants, and starched white shirt and adopt the stance of an air force officer, always at the ready, who happened to be wearing civilian clothes instead of his pilot's uniform. Each night he rubbed his hair with brilliantine cream and wrapped it in a black hair net. He went to the barber very regularly to ensure that his sideburns and the hairline on the back of his neck were meticulously shaped. He shaved his mustache so carefully that it seemed as if he had painted every strand of hair on his upper lip. He polished his black and squeaky shoes with liquid shoe polish and made them shine even more brightly than those of army officers. He would lean against the Mercedes, rest the tip of one shoe on the side of the stone pool, and dust off and

shake out the creases in his well-ironed trousers. He would stand at attention even for Nuri. With four fingers, he would press a matchbook against
the palm of his hand and with a semicircular movement strike a match.
He would press a knife blade against his hand and push it so deeply into
his palm that Nuri believed the blade had cut him, but then he would suddenly turn up his uninjured palm and start laughing.

Nuri had not yet fallen asleep when he heard the creaking of his door.
Grandpa Senator entered and took a couple of steps toward Nuri. His alert
and secretive glance was focused on something outside Nuri's range of
vision. He had a narrow, elongated nose whose tip turned upward. His
straight hair arced back smoothly from his forehead, changed into an
evenly distributed gray along his temples, and spread around his head in a
way that made him resemble a fighting cock. He said, "Are you asleep?"

It was not clear what he wanted with Nuri. He wrinkled the corner of
one eye and said, "It seems you are asleep, child. Why go to sleep so early?"

"I was just resting."

"If you are sleepy, maybe I should leave."

"No, it's not important."

The Senator put a fingertip under his shirt and started scratching
himself. "I have been meaning to talk to you alone for some time, but I
have been very busy. I never get everything done."

Nuri drew himself up and asked, "Do your 'private guests' help you
in the elections?"

"You have to work very hard and please thousands of people. But
these things don't concern you, and it's better for you not to get mixed up
in them."

"Mr. Shariat asked me to join you."

Grandpa Senator closed his eyes in assent and nodded his head a few
times. "I know, but you have to be careful with wheeler-dealers like Shariat. They are only after their own best interest. They take advantage of
people's innocence. Anyway, I wanted to see how much of your official
greeting you had already memorized. There are only two weeks left to
the Fourth of Aban."

Nuri nodded hesitantly. The Senator resumed talking. "For sure, by
now you know the greeting by heart."

"For sure."

"Why don't you recite a little bit of it for me?"

Nuri sat up straight in bed and began. "Your Majesty! This person
. . ."

The Senator jumped right in. "'This person' is bureaucratic. It's better
to say 'your servant.'"

"Your Majesty! Your servant who has been granted the honor of your
presence . . . "

"'The servant of your court' is both more elegant and graceful."

"The servant of your court who has been granted the honor of receiving your presence wishes to take this moment to offer his proud and
ecstatic welcome on behalf of the principal, the students, and their parents
to Her Majesty upon her imperial arrival and to ask the Almighty for the
longevity and happiness of the royal family. It is said: 'The stooped shape
of the universe was straightened up in joy when the Mother of Time gave
birth to a child like you! Ancient Iranians have always guided us toward
admiration of kings, the love of our nation, and to good thoughts, deeds,
and speech. . . . '"

Grandpa Senator nodded quickly. "Not bad. Who helped you?"

"Nobody. I wrote it myself."

"Bravo, your literary talent is not bad either. Yet there is no harm in
taking precautions. In my opinion, it would be a good idea to show your
speech to your literature teacher as well so that if there are small problems
in it, he can fix them. I have written a literary piece myself. Did you know
I am a writer?"

"No."

"They say I have a real way with the pen. I have written something
new recently. I want to ask a calligrapher friend to copy it onto a plywood
tablet in India ink. Do you know how to carve out the words with a jig-
saw? If you know how, I myself will cover the backside of the plywood
with a piece of gold-leaf paper and put it in an inlaid frame."

"I have the saw. Only the words can't be too small. Plywood is thin
and cracks easily."

"Why don't you work on it for now? If it turns out nicely, you can offer
the whole thing framed to Her Majesty on behalf of the students. Maybe

she will give you a prize." He stood up and with a satisfied look examined Nuri. "It seems to me you are sleepy now. Go to sleep. I'll get back to my work. Good night."

The Senator turned off the light and left the room. In the silence, it seemed to Nuri as if a huge burden were being lifted from his shoulders. He lay down on the bed and freed his mind to think about whatever came into his head. Real democracy was possible for him only in privacy, away from censors, inspectors, and guides. He thought, What kind of trick was he going to use to carve such small print into thin plywood? Why had Grandpa Senator never during that whole conversation alluded to Nuri's studies and his repeated absences from school? Disconnected thoughts devoid of any logical links to each other rushed into Nuri's head. He saw Soraya's frowning face. Her wounded expression was like a secret invitation to him. He thought of the storage room, the cool alleys of Dezashib, strangers who returned home late at night, the lights in New York City's Times Square that flicked on and off like an electric billboard in his imagination.

From the alley came the voice of the neighborhood ice cream vendor. To Nuri, Dezashib seemed beautiful and calm under the spell of the dark, alive and far away from everywhere. Rocks of all sizes, in the shape of eggs, had slid down the slope of the mountain to the edges of the paved road. He saw things from multiple perspectives that made connections between the familiar and the unfamiliar. To see something from a new angle suddenly was like making an unexpected discovery: "I see! So that's how it is! Why hadn't I realized this up to now?" That was real life—in other words, a sense of familiarity in the face of alienation.

Perhaps the secret of Madame's success was how the unknown always reminded her of the familiar in her own homeland. She was not like Badri Khanom and Dr. Jannati, who didn't have even a nice memory of American peaches and grapes. And all that because the American fruit was not as soft as "our own Iranian peaches and grapes." As Badri Khanom said, "No! No place is like our own country. If you ask me where I would choose to sleep instead of those fancy-dancy hotels, my answer would be simple. I would say I prefer the run-down huts in Naziabad to all that glitter."

Perhaps with the passing of time life became easier. Maybe Nuri would become more patient, and one day he would finally understand why feeling like a stranger has nothing to do with where you live. Why some people, no matter where they go, remain foreigners, even in their own country. Why the heart of a foreigner is always a hollow of longing and desire.

Nuri cautiously went up to the storage room on the third floor. He opened the door a crack. The clothes cupboards, the long mirror, and the mannequin were in their usual dusty places. The quiet and cool air was just perfect for forgetting the outside world and all that tormented his soul. Nuri looked among Madame's knickknacks. He picked up two pairs of nylon stockings and an old photo album to keep for himself. With dust-covered hands, he stuffed the stockings into his pockets and paid no attention to dirtying his white trousers. He was thinking about nothing, no one, and no particular place. Only a distinct urge prodded him on. He longed for places that from a certain perspective didn't really exist. Their most important attribute was that they always reminded him of other places and hinted at mysterious people.

As he passed the kitchen, he noticed Black Najmeh. He hid the photo album behind him and smiled for no good reason. Najmeh was busy at work and didn't notice him. So much the better. Perhaps his luck had turned, or as they said on the radio, "the chickadee of his recognition" was calling out to him. He left the garden, and when he got to the public telephone booth, he dropped in a dozari coin and dialed the Tahmasbis' number. He recognized Mrs. Tahmasbi from the warmth in her voice. "Who are you, sir?"

"Nuri. Nuri Hushiar."

"How wonderful! What has happened that you remembered the poor people? Where are you, Agha? Our eyes are brightened. Why don't you ask about us anymore, Naneh-jun?"

"But I am always bothering you. How are you?"

Mrs. Tahmasbi had not yet finished her next sentence when she began complaining about Soraya with her usual maternal "Naneh-jun," except in a joking and sarcastic tone that betrayed her secret affection and made "Sori-jun" into a spoiled but adorable child. "Naneh-jun, you are no stranger.

This girl is just driving me crazy with her shenanigans. Tell me why this girl pays everything and everyone so little mind? She pays no attention to her appearance. I don't understand anymore. She doesn't even budge enough from her spot to keep up appearances in front of strangers. From morning to night, she lies on her bed half-naked, dressed in a flimsy dress, and reads novels. She won't be able to secure a future this way. Please don't imagine I am making this up on my own. Whatever I am saying is exactly what she herself says. And then when suitors come asking for her hand in marriage, she rushes about and in that same half-naked state throws her fur coat over her shoulders, walks downstairs barefoot, and sits tailor style in the guestroom in front of them." She paused. "Oh, Naneh-jun, what kind of behavior is this? After all, shame is a good thing!"

Then she turned the subject to the marriage ceremony of "Sori-jun" and Mr. Shirzad. When she remembered the bit at the ceremonial wedding vows, she got goose bumps from shame. Especially that moment when the poor *akhund*, in the customary manner, had asked the bride three times whether she consented to marriage. The third time, "Sori-jun" had stood up and in front of everyone had taken off her wedding dress and put a stop to the celebrations. Mr. Shirzad's face had gone pale as plaster, and without saying good-bye he had left the apartment. He didn't even return to the apartment to take back the diamond ring and the silver mirror and candleholders. Mrs. Tahmasbi paused briefly in case Nuri wanted to say something. Nuri said, "Strange, but why?"

"Why? How should I know, Naneh-jun? You have to tell me why. A mature and thinking person doesn't change out of her wedding dress in the middle of the ceremony and doesn't kick her bright future into smithereens like a jackass. And with a husband like Mr. Shirzad, who has a secure and respectable position and future with the secret police! He had the latest model of Toyota that even a director general couldn't dream of owning. In the evenings, he went to the Intercontinental Hotel in Iran-e Novin Street. He ordered Chivas Regal whiskey. The policemen at the street corners respected him. He had even promised the Colonel a raise. He was going to buy us a villa in Ramsar where we could retire and in our old age sit on the beach and breathe easily. And then this crazy girl . . . "

Nuri asked about Buki. Mrs. Tahmasbi sighed and said she had no idea where he was. She had no idea where that kid went on Friday evenings. She said all this in an easy tone as if she and Nuri were the same age and had been best friends. She started her sentences in the middle and without any introduction. "We received the result of the Colonel's urine test . . . ," she would say but not give any explanation as to what the urine test was for and to whom it had been returned.

Nuri asked about Buki once again. Mrs. Tahmasbi said in a changed tone, "What do you want Buki for, Naneh-jun?"

"I thought maybe he has come back, and we could go somewhere together."

"If you are feeling lonely, come here and see us. Talk a little bit with Sori-jun until Buki comes back." She paused again and said, "Sori-jun says hi and asks were you not supposed to bring the album?"

Nuri feigned ignorance. "Which album?"

"The album with the old pictures of Vienna. The pictures of Madame and the Senator's engagement. You yourself sent a message that you would be coming this week to show us the album."

"Oh, that album."

"You weren't so unkind before."

"I apologize. Please tell her that when I have time, I'll bring her whatever she wants."

"Why don't you bring it right now? Tajrish is but two steps away from here. Mr. Ra'oof and the Colonel say hello as well and ask why do you only come to see Buki? We, the old, decrepit people, don't count anymore?"

"Don't put me to shame, please."

"Sori-jun says she will never talk to you if you don't come."

Fortunately, all the formalities didn't take long. Nuri hung up to go sightseeing alone on the Tajrish Bridge, to treat himself to an ice cream, a corn on the cob, or walnut kernels and to wander around aimlessly and in peace among other people on their outings. Then he would follow someone to see where he would end up.

It seemed that he was becoming once again obsessed with a desire to go the Tahmasbi apartment. What a bind he had gotten himself into!

If Buki were the type to stay home on Fridays or at least let someone know where he was going and when he would return, Nuri would be better off. He would use the excuse of seeing Buki to go to the Tahmasbi apartment. But on a Friday he didn't have anyone there to keep him occupied until Buki returned. Most of the time Cyrus was tied up with pretty Pari or was off somewhere having fun or was busy running around trying to get an exemption from military service. Friday evenings, Mrs. Tahmasbi and the Colonel went out to the movies and left Soraya alone in the apartment because she wasn't interested in movies. Until she found a fiancé to lift her out of her torpor, she wouldn't change her clothes or go out on excursions. This was the main problem. Being alone with Soraya in that apartment was not proper, and it was better for Nuri to postpone visiting the Tahmasbis.

Only once before had he summoned enough courage to go see Soraya when she was all alone. He had put on his sporty white shirt with the yellow and brown stripes, his jeans, and his Candida shoes, but instead of going to the Tahmasbi apartment he had first ridden his bike off into the fields. He rode as far as the Ghuchak Pass, near the Jajrud River, and the Telo coffeehouse. The gentle and continuous pressure of his feet on the bike pedals had given him an inner sense of confidence. How easy it was to feel free! He had turned his bike around and descended the slope of Pahlavi Avenue so fast that in a blink of the eye the facade of the Tahmasbi apartment building appeared before him. As usual, the apartment door was open, and there had been no need for him to ring the bell. Even then, he was cautious. He had surveyed his surroundings and searched his mind for an excuse he could present for being there.

From the lights on the second floor, he had gathered Soraya was busy at something in her room. Once again he felt ashamed. Why had he made himself a stone on ice? Why was he acting like a dummy, running away from home and going to people's houses unannounced? The stale air of the apartment had paralyzed him from within. Perhaps this same air prevented Soraya from going out and made her spend most of her time lying on the bed in her room. A room marked by its former inhabitant, a person by the name of Mashallah Fardid, who had rented this same apartment some twenty years ago. Strange reminders of Mashallah's presence, clinging to the walls like an eternal companion, protected Soraya. Nuri remembered all this from childhood days when he had spent most of his time in that apartment. Soraya herself had taken him repeatedly to her room in the hope of putting him in touch with Mashallah. Nuri, who didn't understand this sort of thing, had stared at Soraya dumbfoundedly and asked: "Where is Mashallah, then? Why is the room empty?"

Soraya yelled: "Idiot, why are you so dumb? Mashallah is here." Nuri's lack of comprehension made her shake her head a few times.

But after some years, when he had climbed the stairs to Soraya's room, he had suddenly felt a change in the air. The cold fingertips of an invisible person touched the skin on his neck, shoulders, and face. It felt as if someone's clammy presence were drawing near him, wrapping around his body like a wet sheet. Nuri shuddered. It was better for him to turn around right then and, before anybody found out, leave the apartment as quietly as he had come in. The first step he took down the stairs made a loud creaking. From behind, he heard Soraya's voice: "Who is there? . . . Who's down there? Maman! Baba-jun! Who's down there?"

Nuri had wasted no time. Hurriedly, but with extreme caution and on tiptoe, he had run downstairs and shut the door behind him in a flash and fled into the alley. As soon as he felt the fresh air on his face, he put his hands in his pockets, took wide steps, and started whistling as if he didn't have a care in the world.

But within a day he again got the urge to see Soraya. When he returned from school, he went first into the storage room, pretending to himself that he intended to return Madame's nylon stockings and old photo album. Like a zombie, he walked through the knickknacks and stuffed a few more things into his pockets to present as gifts to Soraya. If he made these raids only one or two times, he still had a chance of getting away with it. But every few days his old temptation came back with the same force. And right in the heat of the exams, while his schoolmates spent every day in the auditorium practicing for the Fourth of Aban celebrations and Her Majesty's visit. Grandpa Senator and Vaziri went out constantly and, as always, came back with a group of wheeler-dealers expert at fixing elections. Black Najmeh and Puran prepared dishes in the kitchen and continuously served the guests freshly brewed tea. The relatives, one or two at a time or in a group, stayed on for lunch or dinner so that they could participate in the official discussions of the cultivation of Aghcheh.

Thursday afternoons, the sound of Madame's organ came down from the third floor and pervaded every nook and cranny of the house. She played snatches of "Wheat Flower, Beloved" for Ladan and criticized her performance of the role of Goddess of the Harvest. It was gradually getting cold. Madame was afraid of sitting in front of an open window in the study and causing a flare-up of her chronic bronchitis, which would stop her from performing songs for three weeks. Instead of a nap in the afternoon, she threw a bath towel over her head and administered penicillin vapors. She asked about Nuri, why he was rarely around and what he was up to. Was he paying attention to his schoolwork? Had he memorized the speech he had to deliver to Her Majesty? In the midst of all this, it was Nuri alone who had nothing to do. Even if before all eyes he walked into the storage room and took out a vault's worth of stuff, he was willing to bet no one would notice.

When he ran into Ladan in the middle of the hallway, he saw her as strangely thin. She had a sincere and angelic look at odds with her heavy makeup. The minute she noticed Nuri, she lifted her hair like a ponytail to cool the back of her neck. She didn't call Nuri "Mamakh," either. On the contrary, she greeted him in the manner of the relatives. She said that at night she couldn't go to sleep for the thought of his riding his bike in the middle of the busy streets, with all those cars making sharp turns in a flash. After that, she went into her own room to prepare herself for the next day's rehearsal.

The garden was quiet, and in the autumn sun it appeared pale. Maybe he should take the bus to Buki Tahmasbi's apartment. By that time, Mrs. Tahmasbi and the Colonel would be at the movies and Soraya would be reading a novel in her room or listening to a radio program, perhaps *Youth and the Radio*. The temptation to find Soraya was in some respects like a desire to tease someone. In his imagination, he saw her exactly as in a movie poster, bare naked in the semidark, passed out on a bed in a room whose walls turned a steely gray in the dusk. Everything would be quiet as if awaiting an unusual event. A bedside lamp created a triangular, umbrella-like brightness over the pages of the novel. The open window exposed Soraya to a kind of secret assault. She was ten years older than Nuri, but sometimes she talked to him so casually that the difference in their ages didn't matter. Soraya moved around her bed softly, like a cat. She covered the naked parts of her body with the corners of her undershirt. She held her head at an angle and, with the simplicity of a child, drew things out of him. What had he found recently in the storage room? She referred to the postcards, old albums, Madame's opera dresses in such exact detail that it was as if she were looking at them that very instant. Nuri's pleasure stemmed from this need Soraya had to talk to him. One day he would take her to the movies, to a café, even to Shokufeh No Café, and spare no expense. The excitement she showed when receiving gifts made him feel as if he were a grown man of means, the kind of man he wished to become. Now he knew Soraya's weakness. Without any pretense, she had asked him directly about Madame's special opera dress. "When is Madame going to throw away her red beaded dress?"

"Why should she throw it away?"

"If such a pretty dress isn't worn, it will be destroyed by moths. She has to keep it in mothballs and then air it out on the clothesline."

Nuri deliberately stayed quiet. Soraya continued. "If Madame doesn't like the purse she used to use for masked balls, why should she throw it away? Bring it to me. I like it very much."

She spoke like a spoiled brat. Sometimes the words in her mouth sounded like kisses.

◆ ◆ ◆ Mrs. Tahmasbi opened the apartment door for him. Her face, all covered with cream, looked moonlit. Her blue eyes shifted around instead of staying focused. Beneath her dyed black hair, the white roots seemed like a halo. She pressed the key chain in her palm hard, as if it might be taken away from her. Why did she need the key chain anyway? How could an apartment whose doors were always unlocked need so many keys? Their friends and even strangers dropped in any time they wanted. The Colonel had a habit of saying to newcomers, "In this house, we don't make a distinction between insiders and strangers. Our door is open to everyone."

Mr. Ra'oof, the Colonel's old friend, dropped in frequently with his grandson, Sasan, and immediately headed to the fridge. If he didn't find

a chicken thigh, a cutlet, or a piece of *kuku*, he would start complaining.
"There's not even a hint of food in your fridge."

Mrs. Tahmasbi was wearing a special flowery, shapeless dress. The
cream on her face made her look tired and listless. But she was not yet
ready to go to the movies. She had to hoist up her wrinkled nylons and
change out of her slippers. On the floor of the hallway were scattered
men's shoes, a tennis racket, and some free weights.

From the left side, the kitchen door opened onto the hallway, and from
the right onto the bathroom, outside of which were a pile of dirty clothes,
a yellow plastic pail, a box of Fab laundry detergent, and a jar of Farah
vegetable oil, all strewn in disorder. The facing wall ended in a combination of light and darkness, giving way to rooms that opened into each
other. Mrs. Tahmasbi called, "Colonel, guess who has just arrived?"

Instead of the Colonel, Soraya answered from the second floor. "Who
is it, Maman?"

Then the Colonel himself asked, "Who?"

Soraya called, "It must be Nuri, isn't it?"

The Colonel and Mr. Ra'oof were busy playing a game of twenty-
one in the guest room. Sasan, Mr. Ra'oof's grandson, was watching their
game from a corner. The Colonel wore a pair of milk chocolate trousers,
an open-collared shirt, and brown socks. His gray slippers reminded Nuri
of an office worker on summer holiday. When the Colonel noticed Nuri,
he stood up suddenly. He rubbed the tip of his index finger over a finger
of the other hand, mimicking the movement of a knife's blade, and said,
"Watch out or I'll cut you!" He frowned in jest. "Nuri-jan, I'll cut your ears
with this same knife."

Nuri replied, "Go ahead."

The Colonel collected the banknotes he had won and put them in his
pocket. Mrs. Tahmasbi said, "Colonel, let's hurry up. It's getting late for
the movies."

The Colonel took the notes out of his pocket and showed them to Nuri
and pointed laughingly to Mr. Ra'oof. "Do you see this Ra'oof? Just before
you got here, he showed me an ace and a king. He threw himself on the
table to rob the bank. I said to him, 'Agha-jun, Your Excellency, wait a
moment! The chicks are counted at the end of autumn.' When I showed

him my two beautiful aces, he lost it. Am I not right, Ra'oof? If I said too little or too much, say so. It won't bother me."

An annoyed Mr. Ra'oof scratched his head absentmindedly. The Colonel started talking again. "Nuri-jun, if you had come earlier, you would have seen his face for yourself. With that pair of wide eyes, exactly like the two unbalanced sides of a scale . . . " The Colonel laughed so hard he couldn't finish his sentence. "Hee, hee, hay, hay, hay . . . "

He slammed his palm on his thigh, and the force of his laughter made him bend down like a spring. In the middle of laughing, the Colonel pulled Sasan's ears to make him scream. When Sasan screamed, his mouth grew twisted, which made the Colonel laugh even harder. With a finger he pointed to Sasan's contorted mouth to make the others laugh as well, but now Sasan started crying and hid himself behind Mr. Ra'oof, and the Colonel suddenly became contrite. To placate Sasan, he took a candy from his pocket and offered it to the child. "Come on, Sasan-jun, come here, Baba-jun. Uncle only wanted to tease you." The Colonel made Sasan come to the middle of the room so that, as usual, they could have a finger-snapping competition. "Sasan-jun, eh, hurry up, Baba-jun, get ready with those fingers to lift your uncle's mood. Hurry up, my dear!"

They stood in front of each other and set to snapping their fingers as loud as possible. It was time for them to leave and catch at least the third screening of the movie. Nuri sat uncomfortably in a chair and held the old photo album on his lap. The new shirt he was wearing scratched his body like sandpaper. He showed the album to Mrs. Tahmasbi and said, "I brought this."

Then Soraya herself appeared at the top of the staircase in a nightshirt and with uncombed hair. As if out of control, she put on a big display of emotion. She walked over to Nuri, placed the palms of her hands on his back, and pulled him exuberantly to her soft chest. But her enthusiasm did not last long. With her usual inattentiveness, she turned away from him. Then she started picking a quarrel. Why didn't Nuri bring a car to take her sightseeing? Why didn't he invite her to the Dezashibi house to see Madame's special postcards? Nuri had not yet reached the legal age and couldn't get his driver's license. Soraya yelled that if Nuri himself didn't have a driver's license, why didn't he ask Vaziri to come and take them for a drive? She pursed her lips and asked, "Do you mean to say it would be beneath Madame and the Senator to put me in their Mercedes?"

On the upstairs hall table, the phone rang, but she didn't pick up the receiver. It was always one of those good-for-nothing, uncultured, uncouth, and lascivious ones calling to tease her. They played silly games. In an Armenian accent, they called her "young *khanom*" and threw in *"gamas, gamas,"* pretending they were speaking a foreign tongue. She could tell from some of their voices that they were university students. They gave her their phone numbers. They said they only wanted to get to know her. Soraya had returned their calls a couple of times. It would have been far better if she hadn't. Every time she phoned, a different person answered and made her an offer of marriage. One of them suggested that they write to each other to better understand each other's feelings, and then he would come and ask for her hand in marriage. Another of the callers spoke heatedly and claimed that he didn't believe in petit bourgeois superficial and meaningless relationships. He insisted that, without the ridiculous ceremony of contractual marriage, they could have their honeymoon in his room that very night.

Now Soraya was quiet, just listening to the radio from her room. She didn't even acknowledge Nuri's presence. After the first song, she began her own nasal recitation of one of Veegen's songs and went back to her room. "Until your lips touch mine. . . . "

It was better for Nuri to leave the apartment to go to the Super Burger or the Texas Pizzeria, which on Fridays were packed with schoolgirls, but he was hesitant. Disappointed, he went downstairs and collapsed into the sofa like plum jam. He squeezed a pimple on his chin and listened to the Colonel and Mr. Ra'oof, who were now getting ready to go to the movies. Mrs. Tahmasbi pursed her lips for Nuri in a wordless form of pleading with him. It was as if she wanted to make up for Soraya's behavior. She also seemed to be hinting that Nuri should look after Soraya until they came back from the movies. "May I sacrifice myself for your moonlike face, Naneh-jun, go upstairs and check on Soraya. You don't know how happy it makes her."

Soraya spoke up from her bedroom. "Maman . . . "

"Huh?"

"Bring me something to eat. I'm hungry." Then she called down, "Nuri, did you bring your Mumzie-Madame's silver earrings as a gift for me?"

"No, was I supposed to?"

"You yourself promised."

Nuri was stunned. "When did I promise?"

"Of course you did. It was you who said Madame wants to offer me her silver earrings. I remember that you specifically used this word 'offer.' I remember very well."

Mrs. Tahmasbi gestured to Nuri not to take Soraya's words to heart. She put one hand on the radio and with her other hand slipped on her good shoes for the movies. Nuri called, "In a week I'll bring the earrings and present them to you myself as a gift."

"Didn't you say that Madame was going to offer them to me with her own hands?"

"Madame or I, what difference does it make?"

"Get out of here, you just know how to make promises."

Mrs. Tahmasbi looked cross. She was beginning to get annoyed with Soraya, although their quarrels were always a sham. Whenever they had a disagreement, Soraya would lie down listlessly on the carpet and put on a show for her mother's benefit. She would stretch her arms and pretend to yawn. She would wrap herself in a thin chador, place her head on her mother's lap, and tuck her knees into her stomach. She would suck on one thumb and, with her other thumb, rub Mrs. Tahmasbi's arm so hard that it turned red. Then, as if responding to imaginary foes, she would say heatedly, "So what's wrong with sucking your thumb? It's great fun anyway."

Mrs. Tahmasbi called, "Sori-jun, do you want me to send Nuri to see you?"

"What for?"

"Well, you are young and can talk to each other, not like us old people who don't have anything to talk about and go to the movies instead."

"I've got to a good part of my novel and can't put it down just now."

Mrs. Tahmasbi turned back to Nuri and put her fist to her lips. "Eh?" Then she changed her expression back to normal. "When we are out at the movies, Nuri will stay here. It's not nice to leave him all alone in this dark room. Sori-jun. You have to treat him properly as a guest."

Once again, Mrs. Tahmasbi made a fist in front of her mouth. "Oh, look." She put the mixed nuts dish on the table in front of Nuri. "Eat some nuts and put some in your pocket for the road. This Sori-jun of ours is such a coquette. This playing coy is all an act she uses to make people pay attention to her. She'll come straight down."

Mrs. Tahmasbi was completely ready to leave, but she still dragged her feet. In front of the hallway mirror, she ran the palm of her hand over her hair distractedly. At last, she turned around to face Nuri and smiled at him. "Naneh-jun, we leave you in charge of this house. Don't let the devil get into you!" She rounded her eyes and bit the corner of her lips. "No tomfoolery, please." Imitating the Colonel, she brought two fingers together like the blades of a pair of scissors. "Watch out or I'll cut it."

The Colonel and Mr. Ra'oof walked toward the door. With each step, Sasan hit his fist against the wall and talked to himself. Mrs. Tahmasbi still didn't want to leave. Several times she threw a worried glance at Nuri and hung back.

... 5 ...

Nuri had a life of his own, and he was not going to wait an hour for Soraya to finish reading her novel. He would not sit idly in the living room without at least considering leaving. Almost daily Soraya borrowed novels from the Shadman Stationery Store. First, she would read in the small room behind the parlor that held bins and for this reason was called the storage room. At noon, Mrs. Tahmasbi would lay out the lunch spread, and the storage room became noisy. Having barely eaten her lunch, Soraya would go up to her own room on the second floor and fall asleep on her bed. When she woke up, she would lie on her stomach and continue reading her novel, as if she were being drawn into an enticing inner world by an invisible force. She chose novels filled with adventures and escapades— *The Pardayans, The Count of Monte Cristo, The Three Musketeers*—or police novels and mysteries about Nat Pinkerton, Arsène Lupin, and Ginguz Reja'i. Most of these books had begun to fall apart, which drew attention not simply to their stories, but also to the old, poorly typeset letters and the yellowing paper on which they were printed.

Soraya devoured these novels with the hunger of someone who has survived a famine. When she finished one lot, she would return to the Shadman Stationery Store and, looking as proud as a person who has won a hundred-meter dash, come home with another armful of novels she had already read several times. Like a dancer, she would drop forward on the floor. She would lie on her stomach, with her legs bent, her bare, pale feet moving rhythmically as she read, periodically taking a sip of water from a glass she always kept beside her. She would turn over, stare at the ceiling, and confess to Nuri that no new novel, no matter how adventurous, could replace the ones she had read before or arouse her curiosity in quite the same way. Then she would ask Nuri why nothing as beautiful as the

99

events she read about in the novels ever happened in ordinary life. "Why do we draw such pleasure from events we don't believe and enjoy the defiance of the laws of physics and the limitations of time and space? Why do we prefer to resort to superstition and the supernatural in our interpretation of events?" She would explain that novels were not just a pastime for her, but that every page was like a window opening onto unbelievable vistas. With each page, she was so changed that she surprised herself and wanted to read each word slowly and carefully.

She worried that Nuri would judge her by her disheveled appearance and not take her seriously. She accused Nuri of being underhanded. She would say that whether you were groomed or unkempt, both were different a means of erecting walls around the self. At the same time, though, Soraya herself barged past other people's walls in any old way her heart desired. She pretended to be a private investigator like Nat Pinkerton or Sherlock Holmes. She would examine Nuri's face closely and stare into his eyes to discover his secret thoughts. Like the Count of Monte Cristo in his prison cell, she marked off the days on the wall of her room so as not to lose track of the time. Like Ginguz Reja'i ridiculing the head gangsters, she would address Nuri as "my dear bagful of hot air."

Nuri would wait his turn. Then, to excite Soraya, he would speak of the Dezashibi house, the storage room, postcards from the Second World War era, Madame, Princess Bertha and Siegfried von Friedhoff, their famous trip to Prague, and the play they had performed for German soldiers. Sometimes Soraya would shut her book and with a listless yet absorbed look forget herself and listen to the stories Nuri told. It seemed as if she had been robbed of the power to move. Once when Nuri asked her why she did not travel to Europe, she pointed to the novels she was reading and said, "I have these, why should I go abroad?"

"Don't you get tired of them? You read each one once, twice, many times. Don't you ever get bored?"

With a surprise that seemed genuine to Nuri, Soraya said, "My world is exactly what you see. I like it. I'm mad about all its nooks and crannies. Am I crazy enough to go all the way to a foreign country only to get homesick the minute I arrive there? *You* are obsessed with going to New York because you have lost something and want to be near your Maman Zuzu.

All those who like you are always looking for something new suffer from being ill at ease with themselves."

"Miss Soraya, why does everything lose its interest for me so quickly? Why do I have to look for new things all the time?"

"It's not true. That's what you think. You've been around Madame and lost yourself."

"No, I swear it's not just in my head, Miss Soraya."

"Of course it is. I know."

"Miss Soraya, you pass judgment so quickly, I can't even defend myself. Whatever I say will have no effect on you."

Soraya shrugged her shoulders. "You asked for my opinion, I told you. I have no patience to argue with you. If you want to argue with someone, go find Buki."

She turned back on her stomach and resumed reading.

Her empty gaze indicated how attached she had grown to her own prison. A place whose appearance had much in common with a temporary city jail—wet walls, peeling plaster, window frames from which layers of paint had worn off, and screens on which a brownish yellow like an old newspaper had settled. The disarray in the room reminded Nuri of the phony souvenirs of someone who had spent a lifetime exploring foreign countries.

Imitating Nat Pinkerton, she would gaze at the mementos on the walls in order to delve into Mashallah's secret life. It seemed to her that Mashallah either had been in hiding or had lived in that room under house arrest. He had recorded some of his memories on the walls in a secret language. These messages were in the simple and careful hand of professional revolutionaries who want to preserve their anonymity—the kind who always carry a revolver in their jacket pockets and keep their fingers on the trigger even in their sleep. Other messages were recorded in such a legible handwriting that they were reminiscent of schoolchildren's homework: "Culture is better than wealth," "Strong is he who possesses knowledge," "Art is the property of Iranians and no others."

Soraya imagined Mashallah around the age of thirty, always dressed in a light-brown, striped suit. He wore a white open-collared shirt under his suit jacket. His hair was pitch black and curled diagonally across his forehead. In addition to the messages on the wall, Soraya wanted to read the classified documents and police records pertaining to Mashallah's interrogations, probably filed away as top secret in the country's Internal Security Office. She wanted to find out about his life. Was he still alive, or was he long dead? Where was he from? Some of Mashallah's messages seemed like a condemned man's last words to his family.

"Nothing is the matter with me. Don't worry too much about me. I leave Gohar and the children in your care."

Subjects that reeked of the passage of time and the futility of all attachment, that enabled Soraya to gain access to a special realm. Even when Buki was still a child, she demanded that he ask the projectionist at Jahan Cinema for a ten-frame roll of a Pink Panther movie. At last, Buki succeeded in fulfilling her wish. Soraya was beside herself with joy. She begged Buki to take the film to the photographer in Lalehzar-e No Street and have a few enlarged photographs printed from it. As soon as she saw the photographs, she burned the roll of film so that no one else would have access to it.

Now, on this particular evening, Nuri could leave whenever he wanted, but no matter what he did, he would probably run into problems. Soraya would interpret anything he did as a confession. When he examined his options, he found only one way out. Setting aside caution, he decided to confront Soraya directly. He would throw himself into fire and water and stand up to Soraya like Tarzan.

Before entering her room, Nuri looked into the wall mirror and ran his hand over the hair at his temples. His smile made his blue eyes appear cold and disdainful. He put the old album under his arm and climbed the stairs at top speed, like a cartoon figure spiraling around so fast that it leaves no trace but a curved line on the screen. With one hand, he hid the album behind his back, and with his other he grasped the nylon stockings in his trouser pocket. He stood straight as an arrow in the doorway of Soraya's room. Soraya, wrapped in a flimsy chador, lay on the carpet reading her novel. She was under the same old lamp whose blue shade had a large burned spot, now covered with a patch cut from an old newspaper. The chador did not cover Soraya's thighs. For this reason, she noticed

Nuri's presence quickly. She first covered her bare thighs, then raised one corner of the chador to just below her blue eyes and said, "How is this?"

"What?"

"Shirzad always said that, if nothing else, at least my eyes were pretty."

She was speaking about her first encounter with Mr. Shirzad. On an overcast autumn day a few years earlier, when the birds were skipping around on the grass, Mr. Shirzad's eyes had met Sori-jun's blue eyes accidentally. Soraya was busy at a pomegranate vendor's cart, helping her mother pick out the biggest and juiciest fruit. Given his devious nature, Mr. Shirzad had spoken as if he were one of the pomegranates so that Soraya could hear him. Without any preliminaries, he said, "O pomegranate vendor, may you be cursed! Why do you torment us by showing us the blue eyes of someone's daughter just to land us in a heap of trouble? Do you enjoy torturing others? You have ruined our reputation!"

Now Soraya's face was puckered like a Gypsy's. Her eyes filled with tears, which welled up at the corners. She tilted her head and said, "Has Your Highness come empty-handed again?"

Nuri waited and did not show her the album and the nylon stockings. Instead, he stood by the door until Soraya brushed her black hair off her face and assumed a calm and ready pose. The greeting she offered Nuri had an interrogative tone. "Hello!" she said.

Nuri answered calmly, "Hello!"

"Why don't you come in?"

"It's OK here."

"Are you afraid I'll eat you?"

Her eyes took on a playful look. She arched her brows and narrowed her lids arrogantly. "Are you annoyed with me?"

If Nuri had had his wits about him, he would have fled without looking back, but the same force that exposed him to danger was now rooting him to the spot. He showed Soraya the album and the nylons. Soraya frowned. "What are these things?"

"Don't you know what they are?"

"How should I know? Do I have special powers of insight?"

"This is the same old album you asked for. The pictures from Madame and the Senator's engagement."

"Oh . . . "

"And these are two pairs of nylons."

She took the nylons from Nuri. With two fingers, she held them in the air, examined them apathetically, and then threw them on her bed. "Oh . . . "

The "oh" came out of her mouth as if without forethought, perhaps not implying anything in particular. She took the album from Nuri and looked through a few pages. She rubbed her fingers over some of the pictures and said, "These parts are pretty. Where is this?"

Nuri approached the bed and said, "This is Lake Lugano, where Madame and the Senator spent part of their honeymoon."

Soraya put Madame and the Senator's wedding picture on the window ledge and looked at it from a distance. In a melancholic tone, she mumbled to herself. "Madame has never returned to Lake Lugano."

"This is their wedding picture, taken by the Danube, not Lake Lugano."

Soraya put the flimsy chador around her face and walked on tiptoe. "How do I look in my wedding dress?"

"Like the moon."

"Get lost. How brazen you are!"

"I didn't say anything bad. Do you remember the night you were supposed to marry Mr. Shirzad? You looked exactly like the moon."

Soraya said, "That's enough. Take a look at this munchkin and how he flirts with his closest friend's sister. A sister who is ten years older than he. You can't get your hands on movie stars, so you're clinging to me?"

"Miss Soraya, I'm talking about the night of the wedding ceremony. You looked beautiful."

Soraya frowned again, but this time for real. "To hell with him! A decent wedding has to be held at the Officers' Club." She took the picture from the window ledge. "I'll keep this with me for a few days. Then I'll give it back. Is that a problem?"

For a second, Nuri thought about the possibility of losing his special relationship with Madame, yet he was too embarrassed to turn Soraya down—especially now that she was eagerly holding the picture close to her chest, smiling at Nuri expectantly. "For three days, this album will be mine, OK? I'll keep an eye on it and make sure it doesn't get even one tiny scratch, OK?" Her eyes glistened. "Now, let's go out for a stroll and get a little fresh air. Do you have any money?"

Soraya was never eager to leave the apartment, especially with a youngster like Nuri whom she did not take seriously. Nuri didn't know what to think. Fearing he didn't have enough money with him, he put his hand in his pocket and quickly counted the folded notes. He blurted out, "Let's go to a café . . . " Then, after a short pause, "Or a movie."

Soraya wrapped the chador tightly around her bare shoulders and squealed as if she were so delighted she could barely contain herself. "Do you want to go to the Parand Pastry Shop for a cappuccino and freshly baked pastry?"

"Is that a bad idea?"

"No, not at all. It won't take me more than two minutes to get ready."

Soraya shoved Nuri out the door, leaving him no choice but to go downstairs and wait for her. He didn't have much money, but he couldn't leave now. Every time he examined the notes inside his pocket, he felt them grow thinner. He was afraid not merely of having too little money, but also that someone might see them arm in arm in the streets and create a scandal.

Wearing high and narrow-heeled red shoes, Soraya descended the stairs. She stepped cautiously, revealing that she was not used to her shoes and felt insecure. Nuri grew confident enough to approach Soraya, take her arm, and help her come down. In return, Soraya brought her face close to his and pursed her lips coquettishly. Nuri was not pleased, but said nothing. He took the pursed lips to be indicative of an uncontrolled longing he didn't like in women—a female craving that made Soraya's face lose its charm. She cupped Nuri's cheek and told him in an exaggerated, childish tone, "Oh, Nuri-jun, how sweet you are! Did Madame order these clothes for you from Europe?"

"I bought them right here from the Safavi Bazaar."

"My mother says your clothes are sent to you from New York. Little did we know that you buy your clothes here. How nice. Let's go to the Safavi Bazaar together one day."

The square collar of Soraya's white dress scooped halfway down her chest. The lower part of the dress formed a starched, pleated skirt that ballooned around her hips. In contrast, her shoes, handbag, and the scarf around her neck were a bright red that in the dusk gave her dress the appearance of freshly blooming jasmine. She took Nuri's arm. Nuri didn't resist, although it was likely that they would run into Naser Shahandeh, Reza Shahabzadeh, or Buki in front of the Parand Pastry Shop. Buki conducted his business around the American Club, but by now he was likely to be hanging out by the Nahid Pharmacy, showing the boys a new picture of Cyrus and pretty Pari, having no idea how Nuri was ruining his family's reputation. Even if Nuri took some pictures of himself and Soraya lying naked next to each other, though, he would never think of showing them to the neighborhood boys. He liked Buki and knew how quickly he would lose his temper over his sister's honor and, despite their friendship, knock Nuri out with one punch in a dark alley behind the university.

The air was fresh, and yet Soraya's hand, clasping Nuri's arm, was drenched in sweat. Nuri talked a blue streak to prevent Soraya from moving away from him. He fabricated a story about Madame's father being a renowned admiral in the German navy who, with the help of a well-known icebreaker called Dunlop, had discovered an island inhabited by cannibal Eskimos in the North Pole. Soraya shut her eyes and, lost in a dream world, repeatedly rubbed her cheek against Nuri's shoulder. Near the university, she dug her sharp fingernails into his arm and said, "Nuri, what if someone sees us? The news will spread in the neighborhood like wildfire."

Soraya's words did not sit well with Nuri, but the harder he tried to pull himself away, the more she clung to him. "Hey, why do you pull yourself away like this?"

"I just wanted to make sure there was enough room for both of us on the sidewalk."

Soraya rubbed her head against Nuri's shoulder and said, "You're quite a rascal, Nuri."

"What makes you say that? I am not at all a rascal."

"Sure you are, Nuri-jun. You're a rascal! I know it very well."

At the end of each sentence, she smacked her lips. She put on a haughty air to make Nuri laugh. Nuri said, "Miss Soraya, I am not a rascal."

"You sure are."

All during this exchange, she kept digging her nails into Nuri's arm. The more serious Nuri grew, the more playful Soraya became. At last, Nuri pulled his arm away from her, and as he bent down, pretending he needed to tie his shoelaces, he said, "Miss Soraya, have you ever seen an American dollar?"

"I hardly ever see our own money, let alone American dollars. What made you think of American dollars?"

"My mother has sent me a new twenty-dollar bill for the New Year, and I have put it inside my math book. At seven tumans a dollar, it must be worth one hundred and forty tumans. If I had it in my pocket, I'd invite you to the Shokufeh No Café."

Soraya looked at Nuri with admiration and said, "I'm grateful to you."

"You're grateful to me? I have had a truly good time. In this cool air and under such a beautiful sky . . . "

Soraya frowned, but said nothing for a moment. Then in a hurt tone, she asked, "Does this mean you want to leave?"

"No. I just wish I had the twenty-dollar bill with me so that I could invite you to better places."

Annoyed, Soraya shoved Nuri toward the edge of the sidewalk. "If you want to leave, go ahead. What are you waiting for?"

Nuri put on a wounded look and said, "Miss Soraya, what's wrong? Why did you give me a shove?"

Soraya tried to calm down. Looking into her pocket mirror, she ran her fingers over her eyebrows and mumbled, "Let me straighten myself up a bit before we go to the pastry shop."

Nuri walked gingerly along the edge of the sidewalk, keeping his balance. "Miss Soraya, do you like the circus?"

"What are you getting at? You bring me here to talk about the circus?"

"I would really like to work in a circus."

"Nobody is stopping you. You can take your dignified self wherever the hell you want and not try to make it look as if you are doing me a special favor by taking me to a pastry shop."

"Do you like pantomime?"

"Are you teasing me?"

Nuri raised his palm and swore, "Eh! Far be it from me to tease you. I just wanted to teach you miming the way our chauffeur taught me." Like someone imprisoned behind a glass wall, Nuri passed his palms over the invisible surface of the air. He puffed up his cheeks, as if he were swimming under water. "Miss Soraya, what am I doing? Can you guess?"

Soraya threw her purse on the ground, placed her fists on her hips, and shouted at Nuri. "Would you like me to tell you what you're doing? Fine, I'll tell you. You are watching your mother's pain. After centuries, I decide to go out to a café. Instead, you're forcing me to watch your silly miming in the middle of the street. Afterwards, you'll probably complain that you've run out of money and we have to head home. This is all a prank; you don't want to spend any money."

Nuri was startled. "What happened?"

Holding her fingers up like claws, Soraya pulled away from Nuri. "If you touch me, I'll scream. I'm not joking. Come on, try it! Why are you waiting? Go ahead, touch me and see what a fuss I'll make. I'll yell 'police.'"

"OK, OK, I won't touch you."

"Even if you don't lay a hand on me, I'll still scream. Scream, scream, scream until everyone spills out of these houses. Do you remember? Do you remember, oh shameless one, how you promised to take me to a pastry shop? Me, who so dislikes going out of the house? Had it not been for Your Ugliness's babbling, I would never have considered coming out. Leave. Go to hell. I know you very well. You're really stingy. Your entire being is caught up in money. You want to have a good time and still not pay for anything."

Stunned, Nuri didn't say a word in his own defense. Were he to raise his voice, Soraya would scream even more loudly. He bent down slowly, picked up her purse, and offered it to her. Soraya didn't take it. Her eyes warned Nuri against stepping any closer. Fortunately, Nuri was still standing at the curb, which was apparently the right thing for him to do. He followed Soraya toward the Parand Pastry Shop. She sat in one of the chairs Khachator put on the sidewalk in the evenings. Distracted, Soraya took a package of cigarettes out of the purse that Nuri set on the table. She held a cigarette between two shaking fingers and lit it. She lifted her nose and exhaled the smoke into the sky. He sat quietly in the chair opposite her. Even an attempt at apology could provoke another outburst in her and create a scandal. Soraya rested her chin in her palm, and with eyes as piercing as needles she met Nuri's gaze.

She said, "You make me so angry I feel like giving you such a slap, exactly the way Buki does it, so you won't know what hit you. I dress myself up for you and come out, then you act as if you're doing me a favor?" She wrinkled her eyebrows and pursed her lips. "Shirzad would give anything to have me just glance at him once or take one step with him outside the house, but I turned him down. He had a piece of land in Arak. He wanted to build a house on it for me, but I didn't accept. He spoke some three or four languages as fluently as his mother tongue. He could translate from English, French, and even that accursed German of yours much better than the rest of you." She raised her hands to her temples. "Whatever you could have asked for was in his head. It was filled with knowledge. When he spoke to me, he recited verses from Sa'di, Hafiz, and Khayyam. He used to beg to be allowed just once to come by himself to our apartment to court me. I used to say, 'Why do you ask me? What does it matter to me? Come if you want to. Why bother telling me? I have a thousand things to do, and I have to see to my own concerns.' Something like that. He would come to the apartment, ring the doorbell, and say, 'Hello.' He would say, 'Sori-jun, I'm sick. I'm in bad shape. Come take me to the Italian doctor who has his practice in Abbasabad.' Neither did I go with him to the Italian doctor, nor did I allow him to get too friendly with me. Even so, he found many excuses to come to our place. He begged, begged to see me. It's not as if I am a child to fall for that sort of thing. My mother liked Shirzad. She insisted on prolonging our engagement, hoping we would eventually get married. She kept saying, 'This kind of decision takes time. You have to observe his manners and actions, see how he deals with other people and what kind of person he is.' And then there was

Shirzad himself, who was madly in love with me. Like a madman he hung around me. My wish was his command. His only flaw was his opportunism. Like the *bazaaris*, he was always trying to find a way to get a foothold in some government office and brag to everyone, 'Yes, me too.' He noticed that people addressed my father as "Colonel." So he had his own hopes. He wanted to become one of us and move up the social ladder. Not that we are some hot shit ourselves, but anyway . . . "

She started to laugh. She brushed her hair away from her face and averted her gaze. "By God . . . people think that I compromised myself. I told Shirzad, 'At the wedding ceremony it must be announced that the bride is the granddaughter of Hajj Gheysar Tahmasbi, who disarmed Sheik Khaz'al under Reza Shah's orders.' After all, we do have a name and a reputation."

They ordered ice cream from Khachator, and Nuri's nerves settled down a little. He stretched out his legs and examined Soraya closely. Her angry eyes now showed traces of fatigue. She began talking about Mashallah. "When I wake up in the middle of the night, I think Mashallah is buried in my room, and I am sleeping on his grave. That he has some life left in him and is heaving a deep sigh. Under my breath I say, 'Mashallah, Mashallah,' and I listen." She patted the back of Nuri's hand. "Nuri, what a nice person you are. I would like you to be happy too."

"Would you like me to be happy?"

"Yes, on your own life, that's the only thing I want."

Nuri stood up. "If you permit, I'll come back straightaway. I have to go to the washroom."

"When you come back, I'd like to talk to you more. I want to tell you things I couldn't discuss with you after you first moved to the Senator's house. You rarely showed up in Amirabad. They said you were spoiled at the Senator's. You were enjoying yourself and had forgotten your old friends."

Nuri walked to the rear of the café. Before entering the washroom, he took a last look at Soraya. She was still smoking her cigarette and gazing indifferently at the passersby.

Nuri walked past the cash register and entered a semidark hallway that led first to the washroom and then through a low door to the loading area. He walked with an innocent look to avoid arousing anyone's suspicions. A weak lightbulb burned in the bathroom, and the burnished mirror under the bulb didn't reflect Nuri's face adequately. Khachator was apparently more concerned with the cleanliness of the front of the shop and paid no attention to the dried spots in the basin, the blackened grout between the white tiles, and the mound of empty Super Cola bottles stored in the washroom.

Without making any noise, Nuri reached the rear of the loading area and zigzagged his way to the alley. No doubt the next day Khachator would complain to Mr. Raji about Nuri, how he had left an innocent girl at his café and without settling his bill had fled the scene. Nuri shrugged. OK. Let him complain. "To hell with him." Mr. Raji was not the type to make trouble. He had gotten along with Nuri in the discussions about the ceremony for welcoming the queen and was likely to take Nuri's side in this matter. Moreover, if there were any need to shout at anyone, Mr. Raji could not have found a better candidate than Khachator himself. Mr. Raji would warn Khachator that if he entered the school without permission ever again, Mr. Raji himself would break his legs in front of the students.

Nuri emerged in a narrow alley lined with overflowing garbage cans. The air smelled sour like pickled cucumbers. When he reached the street, he mingled with the crowd on the sidewalk. Internationally renowned police chiefs on a par with Sherlock Holmes, Arsène Lupin, and Ginguz Reja'i always went out in ordinary clothes and looked no different from others in the streets when they didn't want to be noticed. Like most of his classmates, Nuri wore tight sailor pants and an American T-shirt.

He tried to picture the situation at the café. While waiting, Khachator would cross his bony hands over his apron, fix his eyes on the ceiling, and roll his tongue in his mouth a few times until Soraya paid up. But if Soraya didn't have any money in her purse, she wouldn't be able to settle the bill. It would turn out badly, and the police would get involved. Nuri kicked a watermelon rind in his path toward the gutter. He liked the style of his kick. He sank his hands into his pockets and once more kicked the rind like a champion soccer player. A splatter echoed in the alley. Like a top, Nuri spun around and skidded to the edge of the gutter. "Bravo!"

Dusk spread across the buildings. The sounds of the autumn evening came from afar, burst in the air like noiseless bubbles, and left Nuri with a sense of emptiness. He fixed his gaze on the iron grating above the court-yard walls and walked straight to the far end of the alley. Along the way, he came across a silver car parked diagonally. Facing the wall, he spread apart his feet and kept an eye on the other end of the alley so as not to be caught peeing.

Nights like this, he would stay up late, expecting a call from Maman Zuzu. As soon as he heard the phone ring, he would leap off his bed and beat Ladan to the hallway phone. He wouldn't even switch on the light because in the dark Maman Zuzu's voice seemed to be coming from some-where near, even closer than Mr. Al-e Batul's courtyard. After the initial greetings, after "Nuri-jun" and "OK, Maman, how are you?" they had nothing left to say to each other. Like Americans, Maman Zuzu would hang up without the usual formalities, and Nuri would not have a chance to finish what he was going to say. He hoped his luck was about to turn and his chickadee was about to sing. He would pack up his belongings and go to New York, a place where, as Badri Khanom said, every night is like a national holiday and the streets are decorated with lights. The stores are open twenty-four hours a day. The Times Square ticker con-stantly flashes the latest headlines on the side of a big skyscraper. A city filled with homeless people who spend the nights by dark and distant fer-ries, pull something over themselves, and fall asleep, still hungry. Imitat-ing Humphrey Bogart, Nuri himself would hide under a bridge dripping with rain. He would take his revolver out of his chest pocket and listen for the echoing footsteps of an approaching criminal—the sound of a siren or a gunshot would draw him out of his dream world and give him a pleas-ant feeling like warm water passing over his nerves.

No doubt the New York that Nuri had created in his imagination had very little in common with Mr. Barney Howard's New York. Mr. Bar-ney Howard was Maman Zuzu's American friend whom Nuri always addressed only as "Mr." He played his guitar in cafés in Greenwich Vil-lage, and it was said that he was ten years ahead of his time. In most pic-tures, he wore yellow corduroy pants and a leather vest over his checkered shirt. Tall like the stars of Westerns, thumbs inserted in his leather belt, he had a typical American half-smile that feigned diffidence but hinted at a carefree boastfulness. Nuri never mentioned Mr. in his letters to Maman Zuzu. Instead, he sent silly photos to New York. A picture of himself with a chador draped over his shoulders like a cape, holding a kebab skewer and looking ready to attack an invisible enemy. A picture of Grandpa Senator sitting on a garden bench, behind him an army officer's uniform hanging on the brick wall. The reception hall in disarray after the guests' departure on the occasion of Madame's birthday. His unmade bed showing the hollow left on it by his body. In her letters, Maman Zuzu never mentioned the pictures Nuri sent to her. She sent Nuri pictures that Mr. had taken of her in midaction: holding a platter with a Thanksgiving turkey on it or opening Christmas presents wrapped in ribbon. She still painted a black mole near one corner of her mouth and put on such heavy lipstick that her lips shone as if they were polished. Spearlike eyelashes and eyelids stained by dots of mascara created a pattern resembling barbed wire. Her cocoa-colored hair was pulled back in Spanish style. Perhaps in Maman Zuzu and Mr.'s life, maybe in all New Yorkers' lives, there was something out of kilter. Most of them seemed to be preparing themselves for unusual encounters.

Behind the walls, under fluorescent garden lights, people were talking. An arrogant army officer with all his stars, stripes, and medals passed Nuri and was swallowed up in the darkness. Then, above a multistoried building, Nuri spotted the Shahrzad open-air movie screen on which images jumped about intermittently. Larger-than-life images of actors seemed first to move toward Nuri and then to withdraw into a funnel-like depth. In his present mood, Nuri wasn't sure whether *The Dirty Dozen* was worth seeing a second time. Even so, he cautiously placed his money on the glass counter of the ticket booth. The clerk looked at him and asked, "How many?"

Nuri raised the tip of his finger like an arrow. "One."

People must have been surprised to see a seventeen-year-old youth alone at that time of the night, but after the troubles with Soraya, Nuri just wanted to sit by himself on the moonlit movie terrace and watch the film.

When the lights came back on, Nuri remembered everything all over again. He stayed in his seat for a while and watched the pale movie credits slowly scroll up the screen. People were shuffling out of the rows of seats, and their footsteps faded when they reached the terrace steps. Nuri thought that by now Soraya would have called Buki to her aid. Buki was unfailing in his sense of responsibility. For friends and family, he would stop at nothing. When Nuri got into a row with Naser Shahandeh, Buki would come to his rescue within two minutes. He would stare at Naser Shahandeh so piercingly that Naser would leave with his tail between his legs, wearing his short-sleeved cowboy shirt and the Lee sailor jeans his father had brought him from Los Angeles. Naser Shahandeh was very proud of his father, who was influential in the Foreign Ministry. Whenever his father dropped him off in front of the school in his white Mercedes convertible, Naser would put on airs.

Nuri stopped by a few of their usual haunts, but he didn't see Buki. He walked along the street to find the schoolgirls who were probably at the Super Burger or the Texas Pizzeria. He still didn't see Buki. Had Buki been there, he would have hung about the girls and whistled at them. He would have put two fingers to his temple like the barrel of a revolver and "bang," shot an empty shell into his head. He would have squeezed Nuri's arm. "Hey, Nuri, son of a bitch, do something."

"What?"

"Look at that short one. Or that fat-lipped one! See how that unbeliever is flirting!"

"What do you want me to do?"

"Go on. Tell her how I am mad about her."

"Which one?"

"That short one. The one whose eyes have dogs that look ready to take a bite of a leg."

He would begin talking about Zhila Shabahang. "Zhila is turning into the Saba Alley. Go catch up with her before she reaches her house."

With his gangly body and a deliberately stuck-out stomach, Buki would walk right up to Zhila. His eyes would give her a "thread" to look at him and smile. He pretended to be drunk. He would whirl around and make himself dizzy. He would combine *thread* and *line* and give it an Arabic plural ending. "Thrine! I'm following the thrine into the depths."

Nuri reached the back alleys along the far limits of Amirabad, near the Hotel Continental, Iran-e Novin Street, close to Pahlavi Avenue. From inside the hotel lobby emanated a fast but monotonous jazz tune that all the boys from the lower quarters of the city had learned by now. When the tape was changed, the boys whistled the rest of the tune until the tape was replayed. The hotel bellman, whom they called Ali Shah, dressed in a gray uniform and white gloves, would shake his finger at the boys to scatter them away from the hotel entrance. Nobody paid any attention to him. They stayed put under the green neon lights and spoke to the Americans in their broken English. On the sidewalk, they sold Winston cigarettes, Khorus-Neshan chewing gum, and disguised packets of condoms. One of the pros among them, reputed to have served a prison term, had brought girls for the foreigners. He was writing in his pocket calendar the name and telephone number of the private club where a middle-aged German man stayed. Most of the Iranians there were employees of the oil company. They held bottles of beer, Super Cola, or some other drink in their hands, stood on the sidewalk by the street vendors, and talked. No doubt each of them had a car, but even so, they had taken taxis the short distance from Takht-e Jamshid to Pahlavi Avenue. In the dining room of the Hotel Continental, each of them ordered three chicken kebabs instead of one and left the other two untouched on their table. They talked about a Jeep that a hippie from some foreign country had built himself and used to tour around in. He was asking only twenty thousand tumans and a half kilo of hashish, which seemed a bargain to most of the oil company employees.

Nuri saw Buki in the semidarkness of the Saba Alley. He was standing beneath a window of the Shabahangs' house, looking into Zhila's bedroom. At the sound of Nuri's approaching steps, he waved a hand that looked like one of the symbols in a religious procession. Nuri shouted, "Buki, son of a bitch, where have you been?"

Buki raised a finger to his lip. This neighborhood, like all other posh districts, echoed every sound a few decibels louder. The new houses had been built of gray-striped concrete blocks by the Sanko Company. Their style was somewhere between the sun-bleached white houses with arched ceilings along the southern shores of France and the older Tehrani houses with small garden pools and doorways adorned with green, yellow, and purple cut glass in the shape of an ostrich feather. The streetlight, which now seemed to Nuri even taller than before, shone on Buki's round face, his jutting forehead, and pointy nose. With slow and drunken gestures, Buki beckoned to Nuri. "Come closer. Come closer. Before I forget, let me tell you this one thing. Last night I dreamed of you."

The outline of Zhila's body moved across the windowpane. She seemed to be wearing some kind of white slip. Buki said, "Nuri, I dreamed you were traveling to a remote place by ship. Exactly as you yourself have described, like Sinbad the sailor, one hand on your waist and the other holding a spear, staring at the horizon and moving forward." Mrs. Shaba-hang put her head inside Zhila's room and said something. Zhila quickly threw on a robe and, before leaving the room, switched off the light. Buki asked, "Are you listening to me? Did you hear what I said?"

"Yes."

"OK. Tell me, when are you leaving for the States?"

Nuri glanced down at Buki's feet and noticed a straw-wrapped bottle of Italian wine. He threw an arm around Buki's neck and said: "So, you have opened your own little tavern in this alley."

Buki looked up in the sky and began singing in the scale of Shur. "Whoever loses anchor in the stormy sea of sorrow will commit the ship of the heart to oblivion. 'Ahli' will not grant the heart's desire because of that idol's heavy heart. He who grants our wish is God in his beneficence." He looked at Nuri again and said, "Have you seen Soraya?"

"Soraya? What do you want with Soraya?"

"I was supposed to see her this evening and didn't find her."

"I was at your place earlier this evening. I was hoping you would be there too."

"I had things to do. I have to make ends meet somehow. You've seen that I'm always working."

Nuri asked, "How long have you been peeping around here?"

"Peeping? Just before you came, I was writing slogans."

Buki took a paintbrush from an empty can of preserved pears and wrote on the gray cement wall, "Death to America," "Down with the Shah." He took the straw-wrapped bottle of Italian wine and guzzled from it. Afterwards, he burped. Nuri said. "What's all this? They'll come and arrest us. Let's go."

Buki burped again. "How are you, my sweetheart?"

"That's enough. Get up."

Buki grew angry. "Who the hell are you anyway?" He finished in a more casual tone. "What do you want, you crazy one?" But he pronounced it "creezy."

"Buki, are you tipsy?"

Buki grew quiet and looked at Nuri with a chary gaze as if he were apprehensive about something.

On his trips to the Indiana Complex and the American Club, Buki always checked the trash bins for items that he could sell in the lower bazaar. Among his finds was a half-empty bottle of Hennessey cognac he had presented as a gift to the Colonel. Sometimes in the middle of the night, the Colonel woke up with palpitations and insisted on being taken to the hospital in an ambulance. He worried that he might have a heart attack and would die for lack of attention. In his dreams, he often played backgammon and grew angry with Mr. Ra'oof's blustering. Mr. Ra'oof kept throwing the dice and bragging, "Excellent, excellent. Colonel, for whom have you left your position so nicely exposed? My dear, my beloved, have you lost your mind? I'll get a set of fives and scorch your mustache so that even the hearts of the birds in the sky will be seared with pity for you." Mr. Ra'oof would rub his palms together greedily and throw the dice. "Colonel, say your last prayers! I'm about to hit you hard and destroy you. It doesn't please God to tease a retired colonel of this country so much."

Buki gave the Colonel and Mr. Ra'oof the cognac to take along with their brazier and drinking utensils to Karaj. They would spread a small rug by the river and barbecue offal on the brazier. Mr. Ra'oof would play the *tar* and sing a love tune. Unfortunately, they developed a taste for the Hennessey and asked Buki to bring them another bottle. Buki kept his eyes open while shouting the names of foreign newspapers. He would put his hand by his ear and shout, "Peeper! English peeper?" The Americans would come out of the club tipsy, with their arms around Iranian women's necks. Buki Tahmasbi would continue to shout. "Oh, peeper, peeper. *New York Times* peeper. *Washington Post* peeper, oh peeper, oh peeper!"

Mr. Sanders, who had made friends with Buki, would wave to him. "Hey."

"Oh peeper, oh peeper. *New York Times* peeper, *Washington Post* peeper, oh peeper, oh peeper!"

Instead of a dozari or panjzari coin, Mr. Sanders would put a rolled banknote on Buki's palm and ask in English, "How are you doing? Are you having a good time?"

Buki smiled and answered in English. "Yes, sir! Having a good time."

Nuri drew Buki away from the Shabahangs' house with no resistance. This was something new because ordinarily it was Buki who assumed the role of the leader. On their way toward Cinema Diana, Buki once again started his paper-boy routine. "Mr. Sanders is very nice." He winked and raised a thumb. "He didn't take even one shahi for this bottle of Chianti he gave me. He invites everyone to his apartment. He says I can drop in on him any time, but I'm not up to it. What should I do there?" He pretended he was selling newspapers again. "Oh peeper, oh peeper. *New York Times* peeper, *Washington Post* peeper, oh peeper, oh peeper! You have to get to know people through their actions, not their words."

"How is it that you, who write all these anti-American slogans on walls, gave in so quickly for one bottle of wine?"

"A man is a man. There's no difference between Americans and non-Americans. We're all fighting the American government." He began to laugh. "How is Madame? Does she still memorize Persian proverbs and sayings?"

Nuri's anger was beginning to well up, but he maintained his calm appearance. "What are you getting at?"

Buki's eyes widened in surprise. "You don't know what I'm getting at?"

"How should I know?"

Buki held his face under Nuri's and gave a drunken smirk. "You don't know what Persian proverbs and sayings are? You've never heard 'Time is gold,' 'Spilt water cannot be collected again,' 'When you lose the thread, you are lost,' 'When you throw the dice up in the air, they have to land on the ground again'?"

A few young girls approached them from the opposite direction. Buki told Nuri, "If you say something to these girls, you'll only embarrass yourself."

"Why?"

"Because you don't know how to speak to girls. You have to speak to them in the manner of intellectuals. 'Do you give permission for me to be with you?'" Speaking like a dandy, Buki said, "'You are very interesting. Do you wish for us get to know each other?'"

Nuri repeated the same sentences a few times. "'Do you give permission for me to be with you?' 'Do you wish for us to get to know each other?'"

He looked at Buki happily. Buki took up where he had left off. "'Would it be possible for me to call you by your first name?' 'Should I give my telephone number for you to call me later?'"

"'Would it be possible for me to call you by your first name?' 'Should I give my telephone number for you to call me later?' Perfect!"

"Of course it is."

"Get out of here!" Nuri replied.

Buki rubbed the palm of his hand over his pocket a few times. "We have an Omega wristwatch. May it bring you good fortune, a mere fifteen tumans. We have a pair of folding binoculars with an ivory handle."

Nuri asked, "How much?"

"Twelve. On your own life, my profit will be only two tumans."

Naser Shahandeh was returning from the Nahid Pharmacy, and he glanced at them out of the corner of his eye. When his papa-*jan* had a backache, he would send Naser several times a day to the pharmacy to have his prescription filled. The first thought that came to Nuri's head had no link to Naser Shahandeh and their street fights. At that moment, he smelled the thin autumn air and got a whiff of something like rotten fish and the algae in a garden pool. He had no idea how he suddenly remembered scenes from the mysterious movie

Strangling Hands. He had seen the film a long time ago with Madame in one of the movie theaters in Lalehzar Avenue, before moving to the Dezashibi house. He glanced at Buki with the secret method that enabled them to read each other's thoughts. He didn't gather anything from Buki's preoccupied expression. Nuri slowed his steps, dragged his heels, and prepared himself to block Naser Shahandeh's way "accidentally." As a precaution, Naser Shahandeh put the prescription bag in his pocket and attempted to sidestep them. They didn't let him. Naser Shahandeh pretended to be surprised, as if he had no idea what they were up to, but his sidelong glances toward the street made it clear he was fully aware of everything. No doubt he was looking for a passerby to appear from somewhere and rescue him. Nuri spoke in a tone friendlier than usual. "Greetings. Why are you alone, Naser?" He pointed out Naser Shahandeh's American shirt to Buki. "Look at this silk shirt. You can only dream of having such a shirt. Do you know that his papa-*jan* pays a sackful of money for each of Naser's shirts? If you don't believe it, come and see for yourself."

As if passing a basketball to Buki, Nuri shoved Naser Shahandeh from behind toward Buki. Naser Shahandeh stumbled, but before reaching Buki, he turned around suddenly and took a defensive position in front of Nuri. Calm and collected, Nuri opened the palms of his hands and held them at his sides, apparently allowing Naser to pass. Nuri gave a bitter smile, like a cold-blooded killer—the kind of smile that seems to imply, "Even a knife cut would not make me bleed." He took the paintbrush from the can Buki was carrying and carefully wrote "Death to America" on Naser Shahandeh's shirt. He ran the paintbrush over Naser Shahandeh's face a few times and made him look like Hajji Firuz, the traditional New Year blackface. Naser completely lost his senses. The whites of his eyes grew bigger with every stroke of the paintbrush. He played dead, which turned out to be the biggest mistake of his life. Nuri raised his hand and hit Naser Shahandeh's skull so hard with the brush that it echoed like a yogurt bowl. "You cheat me, motherfucker? Do you like that?" He hit Naser on the head a few more times and said, "Admit it or I'll hit you again. Admit it already!"

Buki stepped forward. "That's enough, Nuri, leave the rest for tomorrow."

Nuri was just hitting his stride. He grabbed Naser Shahandeh's collar and throttled him. "You put Reza Shahabzadeh up to finding me alone in the street?"

Buki tried to separate them. "It's late, Nuri. Let's move on. You have only ten minutes to take the last bus to Tajrish."

Anger gnawed at Nuri's insides like hunger pangs. He wanted to throw himself on Naser Shahandeh and beat him to a pulp right there in the street. He put his fingers inside his pocket and curled them into a fist. The contraction of his fingers incited him even more. He struck Naser Shahandeh under the eye so suddenly that the poor soul had no idea what hit him. The blow was so hard that for a second Nuri's own head spun around, and he imagined that he had hit himself instead. He hit whatever part of Naser Shahandeh's body his hand could reach: his head, shoulders, ribs, and stomach. As soon as Naser saw Nuri's fist approaching his body, he would knot his eyebrows, follow its trajectory with his eyes, and duck his head to miss the blow. When Nuri struck his face, Naser stumbled backwards, bent down, and rose again like a shock absorber. Buki suddenly grabbed Nuri's fist in the air and separated him from Naser. After all of Nuri's blows, Naser Shahandeh neither cried nor begged Nuri to stop. He pretended to be weak to make Nuri feel sorry for him. Perhaps even at that moment Naser was secretly laughing at both of them. Tomorrow he would make arrangements with Reza Shahabzadeh to lie in wait for them in the back alleys of Amirabad and take revenge. Then Buki would try his usual routine. He would put his arms on Nuri's shoulders and forcefully drag him toward Pahlavi Avenue, using the excuse of needing to catch the last bus to Tajrish.

♦ ♦ ♦ Getting on an empty bus did not sit well with Nuri. He moved slowly toward the rear, pretending to be too tired to talk to the driver. He sprawled on a cocoa-colored leather seat full of holes. His fist felt bruised, smarting with a peculiar sense of numbness. A bizarre thought was taking shape in his head that he would not be able to discuss this incident with anyone, even Ladan, Madame, or the Senator. Although perhaps he could tell "Soraya Khanom" because people such as "Soraya Khanom" responded only like a broken record, producing monotonous, scratchy sounds.

Nuri thought about what he would have to say to Madame, the Senator, and Ladan. As soon as he entered the house, the family interrogation would begin. As always, though, he had left open a rear window to be able to let himself in without the need to ring the doorbell and wake others. He climbed the wall, set one foot on the window frame, and quietly lowered himself onto the tiles of the first-floor hallway. The stone pool lights were reflected on the dusty vine leaves and produced shadows on the wall of Mr. Al-e Batul's house. Maybe Badri Khanom and Dr. Jannati were still talking to the Senator about their share of the Aghcheh property. There was no sign of Ladan, but she would not sleep until Nuri returned home. All night she would listen to the radio. Every few minutes she would gather up the hem of her nightgown and walk to the landing in her slippers to see if Nuri had come back. When Nuri arrived, she never raised her voice at him. Even her shouting was more like a pleading. "You're late again, Mamakh! Don't you have exams? When are you going to sit still and study?"

On the brass table in the first-floor hall, some nuts had been left in a dish, and the ashtrays had not been emptied. The nightlight spread a halo as far as the edge of the shelves inside Nuri's room. He took off his clothes and threw himself on the bed. He closed his eyes, but his brain seemed connected to batteries. His thoughts ran faster and more vividly. He could easily hear whispers from the garden, but he couldn't understand a word. His bedsheets reminded him strangely of "Soraya Khanom's" arms, filled out and so tanned that they radiated heat and their scent made his throat itch. He had been stupid. He should have taken Soraya in a taxi from the Parand Pastry Shop to some remote spot—somewhere on the road to Karaj or the road leading to Gheytariyeh and Saltanatabad, to a vast open plain where they could roll on the grass and coil around each other like snakes. Now he thrust his stomach into the mattress and twisted himself in agony. He felt a pain in the unknown depths of his body that suddenly brought his writhing to a halt. He sensed a sharp spasm in the most unfathomable dark depths of his mind.

... 6 ...

Had it not been for the noise in the garden, Nuri would have lain in bed listlessly for another three hours, quietly turning over in his head the events of the past few nights. When he was under a blanket, he felt free of all constraints. Not only was he unfazed by having abandoned Soraya in the Parand Pastry Shop and beaten up Naser Shahandeh, but the very thought of these things seemed so funny to him that he couldn't keep from laughing. Then he imagined he had been hooked to an electric wire, and his mood changed suddenly. He began to plot such interesting and mysterious ways of annoying Badri Khanom that he couldn't fall asleep from excitement. In the middle of Badri Khanom's dervish prayers, precisely where speech was forbidden, Nuri would place on her prayer rug one of the pictures of Cyrus Tahmasbi and pretty Pari making love so that when she lowered her head, her gaze would fall on them, and her prayer would be spoiled. Maybe this would stop Badri Khanom's early-morning ritual of reciting for the hundredth time the story of her three-week tour of New York—especially in that aggrieved tone that blamed Dr. Jannati's nosebleeds for all the problems they had encountered in the course of their trip.

The very day of their arrival, blood had spurted out of Dr. Jannati's nose as if from a fountain and frightened the manager of their hotel. The manager was afraid that Dr. Jannati had been targeted by Middle Eastern terrorists because he was Iranian. He insisted that they find a room in another hotel immediately. Then Badri Khanom, all by herself and surrounded by a bunch of ignorant foreigners, had to debase herself in front of that American idiot and beg and plead with him not to throw them out of the hotel. Following this incident, Dr. Jannati's left ankle hurt so much every night that his knee throbbed with pain until morning. After all that, this so-called mature man turned into a child and didn't look after himself. He paid so little attention to his diet and ate such spicy and garlicky food that he developed a rash all over his body and the skin around his genitalia began to itch. Now, to whom should a woman far away from home turn? How could she explain to these ignorant Americans that they had medical insurance in Iran and that their plan would pay for all services and expenses down to the last shahi? She knocked on so many doors that she managed to procure a special medical coverage card for Dr. Jannati through Social Services. Every day, with a thousand difficulties, she had to pull him out of bed and drag him breathlessly to several different kinds of doctors. In the presence of the doctor, she washed her hands with disinfectant soap, following the latest edicts regarding hygiene, put on a pair of surgical gloves, and took Dr. Jannati's genitalia out of his underpants as if handling butchered meat, turning them in every direction so that the doctor could examine them. The American doctors, with all their claims to fame, didn't know a whole lot. They didn't recognize a simple rash, nor did they heal Dr. Jannati's left ankle.

During those three weeks, only once did Badri Khanom and Dr. Jannati take a short walk from their hotel to Times Square, and even then their walk was ruined by New York City's fetid winds. After they returned to their hotel, Dr. Jannati began to shiver so hard that the chattering of his teeth kept Badri Khanom awake. That night she counted some thirty-five big flies that she smashed on the wall of their room with a rolled newspaper. Amiz Hosein and Shuri Khanom fortunately came to their rescue. They took Badri Khanom and Dr. Jannati to Niagara Falls, where they had spent a few days of their honeymoon—although Badri Khanom did not particularly like the falls. "What is so special about such ordinary falls? That sort of thing works only for a bunch of worthless nouveau riche who want to brag to each other like movie actors."

After Nuri dressed, he tiptoed from his room to the second-floor balcony and looked around carefully. With his first glance, he realized that the garden had been watered and swept for a birthday, wedding, or some such event. Beribboned baskets of flowers, tables bearing trays of fruit and pastry, and chairs had been set around the stone pool at exact intervals. The male guests were on one side and the women on the other. The women were dressed in the latest fashion, speaking to each other with delicate and circumspect gestures. Nuri recognized the local mosque's prayer leader, Akhund Shahsavari, from his white turban and yellowish brown robe. As the *akhund* slurped his tea from a saucer balanced on his fingertips, he kept offering acquiescent smiles to the Senator. Nuri remembered that this was the day Akhund Shahsavari was supposed to welcome Madame to the blessed religion of Islam. A few months ago Madame had started learning the Koran from Mr. Shariat. She attended to all the details of the household on her own. She kept the rooms dusted, swept, and tidy. Even in the heat of the month of Mordad, she never mentioned a word about going to cooler spots. Instead, with the help of an engineer and an architect, she had the layout of the rooms and hallways drawn. She had a new tub put in the third-floor bathroom and the floor covered in blue tiles from Qom. She went to the bazaar with Mrs. Baxter, the wife of the economic advisor at the American embassy, and bought beige lace curtains. She took such pains over the choice of her dress, her haircut, and her hat that the Senator finally began to grumble. A few days before her conversion, she tried on many different dresses and asked everyone's opinion about them. She sat at her vanity mirror, powdered the hollows of her cheeks amply, and thickened the outlines of her lips with a dark purple pencil. She put a plastic cap over her light-brown hair, now turning a straw yellow along her temples, and massaged the wrinkles on her face with a special cream.

Nuri went down to stand among the guests to avoid drawing the relatives' attention. When Madame saw him, she blinked a few times, raised her eyebrows in the "Sorry, I do not follow!" manner of older ladies, and took on an expression that could not be explained as simple surprise. Maybe she already knew about his shameful treatment of Soraya, or she wanted to warn him about an imminent important event. For this reason, the whole time Madame was repeating the profession of faith after Akhund Shahsavari, Nuri didn't take his eyes off the garden gate. He was afraid that the gate would open any minute and Soraya would burst in, agitated and disheveled, and disturb the proceedings. Madame kissed the Koran three times worshipfully and walked under it. Black Najmeh put wild rue seeds in an incense burner and circled it above Madame's head for good health. As soon as the guests' cheers and congratulations subsided,

Madame offered her hand to Akhund Shahsavari in sincere gratitude for all his prayers and blessings. Akhund Shahsavari swallowed a few times and searched in his pocket for something. He fiddled with the pointy end of his beard, lowered his gaze modestly like a young bride who has heard her own praises, and with phrases such as "Forgive me," "Please, do not embarrass me," and "You are most kind," hid his hands behind his back. Madame was stunned and didn't know what to do with her outstretched hand. A few moments passed in great discomfort. Madame put her mouth close to Nuri's ear and asked in an undertone about the etiquette of shaking the hand of a man in a turban. The minute she understood that Nuri was equally uninformed on this subject, she murmured a few things about Akhund Shahsavari's flushed and sullen face. For the benefit of the relatives, who seemed to be a little on edge, she said a few things about the Muslim ritual of donning pilgrim's attire and confessed that, at this particular moment, her state of mind was not all that different from Hagar's when she had trod back and forth between Safa and Marveh. She asked the guests to follow her to the end of the garden to see the gazebo she had had built recently near the old spring.

The Senator said he could not remember when he had last seen the spring. The land on which the Dezashibi house had been built was originally part of the property belonging to the Great Zargham, Amiz Abbas's brother. In his childhood, Amiz Abbas would seize any occasion, especially when his dear now-departed mother was taking an afternoon nap in the basement, to go to the spring and bathe in it—even though the *khanom* had warned them many times that a sprite lived in the spring who would lure and drown children who disobeyed their mother and went swimming alone. And this almost came to pass. Fortunately, the *khanom* chances into the garden, and the minute she spots Amiz Abbas's golden locks spread on the surface of the water like spiderwebs, she hits herself on the head with two hands, tears her collar, screams, and throws herself into the spring. "Abbas! May I sacrifice myself for you, Abbas!" No matter how much she shakes Amiz Abbas, he neither moves nor breathes—that is, until Amaneh Khanom, Amiz Abbas's paternal uncle's wife, the Senator's mother, forces open Amiz Abbas's locked jaws and pulls out his tongue, which had rolled up in the back of his throat. Amiz Abbas suddenly begins to cough, sneeze, and vomit and thus escapes from "certain death." Then within three weeks, at the departed *khanom's* order, workers and well-diggers come and stop up the spring to prevent such a frightful event from happening again in that ancestral home.

♦ ♦ ♦ The next day, hovering between sleep and wakefulness, Nuri spotted Madame watching him strangely from behind the window in the pale light of the second-floor balcony. Listless and bare of makeup, she wore her magenta terrycloth robe and a wrinkled, black lace collar that covered her neck. She had pinned to her temples the curls she had formed in her hair for the ceremony. Nuri didn't expect to see her at that time and place. Perhaps she had gotten wind of Soraya's being dumped at the Parand Pastry Shop. Her smile appeared peculiarly pinched. Perhaps her concerns had nothing to do with Soraya and instead were linked to Mr. Raji and the results of Nuri's exams. But the grades were going to be announced in school on Wednesday afternoon, and no one knew anything about them yet. Nuri didn't think that Mr. Raji would reveal his grades in advance by phoning Madame—especially since he had lately ignored Nuri's absences and his failure to do his schoolwork. If Nuri were in a tight spot, Mr. Raji would act as an intermediary and rescue him.

Every day, after the morning benediction, Mr. Raji took Nuri into his office. First, he would praise Nuri's family's sense of discretion and honor and, after much adulation, ask Nuri once again to recite the greeting Mr. Raji himself had composed for the queen's visit. When Nuri reached the phrase "the most maternal harbinger of the perfection of the Aryan angel," Mr. Raji would nod and close his eyes in drowsy contentment. Nuri would get thrilled and utter the phrases "the beginning of the workshop of life" and "the univocality and unity of feelings of the Creator of Tenderness" with such fervor that he would surprise himself. Finally, Mr. Raji would rise from his seat uncontrollably, assume a proud and royal pose, and, in the low voice adopted by actors who played the role of the famous nineteenth-century minister Amir Kabir, "pronounce" his "satisfaction and gratitude." Although Nuri felt like laughing, he would stare at Mr. Raji so fixedly that his face remained motionless like an African mask.

Perhaps this was what Madame was concerned about. But Nuri was not worried. Even with his eyes closed, he could see the words of the greeting scrolling up in his mind like the credits at the end of a movie. With a voice appropriate for literary recitations, he would declaim: "Your Majesty! Your Oneness, your self-sacrificing servant is most honored to bestow the most sincere, unalloyed, and obliged salutations on Her Majesty's footsteps on behalf of the humble community of students and honorable educators and administrators of the high school and to appeal to the Almighty to accept this most salubrious message of fellowship as a portent of the Aryan luminescence of the ancestors of this land. . . . "

Nuri rubbed his eyes to feign drowsiness. He got out of bed and left the room to go to the bathroom. Madame disappeared from behind the window and watched him from the bench in the hallway. When he came out, she shifted her weight and made room for him on the bench. She crossed her legs and passed the back of her hand under her nose in a way that indicated she was not sure where to begin. She mentioned Soraya's name in passing as if it had no particular significance and she had remembered it accidentally. "My dearrr, I would like to talk to you a little about this girl. If you don't have time now, I will tell you over breakfast. All night long I thought about you. Can you imagine? Can you believe it?"

The tender smile Madame gave Nuri was a change from her stand-offishness of the past few days, especially now that she was apparently finally addressing Soraya's bad mouth and her Chaleh Maidun curses. Madame confessed that for Nuri's sake she had not wanted to respond to Soraya and become the equal of such a shameless "young lady." "Because this lady, with the utmost disrespect and vulgarity, accused Your Highness of stealing. She claimed that Your Highness takes precious objects from the storage room for his friends."

All night long Nuri had not even once heard any sound resembling a telephone ring. So how had Soraya informed Madame of this news? Of course, Madame had an answer for this question as well. In the middle of the night, Soraya had come to the Dezashibi house and with Black Najmeh's help awakened Madame. She made such a racket that the neighbors came out of their houses into the alley. After all Nuri's bluffing, his nerves suddenly failed. Every night he had stayed awake until near dawn, ears peeled to hear the slightest sound coming from a radius of ten meters in the neighborhood, and then this one night he had not heard anything at all. Madame scraped a dried spot from near Nuri's shirt. "Don't sleep in this shirt. It gets wrinkled."

Nuri paid no attention to Madame's advice and returned to the main point. "What have I stolen?"

Madame used a gentle tone. "First Your Highness should take a bath. We have plenty of time to talk later."

"I have to know right now."

Madame locked her hands together. "If Your Highness is worried about Soraya's accusations, I don't believe them." She smiled at Nuri. She spoke of her own worries. "All night long I kept hearing Miss Soraya begging you for the old photo album, nylons, and my red soiree dress. She said that you stole seventy-six tumans from her purse. But your servant has only one thing to say. A person who has seventy-six tumans in her purse can buy her own red soiree dress."

"What's Soraya's point? What does she want from you?"

Madame bent her head and adjusted the hem of her robe on her knees. "She is angry with Your Highness."

"She's nuts. Ask Buki. He calls her 'creezy,' meaning crazy."

Madame took Nuri's hands in her own. "Nuri-jan, what can I do for Your Highness?"

"From that first day, I said I wanted to go to New York to be with my mother. I don't feel like studying here. Help me go to New York."

"New York?"

"Why not?"

"It's not all that easy to leave, my dearrr. Whoever leaves his country experiences death. In the name of God the Compassionate and the Merciful, may His curses be upon the most treacherous Satan. Every departure necessitates a death, and every death a thanksgiving. As the Americans say, nobody enters paradise before dying."

"I don't understand this kind of talk. I only want to leave."

"Allow me to think about it for a few days."

Madame rose to leave. They should permit Nuri to live as he wished. He was not concerned with expedience, security, and safety, but rather a kind of internal truth without which he felt like a fraud. He returned to his own room and tidied himself a little in front of the mirror. An ache, the kind felt after a period of illness, sank deep into his muscles and joints. He seemed to be changing and growing taller in a peculiar way. His face no longer had the roundness and smoothness of a few years ago. His cheek-bones gave his face a sharp and coarse appearance associated only with experienced people.

The thought of staying at home didn't have much appeal for Nuri, especially a few days before the Fourth of Aban celebrations and par-ticularly now that Madame seemed to appear suddenly in front of Nuri wherever he went. When they ran into each other in the corridor, Madame would pause, appear stunned, and then quickly go up the stairs. At night, until very late, her shadow moved across the closed windows of the bed-room. In the afternoons, she would take Ladan into the study to rehearse her Goddess of the Harvest dance and spend hours practicing songs, most of which seemed ludicrous to Nuri.

At 7:00 A.M. sharp one morning, Nuri made his way to the bus sta-tion and squeezed into a full bus. He clung to the hand grip near the rear door and fixed his gaze on the street. It seemed as if something important was taking place somewhere far away. Nuri needed someone like Buki Tahmasbi to keep him informed. Buki knew about everything, whether it happened in the railway station, the lower parts of Naziabad, the heights of Sa'dabad, or the summit of Tuchal Mountain. Like a portable radio, he constantly announced to the other boys the latest events at the bazaar, the American Club, Qazvin Square, or any other neighborhood.

At the Pahlavi intersection, Nuri got off the bus and ran into the school. Because of exams, there were no regular classes. The playground appeared deserted now, unlike during recess. In the office, a few people were talking to Mr. Ebrahimi, the assistant principal. The exam results had been posted outside the office a day in advance. A few students Nuri didn't know pressed against each other in front of the office, moving the tips of their noses up and down the sheets to find their grades. First, Nuri looked for Buki's grades. He couldn't believe that Buki had passed with a grade of eleven. He moved his finger down the row of names, and as soon as he found his own, his heart stopped. His name had been circled in red.

With a grade of five and a half, no matter what he did now, he couldn't prevent failing the semester. He tried to shrug his shoulders and ignore the whole thing. His having failed was unfortunately definitive, but he felt surprisingly calm now. Even when he saw that Naser Shahandeh had a grade of eighteen, he didn't feel incensed. A dull-witted boy's passing was owing to his having studied himself into the ground, and it had no link whatsoever to innate intelligence. Furthermore, if passing was such a big deal, Nuri would have put down a few more words on his exam papers, but he wasn't such a dolt to kill himself for the sake of a grade of eighteen. He was not made for such degradation. He didn't know a single student who had heard the name of even one of Wagner's operas. Only Mr. Mo'idi, the eighth-grade literature teacher who was a member of the Tudeh Party and had known Papa Javad from a distance, sometimes listened to classical music in the Soviet embassy's "Vox" Cultural Society. But only to the music of composers such as Puccini, Verdi, and Tchaikovsky, who were not comparable to Wagner. Like a cartoon figure, he would put his hands on his waist, stand up straight on tiptoe, and, in a Rashti accent, criticize Wagner and the chauvinism and anti-Semitism of the fascist Nazis.

Failing and passing had no meaning for Nuri. Others' praise didn't put a crown on his head, nor did their admonishments lower his standing. The adulation of a couple of insignificant individuals wouldn't affect Nuri as it did other students, who fell all over themselves dancing to every tune to please those same nobodies.

Now, with Madame's help, he had to make his way to New York and join Maman Zuzu. He felt terribly anxious. He liked to be the odd one out among his peers, but he had no taste for being left behind. For what purpose had he come to school today? Was it just to walk past his classroom? Drink another drop of water from the fountain and feel the water drip down to his cheek from the corner of his mouth? Go to the school cafeteria and buy himself a Kim ice cream bar?

The sun shone through the iron grille on the second-form classroom window and lit the floor, making the hallway appear dingier, longer, and narrower than Nuri remembered. Instead of the sounds of the other boys from behind the classroom doors and the Alborz team's soccer game, he heard schoolgirls singing "O Iran, O Bejeweled Land" from a distance in

the Parvin Etesami High School auditorium—drawn out and high, like a
lullaby sung in chorus, mingling in Nuri's mind with scattered images of
the vast and green plains of a remote country. He clasped a column in the
middle of the hallway and, with no particular purpose, rotated around
it. Slowly his head began to spin, and the images in his head separated
from one another and were replaced by the click-clack of a typewriter
in the office. The shadowy figure of the school janitor, holding a tray of
teacups, moved up the stairs. In front of the third-form classroom, a few
boys Nuri didn't know passed a basketball among themselves. He rested
his elbows on a ledge, narrowed his eyes, and closely watched the captain
of the team dribble the ball rapidly to the middle of the court. The captain
quickly pivoted on one foot, raised the ball in the air, and signaled to Nuri
to catch it. Nuri caught the ball, passed it back to the captain, then made
his way toward the office. He was annoyed that Buki had passed. Perhaps
his friendship with Buki concealed his own weak points and allowed him
to hide behind Buki's experience.

The girls at the Parvin Etesami High School practiced in unison the
verses from Sa'di's *Golestan:*

Human beings are parts of one entity,
Who are created from the same essence.
When one part . . . part . . . is pained . . . pained . . . by fate . . .

Nuri took a shortcut along the back alleys of Amirabad to avoid being
seen on his way to the Tahmasbis' apartment. At the far end of the Vesali
Alley, near the Parvaresh Elementary School, an itinerant vendor held his
tray of snack foods in front of two boys so they could survey it closely. Nuri
was afraid of running into Naser Shahandeh and Reza Shahabzadeh. If they
got into a fight, Buki was not there to support him. His only weapon was
the brass knuckles he constantly touched in his pocket. Soraya also walked
this alley in the mornings to go to the Shadman Stationery Store to borrow
novels. If she appeared at the other end of the alley, Nuri would approach
her, greet her warmly, speak about the hurt he had caused her the other
night, and put an end to the whole thing. He was so eager to see Soraya that
his heart skipped around like a butterfly. He walked faster so as to reach
the Tahmasbis' apartment more quickly. He should have apologized like a

decent human being for his awful misdeeds. The very thought shamed him more and made an encounter with Soraya seem almost essential.

The moment he entered Colonel Tahmasbi's apartment, Nuri decided not to mention anything to Soraya about the other night after all and pretend that nothing had happened. There was at least a five percent chance that Soraya had forgotten the whole thing. But this close to noon Nuri was not sure which one of the Tahmasbis he would run into. No doubt Mrs. Tahmasbi went shopping in the mornings, then cleaned house, talked to her friends on the phone, and asked about their news. Nuri was merely guessing because he wasn't familiar with the daily routine in the Tahmasbi apartment during schooldays. When he was at school, even the Dezashibi house didn't cross his mind. Even the days he stayed home sick, the house appeared to him like an unfamiliar, forgotten dream with which he had to become reacquainted slowly. Now that he had entered the apartment hallway, the midday silence made everything seem unreal to him. He thought that if Mrs. Tahmasbi spotted him, she would start talking and keep on going for another three hours. It was better for him to climb the stairs quietly and go to Soraya's room without being seen. But this was risky. He could end up annoying both Soraya and Mrs. Tahmasbi. Up to now Mrs. Tahmasbi had always pretended not to notice Nuri's surreptitiousness, and sometimes in the Colonel's absence she would even encourage his "mischief." He looked into the kitchen anxiously. Mrs. Tahmasbi, dressed in a navy blue dress with black paisley lace, turned her head with an accidental gaze and took him by surprise. She was taking ground beef from an aluminum bowl near the sink, making meatballs in the palms of her hands, and placing them next to each other on a brass tray. Her movements were regular and deliberate. In a pleasant voice, she said, "Nanehjan, why don't you come in?"

Nuri thought of turning around, heading for the alley as fast as the wind, and leaving not the slightest trace behind. He sensed the air to be unusually dense, as if ready to detonate. Without taking his fingers from the doorframe, he slowly moved forward. He noticed Mrs. Tahmasbi's face. She said, "You really have to forgive me. The samovar is boiling, and tea is freshly made. My hands are oily. I can't pour you tea. Please pour one for yourself and one for me as well. I'm dying for a puff of cigarette with my tea. There is so much to do in this house that I don't even have time for tea and a cigarette."

Nuri asked hurriedly, "Is Buki home?"

"Naneh-jan, why should Buki stay home in the mornings? Has he lost his brain to sit with me and listen to my drivel? Let him go after his own affairs, both to earn a living and leave this stable for a bit of a change. After all, he's young; he has desires and has to keep himself happy somehow."

Nuri took a few steps forward, poured two cups of tea, and slid one of the cups and the silver sugar bowl toward Mrs. Tahmasbi. "Do you know where he is?"

Mrs. Tahmasbi threw a sharp glance in his direction. She rolled her head on her shoulders and took a deep breath. "Naneh-jan, oh my, I'm just worn out!" She took the dishtowel draped over the faucet and wiped her hands and face. She placed a sugar cube in the corner of her mouth and slurped a few hurried sips of tea. She held a cigarette between her fingers for Nuri to light. After her first draw, she exhaled the smoke toward the kitchen ceiling as if, from sheer pleasure, all her muscles had gone limp. With the tip of her finger, she took a bit of loose tobacco off her lower lip and examined it. "With the Colonel's measly salary, what better than *kaleh-jush* can I make for lunch or dinner?" She brought her head closer and spoke softly. "Not to waste your time, Naneh-jan, the Colonel's salary—what should I say about his being a colonel?—is only five thousand and two hundred tumans. That doesn't cover even two weeks of our expenses. Every month we have to mortgage a carpet at the bank to be able to pay our rent and expenses."

"Cyrus and Buki make good money."

"One qerun! Then whatever you leave in front of them, they pout like children and grumble at me, 'Maman, whoever eats this food will have no offspring,' or they say, 'Tomorrow if our father drops dead from poor nutrition, you will bear the burden of that guilt, Maman.' Then they say, 'You keep our father hungry, you do this, you do that.' Finally, I come out and say, 'If this is the case, you should look after him. What concern is it of mine? Which one of you has taken a step for me that I should do the same for you? Do you imagine I didn't have a father and mother of my own? Did I come empty-handed into your father's house? On what grounds do you permit yourselves to demand so much from me and expect me to be at his beck and call? Now that you say these things, I'll be more stubborn. You shouldn't say anything and let me look after him to the best of my abilities and according to my own sense of compassion.' But once again they start complaining. 'We'll take our father to Zafarunieh and rent a place for him.' They brag about Zafarunieh to me. They say such wonderful things about the seniors' home, as if it were paradise itself. It's such and so, its plaster moldings alone cost two million tumans, what windows! What a garden! What nurses! Are you listening to me? They say, 'What nurses!' as if a nurse is popcorn you can afford to hire for the Colonel. Then I say, 'For now he is still my husband, and you need my permission to do anything with him. Were I to divorce him one day and leave this house, it would be up to you. You could do whatever the hell pleases you. But as long as I am in this house, I myself will attend to his food and clothing.' Well, it's not as if they are blind. They see how well I take care of the Colonel. Whatever he wants, I put in front of him. For instance, what's wrong with this *kaleh-jush* I am making so decently and nicely for him? You are not a stranger, after all, Naneh-jan. Finally one day they will feel shame. They will come, kiss my hands, and say, 'Bravo, Maman, may your hands not ache.' To be honest, among my children, Buki helps out the most. Whatever he can afford—a hundred tumans a month, two hundred, three hundred—if he can, he'll put in the palm of my hand."

Ordinarily, the minute Mrs. Tahmasbi noticed Nuri, she would start with her "Sori-jun, Sori-jun" and find some excuse to send Nuri to Soraya's room, but now it was as if Soraya did not exist at all. It seemed Mrs. Tahmasbi deliberately avoided mentioning Soraya's name. Nuri said gently, "It seems you are alone today."

Mrs. Tahmasbi frowned. "I'm alone? If they left me alone, I would have no worry in the world, Naneh-jan. Since last night Soraya has been lying about in the storage room like an invalid. She is being stubborn and says she will stay there and read her novel."

"God forbid, she's not ill, is she?"

"Her illness is her horrible temperament that turns people off. Look at yourself. You arrive here like a gentleman and treat her like a decent human being. You offer to spend your own money to take her to a café.

OK, if Soraya were like everybody else, she would have at least behaved well and thanked you. Instead, she acts like a lunatic, screams, creates such havoc, and makes you so miserable that you repent and decide never to see her again. The heck with their youth. What difference is there between the young and others? After all, what about good upbringing and consideration? Another example is our own Cyrus: although he is my own flesh and blood and I love him dearly, would you believe that during this whole time he hasn't even done as much for his father as the head of a pin? Well, of course he hasn't. Never mind kindness and appreciation. Why does he take the hand of this slut, pretty Pari, bring her here without permission, and ask me at my age to put an engagement ring on her finger? And then he expects me to be beside myself with happiness and to kiss his hands because he has brought me a bride." Without looking, she searched in her empty packet of cigarettes. "If this ill-reputed girl sets foot in my house, I'll put her bundle of belongings under her arm and send her packing. Why should we go that far? Our very own Buki, meaning this very close and devoted friend of yours, doesn't even listen to the Colonel. Instead of studying, he's always in the streets, painting walls with slogans that insult the country's king and our sacred national heritage. So, Naneh-jan, what do you say I should hang my hopes on?" She threw the crumpled package of cigarettes in the metal ashtray. She ran her hand over her hair and face, suddenly grew calm, and turned to Nuri. "You shouldn't take Soraya's behavior to heart. You mustn't let her put you in a bad mood."

"Why should I be in a bad mood?"

"Bravo! That's what I'm talking about. Why be in a bad mood? You aren't a child to let Soraya put you in a bad mood. It's far better to ignore it. Let her repent on her own, feel ashamed, and understand that she has behaved badly. After all, by God's blessing, a thousand of his blessings, you are part Austrian. They say Austrians are so tough that all this camel-like preening and coquettishness has no effect on them."

Nuri feigned ignorance. "What has happened? What has Miss Soraya done?"

"How cute! I like the fact that you are so simple and kind. No doubt it's due to Madame's Austrian upbringing and the fact that she has raised you to be so considerate. But if you ask me, I'd say ignoring Soraya's behavior is futile. The local chief of police is an old friend of the Colonel's. As soon as he realized what relation Soraya was to us, he sealed her file and gave it to us to bring home. That doesn't matter. It's our duty to look after our daughter, and we do it. But you just imagine a mother and a father sacrificing themselves, debasing themselves in front of this and that person, and in return having their daughter not even say a simple word of thanks! I say to her, 'My honorable lady, where is your thank you?' She answers, 'Thank you for what? Whatever you have done is your duty.' I put food in front of her, she doesn't touch it. From morning to night, she squats in that same storage room like an Indian yogi, covers herself with a sheet, and closes her eyes to signal she should be left alone."

"Can I go and say hello to her?"

Mrs. Tahmasbi squeezed her hands together and paused. Apparently she was not prepared for such a request. "Naneh-jun, of course you can. This is your own home, and you can go where you please. You know Sori-jun very well. Her mouth doesn't have a proper lock and key. Sometimes it's out of her control. She might up and say something rude and embarrass all of us. Well, you're not a stranger, and you forgive her because of your own good manners."

"Mrs. Tahmasbi, why should I take offense? I'll just drop in on her and ask how she is doing, and if it bothers her, I'll leave quickly." He took a red rose out of a water glass on the sill. "I'll offer her this beautiful flower. She'll be pleased. She'll like it."

Ignoring Nuri, Mrs. Tahmasbi took up where she had left off. "It's not as if this girl came from under a bush. From her childhood, I have always told her, 'Sori-jun, you must not be rude to anyone, even maids and servants. Offending others is a sin that will eventually have to be atoned for.' Do you think she takes it in? The other night she screamed in the police station. We hadn't even reached home before she developed such a headache that even a full jar of aspirin didn't help her. I told her, 'Sori-jun, didn't I tell you? Do you see what a headache you ended up with?' She turned her back to me and pretended to be asleep."

"If I say a little hello and leave, you think she'll get angry?"

After a few moments of hesitation, Mrs. Tahmasbi rose from her seat, and together they left the kitchen. When they reached the entrance to the

storage room, Nuri slowly lifted the hand-painted curtain, but saw no
trace of Soraya. Mrs. Tahmasbi grew anxious and spoke to herself. "Oh
my God, where has she gone? Has she run away? There is nothing this
crazy girl won't do."

"I'm sure she's gone to her own room."

They climbed the stairs and went straight into Soraya's room. The
sun shone like a column of dust through the window and onto the old
carpet, but didn't reach the rest of the room. Wrapped in a white sheet,
Soraya lay on her perennially unmade bed and constantly wiggled the
tips of her toes like a person with a nervous tic. She raised her head, and
the minute she saw them, she gave such a frown that Nuri was taken
aback. He forced a smile and with two fingers held the flower in front of
her face. This was a dreadful mistake. Rage made Soraya's face turn blue.
Her eyes grew puffy, and she abruptly turned away from Nuri. Mrs. Tahmasbi rambled on to smooth things over. "Nuri-jan, didn't I say Soraya
is feeling much better? Now she can do anything she wants. But she has
to take a little better care of herself than she normally does. She is stubborn. She doesn't eat properly and doesn't take care of herself. No matter
how many times I say, 'My dear daughter, you will make yourself sick
again,' she doesn't listen." She turned directly to Soraya and said, "Nuri-
jun has come to ask about you. Get up, Maman! Offer him some nuts so
that he can see for himself how much better you feel. Get up, Naneh-jun!
Get up, already, may I sacrifice myself for you!" Soraya didn't budge.
Mrs. Tahmasbi turned toward Nuri. "Do you see how Sori-jun's face is
beaming? Thank God she is no longer as thin as in those old days. Last
year, because of that ne'er-do-well Mr. Shirzad, she was reduced to skin
and bones. Look at her now and see how, praise be to God, she has filled
out." She put her hands under Soraya's shoulders to lift her listless body.
"Sori-jun does Swedish exercises in the morning. She wants her thigh
and buttock muscles to be as firm as when she played in her school vol-
leyball team and spiked the ball over the net." Mrs. Tahmasbi pulled
the sheet off Soraya's firm and muscular thighs. "What a beautiful body
this daughter of mine has, exactly like the movie stars whose pictures
are printed in *Roshanfekr!* Look, God be praised, it's as if every line in
her body has been drawn with a compass and caliper!" Mrs. Tahmasbi

looked up. "What breasts! They feast the eyes . . . how fullll, shapelyyy, and turned uppp!!! They are flirting with the sky!"

Holding the flower in his hand, Nuri rose unpremeditatedly. Her face still angrily turned away, Soraya twisted the corners of her mouth in distaste. Mrs. Tahmasbi ran up to Nuri. "Naneh-jan, where are you going? Let me get you something to eat." She glanced at the window. "Oh, dust be on my head, it's noon already. I have to check on my *kaleh-jush*."

Nuri was trembling inside, but he maintained a calm appearance and said in a cold tone, "It's late. I have to get back"

"No, I beg you to stay. It's still early. Have lunch with us. Buki will show up any minute now." She turned to Soraya. "Sori-jun, why don't you say something to make Nuri-jun stay for lunch?"

"Leave him be. Let him go. What have you brought him here for?"

Mrs. Tahmasbi bit her lower lip. "Oh my God, may God kill me, Sori-jun! Nuri-jan has come to ask about your health."

"I wish he wouldn't come for another seventy dark years. I prefer the rotten nails of the Mashtis from the lower parts of the city to anyone with blond hair and blue eyes. Let him go to New York to be with his *maman-jun*, who is right now working as a maid and washerwoman for Americans." Addressing Nuri, she said, "In no way do we need people like you. If you wish, go and stay there. Nobody is stopping you." She pointed to Mashallah's written slogans on the wall. "If I want to be with anyone, it's Mashallah, who sacrificed himself for his country and never even bragged about it. Not with a person like you who at the tiniest hint of attention fancies himself on a par with human beings. Who knows you here, anyway? Maman, do you know him? Look at his face, can you tell what he does?"

"Eh, Naneh-jun, what kind of talk is this, daughter?"

Soraya continued in the same vein. "He embarrassed me in front of a bunch of strangers, and I should invite him to stay and have lunch with us?" She looked directly into Nuri's eyes. "Wait and see how I embarrass you. I'll phone that impoverished Austrian Madame, and I'll tell her how you steal whatever you can get your hands on from her purse and the storage room. How instead of going to school, you sit in cafés and spend her money. I'll tell that pimp Mr. Raji that you go to Shahr-e No with Buki, pick up whores, and have your picture taken lying naked in their arms.

What did you imagine? I have kept all your pictures, and I'll show them to Madame."

Nuri was terrified. "I go to Shahr-e No?" Stunned, he turned his gaze to Mrs. Tahmasbi. "I have pictures taken in the nude?"

"Of course. I'll tell the police that at night you write slogans on the walls of the university, impugning the sacred honor of royalty and disparaging the very person of His Majesty. So, what did you think would happen? I'll scatter your life to the wind. I'll destroy you. I'll take such revenge, you'll run like a dog to the ends of the world. . . . You leave me all alone in a café and flee? Wait till I teach you a lesson you'll never forget."

Mrs. Tahmasbi interrupted her. "Hey, kids, who wants tea? It's just freshly made! One of those great teas!"

Soraya twisted her lower lip. "Look at his face, just like a chimp." She stared at him. "In this apartment, you are nobody. No one knows you. If you never come back, that'll be too soon. Good thing I got to know you fast and didn't fall for your tricks. I always told my *maman*, 'There is everybody else, and then there is Nuri. . . .'"

Nuri put his fingers on his chest and lowered them hesitantly, as if he wanted to be sure he still existed. "What have I done?"

Soraya screamed, "' . . . What have I done!'"

She started to cry. Mrs. Tahmasbi turned her worried gaze on Nuri. She hugged Soraya's head and patted it over and over again. "Sori-jun, eh, Sori-jun, my daughter. Hey, my pretty one, you are too old to cry over a little fight like this. God be praised, you are a lady, you have to be a role model for those younger than yourself, ehhh!"

Nuri rose and backed out of the room. Mrs. Tahmasbi noticed. She lowered Soraya's shoulders to the bed and hurriedly ran out after him. When they were midway down the stairs, Soraya cried in protest, "Maman, you broke my shoulders. Where are you going?"

Mrs. Tahmasbi looked back for only one moment, but continued running after Nuri. "Nuri-jan, Naneh-jan, wait. I have to speak to you." Panting, she caught up with Nuri. She pulled from her bosom a small pouch hanging from a string around her neck. Fumbling, she took a few crumpled notes and forced them into Nuri's palm. "Nuri-jun, for you. On your way, go to the Nahid Pharmacy and buy some valerian drops and a tube of aspirin for Sori-jun. Hurry up. When she gets like this, it's out of her control, Naneh-jan. Even if you insist, she won't listen. May I sacrifice myself for you, don't take too long. I'm waiting."

Nuri took the crumpled notes and left the apartment.

... 7 ...

Nuri thought he had best go to the Nahid Pharmacy, buy the medicine, and deliver it to Mrs. Tahmasbi. Few people went to the pharmacy before noon, and then only to post ads for English, piano, dance, and karate instruction on the bulletin board. The chance of running into Naser Shahandeh and Reza Shahabzadeh was not even five percent. They usually had no reason to loiter in the pharmacy, unless Naser Shahandeh's father had just returned from one of his mountain goat–hunting trips and asked Naser to go to the pharmacy for his backache prescription. Most prescriptions were filled after sunset, during the doctors' busiest office hours, or later in the evening when thugs from lower Amirabad got into fights and, after being hauled off to the police station, dropped by the pharmacy. Sometimes tourist buses collided with each other on the road to the airport. The injured would be brought to the pharmacy in order to be quickly bandaged, given a few aspirins, and sent on their way to the airport on time.

Nuri was more irritated about having to return to the Tahmasbis' apartment than about going to the pharmacy. Soraya would start screaming again and harangue him with so many of those Chaleh Maidun curses that he would regret having set foot there. He could still see Mrs. Tahmasbi's worried face as she ran hurriedly down the stairs, caught up with Nuri at the door, and, panting, pushed the crumpled notes into his hand. If he returned to the apartment, she would put on a grateful expression. She would wink, bite her lip, and indicate how helpless she felt about that shameful girl's bad mouth. She would trot out expressions like "Distressful death be visited upon you" and "My body has become death," which, compared to Soraya's curses, seemed more like a schoolgirl's wisecracks. Then she would bite her tongue because the wife of a "high-ranking police officer" should not sully her mouth with such filthy words—unlike Soraya, who would sometimes utter even ordinary curses as if they were military commands. During all his years of service, the Colonel had not come across a single lowly Cossack who could rival Soraya in cursing. "Get lost, motherfucker," "Shut up, you, with a slut of a sister," "Drop dead, old fool . . . !"

At such times, Mrs. Tahmasbi would swallow repeatedly out of shame. She would dry her wet hands on the hem of her skirt and look for some food to offer Nuri. She would squeeze her key ring between her skinny fingers. Her smile would make her teeth look like a skeleton's. Then she would look at Nuri so intensely that she made him uneasy. At the age of seventeen, Nuri was neither the top nor the bottom of the onion. He did not have the slightest understanding about the problems of a perplexing family such as the Tahmasbis, nor could he do anything to placate a long-suffering and needy woman such as Mrs. Tahmasbi.

The streets were crowded and chaotic up to the Pahlavi intersection. Some people walked fast and purposefully, as if toward a fixed destination. Others gathered in groups in front of stores and talked with animated gestures, although their words could not be heard from afar. A formidable stillness seemed to descend on the street and made it resemble a scene in a nightmare. It seemed as if the fruit vendor's cart, the telephone booth, the book peddler's display, and the tied garbage bags had been abandoned because of some calamity. Nuri imagined that the street's apparent calm would soon be upset by a dreadful announcement. He took Mrs. Tahmasbi's crumpled notes from his pocket, threw them into the gutter, and with the speed of light crossed the street.

A few minutes later he saw Comrade Binesh hurriedly walking toward the Hasanabad intersection. He was about fifty or fifty-five years old. In his black tie, starched Arrow shirt, and wool suit, he bore no resemblance to a member of the Tudeh Party. There was a hint of a wink in his eye, as if alluding to a mutual secret. According to Hasani, Aunt Moluk's servant, Comrade Binesh still had quite a bit of appeal among the twenty- to thirty-year-old female party members. He presented them with copies of Chernyshevsky's novel *What Is to Be Done?* or *The Story of Comrade Stalin's Seventh Escape from Prison*. Piecing things together, Nuri had gathered that Papa Javad and Comrade Binesh had become involved in the Haftgel sabotage, the expropriation of funds from the Central Bank, and even the execution of suspicious party members. Nevertheless, it was hard to believe that a traditional woman such as Aunt Moluk would do Swedish exercises and cook European food every day just for the sake of Comrade Binesh. If she wore cotton shifts at home, she put on a two-piece suit and a white shirt with a turned-down collar to attend party activities. She would powder her face, apply a pale rouge, arrange her hair in a halo around her head, and wear diamond-like earrings as large as coat buttons. She had authorized Hasani to take control of the comings and goings of the house. For this reason, Hasani treated Nuri overbearingly. He ordered Nuri to be on the lookout and avoid unnecessarily drawing the attention of the secret police to the old house. When Comrade Binesh's name came up in conversation, Hasani would speak in veiled terms, hinting at a rendezvous after the revolution when suffering Iranians are at last freed—or, in Aunt Moluk's words, when "the yoke of oppression is lifted from the shoulders of the toiling people of Iran."

Comrade Binesh often took detours to Aunt Moluk's house and arrived unannounced, sometimes in an officer's uniform, other times in the robe, turban, and slippers of a clergyman. He would feign absent-mindedness and act as if he had entered the house by mistake. As a precaution, Aunt Moluk had stashed a safari outfit—complete with an umbrella, rain gear, and a sun hat—and a fake beard and mustache in a closet so that if the secret police raided the house, Comrade Binesh would be able to disguise himself as a foreign tourist and leave for safety.

When Nuri reached the old house, Hasani tried to send him away with the excuse that Aunt Moluk was recovering from surgery, but Aunt Moluk herself appeared behind Hasani, dressed in a flowery cotton shift. Slowly and without the slightest enthusiasm she tilted her head, inserted her fingers in her wet hair, and ran them like the teeth of a comb through the hair painstakingly and evenly. Nuri asked, "Aunt Moluk?"

In truth, he had not expected Aunt Moluk to greet him so indifferently.

"Why are you looking at me like this, child?"

"Is something wrong here?"

Hasani said, "The head of our party unit has been arrested. Khanom is worried that the police will raid our house."

Aunt Moluk jumped in. "We haven't stolen anything that the police should be after us. It's the secret police who will come. Suppose they arrest me, what can they do? The worst that can happen is that they'll handcuff me and throw me into the Ghazal Ghal'eh dungeon. My departed mother, Bibi Safa, did much worse things to me, and she didn't hurt me as much as a flea bite."

Perhaps her indifference was just a show she could not keep up for long. She took Nuri to a side room with exposed ceiling beams. The corners of the fading rug did not reach the walls. The damp walls were reminiscent of an old basement and made Nuri shudder as if he had touched the tiles in a cold bathroom. Aunt Moluk was apparently used to the room. She sat on the rug and stretched her bare legs to one side. She pulled the hem of her skirt over her knees and brushed her hair out of her face. "Nuri-jun, how weak you have become! What is this American shirt you are wearing that makes you look like Ali Varjak?"

She looked around for her cigarettes and lighter and, with a nod and a sidelong glance, indicated the hallway behind the room. "I don't know what this Binesh wants from me. Why doesn't he leave me alone? I can't shut the door in his face and shoo him away like a dog." She pulled the hem of her skirt over her knees again and answered her own question. "After all, his life is in danger. In this dump, whoever loves his country is on the run. Only the sycophants have so much money they don't know what to do with it. I don't know what world they live in. What do they expect? Things will not stay the same forever."

Hasani brought them a tray of fried eggplant for lunch. After lunch Nuri showed Aunt Moluk the stunts Vaziri had taught him. He hit his palm on a knife blade several times and turned it up to reveal that it had not been cut. Aunt Moluk was not satisfied and looked at Nuri with a meaningful smile. This time Nuri struck the knife blade harder and cried out. He put his fingers in his armpits and hopped around in a circle. Aunt Moluk asked sarcastically, "Did you learn this from Vaziri, too?"

Nuri put his hands between his knees, doubled over, and nodded in agreement. "I know even more. Do you want to see me swallow a kebab skewer?"

"No, dear. On your own life, I have a thousand things to do. Just before you came, I took a bath and was getting ready to go out."

"I also know how to read palms. Let me read your palm. It won't take more than a minute." He grabbed Aunt Moluk's hand, turned it toward the window, and ran his fingers over the curved and forked lines of her palm. "My, my, what a beautiful palm you have!"

Aunt Moluk protested, "Get out of here. Are you putting me on? Instead of doing these tricks, why don't you take care of your studies?"

She tried to pull her hand away, but Nuri did not let her. "Wait, let me tell you about your future."

"What do you mean, tell me about my future? Do you believe such superstitions?"

Ignoring Aunt Moluk's protests, he rattled on about her long life, her marriage to a handsome man like Comrade Binesh, and the three beautiful chubby babies they would have together. When he mentioned the children she would bear, Aunt Moluk grew pensive and asked, "What did you say?"

"Comrade Binesh won't leave you alone until you marry him."

"Are you joking?"

"What joke?" He pointed to the lines on her palm. "Do you see these? This one is the love line. This one, the marriage line. These creases, children. Each crease means a child."

Aunt Moluk took her eyes off Nuri and looked down at her palm. Finally she said, "Show me one more time. Let me see which ones you are talking about."

"These."

"Really?"

She stretched out "really" in such a way that Nuri grew suspicious. "Am I wrong?"

"If you are a palm reader, then I myself should open a palm-reading shop."

"Why?"

"How can a woman whose womb has been removed bear children?"

"Has your womb been removed?"

"Four years ago in the Najmiyeh Hospital."

"Oh, really?"

"Your Excellency, why do you play with people's feelings?"

Nuri said jokingly, "What difference does it make? Maybe Comrade Binesh will have children by another woman, and you will become their stepmother."

Tears welled up in Aunt Moluk's eyes. She threw a confused glance at Nuri, rose, and rushed off toward the garden.

It seemed he could not come up with something to say that would not irritate her, but he didn't want to leave the house without saying goodbye. So he followed Aunt Moluk into the garden. He saw Comrade Binesh standing on the rooftop, surveying the garden in his safari outfit, and holding a mismatched umbrella. He had the dreamy smile of those who expose themselves to danger but never come to any harm—the kind who walk to the edge of a precipice, cross the street with no attention to traffic, shout antishah and antigovernment slogans in front of security forces, and walk away without even a scratch. Addressing Nuri as if he were a child, Hasani advised him not to worry on account of Comrade Binesh. Comrade Binesh is always vigilant, he said. When Nuri rang the doorbell, Comrade Binesh thinks the secret police have come to arrest him. He quickly takes the safari clothes, umbrella, and sun hat from Aunt Moluk's closet, and, hopping toward the garden, puts on the pieces of his disguise. He climbs the rickety ladder so fast that he misses the last step, and the ladder falls to the ground. For some time, no matter how much Hasani pleads with Comrade Binesh and promises to hold the ladder steady to bring him down safely from the rooftop, Comrade Binesh ignores him.

Now Comrade Binesh leaned his umbrella against the brick vent, sat down by the edge of the roof, took off his hat, fanned his face a little, and put the hat back on. He hugged his knees and then with two fingers searched in the pocket of his vest for cigarettes and a lighter. It was quite windy on the rooftop, but cupping his hands around the cigarette, he was able to light it and ecstatically exhaled a big puff of smoke into the sky.

In a tone tinged with anger, Aunt Moluk called out, "Why are you looking up at the sky?"

"I think it's going to rain. It's very windy up here."

"Rain? With a clear sky?"

Comrade Binesh winked. He held two fingers in the shape of a revolver, aimed at Aunt Moluk, and, clicking his tongue against the roof of his mouth, produced a noise like a gun going off. Aunt Moluk drew Nuri close and said, "Have no fear. He's not in danger. Binesh knows how to come down from the roof. Maybe it wouldn't be a bad idea for you to go home. I'm sure by now Madame is worried about you."

Nuri put on a self-assured expression. "I'm not a child that Madame should worry about me. Suppose she worries? So what?"

"No, Nuri-jun. That's not nice. You have to treat your elders with respect. Do you remember that time you were here, how she worried? She thought something had happened to you and she would hear about it on the radio that night. It's better for you to go home straightaway. I have things to do, too."

She leaned closer and planted a big kiss on Nuri's cheek. Nuri said, "You have to forgive me for not reading your palm correctly."

"Don't worry. Just look after your studies and forget about everything else. I would say you shouldn't even come here so often. You will fall behind in your studies."

"But I miss you."

Aunt Moluk put a hand to her temple and grew pensive. "This neighborhood is not safe. People here are not used to seeing blond and blue-eyed persons who look like foreigners. The oppressed people, those from lower parts of the city, and even the bourgeois *bazaaris* are fed up with foreigners. If they get their hands on foreigners, they'll kill them and throw their bodies in the Karaj or Jajrud River. Whenever you come here, I am on pins and needles."

"Are you saying I shouldn't come again?"

"Of course not. You are my nephew and the apple of my eye. This door is always open to you, and I would like you to come at least once a week so that I can see you. I'm just saying that it might be better to spread out your visits by five to six weeks. And let me know beforehand. What is a telephone for? We can talk on the telephone, too."

The wound in Nuri's palm began to smart, but he didn't want to open his fist and look at it. "OK. I won't keep you any longer. You have to forgive me!"

"Go, my dear, take care of yourself. Give my best to Madame and the Senator."

Nuri left the house.

His sense of compassion began to fade as soon as he reached the Shah intersection. Not that Aunt Moluk had not done strange things in the past, but none was as strange as her shooing him out of that old house with "May I sacrifice myself for you," "May your ills be visited upon me," and "My heart is pinched with the pain of your absence." Nuri shrugged his shoulders. "OK. Fine. Let it be!" What effect could it have on him? None! Kaput! Finito! Like everyone, Aunt Moluk was free to do as she wished. Let her be happy with glorifying Comrade Binesh in front of others and claiming that every Friday she went on hikes with him and other friends who were known to each other by numbers instead of by names. Comrade Binesh had won a silver medal at the Ramsar water-ski competition, attended by world champions, which he had turned down in protest against the participation of Israeli competitors and Zionism's open endorsement of world imperialism. Wednesdays he fixed late-night rendezvous in the outlying trails around the Pahlavi Freeway to contact "mysterious foreign agents." If the secret police ever arrested him, Aunt Moluk would have looked humble and lowered her voice so that the relatives would not imagine she was too proud of Comrade Binesh. After some time, she would try to raise money to help him. She would take a bunch of old stuff from a trunk that had belonged to the departed "Bibi Fati" and assign it exorbitant prices that made your head spin. Ten thousand tumans for a piece of needlework that had been part of Bibi Ghezi's trousseau! Fifteen thousand tumans for Bibi Fati's prayer rug whose lace borders shone even in the dark cloakroom like the jewels in the film *King Solomon's Mine*. She would examine Nuri's face with the suspicion of a retired Ministry of Education inspector, uncertain whether Nuri had grasped the true value of those old treasures or had any appreciation of the lacework.

Aunt Moluk and Papa Javad used to get into such arguments about these family treasures that they would completely forget about others. They would create a world into which no one but themselves could enter. Perhaps the most real event of Papa Javad's life had been his car accident, but Aunt Moluk could not accept that. When anyone mentioned the accident, Aunt Moluk would not even listen. Instead, she would recite a few sentences from the review of Papa Javad's poetry that had been published in an underground magazine: "From the perspective of reactionary reviewers, 'normal accidents' happen without any warning and are completely divorced from the dictates of history and foundational tensions. Consequently, they seek the cause of death of a man like Comrade Javad Hushiar in ordinary events and insignificant daily mistakes, rather than placing it on the level of a 'historical myth' and imperialism's primary motives."

Nuri had not yet reached the Eslambol intersection when he was suddenly overcome by such a pounding rage that he hit his injured hand against the wall. The pain took his breath away. He leaned against the wall, looked at the bony protuberances of his shaking and bloodied hand, and liked himself. The intense rage had almost fully diffused his anxiety. Returning home in such a state struck him as foolish. With one glance at him, Madame would become suspicious. She wouldn't even need to ask him any questions. She would line up a thousand things in her mind and find her own explanation for his injured hand and disheveled appearance. Or perhaps, as in the past few days, she was now sitting quietly on the sofa in the study and would not even inquire about his health. She would place her hands on the armrest of the sofa and focus her tired gaze on him. Why? Just waiting for him to say something and offer an explanation.

But it was getting late, and Nuri had to return to Dezashib.

He opened the first-floor hall door noisily. Madame was on the phone, painstakingly uttering Persian words that she then translated into English. Her dark-olive, sleeveless dress hung gracefully from shoulder straps, girded by a brown belt at her waist and, like a Spanish fan, pleated over her thighs. She crossed one leg over another, circled the tip of one shoe in the air, and threw an admiring glance at her toenails, painted in pearly white polish. She spoke to Mrs. Baxter in a broken English that Nuri had long grown accustomed to hearing. She apparently wanted to replace the reception hall furniture with a modern set: chairs whose seats were covered with coarse straw and had metal backs in the shape of plumage. The drawers of one of the cupboards looked like a filing cabinet, with compartments evenly separated from each other by metal dividers. At that precise moment, she lifted back her hair and confessed that for some time she had been taking care of everything by herself, rearranging the decorative objects on the third floor, except for a few knickknacks she had left untouched on the heater in the study—for instance, an antique oil lamp with an emerald cut-glass stand and cherry-colored glass fuel container that had been part of her trousseau. If she could find a good buyer, she would sell all the old furnishings in the house, but the Senator was attached to them and did not want them sold.

Nuri went to his room quietly to avoid an encounter with Madame. He was only slightly concerned about his failing grades. Most certainly he would be forced to forget about going to New York. He thought Mr. Daftari, the natural-sciences teacher, was much more responsible for his misfortunes than was Mr. Abutorabian, the literature teacher, or Mr. Rahimi, the math teacher. If Nuri could get his hands particularly on Mr. Daftari, he would get even with him. No longer would he be flaccid like plum jam, sell himself to a bunch of brainless locals, and allow them to mistreat him as they pleased. He would not answer to Mr. Daftari, Mr. Abutorabian, or Mr. Rahimi, and he would not fear for his grades. He would welcome the queen with the speech he himself had written, not with the one Mr. Raji and Mr. Daftari had polished up. Nuri would actually have preferred to be left alone to go about his own business. Let some dunce take over welcoming the queen.

Buki knew first-rate, expert smugglers. Nuri would find one of the best among them and somehow make his way to New York. He would wear a Baluchi outfit and effortlessly cross the border in a police truck. His trip to New York would not even cost thirty thousand tumans. This time he would discuss the matter seriously with Maman Zuzu, and he would squeeze the money out of her for his trip. Then when he arrived in New York, he would find a job and pay her back.

He looked everywhere for Ladan, but did not see her. When he returned home late at night, she always asked him where he had been. Now she herself went out every day, looking for a job. Instead of going to the literature faculty, she dropped by the offices of weekly magazines, wrote letters to unknown editors, and sent them samples of her writing. She would probably not come back for another couple of hours. Nuri couldn't think of a way to find Buki, either. He would much rather talk to Buki than to Madame. After his troubles with Soraya, he felt that a distance had grown between him and Madame. On the surface, poor Madame had done nothing wrong. In her gentle and warm European manner, she was patient with him. It was Nuri himself who could no longer stand her constant inquisitive gaze, her pretense at being a Muslim and an Iranian.

As he climbed the stairs to his room, he heard Madame on the phone, still talking to Mrs. Baxter. She was coaching Mrs. Baxter on her Persian grammar. " . . . it is said that Jamshid was the first king who liberated his people from ignorance and instituted laws." After a pause she said, "Hamurabi . . . because of his failure. . . . " Then after a longer pause and in a lower tone, "OK. Iranians are sensitive. You have to respond to their letters quickly. They will take offense if you don't affix their titles to their names properly, heh, heh, heh. I dictate, and you copy. OK? Fine, please begin: 'To my most kind friend, the respected deputy of the minister of foreign affairs. . . . '" She tried to laugh more quietly. "Your Honor's missive has arrived. Your servant was ecstatic and most exhilarated to receive news from your graceful self." Then she said in English, "Don't do that!" She resumed in Persian, "Of course, of course, tell the doctor you have a fever. Tell him that you have not consumed anything for a few days, your back crawls . . . 'crawls'? Like ants walking on your skin . . . 'tingles' is different from 'crawls.' 'Tingles' refers to a pain that has not yet begun. . . . "

Mrs. Baxter spoke Persian like a nightingale even with the Senator and the representatives of the Majles. Her accent made everyone laugh. In Badri Khanom's view, Mrs. Baxter, like all Americans, lacked the charm and grace of Europeans. In the Italian embassy, she had once bragged about her ancestors who had a long history of pirating merchant ships. For this reason, they had chosen "Wreckage" for their family name.

A long time passed after Madame's telephone conversation with Mrs. Baxter. The only sounds that could be heard came from the stone pool fountain and the dried autumn leaves on the brick paths of the garden. Yet Nuri knew that Madame was watching him from some corner. Her perfume wafted into his room with the cool draft from the end of the hallway. It gave the room an imperceptible air of heaviness that was like the invisible presence of a person. Until Madame showed her face, Nuri wouldn't do anything but play on the high bar. And that is exactly what he did. Five minutes had not gone by when Madame slowly appeared in the hall. From where Nuri stood, he could see that she had put her hair in a bun, pinned on top of her head like a ripe tomato. It was clear she was dressed for a party. Contrary to her habit, she wore no rouge. Her only makeup was a dark green eye shadow. She walked cautiously, as if trying to avoid running into something. "I wanted to speak a few words. . . . Am I disturbing you? Your servant will come back in a few minutes."

The more polite Madame was, the more irritated Nuri grew. She walked deliberately and with each step held out her hand as if her skirt were being pulled from behind. She did not take her eyes from the ground for even one second. She seemed to be reaching out to Nuri for help while she watched for objects in her path. Nuri put his hands on his waist and asked in an authoritative voice, "What do you want?"

Madame blinked and continued to reach toward Nuri. She said, "When I stand up, I feel dizzy and queasy. You have to wait a little for me to feel better."

Anger rose from the depths of Nuri's mind like water rising in a well—a strange anger whose source he did not know. Madame's complaints seemed fake, but full of hidden meanings that nagged him. He felt a vague sense of fear. Fear of darkness? Fear of ignorance? Fear of the inner self he could no longer trust? What he said to Madame was more like a rebuke than a simple statement. "No doubt you didn't eat lunch, and your blood pressure has dropped."

Madame smiled feebly. "Don't get so cheeky. Don't try to find a cause for everything."

He asked, "I get cheeky? What do you mean?"

"No, no, no! I do not wish to interfere in Your Excellency's affairs. Thanks be to God, you have become a big man, almost as big as a desert ghoul. You don't need others to give you advice and show you the way."

Even if Madame gave him the news of a relative's death, Nuri would not have been surprised. "What has happened that I should need anyone's advice? If you want to say something, say it."

Madame glanced around for a place to sit. Nuri went into his own room and came back to the hall with a chair. Nodding her head in gratitude, she sat down and said, "You lose your temper very quickly, both because you have failed your grade and because Mr. Raji has replaced you with Naser Shahandeh for the queen's visit. But now I hear you take a respectable young lady to a café, leave her all alone, and flee like a good-for-nothing, knife-wielding hooligan raised under a bush."

Nuri was more stunned by Naser Shahandeh's taking his place in the ceremony than by Madame's admonishing him so angrily. His jaw dropped. He was flabbergasted. He couldn't believe this conspiracy against him. He sensed a knife stab in his back. "Who said Mr. Raji has chosen Naser Shahandeh to replace me in welcoming the queen?"

Madame took on a self-satisfied look and drew back her head. She stared at Nuri fixedly, as if in disbelief, and said, "You mean that the news has not reached His Excellency's ears? Every day it is announced at the bazaar entrance with pomp and ceremony. The whole world knows about it except for Your Excellency, who pays no attention to people around him and to satisfy his base personal desires is willing to do things even the least civilized people in the Third World would abhor. Hooray for knowledge! Hooray for pride! You will probably deny that you know Soraya Khanom Tahmasbi."

Nuri shouted, "Why should I not know her? Don't you know how many times she has phoned our house, screamed murder, and accused us of this and that?"

"Why did you take her to a café? If you took her to a café, why didn't you pay the bill? Why did you leave her alone and flee?"

Nuri searched his mind for a watertight answer, which he found quickly, "Because of the way she screamed in front of everyone—screams that make your hair stand on end! Do you understand?"

Madame's fingers trembled. "Soraya Khanom accuses you of giving your servant's clothes to her as presents. She claims that you impersonate me in front of strangers."

Nuri exhaled with a sound like air rushing out of a punctured tire. "That's it? That's what she's complaining about? I thought something terrible had happened, someone had died, or some calamity had been visited on somebody."

"You are a growing young man and, like all young men, have needs. Perhaps you are too embarrassed to ask for help, but this is no reason to steal my clothes from the storage room like a highway robber. In these few years, this humble servant has done her best to raise you as a responsible and civilized human being, conscious of the boundaries between his property and others'. I have no idea what is wrong with you." She closed her eyes as if to prevent Nuri from contradicting. "Why? In these past years, I have offered you whatever I had with the utmost generosity. In this house, you have whatever you want. Nobody interferes in your affairs. We are only grateful that we are together and can enjoy your presence. Perhaps you do these things to hurt our feelings."

Nuri couldn't believe Madame was scolding him like this. So much for freedom! This freedom was nothing but indifference—a European mode of encouragement that allowed Nuri to do whatever he wished as long as he didn't bother anybody or cause any scandals. He was close to exploding. In the midst of his troubles, he needed a sympathetic person to moderate his excesses. "Do you know, from the first day I came here, I never once felt at home? This is not my place. I'm just a mere tenant."

He berated himself, wondering what was wrong with him. Why was he wasting his time with a foreign woman who didn't understand anything of an Easterner's inner life?

Madame always spoke softly to temperamental and aggressive people in order to calm them down, so now she lowered her voice to a whisper. "Your servant does not deny that you have had a difficult life. You have been displaced. I have spent many sleepless nights thinking about you. Your servant has lived more than half a century among strangers. I have danced to many tunes and grown accustomed to being a foreigner. Who better than I can understand the ups and downs of your life? Your problem is that you already know yourself better than anyone else. You interpret complexities as family secrets and conspiracies against you. The more we attend to your needs, the more you imagine that the world revolves around you and your affairs."

At that moment, Nuri was in need of someone to prevent him from doing something that would probably come to a bad end. Madame did not understand that you could not play with an Easterner's feelings. He raised his voice in protest. "What do you mean, you attend to my needs? Do you imagine that I have this and I have that, I am rolling in riches and plenty, I have whatever I ask for? If that's the case, then why don't I myself feel it? Why do I have to feel as needy as a beggar? You just pretend to know. You think you can become an Iranian and understand Iranians just by embracing Islam and swearing on Saint Abbas. Sometimes I sit on the balcony, and as soon as I remember our apartment . . . "

When he recalled Papa Javad, he covered his face and ran to his room to avoid showing his tears. His foot caught on the edge of the hall carpet, and he staggered. Madame came after him and said, "Oh, Nuri-jun, forgive your servant. I beg you, my dearrrr, I beg you to listen to my statements. I will take you to Vienna for a short trip. Perhaps, away from this environment, you will be healed. Isn't that a good idea? Huh?"

She stood in front of Nuri and spoke hurriedly. She confessed that, like Nuri, she felt she was living in an alien world. She had long been preoccupied with going to Vienna. Fifteen years had passed since her last visit there. Even then, had it not been for an uncle's death, she would probably not have gone. The last time she had visited the city where she was born, she was distracted by an unfamiliar feeling she could not put into words. She would just stare at the snow on the roofs of buildings. Barricades were put up in the middle of intersections, and the sooty facades of buildings, shrouded in green gauze, were being restored. In front of the opera and on trails in the Parada Forest, she came across some police and petrol officers, asking foreigners for their passes. Saint Stephen's Cathedral, with its graying walls, marble pulpit, and lit candles, appeared to belong to another city and another people. Vienna had changed drastically since the years immediately after the war. Now the Viennese went to cafés and restaurants on Saturday nights, ate schnitzel, drank white wine, and waltzed on dance floors.

Nuri tasted his dried, salty tears in the corner of his mouth. In his mind, he saw New York with a large sign forever pointing to the future. The future, not the past. Movement, not immobility. Change instead of stasis. Maman Zuzu smirked at him from her framed picture on the wall. She had a smiling and self-satisfied look. Her hair was cut at an angle in a style that had been fashionable around the years 1945, 1946. In a happier mood, Madame tapped Nuri on the shoulder several times and said, "This too shall pass, Nuri-jan. Nothing is everlasting . . . "

Ladan's voice came from downstairs, "Nuri?"

"What?"

"I want to talk to you."

Madame seemed to have taken Ladan's voice as a sign that she should leave. She held a finger to her lips in a way that was meant to reassure Nuri. She was going to go up to the third floor and had no intention of disturbing anyone. Nevertheless, she hung back, as if she had left something half finished. She addressed Ladan. "Remain the Goddess of the Harvest forever. Do not let life's problems make you anxious. Do not let an ordinary person bother you."

Ladan stood in the middle of the staircase, looking nicely turned out. Waiting for Madame to go up to her room, she shook dust off her dress. Even after Madame had gone to the third floor, she busied herself with her dress until Nuri asked, "What did you want to say?"

"I don't want to talk here. Do you want to go to a night of poetry?"

"What's a night of poetry?"

"Poets gather in the Patogh Theater, near the television station, to recite their poetry. It's great. Let's go together. We'll talk on the way."

Nuri accepted, especially because it was the time when guests usually arrived. No doubt they would want to talk about Soraya. Ladan took Nuri's arm, and they left the house together quickly.

On the way, Ladan avoided talking. Every time Nuri insisted, she said she would wait until they reached the Patogh Theater. In the theater, the poets, some frail and listless, others animated and smiling, came up to the lectern and recited their poems. The first poet had a droopy mustache and a cunning look. He stood behind the lectern and read his poem "Gaits" in a wounded and lingering tone reminiscent of the cadences of a foreign language. As if forewarning someone, he began sarcastically, "Lo!!! . . . " His poem made allusions to government censors. Everyone except Nuri seemed to catch his meaning. The audience broke into spontaneous applause, and Nuri too was swept along. Ladan was bewildered by the sudden change in him. Stunned, she watched him cheer, whistle, and clap. She covered her face with her hands and slid down lower in her seat to hide her laughter. "That's enough, Mamakh. No need to carry on like this."

After the poetry reading, Nuri and Ladan went to the Khorsand Sandwich Shop for something to eat. They sat quietly and chewed slowly. Every time Nuri tried to make Ladan talk, she turned the conversation around to Maman Zuzu and her having been fined. For a simple traffic violation in New York, she had had to pay twelve dollars out of her pocket. She imitated Maman Zuzu throwing an empty Pepsi can out her car window. Then she imitated the surly, hunched policeman gunning his motorcycle and turning on his flashing red light. She wedged the tomato slices into her sandwich after each bite and put her hair back behind her ears every time it fell into her face. She threw a bashful glance at her fingernails and suddenly said that a few days ago Mr. Shariat had grabbed Grandpa Senator's hand and planted a big kiss on it. At first, Grandpa Senator thought that something bad had happened to Shariat or that he had misplaced a digit in the negotiations over the Aghcheh property. He had pulled back his hand and asked, "Shariat, have you gone crazy? What's all this?"

Shariat had pleaded with him to accept him as his servant and to allow him to marry Her Excellency, Miss Ladan. After hearing this request, Grandpa Senator had remained tongue-tied for some time. Instead of dismissing Shariat—may his body be carried by corpse washers—Grandpa Senator had come up with a wishy-washy answer, keeping both the skewer and the kebab from burning. "Let me speak to her and see what she herself says. We have to think about this."

No grumbling! Just a half-assed answer that gave Shariat the illusion that Grandpa Senator was not opposed to his request. Had Ladan herself been there, she would have put Shariat in his place and straightened him out the minute he opened his mouth. None of this hitting both the horseshoe and the nail that emboldened Shariat to ask the Senator directly for Ladan's hand without any sense of shame and propriety. She had not been raised behind an earthenware jar that she should marry a *bazaari* like Shariat, rub his hands and feet at night, and bear him one child after another. "Yuck, I'm getting nauseated." Her hands were tied. If Nuri didn't come up with a solution, she would go mad. She would be finished. "I have to teach this moron a lesson. What nerve! At the age of forty-two, he is not ashamed to ask for the hand of a twenty-year-old woman."

Nuri teased Ladan. "Khormalu, you've lucked out." He imitated old women. "Naneh, may you grow old together."

At last, Ladan laughed and asked, "Do you know why he wears that pilot's uniform?"

"To please your own dear heart, Naneh-jun."

"Yeah? I prefer death to a thousand years of living with a *bazaari*."

"O brazen one, what kind of talk is this? Have some shame."

Nuri bet that Grandpa Senator would send Shariat packing after the elections. Ladan asked, "How do you know?"

"I know because Grandpa Senator's donkey hasn't crossed the bridge yet. I promise he will fire Shariat after the elections. The person who has to worry is me."

"Why you?"

"Have you ever failed exams?"

"Many fail exams, Mamakh. There's no shame in it."

"I don't have any patience for it. Do you know that I was supposed to greet the queen? Now Mr. Raji has chosen Naser Shahandeh to replace me. Do you know why? Because I speak my mind in front of everyone."

Ladan hemmed and hawed a bit. Nuri continued. You know, I'm just not made for this life. This sort of thing is good only for these brainless, new-money Aryamehri types who are always competing with each other and bragging about their cars, houses, and money. From the beginning, I said I was not that kind."

He was amused by fate's games. One day Mr. Raji takes him into his office and praises him to high heaven, as if there were no other like him in the world, then in the blink of an eye he picks him up by the tail and throws him into the garbage!

◆ ◆ ◆ The following Saturday Nuri and Madame were having breakfast when Mr. Shariat came to work earlier than usual. He was pensive. He apparently had driven his 1972 Peugeot, which he usually brought to the Mostowfi Alley on Friday afternoons. Nuri could not figure out why he was wearing an air force officer's uniform or what plans he was concocting in his head with that self-righteous and aggrieved look. For the first time, he was clean shaven instead of sporting his perennial one-day growth. But his hair was uncombed, and he seemed to be growing it long like university students. He mumbled a greeting and forced a smile, obviously out of a sense of duty rather than from any particular concern for Madame and Nuri. He placed some gift boxes and a blue envelope on the hall table and arranged them so meticulously that Nuri thought he was in pain. Not a day passed that Shariat did not enter the Dezashibi house with a pot of yogurt, a bag of Lighvan cheese, a dish of pistachio halvah, a tin of *sohan*, a metal container of Kermanshahi oil, or a sack of *domsiah* long-grain rice. He placed the presents side by side on the table, rearranged them a few times until they were set in a geometric pattern. He seemed to be averting imaginary disorder, or perhaps he was afraid of the absence of balance in space.

On this particular morning, unlike before, Shariat did not lower his gaze and walk away. Instead, he poured himself a glass of dark tea. He sat in a chair by the wall, away from Madame and Nuri. He slurped his tea slowly until Ladan came down for breakfast. He always put Ladan's irritability to a feminine prudishness that belied her deep interest in him. When he saw Ladan's scowling face, he would break into a grin, act coy, and offer her such inane smiles that even Black Najmeh became cross. But this time when he saw Ladan, he blushed up to his ears. With a hand across his chest, he bowed to her, shyly lowered his eyelids, and, with his head still bent, took the stairs to the study. Lately he regained his old self-confidence only in the Senator's company. He would narrow his eyes haughtily and inconsiderately blather about the Senator's election rival, the custodian of Qom, and his money and influence. "What money! What means! How much influence he has in the court." The Senator was alert and did not let Shariat overstep his bounds. The day Shariat asked for Ladan's hand, the Senator had laughed heartily and tried to end things on an upbeat note. Shariat was not used to joking, and he was rarely able to make anyone laugh. He suddenly lost his temper and began to boast that had it not been for his efforts, the shareholders of the Aghcheh land would not have received any money for it and the Senator's plans for the future would have been scattered to the wind. The Senator beat a tactical retreat and brought everything back to normal. Now any chance he had, he referred to Shariat as "the *seyyed,* the descendant of the Prophet" or "the progeny of the Prophet's family." He hinted broadly that Ladan should not disappoint the "poor *seyyed.*" She should not do anything to offend his religious lineage and cause him to resign from his secretarial post. Without Shariat, the Senator's election campaign in Qom would come to a halt. The court, which was not particularly happy with the Senator, would take advantage of the situation and arrange for the name of the Qom custodian to be the one to come out of the ballot boxes.

As long as Shariat busied himself with the presents and the blue envelope, Madame remained at the table and ate her breakfast slowly and graciously amidst the clinking of the knives and forks. But as soon as Shariat had gone into the study, she rose and immediately made her way to the table bearing the presents. She almost grabbed the blue envelope, quickly took it over to the window, and held it against the light. As she mouthed the words she could decipher, she appeared to forget everything else. With the robotic movements of a hypnotized person, she climbed the stairs. Up to that point, Nuri and Ladan had not made the slightest sound, but now they threw glances at each other, trying to grasp Madame's strange behavior. Each day she did something new and different and made them suspicious.

Nuri waited until the time for Madame's afternoon nap. When he thought she was asleep, he went up to the side table on the third floor and looked for the blue envelope in the brass vase where Madame usually kept her letters. Among her key chain, a pair of women's garden gloves, and the broken handle of her pince-nez, he found two envelopes. One of them was the blue envelope. He was about to open it when Madame came out of her bedroom. She had a mysterious and calm look, as if she had been lying in wait to catch Nuri by surprise. In that situation, finding excuses was sheer stupidity. He stood still until Madame approached him and with a look of indignation snatched the envelope from his hand. She turned her masklike face away from him and pointed to the study. Ladan was waiting for them in the room, with her hands clasped in front of her skirt. The anxious hollows in her cheeks indicated that she had been summoned there. Glassy-eyed, Madame sat in a chair and handed the letter to Ladan and asked her to read it aloud. During the few minutes when Ladan read the letter in the same way she delivered the compositions she wrote for the radio, Madame sat still, her head bent, and listened to Shariat pleading most courteously with "Her Highness and Eminence, Madame" not to interpret his statements as signs of disrespect. He swore not only by his own God, but also by Jesus Christ, the Holy Spirit, and the twelve chaste disciples that his paltry offerings did not indicate anything but his best intentions and his wish to show his admiration and reverence. He had never stopped short of sacrificing body and soul in Her Highness's service, nor would he ever in the future. His only reason for writing such a missive was to reveal his inner feelings for Her Excellency, "Khanom Ladan Khanom"—a pining that made him walk all night long, holding a Bible over his head and asking Mary Magdalena to grant him peace and liberate him from this dire agony.

When Ladan finished reading the letter, a silence descended on the room. Nuri was so angry that he couldn't even rise from his seat. Madame leaned her forehead against the palm of her hand and stared out the window in the direction of the garden. Then with her finger she gently and dreamily wiped away the tears rolling down her cheeks. She twisted around her finger a white thread hanging from the hem of her skirt and remembered her gratitude to Mr. Shariat for the good-natured and attentive manner in which he had helped her prepare for her conversion and taught her to recite the Koran. Then, to cheer up Ladan and Nuri, she drew a sigh and swore by Saint Abbas and Jesus, the son of Mary, that Mr. Shariat's suffering would one day end. She blamed it on Iranians' lack of experience and their intense feelings, which know no boundaries in love. Barely having begun to talk, they learn to recite poetry. The minute they meet someone's eyes, they lose their head, cry, and accuse their beloved of callousness and disloyalty. "Had I been one of these beloveds, I would have lost my patience and fled into fields and mountains. In Europe, if every day you were to go to the market and broadcast your innermost secrets with pomp and ceremony, people would think either that a foreign circus has come to town or that you are advertising a hard-to-sell item. So do not confuse European and Iranian lovers. In general, Europeans are terrified of the kind of lover who lingers around their house and faints at sight of them."

She gave a sarcastic smile. Nuri was annoyed that foreign women could not differentiate between sincere Iranians and ridiculous people like Shariat. Ignoring Nuri and Ladan, Madame glanced at a second letter sent by Princess Bertha. She explained that most of the letter was devoted to talk of the charitable donations Princess Bertha had collected for a school called Saint Joseph's in upstate New York. Addressing Nuri, she said, "Bertha speaks of the principal of the school as a close friend. I promise she will use her influence to obtain admission for you into Saint Joseph's College."

Nuri couldn't pretend he hadn't heard such an important announcement. He was constantly looking for the means to make his way to New York, but now he was agitated and could not trust Madame. What if that letter was only a trap intended to keep him needy and dependent? For a long time, there had been no letters from Princess Bertha, nor did Madame mention her past and Princess Bertha as the most popular singer in pre–World War II Vienna. One day in the middle of the renovations, she remembered "The Small Café in Harnal," a recording that she and Princess Bertha had made together before the war. First, Madame could not remember where she had put the record. She made Nuri and Ladan follow her to the storage room, looked here and there among the knick-knacks, and accidentally found the record inside an old photo album. A small photograph of a young Madame was on its cover, wearing a beret, white bow tie, and puff collar. Princess Bertha's picture showed her in full figure and took up more than half of the cover. She stood in the spotlight on stage and held a microphone. Her thick golden hair was pulled back and fell halfway down her shoulders. She wore a silver-spangled sleeveless dress that hugged the curves of her body and made her look like a cobra who has been charmed by the sound of a reed. The tightness of her dress and her voluptuous body had nothing in common with Madame's modest and virginal appearance. Madame's simple dress reminded Nuri of dutiful schoolgirls and better matched Madame's chattering about love and her memories of Siegfried.

The record was scratched and broadcast a nasal duet and a trombone solo as if from a distance. Madame continually smiled coyly at Nuri and Ladan and apologized for the poor quality of the record. She told them interesting stories about Baugarten's open-air theater, Vienner Großer Musikensal, and Restaurant Chez Bertha. She talked about Hermann Leopoldi, the famous Viennese composer who had signed a contract with Hotel Eden in Berlin. Every night for two years during the invasion of Poland, Princess Bertha and Fräulein Frieda performed two sets in the hotel's private cabaret. Because soldiers frequented the bar, it was not an appropriate place for young women like them. Then Madame reminisced about her trip to Prague and told Nuri and Ladan the story of Siegfried being shot. On a snowy night, Fräulein Frieda and the princess performed in the Zola Bar up to the approach of morning. They heard a gunshot from behind the opera building, and the stage lights went off. It took Princess Bertha and Fräulein Frieda two hours to reach the hospital. Their eyes fell on Siegfried lying on a stretcher, dried mud and blood covering a gunshot wound on his right temple. He had black grease under his fingernails and was wearing mismatched wool socks, one red and the other blue. He seemed as heavy as a corpse. Overwhelmed by fear and tears, Princess Bertha stands in the doorway, but Fräulein Frieda approaches what she assumes is Siegfried's corpse, taking off her woolen hat and scarf. Siegfried's eyes are open. Tired and smiling feebly, he examines Fräulein Frieda's face for a sign, as if needing to comfort himself more than her. He says, "I am very sorry. You have to forgive me. I have been shot in the head. Even recognizing friends is difficult for me. I'm sure we know each other because I like you, but I can't place you. If it is not rude to ask, would you introduce yourself?"

Madame wiped tears from her face and smiled hurriedly. She couldn't remember why she had asked Ladan and Nuri to come into the study or what had been the point of reading Shariat's and Princess Bertha's letters. Excusing herself because of a headache, she called out to Black Najmeh to bring her a cup of tea and two aspirins. That was it.

When they came out of the study, Ladan looked at Nuri from the corner of her eye. Her lips were pursed with anger. She asked, "What about me? Isn't there anybody here to speak to Shariat and stop his madness?"

Nuri shrugged his shoulders. He wished he were somewhere else. He would call Buki, arrange to meet him near Zhila Shabahang's house, and invite him somewhere for kebab and *barbari* bread. If Buki didn't want kebab and *barbari*, they would eat a chicken-and-bean sandwich at the Chantilly Sandwich Shop. Why had Buki not contacted him? Why had he not let him know what Soraya had said about him behind his back? Nuri had phoned the Tahmasbis' apartment a few times, but every time Mrs. Tahmasbi answered and presented the excuse that "Sori-jun is not feeling well. She is passed out on her bed."

♦ ♦ ♦ The next day Nuri was sitting on the floor of his room changing his socks when he accidentally spotted Madame through his half-open door. Tidier and more elegant than usual, she descended the stairs. Nuri crept out to the head of the stairs to watch her. In the first-floor hall, the locksmith was waiting for her. She threw a hesitant glance at him—a quiet and shy man who did not appear unduly struck by the grandeur of the house. Madame's sarcastic tone was unusual. "How long does it take to change the locks?" She looked up at the ceiling and snapped her fingers. "Eh, half an hour only? As easy as drinking water? Huh?"

She took the locksmith to the third floor to change the locks.

On the way up, she ran into Nuri. With more than usual emphasis, she called him "Your Highness" and "Your Excellency." She answered his questions perfunctorily and, with European pauses, gave him to understand that once the locks were changed, no one could enter the storage room without permission. Madame had altered much in the past few days. Sometimes she would emerge from darkness and take Nuri by surprise while he was holding a dumbbell in front of the mirror. Other times, looking pale as if she had not slept well, she would stare at Nuri through a window. After a few minutes, she would disappear into the darkness the same way she had suddenly appeared.

Nuri was looking for a way to go to America, but he didn't know how to broach the topic with Madame. Perhaps it was better to ask the Senator. Only Grandpa Senator could pay his expenses. But he was deceiving himself. He still needed Madame. Perhaps she blamed all his misfortunes on his classmates and Mr. Raji. Just like Badri Khanom, who always took her son Shahrokh's side and blamed Dr. Jannati for Shahrokh's poor school performance. "This doctor, this beloved husband of mine, I don't know in which dump he received his degree. Have you ever heard of treating the frailty of youth with a couple of multivitamin tablets? Multivitamins are good for elderly people like himself who have hardly the energy to breathe."

Every day Nuri felt irritable. When he ran into Ladan, he would use any excuse to argue with her. When Maman Zuzu phoned from New York, he would gesture to the others to tell her he was not home. The day Madame finally forced him to talk to Maman Zuzu, he strung a few words together reluctantly. No matter how Maman Zuzu teased him and spoke to him in the manner of street thugs, "What a man! How are you? How's your Soraya-jun?" Nuri remained quiet. In a more serious tone, Maman Zuzu asked, "Doesn't Soraya have a life of her own that she is after you so much?" After a short pause, she said, "In that country, nobody acts according to any rules. Soraya, who is ten years older than you, is after a seventeen-year-old youth, and Mr. Shariat, having eaten our bread, chases Ladan, who is young enough to be his daughter."

Nuri grumbled, "And then Mumzie feels sorry for him, and whenever she hears his name, she cries as if she has heard Siegfried's name."

Maman Zuzu lowered her voice. "The Germans were fooled by Siegfried's Austrian name and blond hair. They thought he was Aryan like them. When he ended up in the hospital and they took off his clothes, they realized he was circumcised. . . . " She swallowed her laughter. "They decided to shoot him again, but they were amazed by his resilience. Three days after being shot, he was still alive and well."

"How do you know these things?"

"From Princess Bertha."

Nuri had no reason to feel sorry for Siegfried. "OK, Maman!"

"What?"

"I want to come to America."

Maman Zuzu sighed dejectedly. "Oh, Nuri-jun . . . it's not so easy. Only Grandpa Senator can send you, and right now he is really peeved about Soraya's craziness. You must know Grandpa Senator by now. He is a traditional person. He is not like your own father and cannot understand your feelings. I bet if Soraya continues her crazy behavior, Grandpa will send an agent to the Tahmasbis' apartment and have her taken to jail. You don't believe me? Wait a little and see what happens."

Nuri gave up and said, "Maman, I don't understand these things anymore. I want to come to America."

"Eh, you are not a child. There is a proper time for everything. When your turn comes, you too will come to America. You have to have a little patience now."

"Maman, I really miss you."

"Me too, Nuri-jun. I miss that moonlike face of yours. What happened to the new pictures you took? Weren't you going to send some of them to me? Put them all between two pieces of cardboard in a large envelope so that they don't get bent and mail them to me right away. May I sacrifice myself for you, Nuri-jun. May I sacrifice myself for your beautiful face. Now. The telephone bill is running high. They say every laugh costs thirty dollars. So I'll say good-bye for now and call you again next week. Say hello to everyone for me. OK? Fine, my dear. May I sacrifice myself for you. . . . "

Nuri hung up.

The biggest difficulty in gaining Grandpa Senator's consent was that in the heat of the elections he was never home. Early in the mornings, he went to the Senate. In the afternoons, he visited his constituency office in Qom and returned home late at night. One day when the telephone rang and Nuri was in a hurry to pick it up, he ran into the Senator going downstairs in the other direction. For a few seconds, Nuri stood still. Grandpa Senator examined him for a while. He neither mentioned Nuri's grades nor asked for any explanation of Soraya's phone calls. He just winked and said, "How small you are, Nuri! In Europe, a tiny person like you takes up either figure skating or horseback riding. . . . "

He went downstairs panting. Did he know anything about Nuri's preoccupations? Had he read his mind? Nuri couldn't figure it out. He put a hand to his mouth and called from the stairway, "Since you don't like Europe, why don't you send me to America?"

The Senator stopped in his tracks before reaching the hall door. With deliberately slow steps, he returned to the staircase. He put his hands on his knees and offered Nuri a facetious smile that barely hid his anger. "Since when has Your Excellency become so accustomed to sightseeing? What has happened that the minute you get bored, you develop an urge to go to America?"

"Because I can study better there."

"What's wrong with this country? Have you been spoiled? Have you been given so much money you don't know what to do with it?"

Nuri had chosen the wrong moment to speak to Grandpa Senator. He decided to wait until the Senator was in a better mood.

That night the guests left earlier than usual, and the garden grew so quiet that the thought of going to the study and talking to the Senator came to Nuri's mind most naturally. He was certain that sooner or later he would have to show his hand and deal with the Soraya episode and his troubles at school. A nebulous light from the alley passed through the trees and reflected leaflike shadows on the wall. The shadows' imperceptible movements made it seem as if something were happening in the corridor. For a while, Nuri leaned his shoulder against the doorframe of the study and examined Grandpa Senator closely. Like a dream vision, he was seated tailor style on a checkered blanket reading a newspaper with a flashlight. The silver sugarcube bowl seemed empty, containing only sugar dust. Scattered around the Senator were cut-glass tea tumblers with a residue of tea leaves, a telephone, a radio, a few volumes of the *Dehkhoda Dictionary*, leather-bound reports of the private meetings of the Majles, foreign magazines, and a thousand other odds and ends. The Senator looked up from his newspaper and, with an expressionless face and a wave of his hand, beckoned to Nuri. "Come here, let's see."

Nuri feigned ignorance. "Are you talking to me?"

He waved his hand a few more times. "Come in. Did you want something?"

"Me? No."

"Don't bullshit me. I'm sure you wanted something from me. Otherwise, you wouldn't be bothering me at this time of night."

"I wanted to see . . . if you would let me go to New York."

At first, Grandpa Senator looked amused and repeated Nuri's sentence a few times. "'Would you let me go to New York? Would you let me go to

New York?' It's as if you were conceived in New York." He frowned and wrinkles appeared around his eyes. He tilted his head. "Why New York?"

"To go to school."

The Senator scratched under his chin, keeping his aggrieved gaze on Nuri. His smooth, olive-colored skin and thin, almost bruised lips made him seem oddly young. His straight hair, disheveled like a poet's, further emphasized his youthful appearance. He said, "With these laughable grades of yours, you will have a hard time being accepted into an American school."

"Princess Bertha knows the principal of an American school, and she has promised to get me a letter of admission."

Princess Bertha had made no such promise, but Nuri thought he had to say this. The Senator rested his chin in his palm and said, "Princess Bertha has promised to enroll you in a school?"

"Maman says that if you permit it, Princess Bertha will arrange for my admission within a week."

The Senator raised his head. The glint in his eyes indicated he was struck by a new idea. "Let me think about it. I'll tell you later, but on one condition."

"What condition?"

"On the condition that I never again see you with this boy Buki Tahmasbi and his sister, that harlot Soraya."

"Why?"

"Do you know that Soraya constantly calls the office of the secret police and reports me?"

"Reports you?"

"No, she reports her pimp of a father! She has found nobody but me who, according to her, slanders the country and the shah. She says I have a deal with Mr. Baxter and his wife to gather antishah intelligence for the American embassy. I am very eager to know where she gets these ideas. Did you make them up?"

Nuri was unfazed. "No . . . "

"So she has pulled the names of Mr. and Mrs. Baxter out of a hat?"

"How should I know? If Soraya wants something, she finds a way to get it."

"Everyone has the right to make a couple of mistakes during his life and to learn from them, but it seems you think the more reckless you are, the more quickly we will send you to New York to be rid of you. He who wants to go to New York has to show himself worthy of it. Do you understand?" He shook a cigarette out of a packet, put it in the corner of his mouth, and lit it indifferently. He shook the match to extinguish it. He narrowed one eye, expelled the smoke from the corner of his mouth, and looked at Nuri with confidence, as if he had just played a trump card. "How long have you known this girl?" he asked.

"From childhood."

"They say she is ten years older than you."

"Almost."

"No doubt you are also an intellectual. You probably read books and participate in political demonstrations."

"What do you mean?"

"I mean you two are the type who have ambitions of becoming world famous. You see suffering as a point of pride, but at the same time you are attached to pleasure, money, and fame. Bravo! If I had the talent, I would be the same way."

"If you mean Soraya, she has done nothing that requires talent."

"This type looks sidelong at anybody's success. If someone gets his hand on some money, this type says he stole it. Do you know how at my age I have to run around and see all sorts of people for the sake of these dreaded elections? And all for nothing. If I knew how, I too would cheat like the rest of them and stop worrying." He couldn't keep from laughing. " . . . Shariat suggests that in this round of elections, because everyone is up in arms, we blame everything on the Mongol invasion." He cupped his mouth, brought his head closer, and in a secretive tone said, "OK. Tell me if this Soraya Khanom is into matters of the heart?"

"Matters of the heart?"

"Why do you play dumb? I mean does she let you enjoy her? If she does, go ahead and enjoy her. It's a free catch." Once again a trace of a smirk appeared around his mouth. "How is she in bed?"

Nuri grew agitated and asked, "What do you mean?"

Grandpa Senator looked at him slyly. "You devil."

Nuri said, "I don't think about these things at all."

"So, what are all these silly things you do these days?" Grandpa Senator drew on his cigarette. "They say you are acting like a thug. You take her to a café. Maybe you are wasting your money on intellectual discussions." Nuri said nothing, and the Senator shrugged his shoulders. "You seem to be sleepy."

Nuri straightened up and said decisively, "No, I'm not sleepy."

"Nonsense, you don't look so good. Go to sleep now, we'll talk about all this later. Good night!" When Nuri had taken a few steps, the Senator said, "Let me think about your trip to New York a little bit."

"We don't have much time."

To indicate his indifference, the Senator turned up his palm.

Nuri returned to his room, feeling dazed. Why had he not stood up to the Senator about going to New York? The telephone rang. Barefoot and panicky, he ran into the hall to answer it before anyone else. When he picked up the receiver, he recognized Soraya's voice. Assuming that Madame had answered the phone, she began shouting, "May your Nuri be struck by a secret arrow! Respectable lady, how have you, with your good-for-nothing European manners, raised this stupid creature to be so gutless? Otherwise, he would not take an innocent and chaste girl to a café, abandon her, flee, and embarrass her in front of a bunch of Armenians. Why don't you ask his useless corpse what Soraya has done to him that he torments her like this? What has he seen from her other than purity and friendship that he burns her like this?" She raised her voice higher, as if she were speaking to Nuri directly. "May you roast in hell to the end of your days, the same way you have burned me. May I see your putrid body on the corpse washers' plank so that I feel better."

Nuri decided to listen quietly to Soraya's raving. She would finally grow tired and hang up. But after a half hour of swearing, she was still going full force. Assuming Madame to be on her side, she gave an in-depth report of all that she had done to pay Nuri back. She had called Amiz Hosein and Amiz Abbas every day and filled their ears with stories about Nuri stealing from the relatives' houses. She had also told them that Nuri had brought her the old photo album, perfume bottle, and Madame's cards showing "disgraceful acts." The relatives should not allow Nuri into their homes. She asked how she could make Nuri suffer, how she could get even with that fool and punish him for what he had done. She was not happy with Amiz Hosein, who did not have the patience to listen to her. Instead of helping her plot her revenge, he turned the conversation around to his own wife, Shuri Khanom, and asked her whereabouts. He posed strange questions, as if Soraya were a secret agent. "Where does a woman go all alone early in the morning? Why does she not come home before dusk?" No matter how much Soraya swore that Shuri-jun was a loyal wife and completely devoted to Amiz Hosein and how much she liked their two-year-old son, Daryan, Amiz Hosein still regretted his marriage to her. What madness led him to marry at his advanced age and after a lifetime of working in the Customs Office? And to Shurangiz, of all people, whose father sold thread, nails, and metal tripods at the Galubandak intersection and whose mother was a masseuse in a women's public bath. "Soraya Khanom, I shouldn't have had a child. I want to ask you, What good is a child for somebody my age?" Out of sympathy, Soraya comforted him, "Amiz Hosein, don't be ungrateful. You will regret it. Ingratitude has a price. Becoming a father has nothing to do with being young or old. God gave Abraham a beautiful child in his old age. . . . " Soraya stopped suddenly and repeated, "Hello? Hello? Hello?" Nuri remained quiet so as to avoid being recognized, which made Soraya more suspicious. "Are you deaf that you don't answer?"

Nuri hung up and ran toward his room. He was halfway there when the phone rang again. If he didn't pick it up, someone else no doubt would, which would cause even more embarrassment. This time he picked up the receiver and hung up quickly. He was only temporarily relieved. He had to repeat this two or three more times until finally the Senator picked up the receiver in the study. As always, he dialed a number. Out of sheer joy, Nuri wanted to kiss Grandpa Senator, although he had detested him a little while ago. For a second, he forgave his grandpa all his sins. He had narrowly escaped certain danger.

♦ ♦ ♦ Shahrokh Jannati came to visit Madame and the Senator three nights before his flight. Like the family elders, he asked about Nuri and when he was going to receive his admission to an American school. Nuri had no reason to be annoyed with Shahrokh. Any brainless person with a rich father such as Dr. Jannati could gain admission into a college, even Harvard and Princeton. Amiz Abbas called from the reception hall, "Father dear, bring a drop of water for my parched throat. I'm dying of thirst."

A few steps away Badri Khanom and Eftekhar Khanom Nabbatchi, the Senator's paternal uncle's granddaughter, were talking about cheap tours to Hong Kong and Singapore. Badri Khanom was biting into a *nok-hodchi* cookie. She wiped her mouth with a tissue, which she then crumpled in her hand. Mr. Mostafa Nabbatchi, who worked in the oil company, was listening to them. He took the fruit basket and lowered it in front of them. Eftekhar Khanom knotted her eyebrows. "No, that's enough. I'll get gas and won't be able to sleep peacefully at night."

She complained about the pain in her hip joint, which had not completely healed after surgery. It was impossible for her to walk, especially without the shoes for which she had paid four thousand tumans. For a few more years, she had to walk with a cane. Even then, the doctors could not guarantee that they would not operate on her again. Then Shuri Khanom entered the reception hall with her husband, Amiz Hosein. She was wearing a dark-green satin dress in a paisley pattern, with sleeves that covered no more than four fingers' width of her arms, an Italian-style collar open down to her cleavage, and a brass chain belt with a large buckle. She had parted her hair to one side. It was short and reached the tips of her earlobes. Her ears were adorned with cast-iron earrings as big as horseshoes. She wore a brass collar that looked like the brim of an officer's hat and covered the scar from her thyroid operation. She made such a racket with her high-heeled shoes that Eftekhar Khanom began to grumble, "Yes? What is the matter with her? Why is it that in front of the youth in the family she forgets her age?"

Shuri Khanom usually wouldn't come to this type of family party. Or if she came, she acted so haughty that everyone grew annoyed. They still remembered the night of her wedding to Amiz Hosein. Early in the evening, she had put both feet in one shoe and insisted on being called by a European name—"Fleur" or "Mercedes" or "Alexandra." They had pleaded with her, "After all, Khanom-jun, these foreign names are not appropriate for an old family." She was not dissuaded. She even referred to the groom as "Daryan" instead of "Amiz Hosein." "Daryan! Daryan! . . . Daryan! Daryan! Daryan!"

The relatives had glanced at each other, wondering if she meant d'Artagnan, one of Alexander Dumas's famous Three Musketeers. None of them had heard such a name before. Moreover, Amiz Hosein didn't look anything like the Three Musketeers. Fortunately, Amiz Hosein did not give in and a year later forced Shuri Khanom to name their newborn son Daryan. A person like him had his own reputation. He was a dervish in the Gonabadi order. There was not a major, general, or senator who did not come to visit him every night. They genuflected in front of him before taking their leave.

To keep up appearances, Badri Khanom had addressed Shuri Khanom in the formal manner. She had referred to her as a respectable lady so that she would understand her own worth and act like a refined gentlewoman. But Shuri Khanom had continued to be stubborn. "Let me tell you something straightaway and make it clear to you where I stand. I am not a respectable lady or some such rubbish. You have to call me 'Fleur.'"

"Why, Shuri-jun?"

"Shuri-jun was taken away by a monster. If you are talking to me, call me 'Fleur-jun.'"

"What for?"

"Because I like it!"

"Eh, eh, eh . . . may God kill me."

"I am free. I'll live as I wish. Don't bother to issue edicts to me."

Eftekhar Khanom had lost her temper. She had hit her fists on her knees and blurted out, "The uglier the monkey, the more coquettish it is."

Now Shuri Khanom walked deliberately to the middle of the reception hall and arrogantly responded to the other ladies' greetings. She stood in front of Shahrokh Jannati and examined him with scorn, as if asking why he didn't offer her his seat. "Have you been raised under a bush, or have they not taught you their ways yet?"

Shahrokh was stunned. He looked around and asked, "Why?"

"Haven't they taught you to offer your seat to newly arrived women?" She pulled up a chair and sat in it. "These kinds of formalities are not important to me. The only things that matter to me are the feelings underlying them." She put a cigarette in the corner of her mouth, and although Shahrokh had already lit a match for her, she merely thanked him with a nod of her head. She took a delicate silver lighter from her own purse and quickly lit her cigarette. She held the brass flap of her leather purse firmly between her fingers and swung the tip of her shoe. "Love goes hand in hand with respect."

Shahrokh winked at the guests surreptitiously, meaning he was not in league with Shuri Khanom. He raised his eyebrows in exaggerated surprise and said, "Is that right? So that's how it is!"

"A crazy person can be both respectful and in love."

Shahrokh winked again and said, "So he can be both respectful and in love."

During this entire time, Shuri Khanom surveyed her surroundings from the corner of her eye, as if maintaining absolute control. Then she rose and followed Madame, who was taking the guests up to the second and third floors for a tour of the renovations. Nuri, who was watching Shuri Khanom, followed her. Perhaps she had a message for him from Soraya. This alone could explain her coming to the family party. She generally preferred to mingle with people who were much younger than herself. Nuri took the stairs and walked past the guests who were returning to the hall. He was certain Shuri Khanom would soon show up. Pretending he needed to wash his hands, he went into the bathroom and shut the door. Some time passed, but he didn't hear anything. He opened the bathroom door slowly and saw Shuri Khanom in the middle of the corridor. Taking advantage of the situation, he climbed the next flight of stairs, and when he reached the third-floor balcony, he breathed a sigh of relief. He had a few minutes before Shuri Khanom got there.

The lights on the Tajrish Bridge made the sky a pinkish orange. The noise of moving cars reached the garden from far away, along with the rare metallic sound of a car horn. Like an invisible eraser, dusk rubbed out the faint outlines and shadows of buildings from the azure foothills of the Alborz Mountains. In their place, lights glittered in faraway windows. Nuri stretched out on an easy chair. In the fading light, his eyes fell on Shuri Khanom, who now stood in the doorway, hands resting on her waist. Instead of offering the usual greeting, like a Spanish dancer she twisted her arms around each other and held them above her head: "Taadaa!"

Her playacting was not new to Nuri. Shuri Khanom always behaved this way with the younger members of the family. She rested the palm of her hand on the wall behind Nuri and leaned toward him. She spoke in a low voice that seemed taunting. "Do you know me?"

"Why shouldn't I? Of course, I know you."

"You're lying. Let me straighten you out right away. Knowing me is not that easy."

"So it's not."

"Tell me, how are you? Why don't you visit your uncle? Why don't you ask about us? We miss you. All the sensible relatives call and ask about our health, but you never do. We only hear about you from Soraya and Buki." The autumn air was so light and cool that the guests' chatter downstairs could easily be heard up there. Shuri Khanom smiled at Nuri and continued. "You are no longer a child. God be praised, you have reached the age to know the proper rules of etiquette. I don't consider myself that important, and I'm not one for formal niceties. I'm so indifferent to them that Amiz Hosein gets annoyed. He says I go too far. I say, 'One's creativity is not in one's own hands. I was born this way and have to live accordingly.' In life, I put a lot of emphasis on compassion. Everyone makes mistakes. You can't condemn her to the end of her life because she has done this and she hasn't done that—this very Soraya of ours. What's wrong with her that they talk so much behind her back? Why doesn't anybody accept that all her actions are the result of her lack of experience?"

"Which Soraya?"

"How many Sorayas do we have? That same Soraya Tahmasbi who, God be praised, I've heard you take to cafés. Why don't you call her anymore? You know very well that Soraya is very sensitive and gets hurt easily. If I were you, I would call her and ask how she was doing. I would prove to her that I am sensitive to her feelings."

"I should call?"

"Why not? What's wrong with calling a friend and making her happy? Will you lose something if you use a couple of simple words to apologize to a friend who's been hurt? Make her feel better."

"Do you know Soraya calls our house a hundred times a day just to swear at me and embarrass me?"

"Oh, dear Father! How simple you are, Nuri-jun!"

"To tell you the truth, if I knew things were going to turn out so badly, I would never have invited Soraya to a café and got myself into such a tight spot. I will not stay here any longer. As soon as it becomes possible, I'll go to New York."

Shuri Khanom threw a sarcastic glance at him and smiled. "Suppose you get your acceptance today, do you think it's easy to leave? Changing countries is not like changing clothes."

"I said, 'I want to leave.' I didn't say 'I want to change countries.' The important thing for me is to leave. I can't stay here and stagnate, listening to thousand-year-old things for the rest of my life. As soon as I receive my admission letter, I'll go to New York, quick as the wind."

Shuri Khanom narrowed her eyes. "Do whatever you want. That's your business. But you have to think of Soraya as well. When she gets up in the mornings, that poor dear sits tailor style on her bed and arranges the photographs from Madame's old album around herself like playing cards. She rests her head on her chin and just stares at the pictures."

Nuri couldn't keep from laughing. "Is that right? Has she told you to report these things to me?"

She turned her head away, putting a lid on the matter. "If I were you, I wouldn't let Soraya get cross with me, but you know best!"

"She puts the pictures on her bed and looks at them? What for? What pleasure can she draw from looking at people she doesn't know?"

"Actually, people we don't know are much more fun than people we do know. Speaking to people we know is driven by laziness. It opens up a comfortable realm for us to relax in and not worry about encountering any surprises. Isn't that so?"

She threw a meaningful glance at Nuri and bit her lip. Nuri shrugged his shoulders. "I get lazy too."

"It's been a week since they started preparing for Cyrus's wedding. Mrs. Tahmasbi constantly goes shopping with pretty Pari and calls her 'Pari Khanom.' Pari wears a new dress each day and brags to everyone. Becoming a new bride gives her some leverage." She took a lipstick from her purse and applied such a thick layer to her lips that they became red like a ripe tomato. "If you can, call Soraya this very night and placate her a bit. A soft fabric needs caressing." She pressed her lips together a few times to spread the lipstick smoothly. She tidied her hair. "Wonderful, how sweet it is here!" She threw an admiring glance down toward the garden. "How nicely you have arranged this place. Like the moon. When you look at these plants, you are reminded of Hawaii." She grew pensive. "You have to back down a bit, be a little more gentle. How old was I when I lost that sweet husband of mine? Anyone in my shoes would have renounced her faith and killed herself, but I soldiered on and finally reached my goal. Thanks be to God, I now have a healthy child and a guardian as well."

She had already started back down the stairs when Nuri shouted, "Shuri Khanom! Shuri Khanom!" She stopped. She turned and said, "Let's rejoin the guests."

In the reception hall, they were dragging the blind Amiz Abbas to the center of the room, begging him to sing "Don't Go to the Dome" with Amiz Hosein. Amiz Abbas stood holding his cane and sang: "Don't go to the Dome, because you have spirit, you have wings, and you are my beloved. . . . " Dr. Jannati played the role of Amin al-Zarteh, and Eftekhar Khanom took on the role of the old spinster. They had a joke competition and asked each other funny questions that the guests answered. "Aghajan, tell me what is as wide as a cave, but whatever goes in it does not come out?"

At a quarter past ten, the party was coming to an end. The telephone rang, and Vaziri picked it up. It was for Grandpa Senator. Amiz Abbas started on his way. With the tip of his cane, he pointed toward the garden. "Do you smell the cool water? It seems it was right here where I slipped on a stone. In childhood, no matter how many times they tell you not to go to the spring alone because you will fall in and drown, you do not understand. For children, going under water is like watching a nickelodeon. It was lucky that my mother arrived. The minute she sees my hair, she asks herself why the water lilies have turned golden. When she realizes that the golden water lilies are my hair, she hits herself on the head with both hands. She screams, calling, 'O Muslims, O people, help! My child is drowning!'" Still holding his cane, he turned his head heavenward and imitated his departed mother. "Naneh Taghi pulls my tongue out of my throat, holds me upside down by the ankles, and hits the back of my poor head so many times I start coughing and vomit a big bucket of water."

He began to laugh aloud, but the guests continued leaving the garden in groups. Black Najmeh and Vaziri started collecting the dishes. The Senator sat on a chair in a corner and tucked his feet under him. With one hand, he held the tea glass between his knees, and with the other he stirred the teaspoon in the glass. He fixed his gaze on something behind Nuri. "Why are you still here?"

"I'm waiting for Ladan to come back."

The phone rang again. Before anyone answered, it stopped ringing. The Senator beckoned to Nuri. "Come here. I told you I was going to think about your trip to New York for a while. First of all, a child your age shouldn't hang out at a stranger's all the time, especially at the Tahmasbis'. Nobody knows what hellhole they were driven from. Acquiring respect is each person's responsibility. If you don't respect yourself, you can't expect others to respect you. You have to think about your studies to avoid becoming a loafer like Shahrokh Jannati."

"If Shahrokh were a loafer, they wouldn't let him go to America."

"That kind of going to America is good only for the offspring of Dr. Jannati. He who wants to go to America has to be studious and industrious. I have thought about it. I'm not shoveling in money that I should send you to America just for an outing. If you pursue your studies and your grades go up, fine, we will send you to America. Otherwise, you will go straight from your school to the Alborz boarding school. End of discussion."

Nuri was shocked. "Grandpa, I won't go."

Grandpa Senator leaned forward and asked, "What did Your Highness say?"

Nuri regained his composure. "Nothing. I wanted to say I can study better in New York."

"He who wants to study can do so in any barn."

Madame approached them, put her arm in Grandpa Senator's, and together they walked slowly toward the house. Black Najmeh pulled open the curtain in the window of her room. Her shadow narrowed diagonally on the opposite wall and made her seem as thin as she was years ago when at dawn she would throw her chador over her head and leave the apartment to buy bread.

❖ ❖ ❖ 8 ❖ ❖ ❖

Nuri was ready to leave, but he couldn't understand why he was feeling out of sorts. Why did the world that stretched from the garden gate to eternity seem so strange to him? Why did it seem so far away? The unfamiliar appeared encircled by imaginary halos. Perhaps his waiting for Ladan was just an excuse to stay home. Ladan was not a child and didn't need to comply with his wishes.

When Ladan finally returned, she greeted him quickly and superficially. She showed him a bouquet of flowers she had brought home for Madame and the Senator's wedding anniversary. As she changed out of her clothes, she talked about the streets being crowded, people gathering in groups on sidewalks, and occasional scuffles between demonstrators and the police. But no shots had been fired. She had spoken to the famous poet M. G. Shabkhiz on the phone for a few minutes and told him how the erratic circulation of traffic had changed. Nuri was reminded of his childhood days spent around the university. No doubt people were now gathered in front of the Nahid Pharmacy, discussing the Asian World Cup Games. The Japanese wrestler Hashomoto, weighing more than three hundred kilos, throws Rahmati so hard that Rahmati's spleen ruptures and he needs an operation. Humba Humba, the African boxer, knocks out Ahmadi in the fourth round. At this precise moment, Soraya was probably listening to the radio in her room or lying on her side reading a novel. Colonel Tahmasbi and Mr. Ra'oof would be playing a game of backgammon over a meal of *chelo* kebab. Anticipating bad news, Mrs. Tahmasbi would run out into the alley every few minutes. Then she would shut the door, take up needle and thread, sit in a corner of the storage room, and sew buttons back on shirts. A handful of scattered images of Nuri's own making. Unlike Ladan and M. G. Shabkhiz, Nuri did not need to brand people as Tudeh, National Front, Third Line, or Fedayee. Ladan was afraid of running into an ordinary killer, like those whose pictures are published in newspapers: Ahmad Doroshkehchi, son of Hemmat, birth certificate number such-and-such, issued from such-and-such district of Dolghuzabad.

Ladan suddenly dropped her mask of indifference and confessed that her passion for M. G. Shabkhiz's poems was frightening her. She could no longer trust herself or Shabkhiz. For some reason, she readily accepted Shabkhiz's craziness. If he wanted to lie on the grass beside Ladan, she would listen to him quietly in a receptive daze. "Khanom, will you permit me to put my head on your lap for a few minutes?" Or "Will you allow me to kiss your lips?" She never asked him, "What do you mean?" Upon reflection, M. G. Shabkhiz's poems made him either a raving lunatic or a calculating and cunning fraud. She read one of M. G. Shabkhiz's poems to Nuri:

> On the throne of the sun
> I travel
> My golden litter chased by the wind.
> May my prayer be lavishly blessed by the pure morning chill.
> I speak of pain.
> And now, I
> And this stormy pond
> And now, my course this tar-beset formidable tide
> Every moment surges to the marble throne of moonlight . . .

Ladan talked a little about her outing with M. G. Shabkhiz to the slopes of Darband Street. She spoke of light shimmering through the trees, the streaming river, and a small, cozy coffeehouse with chairs and tables facing the stream, family pictures, and an image of the shrine of Imam Hosein hanging on the stucco wall, colored lightbulbs wrapped around the neck and horns of a mountain goat, a painting of ducks and geese and women working in a field by a stream that emptied into a lake. Of the salami sandwich and ice-cold beer they had had together and how they had hit the spot. She was about to go to her room to finish an article that was due the next day when Nuri remembered that he needed to borrow money from her to buy flowers and a gift. He asked, "Do you have two or three hundred tumans to lend me?"

Ladan stared at him and asked, "What do you need the money for?"

"I want to buy Soraya a gift to pacify her. Every day she comes to Mostowfi Alley, looking for me and threatening to do this and that."

As she picked up dirty clothes strewn on the rug, she asked, "Why don't you buy her a fifty-tuman gift? A bottle of toilet water or one of those reasonably priced spray bottles of perfume at the Mehran Discount Store?"

"Will you lend me the money or not?"

"You don't understand women. The more you try to please them, the higher their expectations. If I were you, I would forget about Soraya right now."

"If I don't take her something, she'll keep getting on Grandpa's nerves, and he'll stop me from going to New York."

Ladan became exasperated. "You just have to please Grandpa Senator, not Soraya. Put an end to your relationship with Soraya and see how quickly Grandpa changes. The more you pursue Soraya and try to seal her mouth with promises, the more trouble you'll get yourself into."

"Will you lend me the money, or should I stop asking?"

"First of all, I don't have any money. Second, if I had any, I wouldn't give it to you. Do you want me to give you money so that you can get into worse trouble?"

"To hell with it. I'll get it from some other donkey."

He left Ladan's room. To spite her, he would somehow find a way and visit the Tahmasbis. In the middle of the staircase, he ran into Madame. She neither said anything nor took her gaze from him. Her face appeared placid and masked like the face of a stroke victim. The red splotches around her nose and the bags under her eyes made it seem as if she had just washed and dried her face. Nuri thought about borrowing money from her. That was a stupid idea, especially now that a compressed silence separated them like a wall. Without saying anything, Nuri went up to his own room. A few minutes later he heard Madame singing and playing the organ. She sang so softly and effortlessly that Nuri's fear dissipated. He was tempted to go into the storage room and find a few small gifts for Soraya from among Madame's knickknacks. Madame left her keys in the metal vase on the hall table; they were easy to find. But he dismissed that idea. He was changing his clothes when the door of his room opened slightly. Ladan put a bundle of banknotes on the cupboard and disappeared as quickly as she had appeared. For some time, the sound of her bare feet could be heard running down the hall. Nuri decided to go after her, but there was no sign of her.

Nuri would go to the Tahmasbis and sincerely confess his mistakes. Now he had enough money to buy a bouquet of flowers and to return to Mrs. Tahmasbi the money she had given him for the pharmacy.

On the downward slope of the street, he kept his feet on the bicycle pedals, lifted himself from the seat, and traveled as fast as the wind. The numbers on the houses, the water and electricity plaques, and the holes dug in sidewalks for telephone cables all passed in a jumble before his eyes. Until he reached the area around the university, he didn't see anyone who might have dissuaded him from continuing on his path. But when he was about to pass the Amirabad Body Shop, he became anxious about running into Cyrus Tahmasbi. He took a detour by the gas station and the stationery store and passed the children's clothing store and the electrical and household appliance store. The neon Majidiyeh beer sign shone a moonlight blue in the window of the liquor store. Inside the store, a ceiling lamp produced a triangle of light that reflected a brassy yellow on the counter and made the customers' shadowlike outlines appear dim and dingy. The tripe seller's counter was open toward the street. Above the cauldron, green, red, and white bulbs were strung along a black cord and made the empty tables and chairs look drab.

A few steps ahead of him, he spotted Buki getting off his bike to have a look inside the stores. Then he stood on the sidewalk and recorded his accounts in a small notebook, mumbling the figures to himself. If he saw Nuri, he didn't let on. Just before the intersection, he got on his bike and pedaled up their alley.

Nuri had never gone to a flower shop alone. For a seventeen-year-old boy, buying a bouquet of flowers was tantamount to confessing to an illicit affair. The salesclerk attended to him with a kind of *bazaari* shrewdness— as if wanting to know what such an adolescent boy intended to do with a large bundle of tuberoses.

Nuri held the bouquet with both hands in order to present it more easily to Mrs. Tahmasbi. As always, the apartment door was open. He saw no one until he got close to the kitchen where running water and clattering dishes could be heard. Mrs. Tahmasbi was dressed in an ordinary cotton shift. Her legs were bare, and she wore open-toed sandals. Standing in front of the kitchen sink, she took potatoes from a metal colander and peeled them one by one. She heaved sighs of pleasure, as if attempting to satisfy an unquenchable thirst. As she held a peeled potato under the running tap, she suddenly turned and gave a little scream of delight. "Oh my, dust be on my head, Naneh-jun! It's not as if you have dropped in on strangers that you should bring flowers. What is this? Why do you put us to shame?" She took the flowers, held them half a meter away, and smelled them. She filled a brass jug with water and daintily arranged the flowers in it. She stood back and looked at them. "I must show them to Sori-jun. Sori-jun loves flowers. When she sees tuberoses, she faints." She closed her eyes and heaved a deep sigh. "Oh, what a wonderful smell! My head is spinning."

She placed the jug on the kitchen counter. With the back of her hand, she brushed a few strands of hair away from her forehead. She was careful not to touch her face with her wet fingers. The frenetic shifting of her blue eyes was at odds with the gentle movements of her hands. Her clothes were chosen for comfort, not style. She picked up a lit cigarette from an ashtray on a shelf, tapped its ashes, and put it in the corner of her mouth. "Should I pour you some tea?" She replaced the cigarette in the ashtray and forgot to pour the tea. She held the aluminum colander under the tap to wash the potatoes again. "Naneh-jan, where have you been? How are you? I'm always asking Buki about you. He hasn't heard from you, either. I said I hope nothing bad has happened. I said to our neighbor . . . Do you remember Mrs. Malahati?"

"No."

"The one whose son mortgaged their house and went to Canada."

"No, I don't remember any of that."

"Why not? Think a little. I'm sure you'll remember. I told her, 'Shohreh Khanom, have you seen Nuri Hushiar around here?' She said, 'Which

Nuri Hushiar?' Now, whether she had forgotten you or was just pretending, I don't know. In this neighborhood, everyone has developed amnesia.
I said, 'Khanom-jun, how many Nuri Hushiars do we have? Nuri Hushiar
means Nuri Hushiar.' Her eyes glistened. Then she said, 'Do you mean the
son of the departed engineer Hushiar? May I die. May God rest his soul.
What a pity!' We remembered your father very fondly. What a pity that all
his education, because of an accident, for no good reason . . . "

Nuri finished Mrs. Tahmasbi's sentence. " . . . was scattered to the
wind."

Mrs. Tahmasbi was surprised. For a few seconds she looked at him
questioningly. "What do you mean was scattered to the wind? Your father
was quite a character in his own right. Many, many times they wanted
him dead. Thank God the Colonel came to his rescue. But I should tell
you this as well. The Colonel is not at all concerned with people's political views. He says everyone is free to think as he wishes as long as he
doesn't bother others or try to destroy the country. He and your father
used to travel around together a lot. They were supposed to go to Aba-
dan along with Mr. Ra'oof when that accident happened and ruined all
their plans." She shook her head regretfully and puckered her lips. "We
don't understand God's work. Sweet people like your father have to go to
the grave in their youth so that ne'er-do-wells like Mr. Malahati can stay
alive. Your father was not the *bazaari* type who are only after money and
turn into sycophants with their little bit of stolen cash. But these Mala-
hatis are so chintzy that they like whatever they see. They have heard
the Colonel's name mentioned so much in this neighborhood that now
they think they too can consider themselves influential. Your Maman
Zuzu did the best thing by going to America. I hope she doesn't think of
returning soon. Is she missing a brain that she would come back to this
barn and end up talking to people like Shohreh Khanom Malahati? Do
you know what they say about her? They say if Zuzu Khanom goes to
America, why can't we?"

Nuri changed the topic. "Is Buki home?"

"Do you never miss us?" She lifted the lid off a pot. Steam rose up
in her face, and the smell of *abgusht* filled the kitchen. "My tomatoes are
turning mushy. Let me lower the gas a bit." She spooned up a little *abgusht*

and tasted it. "I don't think it has enough salt. It needs more. " She asked, "Did you receive the invitation to Cyrus's wedding?"

"Am I invited too?"

"Of course. If you are not invited, who should be? Mr. Senator and Madame are also invited. We will be very happy to have you at the wedding. Your presence will honor us."

"When is the wedding?"

"The eighteenth of Azar." She took the water jug from the counter. "Let's take the flowers to the living room for everyone to see."

"I saw Buki a few minutes ago. He was heading home."

"He never tells me about his comings and goings. He shows up in the kitchen only when he's hungry or needs his clothes ironed." She walked ahead. "Let me show these to the Colonel. No doubt he'll think Cyrus has sent these flowers to his Pari-jun. If Cyrus does not send her flowers for even one day, she pouts and won't touch her food. I have to cajole her for three hours before she agrees to talk to him. She says men should not be spoiled. Otherwise, they'll ride herd on you."

She bit her lip anxiously and looked at Nuri from the corner of her eye.

Nuri followed Mrs. Tahmasbi's every step. Even when they got closer to the living room, there was no change in the pressing silence. He expected Soraya to be away from all eyes, but Buki never hid himself. He had no reservation about meeting people. The fading red furniture covers, the dark gray spots on the brass samovar, and the obscured patterns of its handles molded a comfortable space within which Nuri could forget himself. In the semidarkness of the corridor, whispers could be heard and cigarette smoke permeated the air. The gray light of dusk passed in front of the living-room door, turned the door frame the color of an overcast sky, and reflected the vague shadows of the Colonel and Mr. Ra'oof beneath the window, two bent heads three centimeters apart. Around them, darkness outlined the furniture in the living room. Mr. Ra'oof was dressed in a white shirt, flannel pants, and slippers. He shook the dice in one hand and with the other took grapes out of a brown bag on the table and put them in his mouth. He taunted the Colonel. "Colonel, dear, wait. Right now I'll smoke your mustache with a pair of fives."

Mrs. Tahmasbi put the jug on the radiator. Almost hurriedly she went from one corner of the room to the other, raised her eyebrows in fake disdain to indicate her impatience. Finally, she shouted at the Colonel and Mr. Ra'oof. "Baba-jun, that's enough. We've lost our patience. Get up, go out. Get some fresh air and liven up."

The Colonel moved his finger from one backgammon piece to another. He could not decide. "If I were Cyrus, I would deposit the money spent on these flowers into a bank account to have something to fall back on when my wife's belly swells up six months from now. Getting married and having children is expensive. . . . Ra'oof, have you said your last prayers? Or should I say them for you?"

Mrs. Tahmasbi interrupted him. "Colonel, you don't even raise your head from . . . " She didn't finish her sentence, but instead turned her face in anger. "There is no God but God, they force me to say something. Colonel, you who haven't taken your eyes off the backgammon board, how can you tell who has brought this bouquet of flowers?"

"I know from their suffocating stench. Whenever Cyrus brings tuberoses for his Pari-jun, I feel suddenly as if I am suffocating in my own house. I don't have the endurance of the old days anymore. I am sick. I have asthma." He lifted his head. As soon as he saw Nuri, his eyes glistened, and he began to laugh. He got up and hobbled a few steps toward Nuri. "How wonderful, Nuri dear! How unkind you have become! How rarely you show up here! Agha-jun, where have you been?"

Mrs. Tahmasbi showed him the flowers. "See how he puts us to shame. Smell this, Colonel. Please, come on, on Sori-jun's life. Take a deep breath! Our house is filled with the smell of tuberoses just like a greenhouse."

The Colonel's laughter slowly changed into successive, deep coughs. "How nice!" He put his nose to the flowers and appeared to grow faint. He stood still for a few seconds before opening his eyes. "Nuri-jan, the next bouquet we will bring for your wedding. We are most obliged. I wish our children were this attentive to their own parents or at least showed a little respect for those who have sacrificed their own lives for the sake of their children's happiness. We have no expectations. We hope only that, if nothing else, at least we should not be hurt by them. I swear by your own dear life, may my own Buki die, I am constantly running around this apartment like a chicken with its head cut off, looking for a cubbyhole with unpolluted air to avoid these coughing fits." He raised his palms parallel to each other and held Nuri's face between them. He planted a loud kiss on each cheek and threw a hesitant glance at the others. Nuri asked, "Colonel, are you feeling well?"

A hurt look returned to the Colonel's eyes. "What should I say? I am still breathing, and we manage somehow."

"You? Looking so happy and fit?"

The Colonel was pleased. He turned to Mr. Ra'oof and said, "Did you hear? He says: 'Looking so happy and fit.'"

"What did you want him to say? You shouldn't take ordinary pleasantries so seriously. Come, throw the dice now. It's getting late."

Nuri noticed a hand-painted curtain with blue patterns against a beige background descending from the ceiling and dividing the living room like a prayer screen. Perhaps the Tahmasbis had a guest who was staying overnight, and they wanted to give him a separate space. A small apartment with open doors had room for everyone and every event. Even if it didn't seem as if they could, they made room somehow. Nuri heard low voices from behind the curtain, soft like bare feet treading on a rug. It seemed as if things were being rearranged. The hem of the curtain moved constantly, and air wafted through—the stale air of leather suitcases and dry herbs. The smell of a rented house with a layer of grease and dust that made the furniture the color of the glaze on leftover soup.

How easily he accepted things! How readily he put himself in control of events! Even Soraya's entrance appeared to him more ordinary than a daily change of clothes and the morning washup. She wore a light brown polka-dot dress, black stockings with runs in them up to her thighs, and heavy shoes that looked like army boots. Impatient and disheveled, like a person who has just awakened from sleep, she walked alongside the curtain. She frowned and without any greeting sat near the Colonel and Mr. Ra'oof on the sofa whose faded red velvet cover looked white, as in old rugs.

Everyone knew that Mrs. Tahmasbi couldn't tolerate such silence. Sooner or later she would do something and create a scene. The Colonel stopped playing. He put his hands on his knees and stared at Mrs.

Tahmasbi intensely, as if he wanted to nail her to the wall. Mrs. Tahmasbi suddenly put her fingers to her lips in astonishment and bolted
up. "Naneh-jan, what are these things called? Oh God, what happened
to the mixed nuts I brought home day before yesterday?" She gave her
voice a tinge of excitement and encouragement. "Sori-jun, look. See what
Nuri-jun has brought us?" She held a finger under one of the flowers and
anxiously swallowed her smile.

Soraya asked, "Don't we have freshly made tea?"

Mrs. Tahmasbi threw a disgruntled glance at the ceiling. "Who has
ever had old tea in this house that this should be your second time?" She
took the jug from the radiator and placed it on Soraya's lap. "They come
from a long way to see you; they spend huge sums of money and bring
you a beautiful bouquet like this. Then you sit on the sofa and ask me to
bring you fresh tea?"

Soraya asked, "Are these special, or have we never seen flowers before?
Anyway, why has this agha come here? If he wants us to sizzle, well, there
is no sizzle left in us. Why doesn't he go after some other unfortunate person so that we can at least breathe easily in our own apartment?"

The Colonel spoke softly, discreetly, and reproachfully to signal that
he was establishing a father-daughter relationship. "Shame on you, girl!
Why do you speak such nonsense, Father dear? This gentleman is a friend
of your brother. His family has always treated us kindly."

Mrs. Tahmasbi sat beside Soraya and said, "Where have you learned
to behave like this, Naneh-jan? Nuri Khan is our guest. Since when is it
customary to disparage a guest in your own house?"

Turning to Nuri, Soraya shouted, "Agha, why have you come here?
After those despicable things you did, how dare you enter our house?"

She left no room for Nuri to feign ignorance. He sat in a chair opposite
her, locked his hands under his knee, and spoke slowly and almost formally. "I have come to see Buki."

Soraya didn't wait. "Why do you drag out your words like Germans
do? Buki is not here. Moreover, he doesn't want to see anyone."

"A mere half hour ago he was on the street riding his bike toward
home."

"You were mistaken. Go back to your own house. What do you want with us?"

Nuri said, "Soraya Khanom, allow me to say something." He rose, rubbing his chin. " . . . I don't want to disturb you. Buki knows me very well. Ask him. If I have said something to hurt you, I apologize. I am your servant." He looked at the others for support. "If I offended you, please forgive me. I did not mean it."

Soraya's anger erupted. "You, you hooligan, you are worse than the rest of them. You are worse than Madame and the Senator. At least they have enough pride to act human. But, by God's power, you have nothing. You don't even have the brains to pass your exams like Buki." Anger made tears well up in her eyes. "Do you want me to tell you? I want you to be so hurt in this world that no matter how you burn, no one will come to your aid." She threw herself in Mrs. Tahmasbi's arms. " . . . Stupid, what had I done to you that you planted me in the café and ran away? Worse yet, that Khachator, Armenian dog that he is, should come and take my purse for ransom and ruin my reputation in front of a bunch of strangers? You have ruined me, O shameful, mean traitor! Wait until this same calamity happens to you, then you'll understand what I have suffered at your hands."

She began cursing again and shouted even more angrily. Nuri's mistake was to offer more apologies. "Buki is my witness. Ask him to come in and prove . . . "

Apparently only one thing could satisfy Soraya: to see Nuri drop to his knees and drag himself through muck. As she said, "I break the horns of self-satisfied and arrogant people like you to make them understand who their opponent is. I know you very well. Now you're using Buki as an excuse to betray and hurt me?"

"I swear on my mother's life, I had no such intention."

"So who was the idiot who left me in the Parand Pastry Shop and fled? To imagine that I would belittle myself and go to a café with a ruffian like you! From now on, if I go out, it will be with thugs from Chaleh Maidun who are more worthy than any Madame and Senator with their unwashed asses. There's obviously something wrong with me that I go out with a dishonorable person like you." Turning toward Mrs. Tahmasbi, she said, "I went out with him because I felt sorry for him. I said let him be seen on the street with me, let him brag a little about the beauty walking arm in arm with him. Perhaps he could be counted among human beings." She turned to face Nuri again. "Now you have to go somewhere else. Nothing is happening here. That piece was taken away by the monster."

The Colonel and Mrs. Tahmasbi exchanged glances. The Colonel addressed Nuri haltingly. "I think it might be better for you to come another day to visit Buki. He is not feeling well today. He has a headache. He has asked not to be wakened."

Nuri apologized. "It doesn't matter. I won't disturb him. If he were awake, no doubt he would prove my innocence to Soraya Khanom."

Soraya attacked Nuri. "Are you deaf, mule? When you have been asked to leave, you should not degrade yourself this much. Don't you have friends and acquaintances around your house?"

Mrs. Tahmasbi and the Colonel half stood, but sat down again. Nuri said, "I'll come another time. I'd appreciate it if you let me know when Buki is feeling better. I'm devoted to all of you."

Deep down, Nuri knew that Buki was behind the curtain, perhaps even watching him with a few others. Nevertheless, when Shuri Khanom stepped out from behind the curtain, he was shocked and stepped back. Shuri Khanom wore a blue dress with a pear-shaped, puffed collar. She went straight to Nuri and said, "Hello, Nuri-jun. Are you well?" She ran her hands under the flowers. "Did you bring these, Nuri-jun? What good taste! Tuberoses are my favorite flowers. One day I paid the city one hundred and fifty tumans for the neighborhood upkeep fees and bought four baskets of tuberoses and a piece of needlework cashmere. Amiz Hosein went wild. 'Khanom, the way you waste money, you will land us on the street with a begging bowl by the beginning of next month.' Nuri-jun, bravo! I am pleased. You have good taste."

Nuri pulled himself together. He said, "It's nothing." He looked at his watch. "My watch has stopped. What time is it? If it's past six, I have to hurry back."

Shuri Khanom insisted. "Stay. Let's have dinner together. It's on me. Let's go to a pizzeria."

"They are waiting for me at home. They'll worry; otherwise I would stay."

"Pick up the phone right now and call Madame. Tell her from me not to worry. I myself will take you back in my car."

"No, I have to go."

Soraya spoke up. "Let him go to his grave." Addressing Nuri, she said, "Uncle, get up, go already. What are you waiting for?"

Mrs. Tahmasbi said, "Sori-jun, Shuri Khanom is right. Let's go out for a pizza. Mr. Ra'oof, will you come as well?"

Mr. Ra'oof nodded. "Why not? I have no prior engagements."

Shuri Khanom whispered in Nuri's ear. "Soraya shouts a lot, but inside she is very sensitive. She's not like me and won't act humble."

Soraya shouted, "Shuri-jun, who says I am sensitive? Why should I be sensitive? You mean because of this cadaver?"

Soraya raised her hand and smacked Nuri's face. Shuri Khanom ran and grabbed her shoulders. "Sori-jun, that's enough. You are going too far. Sometimes, it's better to show some gentility." She turned to Nuri, "Sori-jun's only flaw is her kindness. She trusts everyone quickly. She turns everyone into an idol." She ran her hand over Soraya's face and murmured, "Why do you hurt yourself so much?" She spoke to Nuri in an ordinary tone. "Don't judge by appearances; she curses out of affection. Even her shouts are from affection. Nothing stays in her heart because she is kind. If you go up to her room right now, you'll see how she has arranged the pictures from Madame's album around her bed so that she can look at them whenever she wants. . . . " She looked at Soraya, who was pretending to be asleep in her arms. "Yes, if it were not affection, she would not pay this much attention to details and humiliate herself in front of so many people."

Soraya pulled away from Shuri Khanom's arms and ran up to her room. The Colonel leaned back in his seat with half-closed eyes. Mrs. Tahmasbi put her fist to her mouth. "Eh!"

Mr. Ra'oof stood up, looked into the wall mirror, and brushed his eyebrows. Nuri heard soft voices behind the curtain. If Buki were there, he would pull him out and ask him right there and then why he was cross with him. He didn't know, but maybe he would even get into a normal fight with him. Buki did everything according to secret plans. He would avenge Soraya and get even. It was better for Nuri to leave. Let the Tahmasbis say whatever they wanted behind his back. Good for them.

Shuri Khanom raised her eyebrows. "So, it's not for nothing that I say this girl is sensitive. I know something." She turned toward the Colonel and Mr. Ra'oof. "I promise she will get over this." She addressed Nuri. "Come upstairs with me."

While Shuri Khanom went ahead of him into Soraya's room, Nuri ran a hand over his hair and straightened his collar. From inside the room came the voice of a radio announcer for the *Request Program,* answering letters and playing listeners' favorite records. He stepped to the door and saw Soraya seated on her bed. She paid no attention to Shuri Khanom, who walked toward the window to turn off the radio. Soraya listlessly placed Madame's photographs side by side on the coverlet. Madame and the Senator's wedding picture, with the Senator's spotless summer suit giving him the semiformal appearance of a person at a cocktail party. Madame and Princess Bertha by Lake Como, with faint shadows making Madame's white silk dress seem pleated and starched. Her long white gloves came up to her elbows. Princess Bertha wearing a slippery, bespangled dress and a narrow-brimmed hat whose velvet rippled like lamb's wool. Behind the two women, the hills grew distant from the sandy shores of the lake and faded away.

Nuri waited in the doorway until Shuri Khanom urged him to come in. She asked, "Why are you taking so long?"

Nuri sat on the rug and opened the conversation with a few commonplaces. "What a cozy room!"

He didn't say this directly to Soraya. He focused on the slogans on the walls, written in a felt-tip pen and framed in rectangles and squares similar to designs on tombstones. Strange and marginal memories such as the shade on the hurricane lamp, the crooked antenna of the transistor radio, or the wooden shelves that didn't match each other. Soraya removed a pack of cigarettes from her bosom and held a cigarette sideways in her fingers. Nuri took a match out of the box. "Should I light it?"

Soraya did not speak. Shuri Khanom reprimanded her jokingly. "That's enough, Sori-jun. Why don't you let him light your cigarette?"

Soraya held her cigarette over the match flame and, like old ladies, exhaled a big puff of smoke from her nostrils. Shuri Khanom was so worried that she didn't take her eyes off Nuri while she spoke to Soraya. "Sori-jun, aren't you feeling well?"

"I'm feeling fine."

Nuri interjected, "Are you really, really feeling fine?"

"I wouldn't have said it if I didn't feel fine."

"Would you permit me to say something?"

"You've already said it all. Now get up and go after your own business."

Shuri Khanom jumped in. "Oh, where should he go? He has come to see you."

Soraya raised her eyebrows and addressed Shuri Khanom arrogantly. "I like him so much, but he plays coy with me. . . . From his childhood, the minute no one was watching, he would come into my room and ask me to scare him. He would say, 'Soraya Khanom, say boo and startle me.' I would say, 'You big bear, why do you so much like being scared?' He would grin to make me feel sorry for him and scare him again. He is that same scared and gangly child who now wears American clothes and grows his hair down to his shoulders like a dervish. Then he abandons me in a café and doesn't even show his face for weeks. So you wanted to do something; you did it and made a mess of it. Shouldn't you at least come to see me once and ask what's happened to me during these weeks?"

She spoke agitatedly. Shuri Khanom said, "Sori-jun, you mustn't assume that Nuri's actions are directed at you. Perhaps something happened, and there was a reason he had to leave you in the café."

"This precious guy sees himself apart from everyone. He mingles more with strangers than with relatives."

"On your own life, may my Daryan die, whenever Nuri sees me, he asks about you. He begs to know when Soraya Khanom will permit him to visit her. I say to him, 'She is still angry with you and doesn't have the patience to see you. You have to wait a long time.' Still he doesn't give up. He keeps pleading."

"Don't take his side. As long as you are with him, he is all smiles and jokes. Then he leaves and is never heard from again." She turned to Nuri.

"You always want to be somewhere else. You're always waiting to pack up and leave. What's with you? Why do you come here so often anyway?"

"Because I feel at home here."

Soraya tilted her head and laughed hysterically. "You feel at home here?"

"Why not?"

"Should I hit you on the head?"

"Soraya Khanom, I am your servant."

"Had I said something behind your back? Had I stolen from you? The couple of gifts you gave me, you brought on your own. Nobody put you under pressure."

"I got scared."

"Of what?"

"Of being seen arm in arm with a beautiful and stylish woman like you and going to a café with you right in front of all the neighborhood boys."

"So why didn't you ever lose your nerve all those other times you hung out in our apartment?"

"I was a child then. I didn't understand very well. I thought of this place as my own home."

"Oh, yeah. Already as a child, you were in love with me." She said to Shuri Khanom, "What a lewd gaze this child had! Just the way he looked at you made you want to cover yourself. He would bring me roses and pictures of movie stars. He would sit by the staircase and look under my skirt as I climbed the stairs. . . . He told the neighbors, 'What beautiful blue eyes Soraya Khanom has, but it's too bad her nose is too big.'"

"I said that? To whom?"

Soraya covered half of her face with her hair. "When I passed his school, I don't know how he found out, but he came out right away. He was mischievous even as a child. Their assistant principal measured the circumference of his head with a string to find out when he would reach puberty. Nuri had made a bet with the boys over who would hit puberty first."

Shuri Khanom winked at Nuri. "What a rascal!"

Soraya continued, " . . . He would say, 'Soraya Khanom, if one of these boys bothers you, let me know, and I'll set him straight.' He said he was my bodyguard. He carried a switchblade just in case anyone looked at me askance. If I'm lying, say so." Nuri didn't reply. "No matter what you say and do, you can't hide the fact that you're crazy about me. You're dying to be with me. If that's a lie, say so. Say 'No.'"

Shuri Khanom began walking around the room and took Mr. Shirzad's framed picture, which was still sitting on the table, and put it in a cupboard drawer. She took crumpled white envelopes from the rug and looked for a trash basket. Nuri took a moment to collect himself. He said, "You are like a sister to me. Of course, I have always loved you. Is it possible not to love a sister?"

Soraya bolted up. "Get lost. If you love me like a sister, why do you bring me flowers? Someone as stingy as you doesn't take flowers to his sister. You think we were raised under a bush and don't understand anything? Say what you want, you are dying for just one kiss from me." She brought her face closer. "What will you give me if I kiss you?"

She said it in a challenging tone. Nuri stuttered. "Soraya Khanom, look . . . "

"Are you deaf? Didn't you hear what I said? If I kiss you, what will you give me?"

Nuri laughed. "You want to test me, right?" He was encouraged by Soraya's expression and said in a more serious tone, "Would you really let me kiss you?"

"Why else did I say these things?"

"Maybe you were teasing me."

Soraya raised herself halfway. "Is that so? Who has taught you this humility? Didn't you say all girls fainted at the sight of your blue eyes and blond hair?"

"Did I say that?"

Traces of anger reappeared in Soraya's face. "Get up. Get lost. You make me sick."

Shuri Khanom rubbed Soraya's shoulders. "That's enough. Make up. Let's go out together and have some pizza. You are my guest."

Soraya said, "I don't feel like it."

She suddenly grabbed the lamp and threw it at Nuri. The cord was short, and before hitting Nuri, the lamp dropped to the floor. Soraya laughed heartily. She threw the crystal ashtray at him. It missed his head and landed on the carpet upside down. Then she took the fan, but it was still plugged in. She couldn't throw it. She held it by its base and looked around for something better to throw. "Do you want me to hit you on the head with this?"

Nuri brought his head closer and said to Soraya, "OK. Hit me. Then what?"

Soraya chortled and, turning to Shuri Khanom, said, "He says, 'OK. Hit me, so what?'" She shook the fan threateningly. "Do you want me to show you how? Whatever happens is your responsibility."

Nuri was preparing himself to be struck on the head when Shuri Khanom grabbed his arm and dragged him toward the door. He didn't resist, and together they left the room. When they reached the corridor, he said, "Shuri Khanom, perhaps you understand. What does Soraya Khanom want from me?"

Now Soraya could be heard grumbling. It seemed she was still swearing at Nuri. "Your father is a dog! You've taken his imaginings for real! I prefer a swarthy complexion to blond hair and blue eyes."

Shuri Khanom ran her hand over Nuri's hair. Without looking at him, she went back to Soraya's room.

♦ ♦ ♦ 9 ♦ ♦ ♦

On Friday, Madame invited her Iranian and foreign friends to a picnic
from an hour before noon until after dusk. The guests were free to dress
as they wished, bring along whatever food they wanted, and leave at their
will. Before lunch, they went for a stroll around Darrus and had their
pictures taken. After their return, the women settled the children in the
hall and served them lunch. When the time came for others to eat, the
children were planted in front of the television to watch the World Cup
soccer game. The rest listened intermittently to the announcers' strange
sentences: "Ali Vafa'ii has distinguished himself as a world champion
throughout Asia," or "With his six goals, Sharif Amini has carved out for
himself and his teammates a proud and productive image that has prepared the World Cup for our acceptance . . . "

The men offered each other drinks in the pantry, teased one another,
and clapped to encourage Aunt Moluk and Amiz Abbas to perform
"Don't Go to the Dome." After the performance, their enthusiasm subsided. Traces of fatigue appeared on their faces. Now they clapped unen-
thusiastically. They separated into groups of two or three and arm in arm
walked along the row of poplars. The leaves had turned red, orange, and
yellow and reminded one of the approach of winter. Some of the men fell
asleep in corners of the hall; others held tea cups and talked quietly. Then
the sky developed the sheen of pearl enamel, and shadows began to move
behind lit windows. Young girls could be heard whispering underneath
the trees. The headlights of the city buses rented to transport the relatives
shone like moonlight on the bare branches and the dusty, darkening alley.
Nuri was in the rear of the garden, teaching tricks to teenagers his age:
how to swallow a kebab skewer and how to strike their palms on a knife
blade. Strange questions arose in his mind. Why was he so attached to

remote events? Why did he enjoy being among guests who were in no way connected to him?

Amid all the bustle, Madame remained strangely aloof. She talked about her plans to visit a famous physician in Vienna. When Dr. Jannati's name was mentioned, she pretended not to hear so that she would not have to consult him. She was afraid that Dr. Jannati would give her the wrong treatment, as he had his own son, Farhad, and make her condition worse. A modest smile appeared on her face. She downed a glass of Monk's Syrup in honor of the "giants" of Iranian literature. "The tedium of a life without passion!" she declared.

She took Mrs. Baxter to the third-floor balcony and asked her advice about the birthday party she was planning. She was concerned about a Siberian cold front that she had heard was moving toward the Alborz Mountains and would any day cause a frightful and ravaging storm in Varamin and Shemiranat.

For this reason, she was hiring workers to pitch three white tents with green stripes in the rear of the garden by the old spring, so that if it rained on the day of the party, lunch could be served inside the tents. The Senator and Mr. Shariat thought rain was highly improbable. After that, Madame stopped speaking of rain, but her reserved demeanor indicated that she was still concerned.

◆ ◆ ◆ Early the next morning Madame came to the hall verandah, threw a wounded glance at the clouds, and turned up her palm to make sure it wasn't raining. She suddenly noticed Nuri and asked, "What is Your Honor doing here?"

Nuri was anxious that Soraya might call. He tried to look normal. "I'm going to the pantry to eat breakfast."

"You really frightened your servant. I didn't recognize you. How strangely you look like your father!"

Nuri sat on the edge of the verandah and swung his legs. "How?"

Madame said, "Hmm, your smile. Your father had a similar shy smile that kept him distant from everyone. No? Did I say it right?" She patted the hair along her temples. "Last night I dreamed that the phone was ringing. I picked it up and said, 'Hello, hello, Papa.' Someone hung up. I came to the window and saw an Oriental bazaar. I heard a call to prayer and an owl. In an Eastern setting outside time and place. Are you in touch with Papa Javad?"

Nuri didn't know why he lied. Perhaps to stop Madame from talking too much. "At the beginning, meaning those first months after the accident, I didn't see him. I only heard his voice."

Madame's eyes glistened with delight. "Really?"

Nuri gently nodded his head. "I still hear his voice."

"What does he tell you?"

"He says he is with me wherever I go. He is always with me."

"How wonderful! No doubt you are very happy."

"Very."

"How lucky you are!"

Nuri went in for breakfast, but Madame busied herself on the verandah until Mrs. Baxter arrived. As previously agreed, they were to don black chadors and take plastic shopping bags like women from the lower quarters of the city. Visiting stores, old hostels, and popular theater agencies in Naser Khosrow Street would acquaint Mrs. Baxter with Iranian culture far better than any tourist guide. Madame would take her to arcades near the bazaar that were filled with the smell of brand-new merchandise—with their soot-covered open-beam ceilings, illegible Koranic verses on blue mosque tiles, and a black banner hoisted on a post whose sharp tip waved in the air. They would visit stores that opened onto narrow arcades where they would buy items such as tamarind, finely sifted rhinoceros liver powder, and chutney for making special pickles. Dried mushrooms as large as saucers that they would soak in water so that they could drink their extract as a cancer treatment.

Mrs. Baxter asked, "Madame, are you sick? Why don't you visit Dr. Jannati?"

Madame frowned, and a smirk appeared on her face. Then she said something about the clutter of signs, billboards, and the merchandise in the bazaar that Nuri did not follow. He saw her only from behind, as she took Mrs. Baxter to the mirror and showed her how Iranian women hold their chadors. In a secretive tone adopted by foreigners, she said, "Do not judge Iranians by Third World standards. Even if they don't know

something, they learn quickly." She lowered her voice. "They are amaz-
ingly smart."

Every time Mrs. Baxter tried to hold the chador over her head, it
slipped and made her laugh. Imitating female attendants in an Oriental
harem like the ones in *The Thief of Baghdad, Sinbad the Sailor,* and *Ali Baba
and the Forty Thieves,* she raised her eyebrows, swung her hips, and narrowed her eyes.

After their departure, Nuri grew peculiarly lonely. Black Najmeh
was busy cooking in the kitchen. Her footsteps sounded soft and remote.
A force incited him to go to the storage room. He imagined the framed
embroideries on the wall, the pattern on the hallway rug, and the sharp
band of sunlight come alive, a kind of abnormal metamorphosis with
which he had been acquainted since his elementary school days.

When the phone rang, Nuri didn't pick it up. He thought about Soraya
and how they would eventually run into each other. Impatience tugged
him like an ailment. Any shame he felt was slowly fading. He imagined
a detailed scene of lovemaking with Soraya. He wasn't embarrassed by
looking at himself in the mirror. He brushed up his bangs and let them
fall on his forehead again. He looked at himself indifferently, as if the
reflection in the mirror were not his. He did not take it for real. Most
women didn't like conceited men who spent hours in front of the mirror
adjusting their hair. Perhaps Soraya mistreated him because she thought
he was proud of his looks. Maybe her swearing was meant to deflate his
ego, but the more Soraya abused him, the more tempted Nuri became to
visit the Tahmasbis.

He busied himself for half an hour with the dumbbells and the high
bar. He listened to Black Najmeh ambling about her room. Then he washed
his face and hands in the bathroom sink and put on a pressed shirt and
pair of short pants. With the tips of his fingers he touched the banknotes
in his pocket. His money was running low. He needed money badly. Until
now he hadn't gone after Madame's money; anyway, he didn't know where
she kept it. He grew angry with himself. Why should he always resort to
someone else's money? What had poor Madame done to have to pay for
his impulses? He blamed his impulses on his need to become intoxicated
with desire. He would go to the Tahmasbis' apartment with an armful

of roses, and as soon as he got to Soraya's room, he would strew them all around. He would write in blood on the wall: "Sweet is the moment of nothingness that lasts an eternity."

He tiptoed to the third floor and took the new storage-room key from the brass vase. He unlocked the storage room, put the key in his pocket, and carefully shut the door. It smelled dusty in here, and his mouth became dry and acrid. The air prickled the skin of his bare arms and shins. The old furniture was covered in an exaggerated yellow, green, and jujube red, more suitable for an eastern European Gypsy cart or a scene in a Walt Disney cartoon. When he opened the old chest of drawers, he saw a jumble of women's pink silk underwear. Under them he found glass-beaded silver handbags with metal straps, some of which he had seen Madame carry to concerts at the Rudaki Music Hall. He didn't find any money inside them. He turned his attention to the row of starched chiffon dresses. He noticed a dark-red dress and a woman's green velvet frock coat. He had seen both of them in pictures of Princess Bertha on the covers of old records. The dress was a sleeveless silk with satin lining. It had two braided shoulder straps that tied into a butterfly in front. Princess Bertha wore this same dress in the picture on the cover of the record "A Small Café in Harnal." In the picture, she was locking her hands behind her tilted head and appeared listless. But on the cover of "Chapeau," she wore a starched frock coat that bulged over her breasts. Its hem was shaped in semicircles echoing the curves of her thighs. A pair of black fishnet stockings hugged her legs. She had a small baton under one arm, and with her other hand she tipped a top hat. She had a cheerful look that implied she was proud of her beauty.

Nuri took a plastic bag from one of the cupboard drawers and was about to put the dress into it when he suddenly saw Madame's profile and her silvery hair in the doorway. She wore flat shoes with straps and short socks that came up to her ankles. Her white cotton dress had military-style epaulets. The belt and its buckle were covered in the same white material. Why had they come back so early from shopping? Nuri looked at his watch. It was twenty minutes past noon. He had spent three-quarters of an hour in the storage room without noticing the time.

He didn't lose his nerve. He had long been anxiously awaiting such an encounter. Now that it had happened, he had nothing to worry about. He turned to offer an explanation, but Madame didn't give him a chance. She withdrew her head and left the door ajar. No question, no answer, no reprimand. Just like a villager who mistakenly walks into a room and doesn't have the wits to say hello and apologize. Nuri saw Madame's antics as a kind of European vengefulness. Instead of ambushing him, watching him from the door, she left without saying a word. Why did she not ask him who had given permission for him to go into the storage room?

Nuri put the silk dress in the cupboard and the plastic bag in the drawer. He wiped his dusty hands on his pants. He threw a glance at the bands of light that shone through the lozenge-shaped windowpane and reflected the pattern of an open fan on the opposite wall. Like an ancient building, the storage room didn't belong to anyone in particular. Anybody could take control of it. He put his head out into the hall and listened. Somewhere far away Madame and Mrs. Baxter were cheerfully saying good-bye to each other.

When he came out of the storage room, he was agitated. Maybe before anything happened, he should leave the house. At the bottom of the staircase, he saw Black Najmeh's big frame in the corridor. With secret signs and gestures, she gave him to understand that the coast was clear and he could get out without running into Madame. Little did he know that Madame was seated in a plastic lawn chair in the shade of an apple tree. On the surface, she seemed to be too absorbed in her needlework to notice anyone, but as soon as Nuri stepped into the garden, she called him, dragging out her sentence as if she had caught him stealing cookies. "Nuri-jaaan!"

"Yes?"

"Good day."

"Good day."

He walked toward the garden gate when Madame called him again. "Please come here. Do not be afraid. It's a private matter."

She put the needlework frame in her knitting bag. She took up the gardening shears from beside the hose and looked among the rose bushes. Wherever she saw an interesting flower, she rose on tiptoe, delicately snipped it, and gave it to Nuri. "Please hold this."

Nuri said nothing. Madame showed him a newly opened large rose. "Look how pretty this one is. Should I pick it?"

"If you wish."

Madame's hair was shaped like a tiara in front and tied back in a pony tail. Her palm was bleeding where thorns had pricked it. She sucked on it. "Have I told you that in the world, the only flowers without thorns are artists?" She frowned and leaned her head forward. "Are you in a bad mood?"

"No."

"Are you thinking about something?"

"A few minutes ago when you came into the storage room, you saw me there. Why didn't you say anything?"

Madame busied herself with the flowers. She said, "There was no need."

"Let me tell you . . . "

Madame stopped suddenly. She looked hurt. She shaded her eyes with her hand. "Nuri-jan, unfortunately, your servant is very worried about you. You are young. You have desires. I think you do these things for fun. Allow me to tell you more candidly. You are no different from other Iranians. Do you catch my meaning?"

Nuri wanted to shrug his shoulders and laugh, but he changed his mind. He said in a serious tone, "My desire is to go to New York to be with Maman Zuzu."

Madame frowned. She spread her fingers across her chest and looked at Nuri anxiously. Perhaps Shuri Khanom or Soraya herself had told Madame about Nuri's raids on the storage room and his visit to the Tahmasbis' apartment. "Your servant prays that you not be hurt in this formal setting. Do you follow me?"

She retrieved the flowers from Nuri and took his arm. Together they walked back to the house. When they reached the first-floor hall, there came a smell of half-burned wood and tar from the third floor. The Senator had started a fire in the study fireplace. Every year he tarred the chimney brick, and then when he first started a fire, the tar melted and dripped down into the fireplace. Madame and Nuri parted in front of Nuri's room. Madame went up to the third floor.

In the evening, Madame and the Senator could be heard whispering on the third floor. They spoke softly, in the incantatory tone of a revelation.

They apparently were talking about Nuri and his future, which made him curious. He heard them coming down the stairs. Now they were discussing the price of oil burners and American refrigerators. When they reached the second-floor corridor, they asked Ladan where Nuri was. If Ladan answered them, it was probably in the form of gestures because no words were exchanged. When Madame and the Senator reached the garden, they spoke more openly, walked faster on the brick garden paths. Nuri felt a sense of distance.

The next two hours passed very slowly, as if the hands of the clock had stopped. He listened to the birds chirping, children playing soccer in the alley, and Najmeh humming in the kitchen. But he also heard sounds from the depths of his inner self that berated him for the mistakes he had made in the past few months.

It sounded as if a crowd were moving from the direction of the Tajrish Bridge to the bazaar. Voices could be heard on loudspeakers in every direction. He took out his bike to go to the bridge and have a look. When he opened the garden gate, he was startled. Soraya was leaning against the neighbor's wall, all dressed and made up. She was in the same white dress she had worn the day they had gone to Khachator's café and a pair of white summer gloves she always put on for outings. She acted as if they had run into each other accidentally. She surveyed both ends of the alley with the nonchalance of an experienced woman who is not afraid of other people's perception of her. She approached Nuri and pulled the gloves off meticulously, one finger at a time. Nuri had long thought about such an encounter and had imagined all its details. But now, faced with the reality of it, he felt hesitant. He leaned his bike against the wall and said, "What are you doing here?"

Soraya rose on tiptoe and threw an inquisitive glance at the garden. She appeared uninterested in a belligerent encounter. "Nuri, how big your garden is. Don't you get lost in it? How many lights you have in the rooms. Are you going to light the house up for a party?"

"Next Friday is my grandmother's birthday. A whole slew of our relatives are invited."

"Why haven't you told us? Are we strangers? Are you afraid we'll crash the party? If nobody else knows you, *I* know you very well."

Without Nuri's permission, she entered the garden. She threw admiring glances in every direction and went over to the stone pool. Nuri was worried that Madame and the Senator would suddenly show up, and a row would ensue. He had better get rid of Soraya before anything happened. Using the excuse of going out for ice cream, they could go to the Tajrish Bridge and walk along the Sa'dabad Road for an hour.

Soraya quickly leafed through a small notebook the size of a pocket calendar. The well-used pages folded and curled under her fingers. When she found the page she was looking for, she moved her finger down the column of names in front of Nuri's eyes. "Do you have their telephone numbers?"

Nuri recognized the names of distant relatives. He had not seen most of them for a few years. The retired colonel Ardakani, Amiz Abbas's second brother-in-law, who now taught accounting at the National Bank in Mashhad. Nahid Khanom, the widow of Jahangir Mirza Begi, who had recently returned from a trip to St. Moritz, Switzerland, and wanted to start a charity for disadvantaged children. Hosein Zargham, the Senator's second cousin, who was a physician but spent most of his time practicing calligraphy—on two facing sheets of paper in a bizarre handwriting reminiscent of Egyptian hieroglyphs and equally incomprehensible, he had copied down one of Lamartine's poems he himself had translated into Persian, but when the two sheets were folded together and held up to the light, the incomplete words became whole, and Lamartine's poem appeared in a beautiful Nasta'ligh hand.

Nuri no longer trusted Soraya after her strange behavior, so at first he confessed that he didn't know any of these relatives' phone numbers and then was considering what to say next. Of all the questions he considered, he chose the most stupid one. "Have I hurt you?"

Soraya initially seemed disarmed. Bewildered, she put her notebook in her purse. A smirk pulled down the corners of her mouth. She asked sarcastically, "Am I crazy to come all this way just to hurt myself?" She shrugged her shoulders and threw a disdainful glance in the direction of the house. "I have wanted to come here for a long time. I had imagined this house differently. Perhaps it's the tall trees that make the garden appear so big. How these trees block the view! It seems the garden has no

walls. OK. I prefer smaller and cozier places. I want to be in a cozy environment." She paused. "Are you disturbed that I have come here?"

Nuri stuttered, "Why? Would you like us to go to the bridge together?
I want to treat you to an ice cream."

Soraya laughed. "That one time we went to Khachator's café is enough
for a lifetime."

"Miss Soraya, please don't embarrass me. On my mother's life, this
time will be different. I'm not lying. Shall we go?" He smiled confidently.
"On my own life."

Soraya pouted. "I know your nature. You keep saying your door is
open to me, I can come by any time, but you are lying." She spoke as if
addressing an imaginary person. "Look at him! He thinks he has run into
a bunch of nobodies who will line up outside his house and wait for their
turn to see Madame. It's not like fifty years ago. There are foreign women
wherever you go."

Nuri pretended to be miffed. "This is like your own home. Whenever
you feel like coming here, you are most welcome."

She shaded her eyes with her hand and surveyed the house. "I bet
I can find Madame's storage room on my own. The staircase is through
the hall, right? The stairs climb along the wall to the second floor. On the
third floor, Madame has her tropical plants. On the right side is the Senator's study, then the toilet and washroom. The storage room is on the left.
Isn't that so?"

"Exactly."

"See how well I know this place?"

She began to walk toward the first-floor hall. Nuri ran after her.
"Where are you going?"

"To the storage room. Is there a problem?"

He couldn't think of an answer. "Problem, no. . . . " He inserted his
hands into his pockets and searched for something. "My grandmother
has the storage-room key. She won't be back for another hour or so. Let's
first go to the Tajrish Bridge and have an ice cream. It's getting dark. . . . "

"Didn't you used to say you had the run of the house? But when my
turn comes, you say Madame is in control?"

"Of course my grandmother has the storage-room key. When she comes back, I'll ask her for the key and open the door for you."

He strung together some nonsense he knew Soraya wouldn't believe. He took her arm at least to keep his own balance. Soraya's smile was coy. It invited Nuri closer and at the same time pushed him back. Then she said, "Why should we go to the Tajrish Bridge? I'm not a stranger that you need to treat me formally. If it's for the sake of mountain air, well, there is a breeze here too." She leaned her head forward. "Why are you dazed? If you don't want us to go to the storage room, we don't have to. There's no shame."

"No, no, Soraya Khanom. Do you remember those days when I was always in your apartment?"

"Of course I remember."

"I couldn't wait to have a car, come to your apartment, take your arm, seat you next to me, and drive around with you. Then I used to berate myself and say, 'At your age, when you don't even know how to drive and not even a parrot hops in your pocket, how can you expect to take the beautiful Soraya Khanom out? What nerve you have!'"

"What does 'a parrot hops in your pocket' mean?"

"The five-tuman bill is green. I call it a parrot."

Soraya laughed. "Where did you learn these things?"

He smiled, "I had a vitamin C deficiency. . . . " He rubbed his thumb against his index finger, as if he were counting money. "Vitamin C . . . Do you want me to tell you what I would have liked to do? . . . Ask me to tell you, and I will."

"Go away. No need to play so many games just to say one word."

"Come on. Ask me and I'll tell you."

Soraya played with the fingers of her gloves and looked at him from the corner of her eye. "You are giving me a headache. Go ahead, tell me."

He said excitedly, "I would have brought you to our house."

"Huh? Just like that, you would have taken my hand and brought me here? Wouldn't you be afraid that people would wonder what a young boy is doing with an older girl?"

"Well, you are the sister of my friend. Why should I be afraid?"

Soraya put her fingers on his face. "How mean you are!"

Nuri coughed. "Aha, aha, I wish I could open the storage room for you."

Soraya gestured. "Don't worry about it. I'll open it myself."

"Oh? You'll open it? How?"

"Let's go up. I'll show you."

Nuri was thinking about ways to send Madame to the Baxters' if she showed up at that moment. The more trouble he got into, the more alien the Dezashibi house seemed to him. The walls seemed greasy and filmy like a dirty plate or like their school cafeteria in the afternoon, when the dishes were not cleared from the tables.

In the second-floor corridor, Soraya examined Madame's embroideries closely. If she entered Nuri's room and saw the ashtray overflowing with sunflower seeds and his dirty socks and shirts strewn on the carpet, she would tease him mercilessly.

"Imagine! I thought you lived in a palace." She ran her fingers over one of the embroideries. "You can find junk like this in the Mehran Bazaar and the Ferdowsi Store."

Nuri said dejectedly, "These are very different from the images of boats, palms, and camels drawn on black velvet."

The corridor lamp turned everything a light blue and made the background of the embroideries look like cold cities in Europe. Combinations of images from small cities and villages or, to quote Madame, "pastoral scenes," with trees, forest pathways, cool and semidark places such as the Raso Bar where Amiz Abbas and the Senator had gone on Saturdays for lunch and drank Alsatian white wine. With tall palm branches in gunmetal vases that leaned over the white tablecloths. Soraya made a face and pointed to the image of a naked young man. "Look at this one and how he is showing everything. He has no shame."

Nuri returned to his primary concern. "Why do you call here and there constantly and embarrass us so much?"

Soraya lowered her lids with false modesty. "OK, so I blurted something out. Why should you be so sensitive and get so easily hurt?"

"OK. Why don't you tell *me* these things?"

"Tell you so that you can make promises and apologies and pretend? Don't imagine that just because we're exchanging a few pleasantries here, I have forgotten your horrible deeds. I don't forget anything." She poked her chest with her index finger a few times. "My heart is scorched. You have to be scorched too, OK?" She turned her gaze away and said more gently, almost to herself, "You are deceived by the appearance of most of the people you make friends with. You think that because you have seen each other a hundred times, you are very much alike and compatible. Whatever you see in them, you find in yourself. But being friends with someone like yourself isn't a friendship. The first time I saw Shirzad by the pomegranate cart, well, I was young. I didn't have much brain. I took his aggrieved and innocent look for familiarity. I thought he spoke honestly. He said he was in love with me. He would put up with all my whims. When we were alone, he said, 'Sori-jun, I am crazy about you. When I look into your blue eyes, I get dizzy. I talk to myself. What have you done to me? What do you want from me? Why have you set me on fire like this?' A pile of things, most of which I don't remember. Sometimes he even cried and said, 'Sori-jun, I'm standing on the launch pad right now. They have started counting backwards. When they reach zero, I'll launch myself head first.' But when you looked into his eyes . . . ", she ran her hand through her thick hair, " . . . they were filled with lewdness. It was as if he wanted to eat me like a peeled peach. I don't mince words with anyone. I told him, 'Shirzad-jun, go after somebody who is in love with you. If you stay with me, you will be ruined.' Do you understand? Now listen to his answer, see what he says. He says, 'I'm devoted to you. Do we have to pay for this girl's cunning out of our own pocket? If you weren't as bad as myself, how could you have understood my nature?' Do you see how rotten he is?"

"Maybe if you hadn't found so much fault with him, your marriage would have gone through."

Soraya shrugged her shoulders. "For me, it's the desire that is beautiful, not having the object of desire. But let me tell you this. He who is greedy is scared. The more generous Shirzad was, the more he revealed his frightened nature. Ask me why and I'll tell you."

"Why?"

"He liked playing tricks. He was afraid that something would happen. He would reach a fountain, and because of his thirst he would dive in head first." She gave her voice a more private tone, as if she were addressing Shirzad himself. " . . . OK, man, if you want to do something, do it. Nobody is stopping you. In love, there is loyalty, affection, and patience. You aren't the only person in this whole wide world whose hopes have been dashed. There are others who are roaming around, looking for their lost love." She took Nuri's face between her palms and brought her lips closer. "My dear one, I am not the type who will forget in a week the wrong done to her."

She said this without any anger, but with a proud drunkenness. Her reprimands seemed superficial. Deep down, she was challenging Nuri. He didn't miss the chance and impulsively grabbed her wrist. "Let's go. Let me show you things you have never seen before."

They walked toward the cupboard full of decorative objects. Nuri pointed out all the antiques: a set of sherbet glasses, a pair of tall oil burners, three glass candle burners, silver holders for glass teacups with a paisley design, especially the crystal glasses made in czarist Russia that were the color of sour cherry along the rim, but had faded into a candy green at the bottom. Soraya pointed to the candle holders and asked, "How much do these go for?"

Nuri was disappointed. He drew back and said superficially, "Fifty thousand tumans? Sixty thousand? How should I know?"

"Why do you pull back? Play your games with someone who doesn't understand."

She took off, running to the third floor with her arms and legs flinging back. When she got to the storage-room door, she took a pin out of her hair, inserted it into the lock, and opened it. She held the hair pin up with two fingers. "After you, sir."

"With this tiny pin? How?"

She arched an eyebrow, implying, "See, but don't ask."

The storage room was dusty and filled with knickknacks, like a pawnshop or the storeroom of a customs office. The desk lid was rolled back. Nuri showed Soraya the small drawers in which Madame had stored a jumble of push pins; paper clips; plastic, pearl, brass, and leather buttons; large cast-iron nails; and old coins. There were other items whose function was unclear: the statue of a masked clown on a stand, holding a torch; a Hungarian cradle and a guitar with a yellow and red paisley design; meter-high columns of dusty china dishes; old Czech oil lamps that had turned a mummified black. Soraya put her hands on Nuri's shoulders, tilted her head, and asked, "If I ask you something, will you tell me the truth?"

"What?"

"Why has Madame stayed here?"

"What do you mean? Obviously because her husband and family are here."

"What if Madame is a spy?"

Nuri was taken aback. "Spy? Why?"

"If you were in Madame's place, would you have been happy leaving everything behind for the sake of this barn? In this foreign city where you don't understand the language, your language isn't understood, and everyone you run into first wants to know where you are from and what your nice accent is?"

"So, what about the rest of us—me, Ladan, my mother, and my grand-father? She has relatives here. No one would spend forty years in Tehran just to spy."

Soraya shifted her weight and turned her gaze away. "OK. Let's assume she's not a spy. There must be something wrong with her to spend forty years in this dump with your grandfather. She herself brags about her life in Vienna, that she sang on Cardinal Ineritz's birthday, Herman Leopoldi wrote songs for her, Kurt von Schuschnik, the Austrian prime minister, was a friend of hers. You would have to be sick to leave all that to come and live in this Tehran. What for? Who was the boy she says was killed in Prague by guerrillas?"

"Siegfried? Siegfried von Friedhoff. . . . "

"That's him. Siegfried von Friedhoff! What a beautiful name! Do you remember the pictures of him in Madame's album? Those narrow eyes whose depths were as clear as a spring." She laughed. "What blond hair! If Siegfried had run into me, I wouldn't have let him go." She withdrew. "Have I offended you?"

"Why should I be offended? What did you say that I should be offended by it?"

"How should I know? Maybe you didn't like my talking about a handsome Austrian man or your grandmother's friends?"

"You didn't say anything bad. If you're saying my grandmother was in love with Siegfried, so be it. What's wrong with two people loving each other? What's good about Madame is that she's not afraid of strangers' love. She has the nerve to leave everything behind and live here because of her love."

Soraya arched her eyebrows. "So that's how it is. Everybody does as he wants and doesn't need to answer to anyone?"

"Love is not a crime. Is it bad if I kiss you? Will you be cross? Whose business is it anyway?"

He came closer to Soraya, then pulled back quickly. Soraya shouted, "Oy, what's with you? Where are you going? Wait a minute."

She threw her arms around Nuri's neck. "How sweet you are, Nuri! You are a piece of the moon. Do you know why? Because you have been raised by a foreign grandmother."

"My grandmother doesn't see herself as a foreigner. She wants to do everything Iranian style. Had it not been for her love of Iran, she would have packed her bags and gone back to Austria long ago. Not a day goes by that a bomb doesn't explode in the streets or some demonstration doesn't take place. Had you been a foreigner, would you have stayed here? For whom would you have risked your life? My grandmother has lived in this house for forty years. She is a better Muslim than you and I. She holds a Koran over her head every midnight and speaks to her God." He was taken aback by Soraya's smile. Perhaps she understood that he had exaggerated the bit about the Koran and Madame's prayers. He asked, "Why are you so happy?"

"Sometimes you are so good, I can't believe it."

"What did I do?"

"I won't tell you. It'll go to your head."

Nuri put his face against Soraya's. "On your mother's life, tell me."

"Should I tell you and spoil you? Do you imagine you've become hot shit?"

"Miss Soraya, Miss Soraya . . . I promise . . . "

Soraya made a face. "'Miss Soraya,' what drivel. You are so loud that the neighbors will hear you."

Soraya's half-joking reprimands excited him. "I promise. Nobody's at home. Rest assured."

"Shut up! Shut up! Shut up! Madame has really spoiled you. I bet she likes you more than Siegfried. They say that once a month she writes a letter to Siegfried and mails it to a cemetery in Prague."

Noises could be heard approaching the third floor. Soraya withdrew, and Nuri ran quickly toward the burlap curtain in front of the rows of clothes hangers. He stepped cautiously onto a stool by the door. Through the window, he saw the Senator and Mr. Shariat walking quickly toward the study.

The Senator spoke out of the corner of his mouth. As he talked, he waved about a lit cigarette that he held between two fingers. With both hands, Mr. Shariat held a shoe box and a wad of banknotes. He wrinkled his forehead in surprise and shook his head, as if in disbelief. They had heard bits and pieces of news. The shah was desperately looking for a new prime minister, and it was rumored that he was going abroad for medical treatment. For this reason, Mr. Shariat was constantly on the phone buying shares for the Senator from the Paris, London, and Berlin exchanges, which he then transferred to the Mutual Bank in New York. Badri Khanom and Dr. Jannati wanted to sell their share of the Aghcheh land to the Senator and send the money to America for "poor" Shahrokh. The Senator was dragging his feet, though. He couldn't believe that an Iranian student could make ends meet with a handful of dollars at the rate of seven tumans to a dollar. Why didn't they go to Canada, where their expenses would be lower? Moreover, Canadians were more generous than Americans. At the beginning of every month, in addition to room and board and medical expenses, they gave foreigners a certified check for pocket money as "social security." Canadians had an amazing interest in Iranians. Among all Middle Easterners, Iranians were seen as the most elegant and talented. But Badri Khanom preferred to emigrate to places such as England or Germany where people were not as ignorant as Americans. The only thing wrong with Europeans was their stinginess. They didn't give enough social security to foreigners at least to see a movie once a week or to have a simple *chelo* kebab in an Iranian restaurant. Instead, they expected an honorable fifty-year-old woman such as Badri Khanom to wash dishes or wipe and shine floors in dirty and damp restaurants, like poor blacks.

Soraya walked toward the clothes cupboard and a few minutes later emerged from behind the curtain. She held Madame's taffeta dress on a hanger in front of her. She whirled around and asked, "How is this?"

"Where did you find it?"

"In the cupboard." She put a long cigarette holder in the corner of her mouth, as in the old Second World War–era fashion magazines. She placed the palm of her free hand on her hip and swiveled her hips exaggeratedly as she walked about. "Honorable ladies and gentlemen, please applaud the angel of Prague opera, Fräulein Frieda Almstead, in whose honor Kurt von Schuschnik, the prime minister of Austria, drank champagne out of her shoe. . . . "

When she signaled to Nuri to clap, coins suddenly fell from her leather handbag onto the floor. Nuri knelt on the dusty floor and looked under all the metal shelves covered with spiderwebs. Finding the coins was not that important, but he didn't have the energy to stand up. He lowered his shoulders slowly to the floor and lay down parallel to two metal shelves. She bent over him, and he felt the heat of her body. He heard the rustle of her dress as she lay down close to him. His head began to spin. He felt his face burning. Soraya asked sarcastically, "Why are you lying down on the floor?"

She was lying a hand's width away from him and looking at him derisively. The yellow ceiling light made the hair on her arm appear like rows of golden ants climbing over each other. Her body smelled of fresh sweat. Whatever he said would put him at Soraya's mercy. He asked in the tone of a child, "What are you going to do to me?"

He tickled her to break the ice so that they could embrace each other, but Soraya ignored him. She turned on her back and bent her arm over her forehead. Nuri didn't give up. He repeated his question innocently, "What are you going to do to me?"

Soraya lifted her head and said, "Don't you want to lie on top of me? What are you waiting for, then?"

Nuri's throat was parched. He stuttered, "Oh, Soraya Khanom . . . "

Soraya rolled toward him. She tilted her head and examined him patiently for a while. "If you are so eager, why are you so clumsy?"

"I'm clumsy?"

Soraya pretended to warn him. "Do you imagine yourself strong and capable of subduing me? Huh?"

He saw the moisture around Soraya's eyes clearly, as if her face had been put under a microscope. He touched her cheek with his fingertips. He lifted his head and planted a kiss on her neck just above the shoulder. He heard the sound of heavy trucks, eight-, ten-, and sixteen-wheelers whose high beams cut through darkness. Behind them, he could hear the din of a disorderly crowd. It seemed to him that the sounds came from far away. From rooftops, from behind walls, from the Tajrish Bazaar, he could hear a plaintive chorus of "God is Great"—a plaint filled with rage, helplessness, and desire that made his hair stand on end. Soraya called to him. "Nuri, what's happening?" He was mesmerized and couldn't answer her. Soraya said, "Have you lost your mind? Why are you looking at me like this?" Now he could hear pots and pans being hit against each other inside gardens and the chants of a Koran reciter being broadcast on loudspeakers. He didn't understand why Soraya became angry with him. "First you play coy to make me feel sorry for you. Then you suddenly freeze?"

She smelled of the dampness of perspiration, the salty smell of musty woods. "Soraya Khanom, Soraya Khanom, I am grateful. I am most grateful. For everything. Say whatever you wish. Your words make me both happy and sad. I don't know if this is good or bad. I've been waiting. I've waited a long time. Now I understand why. I have nothing else to say except that you are very dear to me. Very dear. Even if all this doesn't exist, it's fine. It doesn't matter. A demigod has to know everything. Even if he knows, what's the use? What does it prove?"

"Nuri, what's with you?"

"Destruction is easy for you and me, but who has the power to remake things? You are wonderful. You can do as you wish, judge as you wish, even if it is unfounded. But my feelings are my own, they will remain absolute. In this world, no one has thought about someone as much as I have thought about you. I am a bit of a rogue. This is no playacting. At least accept this confession from me. In this world, nothing is detrimental. Whatever is must be that way. All my antics are very serious. Even more serious than dying . . . I say these things for my own benefit, they are confined to me. They don't concern you."

Soraya rose and said, "How crazy you are, Nuri. If I were you, I would become a movie star. You have the looks, anyhow. You can play the role of foreigners in movies." She kissed him. She put her wet lips, moist with lipstick, on his cheek. "Oh my, what a face! How delicate! If you don't call me, I won't like you anymore. It won't take long for me to miss you."

She straightened her dress and hair. Using two fingers, she shut her purse and then left the storage room without saying good-bye. Nuri listened to her steps in the hall and on the stairs. Silence once again replaced the chants of "God is Great" and the sound of trucks moving away. Being free was like an internal quarantine that fenced him off from others.

... 10 ...

Nuri felt the void Soraya left behind lingering on his skin. He couldn't believe that a mere few minutes ago their bodies had been close and they had kissed. It might not have been as beautiful as kisses in movies, but it had made his head spin. Despite her curses, Soraya still liked him.

He was plunged into the kind of excitement he felt after he had attained an illicit goal—like on the occasions when Madame ran from room to room looking for a pair of earrings, a bracelet, or a brooch she had mislaid that Nuri knew exactly where to find, but instead would become sly and feign ignorance.

He surveyed the corridor from behind the glass panes above the storage-room door. The Senator's sports jacket was hanging on the coatrack. As on most days, he was probably in the study with Mr. Shariat, discussing politics. Their conversations would have nothing to do with Nuri and Soraya. But the damp leaves on the tropical plants worried him. It meant that Madame had returned and watered the plants, but had not looked for him. Light reflected on the opaque panes above Madame's bedroom door, indicating she was busy with something in there.

Nuri thought of phoning Buki to fix a rendezvous on the slopes of Amirabad. They could wander around together. Unfortunately, he had agreed to go to a film festival with Ladan. Who felt like seeing films? He wasn't in the mood, but he would hurt Ladan's feelings if he didn't go.

He had a half an hour or maybe a bit more before her return. He went to his room to get ready, but the thought of Soraya's visit continued to weaken his resolve. He stared at himself in the dresser mirror. A few days' growth of whiskers shaded his chin. He looked as if he hadn't washed his face for a couple of days. Hair sprouted from a row of pimples at his jawline. He ran a finger over the bumps and tried in vain to squeeze a few. He

219

applied Noxzema to them, both to soothe his skin and to establish physical contact with it, as if to gauge the reality of his own touch.

The lights along the sides of the stone pool shone through the leaves and branches of the apple tree and reflected artificial leaf shapes on the kitchen wall. He noticed the outline of Madame's body seated in a straw chair beneath the window. She wore an open-collared dress with a floral pattern. She appeared calm, as if ready to receive her foreign guests. Her legs were bare. Her hair was combed and tied into a hairnet that dangled from the back of her head like a sheep's tail. She wore flat cork shoes, and she had crossed one leg over the other. She moved one ankle in a circle absentmindedly and, leaning her head back, said, "How pale Your Excellency's face has become. I am shocked!" She squeezed a handkerchief in her hand. She narrowed her eyes and stared at Nuri. "Exactly like a Kabuki dancer." She shook her head. "No. No. No. The mask of an African god. No. No. No. How Your Excellency surprises me!"

With her free hand, she took her glass of Monk's Syrup from the table. Nuri was surprised to see her there. He shuddered as his finger touched the Noxzema on his face. He felt hypnotized. His voice sounded strange to himself, as if generated by a computer. "What are you doing here?"

Madame stretched out her legs and held them up parallel to each other. She threw an admiring glance at her shins and ankles. "I apologize. You have to forgive this old lady for interfering in your personal affairs. . . . " She pretended not to be paying close attention to Nuri, although she was clearly watching him. "Your servant and your grandpa have decided to send you abroad. Maybe you will study better there."

It took Nuri some time to grasp the true meaning of what she had said. He asked slowly, dragging out his words as if speaking in a foreign language, "Do you want me to go to New York?"

Madame threw back her head abruptly. A muscle in her neck contracted and stood out like an oblique line. "Grandpa has obtained a passport and airline ticket for you. In two weeks, you go to Saint Joseph's School in New York."

"I'll be going to Saint Joseph's School? In New York?"

"In the state of New York, not the city."

"Why shouldn't I join Maman Zuzu in New York City?"

"No. No. No. New York is not a good place to study. You have to study somewhere outside the city to avoid being led astray by bad friends. Saint Joseph's School is near New York City. Whenever you want, you can visit Maman Zuzu. It's very easy." Her eyes glistened with excitement. She drew closer. "Nuri-jan, think about it. You are going to America. Do you understand what I'm saying? America! Meaning you are leaving home, OK? In other words, you are going to travel across mountains, seas, and continents. Whatever you wish," she snapped two fingers, "you will attain quickly, OK? Oh, how happy I am for you. The opposite is true for me. I won't be happy here without you." She sighed and grew pensive. "When your Maman Zuzu was young, she liked the story of Sinbad the Sailor. She always wanted me to tell her about his strange and frightful sea voyages. She would say, 'Repeat it, Mumzie. What seas does Sinbad's ship cross? Which bizarre creatures does he combat? Which sirens' songs enchant him?' Nuri-jan, my dearrr, I wish you had been there and seen the hints of long voyages and exile in the wide, wild eyes of that child. It was as if she heard songs from faraway seas, enticing her to long journeys. Our lot is to travel far so as to appreciate our own home and to sing in exile: Until when? Where? What a long journey! Yes . . . " she pointed to the ground, "yes, right here. Right here Maman Zuzu and I played hide-and-seek together. We blindfolded ourselves and chased each other in the dark." She placed her palms on the hair along her temples. "When she found me, she would tell me, 'Mumzie, sing for me.' I would hide behind the curtain, and she would say, 'Mumzie, sing for me.' I would make my voice hoarse. She would say, 'Mumzie, sing for me.' I would sing scary songs to frighten her. She liked to be frightened. She would dig her fingers in her cheeks and scream with phony fright."

The telephone began to ring in the hall. Nuri was going to pick it up when Madame grabbed his arm. Nuri asked, "What is it?"

She looked at him beseechingly. "Do not hate me, I ask you."

"Not hate you? Why?"

The telephone continued to ring. Madame hurriedly put her handkerchief to her nose, shook her head, and blew her nose. She asked Nuri very quietly, "OK? Do not hate your grandmother, OK?"

Nuri threw up his arms. "Why should I hate you?"

Madame lowered her head and, playing with her handkerchief, mumbled in a childish tone, "I am very grateful. May God give you a long life and save you for your mother. I wish you success."

Nuri hurried into the hall. He reached the telephone table and quickly picked up the receiver. The line was dead. He didn't know why. Then he hung up, and the telephone rang again. When he picked it up, he heard Soraya's voice. She spoke hurriedly. "Nuri, is that you?"

He spoke deliberately. "Is that you? Where are you? Are you home?"

"Can you believe it? An hour ago I was at your house. Now I am in my own room. I have opened my window. There is a breeze, and it's cooling me down."

"How quickly you got home."

"Do you know what? I say home is the best place, and one should never leave it. I don't understand why most people can't stay put in their homes. They spend thousands of tumans to travel thousands of kilometers away from their home to some foreign place. Then having barely reached there, they get homesick and want to return as soon as possible. Do you know Said Anasori?"

"No."

"He is a close friend of Cyrus. He rides a motorcycle. The one who wears dark glasses."

"No."

"What do you mean, no? How could you not remember him? You have seen him a hundred times at our place. Never mind. I saw him on the Tajrish Bridge, near the Golden Earring. He insisted that I get on his motorcycle and have dinner with him around Zafaraniyeh. And with this bad habit of mine, I said, 'It's free, why shouldn't I go?' I had forgotten how fearless Anasori is. He guns his motorcycle, and we take off like a bullet. On that terrible road filled with potholes, thank God his tires didn't blow out. I said, 'Anasori, what are you doing? Is your body itching for the angel of death? I'm dying of fear. Slow down a bit!' He didn't slow down and took a detour into a field that turned out to be very nice. It was so green and beautiful that I suddenly became hungry. I'm like this. Looking at wild nature whets my appetite. Anasori knew a cozy café he said was ideal for dinner. I said, 'No, Anasori-jun, I have a rendezvous at seven. You have to take me back to the apartment right now.' He said, 'OK, call.' He stopped by a telephone booth, but we didn't have a dozari coin, and it was getting late. I insisted that he bring me back. To cut a long story short, after a whole lot of pleading and promises, he took the road by the Karaj River, and we got back here within half an hour. I was so exhausted I lay down for a few minutes. I don't know why I couldn't fall asleep. I told myself that had it not been for you, I would not have had any trouble. I put myself through all this just for you. It's you who is ruining my life. You didn't expect me to call you, right? Why don't you answer? Are you deaf?"

"No."

"Then why don't you say something? Shouldn't I have called?"

"I can't talk right now. My grandmother is waiting close by. They want to send me to America."

"You're lying."

"I swear. They've enrolled me in a school."

"You're lying."

"On my mother's life . . . "

"OK. You're right. I am the one for whom things turn out badly. I throw myself in fire and water for nothing—just so that we can talk for a few minutes. I wish I hadn't phoned you and made you imagine you are some important shit."

Nuri grew alarmed. "Soraya Khanom, let me finish what I was going to say. It won't take long. Please accept this from me. I can't get the thought of you out of my head. This is very important. You are my god. How can I enter into a battle with my own god?"

"If I am your god and you have such faith in your god, why have you lost your head with a flimsy promise from Madame, and why are you in a hurry to pack your bags to go to America?"

"Soraya Khanom, nothing matters to me as much as you do. I won't go to New York. I'll go wherever you go. Wherever you are, I too will be. I have nothing else to say. Believe it or not, I'm staying here."

"When you talk like this, what can I say? What kind of friendship is this? Why do all good things make me think of you? Mountains, trees, the sky, the sweet smell of grass, each flower I pick smells like you. Wherever I go, I see you. My friendship with you knows no premeditation, no quarrel or makeup. When you are not here, I look at the old pictures. It's not just you I think of. The whole of your life, the life of people you have grown up with, who know you and remember you from afar—I see all of them in front of my eyes. If you want, I can return the pictures to you, but I want to keep them for a while. I want to look at them. Sometimes I feel so close to you, I am filled with you. When I shut my eyes, I see that you are with me in this same room. I stretch out my hand, and I can feel your hands, the soft fuzz on your upper lip, your happy and sweet face. I bring my face closer and kiss you."

Nuri was breathless. He asked, "Are you teasing me?"

"Oh, Nuri, with what nectar did you infuse my body? A friend closer to me than myself. As I sit here, you envelop me like a soft cloud. We Eastern women need to be enveloped. A naked person is distracted and made cross by her own nakedness. I have never seen you bitter and hopeless. No matter how I search my mind, I can't remember you even hurting me."

Mrs. Tahmasbi's voice echoed in the receiver. "Sori Khanom, Naneh-jan!"

Soraya spoke rapidly. "It's my mother. She is running the water in the bathroom. She is calling me to go wash my shirt." She answered Mrs. Tahmasbi. "Maman, I can't come down. You start without me. I'll come later." She told Nuri, "Do you hear the voice?"

"Your mother's voice?"

"No. This melancholy voice coming from the alley. Listen. How beautifully it sings. Oh, my God, what sorrow and feeling."

Nuri could hear only cars moving in the street. "I don't hear anything."

Soraya heaved a sad and unbelieving sigh. "I don't know what instrument is accompanying the song. A mystic instrument, a lovesick instrument whose sound emanates from the alley and makes you dizzy. Some women have come into the alley from their yards to listen to the voice." She shouted to the neighbors. "Khanom, who is singing?" A woman answered, but Nuri couldn't make out her words. "She says no one. I hear it with my own ears, but this lady says no one."

Nuri was beginning to hear the singing, but it was weak and distant. "I hear it too. Is it poetry?"

"'Show your face. My garden is desire.' . . . Do you hear it? What a
tumult they cause with a few ordinary words! How they soothe your heart
like a thousand air conditioners! It's the voice of a dervish. It says, 'I'm a
dervish. I am a dervish. I'm a devotee of Ali.' The neighbors are coming
out of their houses one by one. The dervish is emerging from among the
trees in the alley. What disheveled hair he has! One of those lunatics who
suddenly go into a trance and become ecstatic. But he doesn't carry any
instruments. I don't know how he can sing without moving his lips. . . .
Oh, he's not the one who is singing. Did you hear what I said? The song
is being broadcast from a transistor radio he is carrying on his shoulder.
Nuri, can you believe it? All this from a transistor radio? Did I hurt you,
Nuri-jun?"

"I am only listening to your voice."

She began to laugh. "You sing quite well yourself. Come over here and
sing. I'll record it. Are you coming?"

"Definitely."

"Don't take long. I'm waiting."

She hung up so quickly that Nuri was jolted out of his daydream. He
shouted, "Soraya Khanom!"

He redialed the Tahmasbis' number. The line was busy. The third
time he dialed the number, he noticed Madame. She was waiting for him
on the landing. She clung to the banister and asked, "Who was it?"

"Soraya."

"Swearing again?"

"No."

"So, why do you look unhappy?"

"I'm not unhappy. Ladan will be back any minute now, and we'll have
to go out. I haven't even changed."

Madame seemed pacified. "You always wanted to go to New York.
Are you not happy about going to Saint Joseph's School?"

Nuri grew pensive. "I don't know." He repeated, "I don't know."

Madame nodded in agreement and allowed Nuri to pass. Lost in his
thoughts of Soraya, he went up to his room.

No more than a quarter of an hour later, Ladan put her head in his
room and asked, "Mamakh, are you ready?"

Nuri rose. Ladan looked around the room and asked, "Why haven't you turned on the lights? It's bad for your eyes to sit in the dark."

If he went to the film festival, it was not to watch films or listen to Ladan and her friends. He just wanted to be alone in the dark theater.

They walked fast toward the middle of the Mostowfi Alley. When the Tajrish Bridge lights became visible, Nuri suddenly decided against going to the festival. He slowed down deliberately. As they reached the incline at the end of the alley, Ladan began to grumble. "Why do you walk so slowly, Nuri? I'm losing my patience. We'll be late."

Nuri said, "So what if we're late? What happens? To hell with *The Godfather*."

"Why do you attack me like a rabid dog?"

"I don't feel like going to a movie."

"Fine. Nobody issued you a formal invitation."

"Go by yourself. I have something to do."

"What do you mean, Mamakh? If you didn't want to come, you should have said so before. I would have gone with Shabkhiz. Nobody forced you."

"Why don't you go alone? You're not a child to need a chaperon."

"If you don't want to come, fine, say so. No need to give me advice."

On Pahlavi Avenue, a crowd was carrying religious banners and icons. Nothing could be heard but footsteps and occasional coughs. Nuri whispered in Ladan's ear, "Are they going to the festival too?"

Ladan lowered her voice. "I think it's the Turks' procession. They are headed for the Hoseiniyeh in Javadiyeh."

"What for?"

"To protest."

"To protest what?"

"To protest the treatment of those who are in jail and people who have disappeared."

"The ones they show on television?"

"Do you watch television? You seem to be always thinking about getting your passport to go to New York."

Nuri laughed. "*I* go to New York? No way."

"You mean you don't want to go to New York? So what was all that pleading with Maman Zuzu about?"

"I won't go to New York. If you don't believe me, ask Mumzie."

Ladan put on a half-pouting expression and said in jest, "That's enough. From the moment Shahrokh Jannati left for America, not a single day has gone by that you haven't moped about going to America. Maybe you don't like the fact that they have registered you at a Catholic boarding school. You're afraid that if you go there, they'll force you to study day and night. Of course, it's obvious. Grandpa is not brainless. He wouldn't give you bundles of money to spend in New York. Saint Joseph's School is made for lazy halfwits. You have to wear a uniform all the time, shave your head, and polish your shoes."

"Why are you so worked up over it?"

Ladan lost control. "Why not? Grandpa has handed his brains over to Mr. Shariat, who keeps at him from dawn to dusk to liquidate his assets, send his money to foreign banks, and get himself to a safe place before things take a turn for the worse. Grandpa accepts all this as if it were Koranic verses. He listens to it all. When he finds me alone, he says I should marry Shariat, meaning a man well beyond ugliness and twenty-five years older than I."

"Really?"

"His Majesty, who doesn't study and spends twenty-four hours a day on the streets, gets sent to America with pomp and ceremony, to a boarding school nobody has ever heard of. But when my turn comes, Grandpa says to me, who have never in my entire life never had a grade lower than eighteen and am second in my class, 'What's the use of going to university? Why don't you marry Shariat and make *abgusht* and *eshkaneh* for him every night?' If you were in my place, you would have run away a long time ago and never looked back."

Ladan walked faster toward the crowd. Nuri didn't feel inclined to move. He stood there for a while. When Ladan disappeared, he turned back.

The crowd was turning into a tree-lined alley with a green Shemiranat jurisdiction sign. Headlights occasionally lit the words on the reflective sign and threw oblique shadows into the depths of the alley. Nuri was overtaken by an emotion that was neither fear nor anticipation. It was more like a pleasurable apprehension that always gripped him when he was alone or in unfamiliar places. He would follow a stranger along the Shemiran alleys. Imitating private investigators, he would put his hands into his pockets and be puzzled by the sense of déjà vu he experienced in the neighborhoods he wandered through. What prompted him to visit these places? What lost object was he after?

When he found himself walking toward the city center, he knew he had followed a stranger. A turbaned *akhund*, dressed in a black winter robe, paused occasionally by the road, leaned on his cane, and looked up the street to see if a bus was headed in his direction. Passing cars' lights sometimes made his profile resemble the bust of the poet Ferdowsi, though lacking the epic majesty and the scowl of a statue staring down history. A smooth line delineated the *akhund*'s forehead, nose, and lips and made him look calm—a patient person used to waiting his turn. He blinked his eyes constantly. Whenever a bus appeared in the distance, he signaled to it with the tip of his cane, but most of the buses were full. The drivers changed gears and passed him by like stubborn children making faces. City lights were beginning to emerge in the distance. Nuri sighed in relief. After the Pahlavi intersection, he decided to stop following the *akhund*, but when he turned toward the university, the *akhund* did the same and even slowed down to adjust to Nuri's pace. Although he was probably around forty or forty-five years old, his face appeared very young. He surveyed his surroundings cautiously from the corner of his eye. It seemed as if he wanted to strike up a conversation with Nuri. He concealed his embarrassment with a tentative smile. He pushed his glasses up his nose to read a piece of paper he was holding between two fingers. The left lens was covered with a piece of cloth that was wrapped around the black frame, apparently to hold the glasses together. Now, under the streetlight, his face appeared shiny. His skin was sallow and soft like smoky ivory. A sprouty beard made him look almost faded. Delicate, feminine lines defined his features and gave them a special appeal, like innocence elevated to perfection. He pushed the hair on his forehead under his turban and said in broken French, "Bon soir, Monsieur." Nuri leaned forward, but said nothing. This time the *akhund* said in English, "Good evening, sir."

Nuri blinked a few times and asked, "Are you talking to me?"

The *akhund* spread the fingers of one hand and covered his mouth with them. He blurted out, "Oh, you are Iranian."

"Where did you think I was from?"

The *akhund* twisted his lips with his fingers, and his eyes grew wide. "You have to forgive me. My mind is elsewhere. I'm tired. I haven't slept for a few nights. I thought you were . . . ," he tried to fix his gaze on Nuri's hair and eyes, " . . . a foreigner. Your hair and eyes make one assume."

"It's all right. There are a lot of foreigners around here."

"To tell you the truth, in some respects I too am a foreigner. Two weeks ago an important affair brought me from Ghomsheh to Tehran. I had no idea that I would have to spend every day of these two weeks hunting down a foreigner. This person has left something with me, and I have to return it to her. I have gone to most of the hotels and bars where foreigners hang out, but to no avail. Now most of the foreigners know me. As soon as they spot me, they wave and say: 'Hajji, no news yet?'" He put his fist in front of his mouth to stop himself from laughing. "Well, that's a sign of their kindness. We Iranians have a habit of badmouthing foreigners. God is my witness, in this period of time I have seen nothing but kindness, politeness, and respect from these poor souls."

Nuri said, "Tell me your friend's name. Maybe I'll be able to help you."

The *akhund* bowed and spoke in a humble tone that struck Nuri as ridiculous. "You are most kind." He held out a piece of paper under the streetlamp. "For now, read these few lines. I'll tell you the rest."

The paper had passed through so many hands that it looked like an old banknote. Nuri could barely make out the words. "Quel soir, Nina! Quel soir, Nina!" After a few seconds, Nuri repeated the words, "Quel soir, Nina! Quel soir, Nina!"

Nuri realized that the *akhund* was happy to hear the French words. He jumped up and down like a child and repeated in a sing-song fashion, "Quel soir, Nina! Quel soir, Nina! Have you heard that song?" Nuri shook his head. The *akhund* continued. "Yes, this is an old French song. The tape recording . . . "—he inserted his hand into the pocket of his robe and brought out a tape—"this recording of it was entrusted to me by a foreign friend named Nina. Religious duty enjoins me to return it to her, but I can't find her anywhere." He put the tape back in his pocket and grew pensive. "Agha, it's strange . . . I'm sorry, but if it's not too nosy, can I ask your name?"

"Nuri Hushiar."

"God be praised, what a nice name. May God keep us all alert as in the meaning of your name. I was saying that two weeks ago I heard this song sung by this lady. Your Excellency Hushiar, what a night it was when she honored me with her performance! She sang a delicate song for me that I will never forget as long as I live. How strangely ignorant we all are, Your Excellency Hushiar. We don't know what fate has up its sleeve for us. For instance, your servant who has come from the provinces likes to spend the nights out in the streets of Tehran to see everything before returning to Ghomsheh." He looked up at the roofs of the buildings. "How this city has progressed. I went to the bazaar today to buy a small tribal rug as a souvenir for Miss Nina. The shameless merchant asked for two hundred and twenty tumans. Do you grasp my meaning? Two hundred and twenty tumans! If I had two hundred and twenty tumans in my pocket, I would have taken Miss Nina by the hand, gone to New York with her, and invited her to a first-class restaurant. No, this city is not for me. I had better get myself to the Mihan Tour Bus terminal and go back to Ghomsheh before I lose my hat to the wind. I am only concerned that this lady will return to her country and say that Iranians are disloyal, ignorant, and, may I be struck dumb, ungrateful."

"Is this your first trip out of Ghomsheh?"

"This is my fourth trip. My previous trips were for the purpose of buying prayer books to sell in Ghomsheh, Neyriz, and Isfahan. Now I am being given a carrel in the seminary attached to the Sepahsalar Mosque. In return, I pay a small tuition fee."

They were passing by Cinema Diana. The Parand Pastry Shop was unusually deserted. Nuri glanced toward the university. He saw a few people he didn't recognize. He had no desire to run into his classmates. He mumbled to the *akhund*, "So, you are staying here."

"No, I've decided to go back. This is not my place." He lifted his nose heavenward and took a deep breath. "What a nice smell, Your Excellency Hushiar. Do you smell it? What is it?"

Nuri sniffed. "The smell of fresh coffee. Have you ever had Turkish coffee?"

"What a nice smell! Some things have a better smell than taste. I wouldn't mind trying it. How do you order it in the café?"

"No big deal. You sit at a table and order Turkish coffee."

"Is that all?"

"That's all."

"Would you give me the honor of guiding me? Allow me to invite you."

They went into the café and sat at a table by the window, and Nuri ordered coffee. The *akhund* suddenly raised his head and said, "In Ghomsheh, it's customary not to trust Tehranis too much, but this kind of thinking is old-fashioned. They imagine that the minute they step outside the Ghomsheh gate, they'll be at the end of the world. They say that the inhabitants of Ghomsheh are the most intelligent in the whole of the Middle East and are racially closest to the Aryans. When you think about it, we don't really understand our own customs and beliefs. It is said that each generation's vision is shrouded by a veil. Only later generations can see what the earlier ones could not. These old beliefs stem from ignorance and lack of education. Look at us, for instance. I mean Your Excellency and me. One is from Tehran and the other from Ghomsheh. We are sitting here like two brothers and having a pleasant and open chat. I look at you, you look at your servant. Despite all our differences, we are compatriots. The language we speak to each other is like the language of our own tribe. There is no difference between you and me. Whatever is mine is yours, albeit not worthy of you. I bet you have the same attitude toward me. God is my witness, if I had a thousand, ten thousand, even a hundred thousand tumans in my pocket, I would offer it all to you with no receipt, signature, or stamp and return to Ghomsheh with an empty pocket."

"I am very grateful."

The *akhund* put his hand in his pocket and took out a wad of notes to give to Nuri. Nuri pulled back and shook his head apologetically.

"Why not, why don't you want to make a compatriot happy? Why shouldn't you trust me? If there is no trust between us, how can I feel close to you? What difference does it make if a compatriot has black or blond hair? His eyes are blue or brown? A human being has to understand love, compassion, loyalty, courage, and selflessness. He has to feel compassion toward others. This is what matters and remains forever. The rest is nonsense. The most important thing is to feel compassion and be capable of suffering pain."

He brought the notes closer to Nuri, but Nuri shrank back again. "No, thank you."

The *akhund* hesitantly put the wad of notes in his pocket and said, "Did you say you inherited the blue eyes and blond hair from your mother?"

"From my grandmother. She's Austrian."

"God be praised. May God keep you for her." He remained open-mouthed for a while. Then he pushed aside the ashtray and the sugar bowl and said, "Your Excellency Hushiar, I would like to tell you something, but I would like it to stay between us."

"Please, go ahead."

They waited until Khachator served their coffee, added up their bill, and left. Then the *akhund* smirked, lowered his head, and shook it like a limp piece of meat as if to indicate the futility of sitting in a café. But the smirk quickly faded. He craned his neck. "Everyone is startled out of a nightmare at least once in his lifetime. Whichever direction you stretch your hands, they touch nothing. And there is no one to awaken you. My condition is exactly the same. If this has happened to you, you'll know what I mean. You say to yourself: 'OK, she's a foreigner. It makes no difference if she is British, French, or Japanese.' I just don't know what is so different about Miss Nina that has drawn me to her so much. Of course, Americans are completely different from other foreigners. They are so self-absorbed that no matter where they go, they don't seem to take note of others. Even when they are abroad, they shop, dress, and give parties as if they were still in America. Their houses don't have walls. American men go into the street with no underpants. The women have no shame about going out in their undergarments. Perhaps, as some say, they don't have a proper culture and that's why they don't respect others' customs and habits, but I say it's all indicative of their simplicity. Like children who trust everyone. Even if they are cheated, they feign ignorance. They don't draw your attention to it because they don't want to embarrass you.

I have no reason to distrust you. One night I stole this same tape of 'Quel soir, Nina' from Miss Nina's purse. Now, don't ask why. I suddenly got it into my head and stole the tape. I told myself maybe she would like the shrewdness of a person from the Third World. Perhaps she would say to herself that she should not underestimate me. OK. Everyone has a weak point, and if Satan gets under his skin, may God help him. Anyway, God is my witness, Miss Nina did not let on, although she had noticed my crime. She acted generously and continued to talk about her travels across the world and her trip from America."

"Really? I thought she was French. Nina is a French name."

"Her mother is French, but she herself is American. She is one of those blondes with simple and innocent looks. Now, imagine that an eighteen-year-old girl has come from that far away all alone to tour the world on a clunky motorcycle. What courage! If I had this kind of courage, I would get on Miss Nina's motorcycle and tour the world with her."

Nuri had grown used to the *akhund*. He nodded and agreed implicitly with matters that in no way concerned him. He asked, "So, you feel like touring the world with Miss Nina?"

"Why not? I even mentioned it to her. She was going to think it over and let me know. Unfortunately, I have walked all over this city without finding any trace of her. At the very least, I wanted to return this tape and explain to her that I am not one to take things lightly. I didn't steal the tape as a silly practical joke. I wanted to have a memento so that if I suddenly grew doubtful about our encounter, I would have something to prove that I had not dreamed the whole thing. So let's admit that I did something wrong, but believe me it was out of ignorance and lack of experience. I have never wanted to hurt anyone in any way, let alone Miss Nina for whom I reserve a special place and respect. I told her many times: 'Dear Khanom, what have you seen in my worthless appearance and being that you dote on me so and put me to such shame? What attraction could this threadbare robe, loose turban, and broken glasses have for you to make you waste so much of your time on me? Your servant doesn't even know how to use a knife and fork. I don't know how to greet foreigners. I see no reason to receive such attention from a beautiful and precious girl like you.' She always answered me in Persian in a sweet tone that, I swear by the blessed soil of the tomb of the chief of the faithful and by the parched lips of the martyr of martyrs, was more delightful than celestial songs. Your Excellency Hushiar, allow me to speak frankly. Those nights it was as if angels sang to this poor soul. Miss Nina parted her beautiful lips and sang in a voice that I don't believe any living being has ever heard: 'Quel soir, Nina! Quel soir, Nina! Quel soir, Nina! . . . '"

Brimming with joy or whatever his feeling might be called, the *akhund* smiled passionately. He shut his eyes and shook his head. "I told her: 'To what do I owe all this kindness? Am I awake, or am I dreaming?' She said: 'You are a unique man. You have a pure heart filled with love like a child who doesn't realize he is capable of hurting others.' I asked: 'Me?' She replied: 'Yes, you.' Your Excellency Hushiar, had you been in my place, wouldn't you have lost your head? Wouldn't you have fled into fields and plains? Wouldn't you have gone someplace where no one could find you?" He frowned and struck his fist on the table. "But I was stupid. I imagined I could speak openly with an American woman and tell her whatever was on my mind. I asked her to permit me to take a kiss from her sweet lips, those wells of nectar and honey, and remain indebted to her for the rest of my life. She disregarded my insolence and said: 'What's wrong with talking? Why do we have to end up kissing and embracing?' It was out of my control, Your Excellency Hushiar. I forgot myself and overstepped the bounds. I insisted so much that she finally accepted, but on one condition. I said: 'Whatever condition you impose, I'll accept willingly.' She said on the condition that I kiss her with my eyes shut. OK. I'm from Ghomsheh and don't know much. I just shut my eyes and waited a few moments, but nothing happened. When I opened my eyes, she had vanished like a dream. I looked here and there in the streets, in the narrow and dark alleys, among trees and under the sidewalk bushes, but did not find her. That was two weeks ago, and I have walked all over this city and still haven't found a trace of her. Sometimes I get so tired of myself, I think I should kill myself. When your eyes have seen beauty, such a perfect beauty at that, you have reached your life's goal. There is nothing left to live for. Your servant has concluded that the meaning of life is to discover and witness perfect beauty. Everything we do in life stems from love. To remove one by one the veils covering our eyes and to let our sight revel in beauty. After that, life is a pointless waste of time. So what if I live for another fifty years, keeping myself alive with quantities of bread, cheese, and meat? At the end, I'm left with the same bowl and the same soup. Am I not right?"

Nuri couldn't manage even a simple smile as a response. He had noticed a woman pass in front of the café, walking hand in hand with an army captain. The gazes of the passersby were unwittingly drawn to the curves of her buttocks, but the woman's own attention was riveted to the captain. Her laughter was so loud that it could be heard inside the café. The woman had the same white dress and red purse that Soraya usually wore to parties and outings. Nuri couldn't believe how eagerly Soraya clung to the captain. She nonchalantly straightened her dress over her hips and shoulders, wet a finger, and ran it under her eyes absentmindedly as if she were completely absorbed in the captain's words. Nuri rose to leave. The *akhund* grabbed his sleeve. "Your Excellency Hushiar, where are you going? Why have you turned so pale? Did I say something offensive?"

Nuri answered superficially, "Something urgent has come up. I have to leave quickly. I apologize."

He reached into his pocket to leave money for the bill, but the *akhund* stopped him. "Please, allow me. Why are you being so unkind?"

"You have to forgive me. I have to leave. It's an urgent matter."

"It's still early."

"Please permit me to leave."

"When can I see you again? How is tomorrow night at seven?"

"Certainly. Certainly."

Nuri ran out of the café. The *akhund* shouted, "Don't forget our rendezvous! Tomorrow night at seven, right here."

"OK!"

The minute Nuri stepped into the street, he remembered that he had not asked the *akhund*'s name. He had an image of a lock of black hair escaping from underneath the *akhund*'s turban and falling on his forehead, a pair of glazed eyes in a permanent state of surprise.

In the street, he couldn't see Soraya and the captain. It was impossible for the two of them to disappear so quickly. He made his way to the side alley and looked around, but saw no one. He ran to the end of the alley and came out in another deserted alley in the rear of the university. Only where the alley fed into Amirabad Avenue could he see car headlights that moved like the beads on a rosary. He ran toward Amirabad Avenue. As he got closer, he noticed a telephone booth. A short distance from it stood the captain with two other men. Nuri withdrew. It was not wise for him to step into the fray with illusions of rescuing Soraya. He was likely to fall into the hands of a bunch of thugs. He had best survey the scene first.

Soraya entered the booth. With a scowl, she picked up the receiver and spoke fast and in an angry tone. When she talked, she seemed to be chewing gum. She flapped an arm about. Every now and then she threw a worried sidelong glance in the direction of the captain and his two friends, who were making faces at her and razzing her. Her frown issued a warning to them at the same time that she argued with someone on the phone, but the three men didn't heed her warning. They continued to make faces at her and laugh out loud. She suddenly looked weary and hung up.

Here were Nuri and these three drunken, insolent thugs. Like vulgar Cossacks, they scratched their thighs, teased Soraya, and laughed at her. Nuri was afraid that if he acted as a shield for Soraya, he would be beaten to a pulp by the three men. They had their hands on each other's shoulders. They were laughing so hard that their heads drew back and fell forward in unison. One of the men, who wore army boots, walked to the booth, opened the door, and put his arms around Soraya's waist to draw her out. He did this so quickly that Soraya was taken by surprise. Like an insect turned on its back, she waved her arms and legs as the man dragged her out. At first, she didn't let go of the receiver, but it soon slipped out of her hand and dangled in the air. She pulled down her skirt, which had bunched up on her thighs, and offered a half-teasing smile to the man who was still holding her in his arms. Looking like a miffed schoolgirl, she turned away from him and straightened herself. She slid out of his arms, stood on the sidewalk, and said, "Ouch, why did you squeeze me so hard? You hurt me, Father dear." The man tickled Soraya's armpits and made her laugh. Soraya complained in jest. "Get lost, find somebody your own size."

The man bent down, held his pursed lips in front of her face, and said, "You are my size, sweetie!"

The three began to laugh. Soraya looked away and said, "Oh, may God kill me, not in front of everybody."

The man brought his face closer to kiss Soraya, but she withdrew abruptly. He inserted his hand under the shoulder strap of her dress. Soraya covered her chest hurriedly. She lowered her voice. "How silly! I'll scream . . . "

Nuri put his hands in his trouser pockets and crisscrossed the tips of his shoes on the pavement. He felt numb. He saw a marble by the gutter and kicked it. He hopped behind it and, when he got closer, kicked it harder. He got carried away and with the next kick shot the marble to the end of the alley like an ice cube. This time, instead of hopping, he ran to it. He stumbled on a crack in the pavement and almost fell. He grabbed two bars of the metal fence around the university and began kicking the cement wall with his feet. The curses that issued from the depths of his throat sounded like the wails of an injured animal. He leaned against the wall and slid down to the pavement. He was cold. He covered his cheeks with his palms. He felt the weight of his heavy head in his hands, as if it belonged to a mysterious creature. For a moment, he thought someone else was touching his head, like when he was sick and Maman Zuzu had put her palm on his forehead to see if he had a temperature.

A clunky old Volkswagen drove by and left behind an odor of gas that blended with the stench of garbage. Nuri had to abandon himself to instinct and go wherever it took him. When he reached Shahreza Street, he got an urge to find the *akhund* from Ghomsheh. He threw a furtive glance into the café, but he did not see the *akhund*. He walked toward Shahyad Square. Maybe he would run into Buki. He became absorbed in the blinking billboards and the lights adorning the food stores, which resembled a string of pearls looping down from a neck. He felt as if he were in a wedding, being showered by colored tinsel instead of by the customary white coins and candies. He remembered Soraya and her three hooligan friends. How he had thrown in the towel! Fortunately, there were no witnesses to give him away.

He ambled about for a full hour or maybe more. He debated about going to the Tahmasbis' apartment. He recalled Soraya's face in the storage room, like a close-up of a godly image projected on a screen. He felt he was being drawn into the bottomless depths of her dark eyes. His love for Soraya seemed to have more to do with a sense of distance than with familiarity—like a riddle that the more you try to solve it, the more you become enchanted.

He waited in front of the Tahmasbis' apartment for a while and grew calm. Not only was it late, but he also lacked an excuse for a visit. He glanced at his luminous watch. The hands were not moving. It showed eight-thirty, which couldn't be right. The apartment door was unlocked. He opened it with a gentle push. Sweeping darkness drew him into a corridor like the mouth of a large fish. As if touched by something cold, his body seemed to stand out in the darkness. With each step he took, the darkness became less saturated. The draft he felt indicated that he was approaching the kitchen. He smelled a mixture of burning oil, unwashed dishes, and cooling coal in the samovar. Then he heard Mrs. Tahmasbi's bronchial and knotted voice. "Watch out for the garbage can, Naneh-jun. There is a chair by the door. Bring it in and sit down."

She spoke with patience, almost with resignation, as if she were preparing herself to reveal a painful secret. Nuri heard a match being struck and out of the darkness emerged Mrs. Tahmasbi's tired eyes set in black circles, unblinking like the eyes of a statue. She was seated on a stool by the kitchen counter. She raised her hand. She took the glass off a lantern sitting on a kitchen shelf, lit the wick with a match, and replaced the glass. She said, "You have to forgive me. There has been no electricity for an hour. Dust be on their heads! On radio and TV, it's constantly announced that we are reaching the great civilization, so why is it that when it comes to electricity and simple things like that, no one talks of great civilization? I swear on my father's grave, they say these things to placate us. They think we're a bunch of naïve children for whom they can paint sparrows."

She wore her blue plastic slippers. She had crossed her legs, and her bare, chocolaty shins looked dry and chapped. She gently dangled one foot in the air and examined Nuri so closely that he got the jitters. He asked, "When do you go to bed?"

Mrs. Tahmasbi rested her elbow on the counter and brushed back her hair. "We aren't used to going to bed early. Naneh-jan, what made you think of us, the little people, at this time of night?"

If Nuri had had the nerve, at that very moment he would have asked Soraya's whereabouts and put his mind at ease, but he felt awkward. Moreover, he didn't think Soraya would have returned yet. Meanwhile, Mrs. Tahmasbi was staring strangely at his mouth, as if she had suddenly noticed that he had a harelip or something like that. He spoke in a monotone. "I wanted to come by much earlier, but I had problems to attend to."

"What problems?"

"Things are not good at all. The streets are either crowded or completely deserted. Half of the stores are shut. The other half lower their iron grilles as soon as there is any noise. Several times I tried in vain to find Buki."

"Well, you should have come directly to me. I would have found him for you."

"I didn't have time. These battles don't leave me or anyone else time even to scratch our heads."

"May God kill me. Have you too taken up demonstrating and writing slogans?"

He wrinkled his forehead and said, "Well, you can't sit idly by. Just an hour ago, with my own eyes I saw three army officers dragging a beautiful girl into a telephone booth and assaulting her."

Mrs. Tahmasbi struck her palm on her cheek and bit her lower lip. "Eh, may God kill me." She held her fist in front of her mouth. "What a world we live in. You mean right there on the street in front of everybody?" Nuri nodded in agreement. Mrs. Tahmasbi said, "What unimaginable things we hear! Why didn't you call the police or ask people for help?"

Nuri showed his brass knuckles to Mrs. Tahmasbi. "With these very knuckles, I punched one good-for-nothing so hard he didn't even know what hit him. When he tried to move, I planted two more punches under his left eye and one more in his groin. He yelped and fled. When his pansy friends saw this, they let go of the girl and came to tackle me. They held up their fists." He held up his own fists, lowered his head, and fought with an invisible adversary. "One of them tried to punch me in the face. I threw him two karate kicks, and blood spurted out of his nose as if from a fountain. He cursed me and said he would get even with me one day and

make my mother mourn for me. By this time, people from the neighborhood had gathered. As soon as the other two realized things were heating
up, they borrowed an extra pair of legs and fled. . . . "

Mrs. Tahmasbi grabbed her cheek. "Naneh-jan, how fearless you are.
Don't you realize this is a lawless country? Here any fool with a pair of
epaulets and a couple of snots glued to his hat considers himself entitled
to people's property, honor, and soul. Thank goodness you weren't alone.
When these types lose it, they put a bullet through you. Naneh-jan, what
amazing luck that these hooligans didn't do you any harm. What did you
do with the girl?"

"I put her in a cab and took her to her home in Yusofabad."

Mrs. Tahmasbi mumbled, "Thank God. I swear by the light of this
lantern that every night when I put my head on the pillow, I think of you.
You know that Buki does not have a good head on his shoulders. Out of
stupidity, he makes himself the bean in every soup, does strange things,
and exposes himself to danger. He gets entangled with people who can
handle a hundred his size. I can't fall asleep until he comes home at night.
I can't sleep at all. I have terrible thoughts. I ask myself what my darling
child is doing in the streets. What has happened to him? In the mornings, I'm afraid to open my eyes and find his picture in the papers, lying
face down in a gutter somewhere outside city limits, police tape around
his body, and officers taking pictures of him. Nobody is dependable in
this house. None of them comes home at dinnertime. Buki's comings and
goings are haphazard. Thank God, at least Cyrus has established his own
home. Maybe Pari Khanom"—she threw a meaningful glance at Nuri, and
a smirk appeared on her face but faded quickly—"will put some order in
his life. Teach him to go to bed at a regular hour every night and get up
at the same time every day. Sori-jun alone always returns around ten or
eleven. Barely having eaten dinner, she puts her head down on a pillow
and falls asleep like a charmed spirit."

"Is the Colonel home?"

"What difference does it make to me whether he's home or not? Most
nights he reads newspapers and magazines in his room until midnight.
I am the one who has to stay up every night until they come home. May
God kill me, I forgot to pour you tea. Would you like some?"

"Thank you, don't trouble yourself. I didn't come here to have tea. By the way, where is Soraya Khanom?"

Mrs. Tahmasbi shrugged, wrinkled the corners of her mouth, and poured tea into a cup. "What should I say? Not everyone is like you and worries about others and is concerned about his mother. Naneh-jun, I am really thankful to you. How nice that you remembered us and came here. Please have this cup to make me happy. I imagine Sori-jun will be showing up soon."

"I swear I am not just being polite, Mrs. Tahmasbi. I don't drink tea at night."

"Just have this one cup for my sake. As the Colonel says, tea has to be drunk before sleep. It sharpens your mind."

Nuri glanced toward the kitchen door and said softly, "I have a rendezvous with my superior. Let's leave the tea for another night."

"Why do you speak so softly, Naneh-jun? Nobody is home to hear you. I am all alone. I sit here to drink tea, smoke a cigarette, and do my work. Maybe chop an onion, wash a dirty dish. Please take a seat until the kids come home."

Nuri sat in one of the four blue plastic chairs around the table. The minutes passed slowly and in silence. He had given a fake version of the encounter between Soraya and her three friends and now he had to tell the truth. But Mrs. Tahmasbi's tired, other-worldly look dissuaded him. Her ignorance of what was happening made him feel sorry for her. She put the teacup and sugar bowl on the table with the movements of an automaton. Without making any noise, she returned to the sink. She said, "Naneh-jan, for some time I have been looking for an opportunity to talk to you about your future." She stressed the word *future.* "You have to think of me as your mother. You were raised on my own lap. You were never just a neighbor's son. From the day Zuzu Khanom went to America, I have been thinking about your future. I myself was fifteen years old when I married the Colonel. I had to live with my mother-in-law, two old-fashioned sisters-in-law, and a bunch of other oafs in a tiny place. God is my witness, there was not a single day that I didn't lift my head from the pillow and cry and ask God how long I would have to endure my in-laws' put-downs. If I say there is not a compassionate person in the Senator's house, I have no bad intention. I have always told the Colonel that if that accident had not happened, we would have been neighbors today and at least would have kept an eye on you from a distance."

"Of course, you are like a mother to me. When I don't see you for a while, I swear to God I miss you."

"You don't know how much Sori-jun is taken with you. This same girl who doesn't even submit to God pleads with me once a week to go to Qom and take a prayer written with saffron on a piece of cloth to tie to the shrine of Saint Ma'sumeh so that she will get her wish."

"What wish?"

Mrs. Tahmasbi patiently held a match under her cigarette and narrowed one eye to keep the smoke out of it. A mischievous smile pulled up the corners of her mouth. She crossed her legs and said, "Among all her rich and elite suitors, she is interested only in you. It would not be a lie if I told you that she has written a hundred letters to you. She stays up until midnight in her room to write to you. She hasn't mailed even one to you. Well, what can I do? If she writes these letters, it's just for her own sake. God forbid that someone should read one of them. You're not a stranger. You know how important her reputation is to her."

Nuri blurted out, "She writes me letters?"

"Don't make her wait any longer. She is sensitive. She'll get hurt."

"Is she waiting for me? Why?"

"You just have to declare your intentions."

He didn't fully grasp Mrs. Tahmasbi's meaning. He asked, "How should I declare my intentions?"

Mrs. Tahmasbi put out her half-smoked cigarette and gulped down her tea. She gathered the cups and saucers, rinsed them under the tap, and said, "Naneh-jan, when do the Senator and Madame intend to come and ask for Soraya's hand?"

"To ask for Soraya Khanom's hand?"

"What's this 'Soraya Khanom'? Try saying 'Sori-jun' once. It's much prettier. Never mind. There is no way to make Sori-jun take an interest in another man. May this never happen, she says she would rather be buried without a shroud than to marry a nobody like Shirzad. Well, she is right, and we agree. But a young girl can't sit in a corner for an eternity waiting for some news from you."

Nuri lowered his head. "Mrs. Tahmasbi, you know very well that I haven't even finished high school. I am ten years younger than Soraya Khanom. I haven't yet reached the marriageable age."

"In this day and age, no one worries about birth certificates. Isn't our own king ten years older than Shahbanu? Was she dumb to have married him?"

She suddenly broke into laughter. Nuri waited until she finished laughing. He said, "The husband can be older, but if the wife is the older one . . . then?"

"They say in France it's customary for men to marry much older women. . . . " Noises could be heard from the direction of the alley. She paused and asked hesitantly, "Naneh-jan, where are those noises coming from?"

"I think from the alley."

"Do you hear them too?"

Nuri recognized Soraya's voice coming closer. Repeating short sentences sounding like "Shut up" and "You'll wake the neighbors," she was urging her companions to be quiet. Nuri said, "I bet that's Soraya Khanom."

"Is that Soraya's voice? Really?"

"I bet it's her."

Soraya's disheveled appearance was a sign of temerity. She was not afraid of anything. She took uneven steps toward the kitchen. Whenever the three men in the alley shouted something, she smiled and put on a humble expression like a young bride who has heard her own praises. Now their voices could be clearly heard from the alley:

"Sori-jun, why are you hiding?"

"Sori-jun, you who came from India, were this big and grew this big . . . "

"How big is my dear, how big is my darling, how coy you are!"

Soraya was looking for a place to sit when she suddenly lost her temper. She rushed back to the door with firm and decisive steps. The minute she opened the door, she shouted, "If you don't leave, I'll call the police."

The three broke into laughter. One of them screamed like a little girl. "Didn't you hear? Are you deaf? She'll call the police, and they'll take care of you once and for all."

The second joined in: "Bread, cheese, and herbs . . . "

The third chimed in, "Don't shudder when you see the policeman . . . "

The first one: "The policeman won't do anything to you . . . "

The three together: "He'll take out his stick. . . . "

Soraya grew quiet. She returned to the kitchen with slow and half-hearted steps. Mrs. Tahmasbi wanted to say something, but anger seemed to have rendered her speechless. She spat into the ashtray and shuffled in her plastic slippers to the apartment door. After a few moments, she could be heard shouting, "Don't you have lives of your own?"

The captain answered Mrs. Tahmasbi quietly. "Greetings."

Mrs. Tahmasbi continued. "The only thing you know is to find an innocent and naïve girl alone and pester her. There's a limit to obscenity."

The captain spoke politely in a tone that betrayed shock, "Khanom, please forgive these boys. If they said any nonsense, it's because of their ignorance." He turned to his two companions and ordered, "Get on your way."

"What did we say, Said-jun?"

"Put your heads down and walk to the street. I'll join you in a minute."

Their steps could be heard down the alley. After a while, the captain shouted, "Have you been raised in a barn? Why haven't you bid the lady farewell?"

They started laughing but quickly stopped. The second one shouted, "Good night, farewell."

Mrs. Tahmasbi slammed the apartment door and returned to the kitchen. When she walked by Soraya, she ignored her. Only their shoulders touched slightly. Soraya's gaze had grown filmy, as if she were roaming other worlds. She brushed back her hair, took a tube of lipstick, a small brown case, and her key chain from her purse, then tossed them back in without looking at them. She stood in the middle of the kitchen for a few moments, looking dazed and distraught. Suddenly throwing herself into a chair, she began to cry soundlessly. First, her shoulders began to shake.

Mrs. Tahmasbi pleaded with her. "Get up, Naneh-jun. Let's go upstairs. Put on a comfortable dress and lie down." She threw a hurt glance at Nuri. "Evil eyes will do their damage. These people, may they die a painful death, can't see a beautiful girl without tormenting her. They won't leave her alone."

She put the palm of her hand on Soraya's head and gently patted it, running her fingers down her hair. Nuri said, "Do you know who has given her an evil eye?"

"I don't know; otherwise, I would've settled my score by now."

"I wish you knew." He suddenly felt choked up. He spoke faster. "Soraya Khanom should not go out alone. A bodyguard should accompany her at all times."

Soraya snorted and protested. "Nuri, can't you call me by another name? What's this 'Soraya Khanom' shit?"

"What should I call you?"

Mrs. Tahmasbi seemed to have become excited by Soraya's words. She answered, "Well, say 'Sori-jun, my dear, my beauty,' what difference does it make? Don't let a bunch of jealous people ruin your relationship. There is no shortage of jealous evil-wishers in this country. God is my witness, not a bad word has escaped this girl's mouth. She has never hurt anyone. She has never been ungrateful. It's no nonsense when I say Sori-jun is different from these superficial girls running around everywhere. These so-called humble girls just know how to run around with lewd people from morning to night."

She brought her chair closer and threw her arm around Soraya's neck. She had a hard time reaching and had to bring her chair even closer. Soraya didn't move an inch, but slowly lowered her tilted head onto her mother's shoulder. Her eyes closed, and she seemed to melt into her mother's arms. She put her thumb in her mouth. Mrs. Tahmasbi threw a proud glance toward Nuri. "Nuri-jan, don't just stand there. Come a step closer and help me take Sori-jun up to her room. Poor thing is collapsing from fatigue." She brushed Soraya's hair away from her eyes and grew absorbed in her flushed face. "Sori-jun, how lucky you are to have Nuri here. He'll bring you whatever you need."

Nuri said, "Whatever you wish, I'll bring to you."

Mrs. Tahmasbi bit her lip and winked at Nuri. "Come closer. Don't be afraid. Support her under her arms. Let's take her upstairs."

The entire time Nuri helped Soraya up the stairs, she didn't resist or utter one word of protest. Only occasionally when their arms touched was a secret dialogue established between them. Polite contact that lasted up to the middle of the staircase. Then they pulled their arms apart, as if by some implicit agreement, and walked the rest of the way firmly. Unaware of all this, Mrs. Tahmasbi climbed the stairs, grumbling about the absence of electricity. "I'm afraid this darkness will cause an accident. Watch your step. You have to be a cat to walk in this darkness. Why don't you wait a minute. I'll go to the kitchen and bring the lantern."

After Mrs. Tahmasbi's departure, a silence fell—the kind of silence in which you can hear the other person's breathing, the kind that demanded response and action. Nuri needed distance in order to talk. He drew back. That was a mistake. A void was left on his skin where Soraya's arm had touched him. He felt a need to fill that void. Then Soraya suddenly pressed her chest to his. She whispered into his ear, and her warm breath tickled. "Nuri-jun . . . "

"Huh? What?"

She threw her arms around Nuri's neck, pulled him closer, and said, "Why do you talk like this?"

"How?"

"Like Shirazis."

"Do you dislike it?"

"Sometimes I like it. When you say 'Soraya Khanom,' it's as if you are speaking to a mature woman. I get embarrassed. Do you remember how shy I was when you were young? You'd think I wouldn't be shy now. We're past all that. If I want to dance with you, why shouldn't I?"

The lantern appeared in the staircase and gradually lit up the corridor. Mrs. Tahmasbi herself emerged from the darkness, holding the lantern above her head. When she climbed the stairs ahead of them, Soraya wrinkled her nose and stuck her tongue out at Nuri. Mrs. Tahmasbi had no idea what was happening behind her. She continued to mumble. "When an evil eye strikes something, it's ruined. It never fails. Once in the beginning of winter, the departed Bibi Ghezi came to our house. She looked at our persimmon tree and praised it: 'What big persimmons your tree has produced.' That was it. As God is my witness, every week we used to hire a worker to shake the tree. Nobody could make the fruit drop from the tree like he did. The next year the tree dried up completely. Not even a leaf, let alone persimmons. We hired Mashadi Ali. He sawed that tree, cut it into firewood, and sold it at one qerun a load."

They entered Soraya's room, and Soraya plopped down on her bed. She took off her red shoes, looked into each shoe and sniffed it, shook dust and pebbles out of it, and threw it down on the floor. She rubbed her feet, which had turned beet red. Then she lay on her bed.

Mrs. Tahmasbi smiled contentedly and placed the lantern by the bed-side lamp. Then she went over to Soraya and leaned beside her on a pillow. Although Soraya's eyes were shut, she seemed to be paying attention to all that happened around her. She put her forearm on her forehead, opened her eyes, and, as soon as she noticed Mrs. Tahmasbi sitting so close to her, pulled away. Mrs. Tahmasbi opened her arms to embrace Soraya and began cooing. Soraya shouted, "Why don't you leave me alone?"

Mrs. Tahmasbi froze. She threw a pleading glance in Nuri's direction and said, "Naneh-jan, what did I do?"

Soraya pulled herself up, planting her hands and knees on the bed. She lifted her head and barked at Mrs. Tahmasbi, "Why are you sitting here? When are you going to get lost?"

In response, Mrs. Tahmasbi pursed her lips and once again reached out to hug Soraya. In a flash, Soraya slapped Mrs. Tahmasbi's cheek. For some time, no one moved or made a sound. Then Soraya shouted at her mother, "I don't want to see your ugly face in this room ever again. Do you hear me? Get lost!"

Mrs. Tahmasbi put her palm to her flushed face. It didn't take long for tears to start rolling down her cheeks. She rose suddenly and ran out of the room. When she reached the stairs, she began sobbing. Her sobs could be heard for a few seconds.

Nuri wasn't happy to be alone with Soraya. He felt embarrassed and didn't know whose side to take. Without thinking, he rose on his knees and opened his arms. He had not yet touched Soraya when Soraya threw her arms around him and kissed him on the lips. Mrs. Tahmasbi's voice came from behind the door. "Soraya-jun . . . " She sobbed like a mother-less child. Her sobs made her sentences choppy. "My Soraya-jun, oh, my Soraya-jun, are you listening to me? What did I do? What did I say? If I said something, OK, I'll pay for it. It doesn't concern you. Do you know why, Naneh? What mother would be happy when her darling child is not? Someone I myself taught to walk, someone I toiled for, someone I stayed up nights and cared for? I don't expect anything from you. Are you listen-ing to me? Did you hear what I said, Naneh-jun? Do as you wish, may it all turn out well. Naneh, OK . . . ?"

Soraya barked at her, "Tell me, what is it that you want from me, Maman?"

"Your happiness. I only want your happiness. Your happiness is my happiness, Naneh-jan. I would like to see your face shine with happiness like the moon. My only joy is to sit in a corner and watch your moon face. What harm does that do you? Will you let me come in? Should I come in?"

Soraya turned toward the window. The deep wrinkles in her brow slowly faded. She still looked angry. Mrs. Tahmasbi started again. "Should I come in?" A few seconds passed in silence. "You won't be angry if I come in? You won't hit me, will you?" There was silence again. "Sori-jun, you know very well I'm nothing without you. Nothing, nothing. Let me tell you why I'm suffering this way. People are jealous, Sori-jun. They can't stand anybody's happiness. When they see us, they become jealous. They say: What's so special about them that they should like each other so much? If anybody should be happy, why shouldn't it be ourselves? You shouldn't let them get their wish. A mother is different from other people. Without any complaint, a mother will sacrifice herself for her child's hap-piness. One day you'll become a mother and you'll understand. All of a mother's wishes are in a glance. Her only joy is to look at her child's beau-tiful face. My Sori-jun, may I sacrifice myself for you, can I come in? Will you let me . . . ?"

Soraya said in a gentler tone, "Fine, so you come in, then what?"

The door opened, and Mrs. Tahmasbi entered. In her hand, she carried the yogurt bowl she usually used to dispel evil eyes. Inside the bowl was an egg and a piece of charcoal. Looking aggrieved, she approached the bed slowly. She placed the bowl gently by the bedside lamp and forced a smile. She began crying and tried to stop herself. "Sori-jun, these are tears of happiness. I'm proud of having a precious girl like you." She turned to Nuri and said, "This girl's heart is purer than a mirror. May I sacrifice myself for her beautiful body. May all her pain and disease be visited on me." She bent down to kiss Soraya. Soraya withdrew in disgust. Mrs. Tahmasbi said quickly, "Sori-jun, you don't like it? Fine, I won't kiss you. It's more than enough for me to sit here quietly." Then she put the egg between Soraya's fingers and spoke the names of people she knew. Soraya smiled coldly at Nuri and shrugged her shoulders, as if to say she couldn't stop this crazy woman. But then she was like wax in Mrs. Tahmasbi's hands. She didn't resist in the least. As Mrs. Tahmasbi pronounced each name, she drew a circle on the egg with the charcoal. "Shuri Khanom."

Soraya repeated Shuri Khanom's name, but the egg didn't break. Then they turned to the names of closer relatives and acquaintances— pretty Pari, Cyrus, Buki, Mr. Ra'oof, the neighbors, even people in Nuri's house, Najmeh and Ladan. When they reached Madame's name, the egg exploded in Soraya's fingers.

Mrs. Tahmasbi threw a meaningful glance at Nuri, but said nothing. Soraya threw back her head and laughed heartily. "Didn't you say you wanted to know the name of the jealous person? What are you going to do now?"

As Nuri looked back and forth from Mrs. Tahmasbi to Soraya, he tried to laugh, too. Mrs. Tahmasbi swallowed her smile. She rose. "Do you need anything I can bring you?"

Soraya asked, "Do we have any cake?"

"Even if we don't, the Fard Pastry Shop is close by. I'll go buy some. Keep your ears peeled for the doorbell until I come back."

She had barely left the room when she returned. She stuck her head in the door and said to Nuri, "You really have to forgive me. If Madame's name came up, don't take it seriously. The educated people today say they don't believe in such superstitions anymore."

She drew back her head and ran down the stairs.

... 11 ...

First, Nuri heard a man's footsteps in the alley, apparently rushing home late, then a woman's voice calling someone from within one of the neighboring houses, followed by a car horn that seemed to be suspended in the air for a few seconds. The empty silence left behind made him more conscious of scattered and incoherent sounds, like vague whispers from behind a closed door.

He sat down with his back against the wall, hugged his knees, and pretended to be on the lookout for Mrs. Tahmasbi's return from the Fard Pastry Shop. "I don't think the pastry shop will be open this late at night."

He said this to bring his unusual circumstances into some kind of order—especially now that Mrs. Tahmasbi had spoken of his marriage to Soraya as a fait accompli. He thought about the silly things people did when they were engaged—offering bouquets of flowers, going on late-night outings, and kissing each other in front of everyone—and he shuddered. The minute a couple exchanged engagement rings, their relationship became formal. The relatives would place a distance between themselves and the couple, allowing them to play the roles of bride and groom like a pair of movie stars. Nuri preferred a more accidental contact. He wanted to get closer to Soraya in privacy and with a veneer of innocence. Their own apparent nonchalance made him feel secure.

Despite his apprehension, he was completely overtaken by the desire to caress and kiss her. In order to restrain himself, he recalled Soraya's slapping Mrs. Tahmasbi. With his mind's eye, he saw Soraya's hand curve back, swing forward after a short pause, and strike Mrs. Tahmasbi's face so hard that her head bobbed like a spring.

Soraya asked in a slightly shaky voice, "Why are you so quiet?"

Nuri answered, "What do you want me to say?"

250

He was surprised by his confrontational tone. Maybe he wanted to cause a rift between them. Soraya rolled over on her bed and inched closer to Nuri. She asked, "Why are you frowning like this?"

"Like what?"

"Maybe you regret having come here."

Nuri said, "I don't frown for just any reason."

"Eh? What is your reason?"

"When I see you on the street with a bunch of hooligans. Where do you find these degenerates?"

"Which degenerates?"

"The ones who follow you around on the street."

"Do you mean Anasori?" She lowered her eyelids and, looking at her fingernails, asked sarcastically, "Are you by any chance jealous?"

Nuri said, "If I were you, I wouldn't be so friendly with such people."

"Does it hurt your sense of male pride, Nuri-jan?" She planted her elbows on the bed, rested her chin on her palms, and smiled like a coy child. "Am I not your pride? Why don't you call me your pride? Narrow your eyes a bit more and let me see."

"Why? Are you crazy?"

"Come on, narrow them. You look exactly like James Dean."

Nuri chuckled. "Don't tease me. I want to say what's on my mind."

Soraya sat on the bed tailor style and said, "OK. Say whatever you want. I won't talk anymore."

"Whatever I want?"

"Whatever."

"You shouldn't allow such thugs to treat you like . . . "

Soraya stopped laughing and asked, "Like what?"

He spoke quickly. "Like an ordinary woman."

Soraya shouted, "Why don't you finish what you were going to say, you idiot? Didn't you want to say 'like a whore'? OK. Say it. Who are you afraid of?"

"You misunderstood. Let me explain."

"Such big shit coming out of the mouth of a little munchkin like you!" She pressed her fists into her thighs and leaned forward threateningly. "If you mean that I have no idea when I'm dealing with degenerates, then why did I get involved with such a rude person as you? You men are all alike. You sacrifice everything to your desires. This Anasori believes himself a close friend of Cyrus, right? So why does he forget that there is a woman named Soraya when he gangs up with his friends? In the Khajik Grocery Store, I keep telling him, 'Father dear, I'm late. I have to go home.' It's as if he doesn't hear me. He just keeps pouring arrak in his beer mug and downing one shot after another. He tells his friends jokes at my expense. You men are really rude. You make a show of respecting women. You open car doors for them, but as soon as you find them alone, you show your vile nature. God forbid that someone pay a little attention to Iranian men; they think the whole world is entranced by them. They overstep the bounds at their whim. Complaining to the police is useless. They're no different from other men. They'll say: 'If there wasn't something wrong with the woman, she wouldn't be drinking beer with people like this.' They'll say: 'Respected lady, what were you doing in a tavern with three thugs?' Implying that the tree itself is blighted, and it's the woman who incites the man. Then when things turn serious, they wink at their friends shamelessly and brag about the pretty chick accompanying them. Anasori keeps bragging to his friends that Sori-jun is crazy about him, Sori-jun is just dying for him, and a bunch of other drivel to egg on his friends until they start repeating the same nonsense. It's a pity I didn't manage to dash their brains out." She waved her finger in Nuri's face. "Just wait, I'll get even with them. Just wait until Cyrus sets foot in this house, on my mother's life, I'll tell him: 'I spit in your face, you pimp! This is how they treat your sister? You just stand there holding your finger in the air to see which way the wind is blowing? If they had done the same to your pretty Pari, would you have been as gutless?" She pressed her palms against her eyes to stop her tears. "Sometimes I get so angry that I feel as if I'm suffocating. Why don't women have the right to have simple friendships with men? Why do we have to put up with a hundred insults for the sake of a simple outing?"

Nuri said hurriedly, "Soraya Khanom, tell me what to do! I swear to God, I'll do anything you ask. Believe me. You tell me and I'll do it."

Soraya took Nuri's hand and caressed it. "No. No. No. Don't you worry. I just needed to vent my anger. You're different from these ordinary, gutless people. I wish you had been in the grocery store to stand up to Anasori and his friends. You would have showed them . . . "

She kissed Nuri's palm and placed it on her cheek. "Nuri-jun, everybody is running around trying to go abroad, but you sit here by me and speak your sweet words. I'm really thankful to you." She kissed his cheek. "You have to go to America. If you stay here, you'll waste away."

"You mean . . . you're saying . . . you'll be happy if I go?"

Soraya smiled, "What do you want me to do? Should I fall all over you and plead with you to stay?"

"Why shouldn't we go abroad together?"

"We're different. I get used to places and take root, but you get bored quickly and need to move on to other places."

"That's it?"

"That's it."

Soraya's averted eyes made it seem as if she were looking at the cracked blue plaster walls of her room for the first time. At the posters she had pinned on the cupboard door; Mashallah's messages written on the wall on parallel lines inside rectangles; the books piled up on the floor; a bust of Beethoven, a camera, and a metal flute placed beside each other on a shelf near the door. A bunch of used furnishings so mismatched that they couldn't possibly belong to one place, person, or generation. She patted the bed, inviting Nuri to lie next to her. Nuri asked, "Why?"

"Don't worry. Just lie down."

Nuri lay down, but didn't lower his head. "I'm not comfortable like this. It would be better for us to sit up."

"Don't play coy. Lie down."

He put his head on Soraya's lap. "May I?"

"Enough already."

Without thinking, he threw his arms around her. When he felt her breasts against his chest, he seemed to forget himself for a moment. He watched himself from afar with a cold and calculating curiosity, as if he were a stranger. Only the internal voice that always distanced him from himself reminded him, "Look, Brother, see where you have ended up." He didn't have any time to waste. He had to get to the crux of the matter as soon as possible, but the intensity of his desire made him clumsy.

He shook like a partially paralyzed person and hurriedly rubbed Soraya's back and buttocks with his hands. "Soraya Khanom, allow me, allow me to kiss you. Just a small kiss that I'm dying for."

Soraya said, "Nuri-jun, slow down. What has come over you?"

She drew away from him. Nuri didn't stop. He dug his fingers into Soraya's shoulders and pulled her toward himself. "Just one more minute . . . "

Soraya freed herself. "That's enough. Do we always have to end up kissing?"

"Without kisses, it's unfinished." He made a face. "Who accomplished the task? He who completed it."

He didn't know whether he was at the beginning or the end of the task. What did he mean by 'the task'? The memory of a strong perfume lingered in his mind, but it couldn't belong to Soraya. She never went to the shops in Mohseni Square, complaining that the shop owners dressed worse than movie stars and adorned themselves with a thousand trinkets. She usually bought her perfume from discount stores in Mehran Alley or from makeup sellers on lower Lalehzar. One of the faults Madame found with Soraya was linked to "these unusual Iranian customs." Once in the middle of one their arguments, she had asked Nuri, "My dearrr, what's the name of Soraya's perfume? It turns my stomach." She suddenly thought of something and added, "Why do Iranian men use depilatory cream? What use are hairless legs hidden under trousers?" She proceeded to talk about women's excessive use of makeup and their so-called fashionable clothes. She proclaimed that such women either came from the lower classes or had been so westernized that they had no values of their own.

Nuri had responded, "So why have you wasted your life among these strangers?"

"We strangers find our lost ones among strangers."

Soraya had completely freed herself from Nuri. She moved to the end of the bed. "Come here. Sit next to me, but behave."

Nuri nodded perplexedly and moved closer. Soraya mumbled, "Nuri-jan, sit right here beside me, keep an eye on me until I fall asleep, OK?"

"Why?"

"Because I'm tired. Someone has to watch over me so that I can calm down and fall asleep."

Nuri nodded in agreement, hugged his knees, and kept his eyes on Soraya. A few minutes later she began snoring. Now he had nothing to do there. He had to flee without drawing any attention to himself.

His first obstacle would be Mrs. Tahmasbi, who might have returned from the Fard Pastry Shop. Then there were the other Tahmasbis, who might have come home also. Nuri couldn't be certain which one of them he would encounter at the bottom of the staircase. The last bus to Tajrish had long departed, and he had no other means of getting home. He heard the apartment door open all of a sudden. The Colonel shouted, "Nossi, Nossrat Sadaat . . . "

Mrs. Tahmasbi stirred in the hall and quickly ran down the stairs. "What are you doing, Colonel? I'm here. No need to shout."

She spoke softly and finally persuaded the Colonel to lower his voice. "What has happened?"

"Sori has just fallen asleep. If she wakes up now, she won't sleep again."

"Can you slice this watermelon for us? Ra'oof and I want to play a few rounds of backgammon."

Nuri rose to look for a way out of the room. In the dark, Soraya might not recognize him. She might be startled by him and scream. He thought about lying down by the door and spending the night there, but then Soraya rolled over. Her skirt slipped up her thighs. He placed his hand gently on the curve of Soraya's leg.

He recognized Buki's hurried footsteps in the corridor. A silence descended on the apartment, as if sucking all sounds out of the air. Then the telephone rang, but the whir of the electric fan prevented him from hearing the exchange. When the doorbell rang perhaps half an hour later, Nuri was even more surprised. No one needed to ring the doorbell to enter the Tahmasbis' apartment—unless it were a stranger. Then he heard the Senator's voice. At first, he couldn't believe it. The Senator was berating one of the Tahmasbis. Nuri's first thought was that he had been set up. Obviously, the Tahmasbis had planned to bring him to the apartment, throw Soraya in his arms, call the Senator, and obtain his consent for

Nuri's marriage. He had no choice but to flee. But the Senator was shouting from outside the apartment door, and Nuri's exit was blocked. The Senator spoke as if he were giving orders to a bunch of hired hands. "Why doesn't someone open the door?"

The Colonel's voice could be heard. "Your Excellency Senator, there is no need to ring the doorbell. This little hut is not worthy of you. Please come in."

The Senator shouted, "You know very well that Nuri is not allowed to stay out this late at night."

The Colonel said, "Your Excellency Senator, first have a glass of soft drink or something. I promise to turn Nuri over to you safe and sound."

The Senator spoke more softly, but in the cold and proud tone that always put a distance between him and others. "I am grateful. I don't drink anything this late at night. Please, call Nuri. We have to return to Tajrish."

Nuri didn't have much time left. In a few seconds, they all would come into the room and catch him. He searched every corner. He looked out the window and even threw a glance toward the pavement, but he wasn't capable of jumping from such a height. His efforts woke Soraya. Half asleep, she sat up and fiddled with her earlobes, trying to remove her earrings. "They won't even let you have a short nap. Nuri, ask my mother for a glass of water. I'm dying of thirst."

She lay down on her side, pulled her knees into her stomach, and began to snore. Then Madame's heels could be heard in the corridor. "I offer my apologies. It is late. We did not know where to mend. Among all our acquaintances, we only mended to you."

Grandpa corrected her mistake, " . . . turned to you."

"Forgive me, we turned to you. Raising children is more difficult here than raising cattle in Austria. No place is safe. Ali-jun, it's very cold here."

Colonel Tahmasbi said, "Your Excellency Senator, I was in the police force. Maybe I can help you. Would you please tell me when you last saw Nuri?"

The Senator set aside all pretense of politeness. "Your servant has not come all the way from Tajrish to be interrogated by you. You have to tell me where Nuri is."

"As it turns out, his generosity has diminished lately. He has not come by to see us for some time. Nossi-jun, isn't that the truth?"

Mrs. Tahmasbi answered the Colonel so softly that Nuri could not hear her. The Senator asked, "Colonel, do you know that kidnapping is a crime?"

"Your Excellency the Senator, please believe that I am not misleading you. We are very fond of the respectable Zargham family. We are proud of exceptional people like you."

"Please, there is no need to lie."

Madame said hurriedly, "Eh. Eh, Ali-jun. The Colonel is an honorable person, and he is our host. You owe him respect."

The Senator shouted, "You call this honorable? An honorable person would not lead a child astray and unload his tainted daughter on an inexperienced young boy. Colonel, your servant does not have the patience to argue with anyone. Either you turn Nuri over right now, or I will order a complete search of your house."

The Colonel's voice shook. "Your Excellency, may this in no way reflect on you, your servant's brain is not so damaged as to forcibly confine your grandson in his house. If you do not take my word for it, fine, I turn the house over to you. Search wherever you want. We are not guilty."

Nuri didn't understand whether he was prompted by fear or courage. He knew only that they were climbing the stairs and would soon be at Soraya's door. He had to take action. He pushed open the door and stepped boldly into the corridor. His first sight was the Senator, climbing the stairs decisively in his white silk suit. Madame was right behind him. She wore her purple robe, rabbit-tail slippers, and black hairnet. Her appearance indicated that she had set out in a hurry, without time to change clothes.

The Senator froze when he saw Nuri. "Nuri?"

Nuri answered, "Yes."

The Senator threw an angry glance back at the Colonel and said, "I thought you hadn't seen Nuri lately. So what do you call this?"

The Colonel held his hands out like a pair of parentheses. He turned to Mrs. Tahmasbi and asked, "Nossi, did you know Nuri was here?"

Mrs. Tahmasbi said, "Colonel, what's with you? This is like Nuri's own home. Our door has always been open to him. Whenever he venerates us with a visit, he brightens our eyes. We are honored." She turned toward Madame and the Senator. "You have been most kind, you have honored us." She told the Colonel, "Oh, may God kill me, Colonel, have you not offered Madame and the Senator anything?"

"What did you want me to offer them?"

"What happened to the watermelon I sliced for you? Couldn't you have offered a few slices to Madame and the Senator?"

"The watermelon is gone."

Mrs. Tahmasbi rolled her eyes in surprise. "Really? That big watermelon is all gone?" She turned toward Madame. "Can you believe that these two men put that big watermelon in front of themselves and ate the whole lot in half an hour?" She turned again toward the Colonel, "Have you survived a famine, or can't you ever get your fill? OK. You could have put a little aside for guests. . . . " She turned to the Senator. "You are my witness. He'll sacrifice himself to his belly in the end. The doctors advise him: 'Colonel, please watch your food.' On the surface he says: 'Fine.' But when my eyes are averted, he goes to the fridge and eats anything he can find there. Then he moans, 'Nossi, help me, I'm going to explode.' And I say, 'Fine, go ahead and explode and leave us alone.' You can't treat a man his size and age like a child."

Madame drew back. The Colonel was still explaining. "Am I a magician that I should know Nuri-jan is here? If I had known, I myself would have called the Senator and let him know so that he wouldn't worry."

Mrs. Tahmasbi chimed in. "Nuri-jan is no different from our own children. From his childhood, he has been in this apartment and mingled among us. He is not a stranger that whenever he comes here, we have to inform a hundred people."

The Colonel took up where she had left off. "I had no idea, Nossi. . . ." He tried to take the Senator's hand. The Senator snorted. The Colonel ignored that and continued, "I admit that you are right. If you have any commands, I am at your service. I have only one small request. Please let Soraya be. Older people make her do things that she would never do on her own."

Soraya was asleep on her bed, one leg bent at the knee, the other curving delicately toward the wall. She looked as innocent and vulnerable as a child. Mrs. Tahmasbi hurriedly entered the room, knelt by the bed, and hugged Soraya. Soraya turned her face away. Now it was the Senator's turn to step closer and look around with a disapproving gaze. He addressed the Colonel, "This room smells of alcohol. The *khanom* has been drinking."

The Colonel was shocked, "Do you mean Soraya?"

The Senator nodded. "Look at her cheeks and how flushed they are. That's from drinking too much."

Mrs. Tahmasbi mumbled, "It's fever that has flushed her cheeks. Sorijun does not drink. If you touch her head, you'll see that it's as hot as an oven."

The Senator lifted his nose into the air and took a few deep breaths. "Don't you smell the alcohol?" He asked Nuri, "What about you? Have you been drinking too?"

"Me? No!" Nuri protested.

The Senator said, "For now, go to the car. We'll talk later. Vaziri has parked in front of the building."

"Grandpa, allow me . . . "

"Didn't you hear me tell you to leave? Are you going to go, or . . . "

Nuri lowered his head and went downstairs reluctantly.

Vaziri had parked under the streetlamp. In the dark, his carefully combed hair glistened. He smelled of cologne and brilliantine. He was polishing the front fender. When he saw Nuri, he pulled back his shoulders, opened the car door for him, and gave him the kind of smile actors offer their counterparts. "Stretch out on the front seat."

Nuri asked, "How did you know I was at the Tahmasbis'?"

Vaziri wiped the sweat off his brow with his forearm and said, "Ladan was the one who kept worrying that you would miss the bus and not be able to return to Tajrish." He imitated Ladan: "Mumzie, Mumzie, it's really, really unsafe. . . . "

"Do you want me to tell you what burns her? I'm going to America, and she's staying here. But if only she had told me that, I could have answered easily. I would have said, 'You go to America. I'm not the type. I will study right here.' Don't you agree that I will study better here? You have to tell Madame and Grandpa Senator that."

"Should I tell them that you should stay in Iran?"

"Why not? They should let me go to law school. They'll see how well I study. You know me. I have to want to study, not be forced into it. Tell them these things. See what they say."

Vaziri shrugged his shoulders. "For now, you just stretch yourself out. Let's see later."

"If they don't let me, to hell with it."

Nuri stepped into the car and stretched out. Vaziri stood by the open door. Waiting for Madame and the Senator, he drew noisily on his cigarette. Then Madame and the Senator appeared in the apartment doorway. Grandpa Senator had his hand on Madame's shoulder. As they approached the car, Vaziri mumbled to Nuri, "Start moaning."

"Moaning?"

"The kind of moan for stomachache or backache."

"What for?"

"They'll worry about your health. They'll forget the business with Soraya."

Vaziri opened the back door for Madame and the Senator. When they were seated, he sat behind the wheel and started the engine.

Although Nuri moaned most of the way, Madame and the Senator ignored him. The few sentences they exchanged concerned the Tahmasbis' apartment. Madame asked, "Did you see the framed painting on the wall?"

"I think it dates back to Mrs. Tahmasbi's great-grandfather, who was killed in the Khaz'al battle."

"What a narrow staircase! There was hardly enough room to walk."

"How squeaky the steps were."

"Their apartment is not new. They have to look after it; otherwise, it will deteriorate quickly."

The entire way Nuri didn't take his eyes off Vaziri. When Vaziri was tense, he would get a twitch in his eyes and drum his fingers on the dashboard. Now his profile looked calm even in the dark. He was steering with his forearm instead of his hand. Madame and the Senator asked Nuri no questions, nor did they reprimand him.

Nuri's thoughts turned to the dusty and empty spaces in the lower quarters of the city—Electricity Avenue, Execution Square, the quarries around the cement factory, and the uneven edges of the ghettos serrated like an atlas by the crisscrossing of sewer lines. The thought of leaving these places behind made him feel as if he were coming to a dead end.

Going to the Tahmasbis' apartment was not such a big sin. Buki did far worse things, and no one reprimanded him. Moreover, compared to the Senator's political machinations, Nuri's antics seemed like child's play.

Nuri heard Maman Zuzu's name. He perked up his ears. The Senator asked, "Why did she call?"

"Your servant called *her*. In response to whatever I said, she laughed and talked about money. She insists that we make a piggy bank for her."

"Piggy bank?"

"Instead of buying her gifts, we should put the money in a piggy bank. It's expensive to live in New York, and she won't receive her diploma for another year."

Reflected in the rearview mirror, the Senator's straight hair flowed back from his forehead and spread around his face, making him look like an eagle. He held his head erect with a kind of wounded pride. "Zuzu was never the kind to beg for money. What's the use of a piggy bank for a middle-aged woman? Why doesn't she open a bank account?"

"Where would she get the money?"

"They keep saying she won such and such an award, but she has never sent us her grade reports. What about Mr.? Why doesn't he help her?"

"Barney has gone to Nashville to take part in a bluegrass festival."

"Bluegrass?"

"How should I know? It's a kind of rustic American music."

"The same Barney who used to call three times a week last winter to borrow twenty-five thousand dollars from us? Do you remember? The minute you picked up the phone, he shouted in his American accent: 'Your Excellency, Senator, a millionaire farmer, an important political figure, a lover of the arts and artists, why don't you lend me twenty-five thousand dollars to finish my film?' He says he's a famous movie director and claims to have won a prize at Cannes. His latest film was Princess Bertha's life story whose script Parviz Sayyad wrote for him. I tell him: 'My dear agha, give me a few days to think it over.' He shouts: 'There is no time left for that. If I don't shoot the film by tomorrow, the snow will melt. We won't be able to shoot the winter scenes. We don't have the budget for artificial snow.' When he phones the following week, I tell him: 'Mr. Director, genius artist, now that all the snow has melted, why are you in such a hurry to borrow money?' He says: 'Send whatever you can. Fifteen thousand, five thousand, or one thousand dollars.'" Madame and the Senator laughed. "Wandering from city to city and playing guitar in this and that bar don't make you an artist. I'm not sure about this Barney. He's not the type to settle down and have a family."

Nuri turned and asked, "How is Maman Zuzu?"

For a while, Madame and the Senator just looked at each other. Then the Senator said, "We'll talk when we get home."

He took a small notebook from his chest pocket and held it open in front of Madame for her to read. Vaziri, still on the lookout, winked at Nuri to reassure him.

Vaziri parked the car near the stone pool. Madame and the Senator stepped out and walked toward the first-floor hall. Nuri remained seated, trying to think of an excuse to strike up a conversation with them.

Finally, he followed them into the hall. For a few moments, he listened to their footsteps slowly moving up the stairs. Madame shouted from the third floor, "Good night."

Nuri gave up on the idea of convincing them tonight that sending him abroad was a mistake. He answered, "Good night."

He climbed the stairs quickly, then tiptoed to Ladan's door. He coughed a few times to wake her up. He heard her roll over on her bed, then she said in a tired voice, "Mamakh, there's no need to put on an act. If you want to come in, OK. Come in, the door is open, but be quiet so you don't wake the others."

Nuri stepped into the room slowly without switching on the light. He squatted down by the door. Ladan asked, "What has happened? Why are you so quiet?"

"You said I should be quiet."

"Do you want to pick a fight?"

He put aside all pretense. "Did you send Grandpa Senator and Madame to the Tahmasbis' apartment?"

"Yes, of course. You don't tell anyone where you're going or when you'll be back. The minute you're asked a question, you jump on a person. You wanted me to say nothing so that you could get yourself hurt and we would hear the news indirectly?"

"So, you finally got even with me?"

"What for?"

"Because I didn't go to the film festival with you."

"Get lost. Big deal. You think only about yourself."

"Did you expect me to think about you?"

"Think of your poor grandparents. They walked up and down the alley for two hours waiting for you to come back; they called the police and phoned all the relatives. Who do you think they do all this for? They hope only that one day you learn to think of others. Have you looked around once to see how everything is turning upside down?"

Nuri moved closer to Ladan. "If you're so worried about Grandpa Senator and Mumzie, why didn't you call the Tahmasbis yourself and ask me to come back sooner?"

"Did you want me to call people in the middle of the night and wake them up?"

"If you didn't like waking them up, why did you make Grandpa and Mumzie go to their place at midnight, shout at them, and humiliate them publicly?"

Ladan turned her back to Nuri. "It's none of my concern. I'm neither the top nor the bottom of the onion. If you have anything to say, take it to Grandpa and Mumzie. I have to go to sleep now. I have a lot to do tomorrow. Good night, Mamakh. Shut the door behind you."

She rearranged her head on the pillow and pretended to be asleep. Nuri blurted out, "Dust on the head of the idiot!"

Nuri went to his own room and lay down. For an hour or two, he tossed and turned. A cool, light breeze caressed his body.

Light flickered in the sky like streetlamps automatically switching off at daybreak. Nuri knew he shouldn't bother Madame and the Senator so early in the morning. He should shower first and dress in freshly pressed pants and shirt. Instead, he took the stairs to the third floor. He hoped that he could make Madame understand his inner feelings. Perhaps she would find a resolution or at least postpone his trip to America. He reached Asali's cage. The parrot was perched on the metal bars. He spoke from the depths of his throat, "Give me a kiss, hurry up!" Nuri held a couple of sunflower seeds in front of him. Asali ignored him and repeated, "Give me a kiss."

Nuri was so sleepy that he could barely keep his eyes open. The pattern of the cage seemed opaque to him. He lowered the red cover over the cage. In the dark, Asali stopped talking. Nuri glanced around. He wished he could sprinkle cold water on his face. He felt hunger gnaw at his stomach. He leaned against the wall, slid down slowly, hugged his knees, and fell asleep by the bedroom door.

When he opened his eyes, he felt out of place. The Senator's sports jacket was hanging on the coatrack. Then he saw Madame in the middle of the corridor, ephemeral as a ghost and holding her cane with a shaky hand. She looked him over with a glazed and surprised look. Her gaze made him get up. When he approached her, she drew back her head in warning and prevented him from moving closer. Nuri was frozen to the spot—not only because of her warning, but also because she had no makeup on. She never left her room before putting on her makeup. She used a special brand of rouge and powder that gave her face the appearance of new merchandise—the kind Nuri was reluctant to touch. The relatives grumbled about Madame's heavy makeup and how it made her look like an Armenian witch, but Nuri thought that without makeup she seemed ten years older. With her wrinkles and pale complexion, she bore only a vague resemblance to herself. Instead of the purple robe, she wore a white cotton dress. She wriggled and bobbed like a puppet. She tried in vain to reach the banister. Her hand moved like a starfish on an invisible surface. She looked around hurriedly. Nuri asked, "What do you want?"

Now she beckoned to Nuri. "Please come a little closer. Please help me. Cast kindness only into the Tigris . . . "

He supported Madame under her arms and took her to the study. Livelier than before, she sat in the chair by the fireplace. She narrowed her eyes and said, "Your Majesty is tired." Nuri shrugged. Madame grew pensive and said, "Strange events repeat themselves." She forced a smile, apparently to comfort Nuri. "I have been thinking these past few days about your trip. I felt the same way years ago in Vienna. The night of my engagement to your grandpa I didn't sleep a wink. I had leaped, but I did not know from what height. The whole night I saw images of your grandpa in front of my eyes, and I wondered who he was. Why do I want to marry a tyrannical Eastern man and go to a place I don't know? Who is this demon? In which Eastern harem will he enslave me? In what deserted hell will he put me to work? Princess Bertha stayed up with me the whole night and comforted me: 'Frieda, accept it. Frieda, don't be stupid. After Siegfried, after this ruinous war, after the destruction of Europe, Vienna is not a place for you.'" Madame played with her Allah necklace. "Perhaps I now would have been in Salzburg in a building near our farm, sitting on the same verandah where my grandmother sat and did her knitting. That last year, the snow was melting. Our cat, Münster, rubbed against my grandmother's legs as she fed the chickens. The chickens were afraid of the cat and would not come close. Blue smoke rose from the chimney, and the smell of wood fire permeated the air. My grandmother had had a stroke and could not speak. Everyone wanted to know how we had learned to communicate through mime. Sometimes our neighbors would come over to watch our pantomime. They put our picture in the papers." She inserted her hand in her bodice and pulled out a silver locket hanging at the end of a chain. She took a folded piece of old newspaper from it, showing a photo of herself miming to her grandmother. When she unfolded the paper, a picture fell out. At first, she didn't want to show it to Nuri. It was a small picture, no bigger than a finger joint, torn across the middle and glued together on a piece of cardboard. After a moment of hesitation, she picked it up and held it in front of Nuri. He recognized Siegfried von Friedhoff from his blond mane. He wore a military uniform, had a helmet under one arm and a rifle in the other hand, and stared frozenly into the camera. Madame lowered her eyelids and asked, "Do you remember Siegfried von Friedhoff?"

Nuri nodded. Madame refolded the piece of newspaper and put it back in her locket. But she held the picture in her fist. Nuri asked, "How many years have you kept this old picture with you?"

Madame folded her fingers over the picture to hide it. "Would you believe it's been fifty years? No, much more."

"He's a handsome man."

Madame said excitedly, "He looks like you, right? Like yourself, right? Right?"

"Me?"

"Yes, Your Excellency!" She looked first at the picture, then at Nuri. She brought the picture closer to Nuri. "Please accept this unworthy gift from your servant."

Nuri pulled back. "You want to give this to me?"

"If you don't like it, present it as a gift to Princess Bertha on my behalf when you go to America. I would be most grateful to you."

"I won't go to America."

Madame pressed the photograph into Nuri's palm, frowning. "The choice is not yours. When Grandpa says you must go, you have to go wherever he sends you."

"No way, I won't go to America."

Madame sighed in frustration and planted her hands in her lap. "My dearrr, don't imagine that it's easy for us to send you to America. We too have feelings. This house will be empty without you. It will be painful to come into this room when you're gone. But your servant and Grandpa have grown old. We are no longer capable of raising you. I myself am sick. Three days ago the doctor recommended surgery. Sooner or later I have to go to the hospital."

Nuri put the photograph on the side table and asked, "Surgery for what?"

"It's not important."

"Why not?"

"I said it's not important. How stubborn you are!"

"I won't leave until after your operation. I'm not a child that you need to hide things from. If it weren't important, you wouldn't hide it from me."

"You go on to America. If something comes up, you'll come back to Iran."

"If I go, I won't come back. I'll never see you again."

Madame grabbed Nuri's wrist, indicating he should sit down. "The operation is to stop the bleeding in my bladder. It's not dangerous. But my heart flutters for you. The first few days away from home are hell. I don't know why I remembered Siegfried. Healthy as he was, he wasted away in a foreign land. When his last letter reached Vienna, he wrote that the Communists in Prague were unkind to the Nazis. Siegfried lost his self-confidence and believed he was nearing the end of his life. He was afraid that if he shut his eyes, he would never wake up."

"Don't you want me to go abroad?"

"Of course."

"So why do you issue all these arguments against it?"

Madame froze and grew pensive. "Because you are dearrr to me, the apple of my eye. Do you remember the day you came to this house?"

Nuri smiled and leaned back in his chair. "You sang Brünnhilde's song on the third-floor balcony."

She leaned forward in her chair and held her fingers in the air like claws, ready for a signal from an imaginary conductor. But instead of playing the organ, she sang a wordless song. So softly and nasally that Nuri was reminded of their Thursday organ practices. He would sit on the stool, and Madame would wave the old baton in the air to the rhythm of the music. She would fix her gaze on the door in order to allow him to concentrate on his music. Then Nuri would think of the depths of still waters that appeared enchanted in the dusk. The pale sky would undergo an alarming but strangely calm transition. The plaster face and lowered gaze of the Virgin of Solitude would quietly await a hidden voice.

He couldn't believe that after so many years Madame could affect him so. Her song welled up from her inner depths and left Nuri no room to flee. From the opening to the closing note, sung in a voice like "Ouuuu" that vanished in the dark, Nuri sat there mesmerized and listened to the song. "Ouuu. . . . uuuu."

His going abroad was part of his destiny, which he couldn't understand but recognized as absolute. Perhaps in a few years, with more experience, he could turn things to his advantage. For now, he couldn't find such a miracle within himself. How quickly his bright future became accustomed to darkness! How quickly it faded and sentenced him to an irrevocable fate!

Fortunately, the creaking of the door broke the silence. The Senator, wearing his blue pajamas, entered the room. When he saw them, he took the toothbrush out of his mouth and wiped toothpaste from his lips. He stepped closer and asked, "You're practicing this early in the morning?"

He pulled up a seat, plopped into it, and placed his toothbrush in his pocket. He asked Nuri, "Did you sleep at all last night? How long did you sleep?"

Maybe things weren't as bad as Nuri had imagined. He shrugged and said, "I slept a while."

Grandpa Senator winked at Madame and addressed Nuri, "What will you do in America? They say that in America people don't have time to sleep. They have to work all the time."

"I'm going to America?"

Grandpa winked again at Madame. "Imagine, two weeks from now you'll be eating fried chicken. When you think of the distance, you get dizzy. Imagine from here to New York." He lowered his head and grew lost in his thoughts. "In the past, it took a month to go to Europe, but now travel has no meaning anymore. You leave here on Friday, and Sunday night you arrive in New York. In our time, distances were real. Distance was measured by the hand. But now everything has changed. I bet that in ten years the problem of time will be solved as well." He raised his head and looked at Nuri. "I wanted to be born in the twenty-first century so as to see how they resolve the problem of time. Maybe in the twenty-first century going from Tehran to New York will take only a few seconds. They'll plug themselves into a wall outlet and in the blink of an eye find themselves in the customs line in New York, in front of an American officer inspecting their passports. Maybe even customs, borders, and such things will be abolished, and the entire world will become one country." The Senator laughed. "Nuri, are you happy about going to New York?"

"I don't know. Nobody has told me when I'm leaving."

The Senator glanced at the wall calendar. "Not this week. Friday night of the following week. You reach Paris at midnight. The next day you leave for New York."

Now their conversation was becoming more private, and Madame didn't participate in it. She watched Nuri from the corner of her eye with a strange, fixed stare, as if she were conveying a message to him.

She seemed to be criticizing him for not standing up to the Senator. Nuri had no choice but to shout out his decision against going to New York. That was his intention, and he opened his mouth to declare it when the Senator rose from his seat and took a passport from a desk drawer. He wiped its shiny purple cover a few times with his hand. Apparently, he liked its new, clean look. He bragged about how the passport had been obtained with one phone call. He waved it in the air and struck it against the edge of the desk. "I told him on the phone: 'Your Excellency Ghotbi, this request of mine is not like any other. It's very important.' He said: 'Of course, Senator. You are our master. No need for such words. . . . Had it not been for you, the legislation legalizing cultivation of poppy seeds would never have passed the House.'" He examined the passport with admiration. "He is a wonderful person. He never forgets that he grew up on Shahpur Street."

He invited Nuri to have a closer look at the passport. Nuri felt Madame's gaze weighing on him. He said, "Grandpa, going to New York is not all that easy. Now I have a thousand . . . "

The Senator laughed. "What do you mean your going to New York is not that easy? It might not be easy for the Tahmasbis, but they are different from us."

"Grandpa, I meant to say that I'm not ready for it . . . "

The Senator frowned. Perhaps he hadn't understood Nuri's words. He shouted, "What are you waiting for? Don't you want to have a look at your passport?"

Nuri rose quickly and walked over to the desk. He tried to avoid Madame's gaze. Nevertheless, it seemed as if she were secretly shouting at him and accusing him of gutlessness. The Senator shook the passport in Nuri's face. "Do you know what this is?"

Nuri said reluctantly, "Grandpa, I would like to talk to you."

Grandpa Senator wiped the tip of his nose with the back of his hand. "Enough! When I need an explanation, I'll let you know. There's no need for you to worry unnecessarily. If you're concerned about last night, it's over and done with. It's in the past. Look at what I've brought you."

Nuri waved the passport away and protested. "I have to explain. It's important."

The Senator raised his voice. "I told you once. I don't want to hear from you again. Look at this passport."

Nuri was standing at the edge of a precipice, and Madame was trying to prevent his fall with her frightened gaze. He addressed the Senator. "Grandpa, I don't want to gamble with my future."

Grandpa pointed to the passport and asked, "Do you know who took your picture? Mr. Shariat has bought a camera recently, and he follows Ladan around and snaps pictures of her. I told him, 'OK, why don't you take a couple of pictures of Nuri as well? We'll frame some of them and send the rest to the Passport Office to have his passport issued quickly.'" He leafed through the pages of the passport and opened it to the page with Nuri's picture. "It's not a great picture. Nothing like the pictures he takes of Ladan. I say if he had put an empty metal can and a tray of *bamiyeh* in front of you, you would look exactly like Asghar the Killer . . . "

He broke into laughter, took his toothbrush from his pajama pocket, and got ready to leave. Nuri asked, "What happens if I don't want to go to New York?"

Grandpa Senator lifted his chin and lowered his eyelids. "Fine, if you don't want to, but you have to start thinking about getting a job and your own place." Before leaving the room, he took Madame's hand and kissed it with such warmth and emotion that Madame half rose out of her chair.

"Frieda, the queen of my heart."

... 12 ...

Nuri was surprised by his own hurried exit. He didn't bid Madame farewell or offer even a perfunctory bow. And instead of her customary "Your Excellency," "Your Majesty," "I am most obliged," or "You are most welcome," she watched his departure silently. When Nuri reached the corridor, he was overcome with an embarrassment that he could relieve only by biting his lip. The memory of Madame's disappointed gaze weighed on him, asking why he had not stood up to Grandpa Senator, but Nuri thought that he had done nothing to deserve her reproachful look. Instead of indicating her disapproval, she could have asked him to stay in the study, given him her usual half-hour of advice, and comforted him. Listening to her German accent and her poetic Persian would have restored the bond between them.

" . . . My dearrr Nuri, I am afraid that, God forbid, you might beseech the Prophet to reveal by what authority Grandpa is sending you to America. Your servant will declare that Grandpa has your best interest at heart and has sincerely prayed to God for your protection. I plead with you, do not pride yourself on the pain you suffer, as do most Iranians. Do not boast and assume that you are above others. Otherwise, you will make of this pain a shrine that will further entrap you in self-centeredness."

Nuri wondered why he persisted in his childish behavior. Perhaps tomorrow or the day after he would find an opportunity to tell the Senator forthrightly that he had no intention of going to America.

An image of Soraya appeared in his mind's eye and made him feel like prey at the mercy of a hunter. He sat on the edge of his bed and thought about changing his clothes. He chose his sailor jeans, yellow shirt, and brown jacket with epaulets for the combination of blue, yellow, and brown that complemented his blond hair. He counted his money. He

271

had enough. He dialed the Tahmasbis' number, but nobody answered. The Colonel and Buki must have gone out. Usually within a quarter of an hour of their departure, Mrs. Tahmasbi went shopping, leaving Soraya alone. Then Soraya often dropped by Amiz Hosein's house to visit Shuri Khanom.

Nuri hurriedly dialed Amiz Hosein's number. He gathered from Shuri Khanom's nasal voice that she had been asleep. "Hello?"

"Shuri Khanom?"

She didn't seem to recognize Nuri's voice. "Who's speaking?"

"It's me."

She shouted, "Oh Nuri, is that you? Why didn't you say so? When I heard the phone this early in the morning, I panicked. Wait a second. Let me get my cigarettes. I have to have a puff before I can open my eyes." Nuri laughed as he heard Shuri Khanom's first inhalation. "I'm all set now. So, what made you think of us?"

Nuri asked, "Do you know where I can find Soraya?"

Shuri Khanom yawned. "Where did you want her to be? She's probably in her bed, reading a novel." He heard her throaty laughter interrupted by a cough. "Eh, you don't give a person a chance to have a cup of tea. What's up? Why are you in such a hurry?"

"I'm sorry. If it weren't necessary, I wouldn't have disturbed you. I phoned the Tahmasbis' apartment. No one answered."

"Who would, this early in the morning? Not everyone is like me. Now, do you absolutely have to see Soraya?"

"Yes."

"Why?"

"I'll tell you later."

"Eh!" Her silence indicated that she was not satisfied with Nuri's answer. Nuri said nothing. "Call her in an hour. I'm sure she'll answer."

"Thank you. Good-bye."

"You wake me this early in the morning, and as soon as you get what you want, you hang up."

"I have to, Shuri Khanom. I'm not lying. I have no choice."

"Fine. No need to preach."

He waited an hour to phone the Tahmasbis' again, but there was still no answer.

✦ ✦ ✦ Around dusk, he left the house with no particular plan in mind. He came across children and chador-clad women surrounding a juice seller. He noticed that the blue paint on the old bench under the Ansaris' acacia tree grew more faded every year. He reached a vacant area fenced in by plywood. Blades of grass grew along the base of the boards and made the empty space, now used as a parking lot, resemble a forgotten garden. He saw a balloon stuck on the electric line. If he went to the lower quarters of the city, he had no more than a ten percent chance of running into Buki. Only in the afternoons did Buki go to Naser Khosrow Street to deliver merchandise to the shop owners. In the evenings, he hung out by the American Club or Hotel Continental. He would wave foreign newspapers above his head and shout: "Oh peeper, oh peeper, *Washington Post* peeper, *New York Times* peeper, *Herald Tribune* peeper . . . "

Nuri spent two hours in Iran-e Novin Street, waiting in front of the American Club and chatting with the hotel doorman, but there was no sign of Buki. The pavement ran as smooth as the palm of a hand past military vehicles, armed soldiers, and billboards, and then narrowed into a dusty space. A group of people carrying signs and banners turned into Shahreza Street and moved toward Takht-e Jamshid and the American embassy. Only the scraping of their shoes could be heard on the pavement. They walked as if responding to the trumpet call of the angel of resurrection.

Nuri spotted Buki in the crowd. He wore dark glasses, and his face gave nothing away. Nuri became agitated. In the past two or three months, he had missed Buki terribly. If he could have mustered the courage, he would have flown to him and shouted, "Hit it here, Buki. Where have you been, you son of a dog?" But Buki's unhurried pace checked Nuri's enthusiasm. When Nuri caught up with him, Buki put a hand on his shoulder and kissed him on both cheeks formally. There seemed to be an icy distance between them. Nuri struck Buki gently and pretended to run away. Buki slowly removed his dark glasses, blew on the lenses, and wiped them with his sleeve. He examined Nuri from the corner of his eye, as if asking, "What's the meaning of these silly antics? Why do you so childishly imitate movie stars?" Nuri cringed. He glanced back at the crowd, trying to gauge their reaction. He smiled nervously and asked in a friendly tone, "In what grave have you been? Why do you hide when you see me?"

Buki put his glasses back. A gentle smile spread across his face. He said, "They say you want to go to America."

Nuri answered hurriedly, "It's just a rumor."

Buki didn't not appear convinced. He said, "New York, Los Angeles, Arizona, and Indiana . . . " He stretched out "Arizona" and "Indiana" mockingly. "Not every sissy can pick up his bundle and go to America. Why would you stay here anyway?"

Nuri said, "What an ass you are. This is my country."

Buki inserted his thumbs in his belt and threw a sarcastic glance at the crowd. "It's pointless for you to stay here, Chief. If you stay, you'll have to settle your accounts with these people."

Nuri asked, "What do you mean?"

"Whoever stays here will have to settle his accounts with the people. Either you roll up your sleeves and join the fight, or you leave. This middle-of-the road business is silly. You're either with us or against us. You say you don't belong here, OK, Chief. Go to America."

"Who asked you whether I should stay or go?"

"There's no need to ask. The people are fed up with the government, and they are fearless. You're welcome to join in. Otherwise, leave. May you come to a good end."

He didn't mention the events of the previous night. Nuri decided to leave well enough alone. He suddenly felt queasy, like a child who has eaten something that doesn't agree with him. When they finally shook hands, neither one wanted to be the first to withdraw his hand.

Nuri was left behind in a crowd of black-clad people carrying slogans and pictures of various political leaders. Their black standards resembled objects excavated from an ancient city and perhaps part of a ritual sacrifice in honor of a great idol. Rough and primitive images like paintings in a coffeehouse, unrealistically obscure and one dimensional: the Day of

Judgment, the dead dressed in white burial shrouds and rising from their graves, and Satan with his fiery bludgeon.

He reached three telephone booths standing in a row. He entered the first one and dialed the Tahmasbis' number. Soraya answered. The line was weak. He strained to catch her words.

"Nuri . . . huh? Nuri . . . is that you?"

"Oh, I'm so glad I found you." He heard a sound like two clay objects struck against each other. "Soraya Khanom? What happened? Has the line gone dead?" He waited, but heard nothing. "If you can hear me, hang up. I'll dial again." A few seconds later he heard Soraya's calm and regular breathing. He said, "I've been looking for you since early this morning. Where have you been?"

"I've been here . . . I didn't go anywhere. . . . Last night after you left, I drank a glass of milk. I couldn't fall asleep."

"I wish I had stayed there last night. I didn't expect Madame and the Senator to show up. My problem is that I don't have control over my own life."

"Whenever you leave me, do you know what I think about? Don't say you do. I think only of your body. I say to myself: 'How can this little Nuri grow so tall in a few months?' Until recently I thought you were still a child. Do you remember how you used to tease everyone and play at being an adult? The past is past. It's impossible to return to the world of childhood. You can't ask yourself, 'Why didn't I do this and that? Why did I let such a simple friendship slip away?'"

"Soraya Khanom, we can have whatever we want. We just have to . . . "

"The problem with you is that you keep wanting to reassure others. Let me come right out and tell you. Now that you're going to America, I'll be left alone. You are the distance between me and death. No need to give me advice. It doesn't suit you. I know that it's not good to be so attached to a person. You'll go to America and settle down, whereas I, even now, feel suspended in air, as if I were uprooted like a thistle bush. I'm not saying you shouldn't go. You have to go. I ask only that we be happy these last few days you are here. After you leave, we'll cope somehow."

"I have no intention of going anywhere, let alone America. Did you hear what I said?"

"Yes. All right. You're deafening me."

Nuri was growing angry. "I have other things to say. You have to listen. Last night I stood up to Grandpa Senator and said, 'I will not go to America.' I said, 'I won't go anywhere without Soraya. Soraya is my soul.' Did you hear me?"

"Yes."

"Grandpa stared me in the eyes. Maybe he wanted me to drop to my knees and say, 'I'm sorry, I eat shit . . . please forgive me. I apologize.' I won't fall for that kind of trick. I got even bolder and said, 'I am no longer the simpleton of a few years ago. I'll determine my own path, you'll decide yours.' Soraya Khanom, did you hear me? Didn't I do well?"

"You're kidding, Nuri."

"Why would I be kidding? Leave your laughter for when we're out of this muddle. This country is a mess. People are fed up. Maybe you're right. Do you know what my papa used to say? He would say, 'Many prefer to go to America. Let them go. Each person has the right to choose his own path. But this is my country. I'll stay here. I'm not afraid of the secret police or anyone else, not even Nixon himself.' If Papa Javad were alive, he would probably take me to demonstrations. Maybe we would have gone to the party divisions together; he would have introduced me to the party life a little. He once showed me some rolled sheets of paper on which he had written some secret codes in cuneiform. When you held them under the sun, the figures began to move like ants. But he didn't read it to me. He promised to read it to me when I got older."

Soraya interrupted him, "Wait a minute. When did you join the opposition?"

"I can't tell you. This is not the time. Now I have to look for a place for us."

Soraya chuckled, "We're going to get married? You and me? For real? Where are you going to get the money? Are you sleeping on the legendary Gharun's treasure?"

Nuri head was bursting with pain. He said, "Who's sleeping on a treasure? It's my inheritance I'm relying on."

"Slow down a bit. Why do you shout?"

"I shout so that you can hear me. Do you hear me?"

"Of course I hear you. What do you want to say?"

"The only thing left of my father's estate is the Aghcheh land. I want to sell it. It's worth a lot of money. . . . Why do you laugh at whatever I say? If you don't believe me, I'll show you the signed and certified deed."

"Just like that? You'll sell the land, put the money in a bank, and we'll live off that for the rest of our lives? What about Madame and the Senator? Will they let you marry me?"

Nuri asked, "Soraya Khanom, why do you laugh at me? What's so funny? I can't even finish a sentence before you start laughing. After all, I have a right to say what's on my mind."

"OK. I won't say anything. Say whatever you want."

"It's none of their concern whom I marry. It's I who am going to marry, not them. You tease me so much, I can't talk to you seriously."

"Go on, go on, Nuri."

"In the last little while, I have started buying and selling land. There's big money in it, especially if I take up farming. I mean with modern machines, not ancient plows and tools."

"I bet next week you'll be eating hamburgers and pizzas in New York. You won't even remember that there's a person called Soraya in the world."

"I'm not one for going to America."

"OK. If that's the case, I'll take back everything I said. Don't go. Stay right here."

"Are you serious?"

"Why should you go to America? You don't have anyone there to look after you. Even your Maman Zuzu has become an American. Maybe you won't even recognize each other. Nuri, listen."

Nuri asked, "What?"

"Let's go on a picnic near the Gachsar Spring on the road to Chalus. We'll spread a blanket by the spring, listen to the rushing water, and dance together." She paused. "Let's go, your laziness."

"You are so mature. I sometimes ask myself who you are. What do you want with me?"

In his present state, it was dangerous to see Soraya. The minute he saw her, he would fall apart like an old wreck. Suppose she held his hand and kissed him. He didn't expect much from her. He just wanted her to tend his inner wounds with compassion.

Only once before, after his first-form final exams, had he felt this fragile. He had been given his grade report, and he had hurried home to show it to Madame. He had found her on the third-floor balcony, sipping her Monk's Syrup and talking to Asali. She was happy to see him. He handed her his report and stood still, fixing his eager gaze on her. After a few moments, Madame heaved a sigh of relief and rested the report on her lap. Her face took on a calm expression. Nuri heard her voice as if from a distance. "Your servant, your grandmother, is most delighted. With these brilliant grades, you have achieved a colossal success and distinguished yourself among your peers. I am ecstatic. How should I say it? How do they say it? Lifting my proud head to heaven, I pronounce to humanity and the world that this Nuri is our dear grandson. I congratulate you on your sweet success, applaud your forefathers, the very founders of this family, and I pray for a bright future for you. What else should I say, Nuri-jan? I apologize. As the poet says, 'You are the object of my desire. The Kaaba and the temple of idolaters are but excuses.'"

Nuri had felt shy because he saw Madame as a foreign woman. He was about to refill her glass when his foot caught in the carpet. He stumbled and fell in front of Asali's cage. Fortunately, the carafe did not break, and no syrup spilled on the rug. He was more concerned about having revealed his inner anxiety to Madame. He rose to go to his own room. Madame asked, "When will you come back?"

"Please wait. I'll be right back."

Of course, there was no way he was going back.

♦ ♦ ♦ He didn't need anyone's permission to visit the Tahmasbis. He considered Soraya his, and her room his absolute domain, so he left the house quietly.

When he entered the apartment, he kept his fists in his pockets. He walked purposefully. No one seemed to be home. The rooms were so empty that he was incited to steal something. He rifled through the drawers for something forbidden. The thought of finding such an object excited him. He went to the living room cabinets where Mrs. Tahmasbi stored treats for guests. He chose a few big almonds from the nut dish and ate them quickly. He also took a piece of baklava and three sugared mulberries to eat later. He had not yet shut the cabinet when he felt he had to pee. He ran to the bathroom in the corridor. He ate the baklava and sugared mulberries right there. He took his time in order to calm his nerves. He returned to the corridor. The smell of fried onions and fenugreek came from the kitchen, a stale scent that made him feel a little sick to his stomach. Why was he so worried? Why was he always secretly preparing himself for one-on-one combat? He clutched the banister and climbed the stairs very slowly, as if he were Sinbad the Sailor, returning from twenty years of sea voyages to settle his accounts with a bunch of disloyal friends. He looked into Soraya's room. As always, Soraya lay on her bed reading a novel. The creaking of the floor startled her. She put her book face down on the carpet, looking as if she had been caught red-handed. Nuri was concerned that she might tease him or shout and bring the Colonel and Mrs. Tahmasbi out of some hiding place. But Soraya's look encouraged him to approach her. When he reached the bed, he tried to thank her with a few formal expressions. He knelt by the bed, lowered his head, and as soon as his lips touched her feet began sobbing—sobs that shook his entire body. Even his kisses were not completely within his control. After each kiss, he stared into the distance and savored its taste on his lips. At last, he brought his face close to Soraya's. She embraced him and caressed his neck.

♦ ♦ ♦ Until a few days before his departure for America, whenever Nuri visited Soraya in the evenings, the Tahmasbis left the apartment, excusing themselves to go to a movie or visit friends. It was normal for them to go out. Most people left their houses around that time. Looking like paper dolls, the women were dressed in autumn shades, coifed and made up, and walked arm in arm with their husbands. Their perfumes permeated the air. The men opened car doors for them and drove them to pleasant spots such as the Tajrish Bridge and Darband. They would stroll about, have dinner, and return home around nine or ten at night. But Nuri couldn't believe that the Tahmasbis' outings were not deliberately planned to give him time with Soraya. Whatever the reason, he was happy to be alone with her—especially the first nights when Soraya hugged his head and caressed his hair in total silence. She said nothing. A ghost from an unknown world who communicated with him only indirectly. Nuri was free to embrace and kiss her. The only condition was that he be gentle. He did his best to comply. Only once did he put his hand under her collar. He suddenly felt as if he were watching the scene from outside. When he touched her breasts, his head began to spin. He grew so excited that his eyes bulged, rotated in their sockets, and grew dim. He got flushed and ripped the front of her shirt. He bit her lips and mauled her like a wild boar. At first, Soraya didn't stop him, but then she abruptly drew back. She struck one foot on the floor. He asked in surprise, "Sori-jun, why?"

"Because."

"Why? Why? Sori-jun?"

He collected himself and sat back. Soraya continued to stare at him with distaste. It seemed she was demanding to know why he had given up so quickly, yet he lacked the nerve to take up where he had left off. Soraya brushed back her hair and said, "Bravo, Nuri. Bravo!"

Nuri had to leave before he made matters worse. But for a few minutes he sat quietly in front of her, hoping she would say something to reassure him that she still loved him.

In the Dezashibi house, he saw what Madame and Mrs. Baxter had bought in the bazaar for his trip to America—a toothbrush and toothpaste, diarrhea remedies and airsick pills, and Samsonite suitcases. A few times Madame had insisted that Nuri accompany them on their shopping trips, but he had declined. When she returned from the bazaar, she showed him her purchases and asked his opinion. Nuri never thanked her, nor did he say anything to prevent her from buying more things for him. After his initial complaints about going to America, he was now overcome with an inability to utter the slightest protest.

For a few days, he felt no urge to visit Soraya. He forced himself to phone the Tahmasbis a couple of times. On those occasions, Mrs. Tahmasbi made a thousand apologies for Soraya's absence. The news of her sudden disappearances didn't affect him much. He felt only a passing curiosity. Why did she need to get even with him? Why did she enjoy teasing him? Half-questions for which he was not terribly eager to find answers.

He did steal into the Tahmasbis' apartment once. Soraya's room felt cooler and less lively, but it was as untidy as before. He walked around the room. Maybe she had left a note saying she had gone out to borrow a novel or could be reached at Shuri Khanom's. There was something like a spirit in the room. He felt confronted with a presence that seemed to put him in touch with events in another time and place. He imagined faded scenes as in old photographs. It appealed to him to think that years ago someone named Mashallah had lived there. He found it difficult to leave the apartment. He descended the stairs and sat on the sofa in the dark living room. He heard the apartment door open, followed by footsteps in the corridor. In the yellow light from the streetlamp, he saw Mrs. Tahmasbi and the Colonel, carrying plastic shopping bags. They switched on the light and threw a quick glance in Nuri's direction. They seemed unsurprised to see him and merely walked toward the kitchen. The Colonel called, "Would you like some tea?"

His offer gave Nuri an excuse to go to the kitchen. He said, "Good thing you came back. How dark it is in here! I got here two minutes before you. I looked for the light switch, but I couldn't find it in the dark."

The Colonel stood by the sink, taking tomatoes from a bag and rinsing them under the tap. Mrs. Tahmasbi stood on tiptoe to reach for cups and saucers on a shelf. They were absorbed in what they were doing, as if Nuri didn't exist, which made him think about leaving. He took long strides toward the door and said good-bye in a loud voice. "Farewell, with your permission I'll go. I have to catch the last bus."

He left without waiting for a reply.

Just before reaching Amirabad Avenue, he saw Soraya and Captain Anasori hailing a taxi. He stopped for a moment. He was not angry. Actually, he felt comforted. He stood by a wall in the dark and watched them. Soraya jumped up and down excitedly every time a taxi drove by. Perhaps it was better for Nuri to approach her right then. He could still count on his blue eyes and blond hair, his knowledge of foreign languages and operatic songs. Whenever he was at an impasse, he could show his winning hand. But now he ridiculed these things. He saw the future as a distant and blurry horizon. The future was for those who had achieved a past.

♦ ♦ ♦ At the airport, Madame and the Senator were busy greeting those who had come to see Nuri off. Every few minutes Mrs. Baxter squeezed Nuri's arm and reminded him to visit her niece Sharon in New York. Then she winked at him, as if he were a child.

Nuri was startled when he spotted the *akhund* from Ghomsheh among the crowd, pausing now and then to ask the other travelers something. When he came up to Nuri, he showed him the same piece of paper he had shown him a few weeks ago. He held the paper in front of him and said, "Good evening, sir."

Nuri pretended not to recognize him and replied, "Good evening."

The *akhund* seemed puzzled. He said, "You look familiar. Have I met you before?"

Nuri shook his head. The *akhund* said, "Do you know a foreign woman named Nina . . . ?" then walked away, looking bewildered.

As the plane took off, the city lights slowly faded from view, and Tehran grew dreamily distant. Strings of lights sparkled on the hills like diamond necklaces. For the first time, Nuri felt happy to be among strangers. He shut his eyes, but instead of sleeping, he remembered the events of the past few weeks. His perambulations through Tajrish and the guests who smiled and winked at him, gave him letters and addresses, and asked him to contact family and friends in America. The residents of his house said the least—especially Ladan, who hid her tears from him most of the time and, before saying anything, dabbed her eyes with a white handkerchief. He spoke with the Senator only on the evening of a meeting with the shareholders of the Aghcheh land. They ran into each other in the corridor. The Senator was cheerful and gave Nuri a hug. Then he opened his fist and showed Nuri five one-Pahlavi gold coins. He threw the coins into the air, caught them, smiled, and put them in Nuri's pocket. Nuri said, "Grandpa, it seems you are feeling good."

The Senator rapped the antiques cabinet and said jokingly, "Knock on wood, why shouldn't I feel great?" He looked up at the ceiling and scratched under his chin. "You are leaving in the nick of the time. When you get there, remember us. In these conditions, who knows what will happen to us tomorrow?"

Nuri took the coins from his pocket. They were so new and shiny that he wanted to keep touching them. The Senator sauntered downstairs, whistling a song.

Madame had acted like a stranger, unsure of herself. Sometimes she would appear like a ghost behind a window. If she ran into Nuri, she put on a happy expression, but when she thought she was alone, she looked tired. Even on the day of the picnic when Amiz Abbas, Amiz Hosein, and Aunt Moluk performed "Don't Go to the Dome," she had sat on the verandah, rested her chin in her hand, and looked at the guests indifferently. When she saw Nuri, she shaded her eyes and asked, "How are you? Are you enjoying yourself?" Nuri nodded. She moved over to make room for him and asked, "Are you homesick?"

"Very much."

She patted him on the back. "You will forget. You are a nice young man." Then she addressed Mrs. Baxter. "Betty, do you know that Nuri is already homesick?"

Mrs. Baxter shook her finger in Nuri's face and said jokingly, "No, no, no . . . "

The relatives would come over to him, some with bouquets of flowers, others with ten- or twenty-dollar bills in envelopes, and they embraced him and kissed him on the cheek. Amiz Abbas pounded his cane on the brick garden path, lifted his dark glasses, and sang "Don't Go to the Dome" monotonously.

Dr. Jannati made as if he were going to dance and mockingly bent his knees. He readied his fingers to start snapping above his head and sang: "May I sacrifice myself for your body, Gholam Hoseini." He gestured to Amiz Hosein to continue. "Take it away, Amin al-Zarteh. . . . "

When Nuri opened his eyes, dawn had broken. The first rays of the sun touched the peaks of the mountains in Turkey. Granite mountains the color of camels, bearing no trace of life except for wild bushes, and leaning against each other like monsters. He suddenly remembered the smell of Damavand mountain air at dawn, dewy alfalfa and potato fields, and an old man who had gone to the spring for his morning ablutions.

He didn't know how to use the plastic food tray, so he left it untouched. Instead, he examined his seat, the nuts and bolts delicately holding the pieces together and reminding him of the dainty pastries of the Fard Pastry Shop.

The plane flew over rectangular green farms and gray hills. Then Paris's sooty cityscape emerged with cars moving like ants in the streets, bridges crossing the Seine in parallel lines, old monuments and tall churches lining the streets. As the plane landed, Nuri wondered what was happening inside those old buildings with brick chimneys. How many years would he have to live there to experience daily life like the French? How long before he would forget being a stranger among people who spoke a language he could only pretend to grasp?

Before changing planes in the Charles de Gaulle Airport, he bought a thirteen-dollar bottle of brandy from the duty-free shop. He was very happy to be on his own in a foreign land. He opened the bottle of brandy on the flight between Paris and New York. He took a sip and offered it to an American man sitting next to him. The American declined politely. He looked like a businessman, dressed in a gray-striped suit, a starched shirt, and a tie. When he talked, a corner of his lip twitched, and instead of looking in Nuri's eyes, he stared at his mouth. He asked Nuri in English how many times he had been to America. Nuri replied in broken English that he was on his third trip, going to the United Nations as an Iranian representative. The man raised his eyebrows. Nuri continued, "With a salary of ten thousand dollars."

The man said, "Ten thousand dollars! A month or a year?"

"A month."

"Ten thousand dollars a month? That's a lot."

The man began reading a newspaper. Nuri looked out the window. He saw a dark and stormy ocean surging under them. His eyes fluttered, and when he reopened them, he was still inside the dark plane. The man in the seat next to him had the newspaper on his lap; his head leaned against the seat, and he snored. Inside the window frame, Nuri saw the torch of the Statue of Liberty and the lights of New York City blinking along the shoreline. He had to think about gathering his bags.

Before arriving at JFK, he had mentally rehearsed his encounter with Maman Zuzu. He would throw himself into her arms so as to avoid any embarrassing pauses. Maybe he would hide among the other passengers and cover her eyes from behind, waiting for her to utter his name. In the past few years, he had thought repeatedly about the first moment of their reunion. He knew America very well and could pass for an American. He could imitate James Dean—especially the scenes in which James Dean became excited like a child, cried in the middle of laughing, stood drunkenly under oil derricks and looked up eagerly, as if, instead of oil, gold were being showered upon him. With his knowledge of Humphrey Bogart and Marlon Brando, Nuri would surpass Maman Zuzu and Barney, to say nothing of American teenagers because Americans are ignorant of the rest of the world. They have been trained to slave sixteen hours a day at work and have no time for any other concerns.

Despite all this, as soon as he came out of customs, he grew apprehensive. As on the first day of school, he looked around for a familiar face. No doubt his agitated expression had already given him away. They would not mistake him for an ordinary American. His fashionable suit and shoes were meant to indicate that Iranians are no different from Westerners and do not make their living as camel drivers and robbers, but now these clothes were becoming a burden. Among the throngs of people awaiting the passengers on the other side of a metal barricade, Nuri began to feel like a foreigner. Some people jumped up and down joyfully; some held pieces of cardboard with names written on them; and others listlessly looked for the person they had come to fetch. Nuri was conscious of sidelong glances that implied he was being observed.

When he spotted Maman Zuzu standing next to Barney, he felt as if he had found his double. She was a bit darker than he remembered her. There were strips of gray in her frizzy hair, making her head resemble a basket arrangement. She wore a flowery blouse and leather sandals, and a leather purse hung from her shoulder. She looked around expectantly. She sighed, straightened her dress, brushed her hair back, hoisted her dark-framed glasses on her nose as if waving away a bug. At last, she jumped and shouted with delight, "May your mother be sacrificed to you, Nuri-jun, how are you? Where have you been?"

She ran toward a young man in glasses who was ten steps ahead of Nuri. She was about to embrace him when she stumbled in surprise. She

held her fist in front of her mouth, stepped back in shame, and threw dis-
believing glances around. She broke into laughter. Looking flustered, she
apologized in English to the young man. He smiled and waved good-bye.
Nuri walked up behind Maman Zuzu and covered her eyes. She stood
alert the way she always did when she came in contact with someone
familiar. "Nuri! Nuri! Nuri! Nuri!" she said in a childish tone. She turned
and grabbed his arm and whispered in his ear, "Maman, where have you
been? Was it a long trip? Are you hungry? Let's get something to eat first.
Then we'll go home."

She spoke like a person ready to reveal secrets. Secrets that had probably taken root in her mind during the years she had been alone and that
now had a reality of their own.

The restaurant was actually an enclosed part of the airport shopping area. A large cafeteria with carts bearing fruit, soft drinks, bread,
and pastries. It looked as if it could be dismantled in the blink of an eye
like a stage set. They sat at a table near the escalator, which moved like
a mirror image in opposite directions, such an orderly movement that it
drew Nuri out of himself. Like a hick, he pretended to be fascinated with
the airport. He examined the other passengers and the signs in order to
avoid Maman Zuzu's gaze. He looked interestedly at Barney's sleeveless
polka-dot shirt, faded blue jeans, and belt buckle painted in American
Indian style. Barney sat quietly across from him, only tapping the heel of
one boot rhythmically. He put his elbows on the table. He wore a silver
ring in the shape of a coiled snake. His eyes were the color of his blue
jeans. His faded blond hair was thin. The gray and henna growth on
his face made his cheeks seem bony and hollow. He looked like a forty-
or forty-five-year-old man eroded from within by a handful of chronic
thoughts. He asked Nuri in English how he was doing. He had heard so
many good things about him from Maman Zuzu. He was very happy
that Nuri had come to America. He was planning to take him sightseeing in Manhattan the next day. Then he said a few words about life in
America. "No doubt life here will be difficult for an important person
such as you. Your grandfather is a senator in Iran and a close friend of
the shah. You are part of Iran's social elite and enjoy many advantages,
but most of us Americans are ordinary people."

He pursed his lips and pointed to the people sitting around them. Maman Zuzu seemed to be happy with this turn of events. She offered them a hopeful smile. The smell of frying oil made Nuri feel sick. He saw himself as a stranger in a carnival. The waitresses wore bizarre costumes in light shades of blue, red, and lime green. Their red pillbox hats gave them the appearance of toy soldiers in Napoleonic uniforms. Their skirts, resembling short Scottish kilts, covered no more than a hand's width of their athletic, cream-colored legs. Nuri's gaze was drawn to their short white socks. He was anxious about misusing the plastic fork and knife. Not only the waitresses, but also Maman Zuzu and Barney threw curious glances in his direction and seemed to take note of his every move. He asked questions and pointed at commercial signs just to divert attention from himself.

On the ride to Bridgewater, where Maman Zuzu and Barney lived, he felt as if he were on a roller-coaster ride. The rush of colors and lights made him dizzy. Their car seemed to glide from one highway into another. Roads twisted above and beneath them. Drops of rain dotted the windshield. Billboards continually turned on and off. The rush of noise and movement faded as they reached quieter streets, which seemed so distant and dreamy that at last Nuri calmed down.

The car jounced into a garage where a naked bulb burned. The house was small with white siding. The old basketball pole had obviously not been used for a long time. Nuri jumped to imitate shooting a basket. Maman Zuzu laughed. Barney put his palms in the rear pockets of his jeans and stared with his mouth half-open—he had forgotten his house key. He took a stool from near the basketball pole and placed it under a window and, with Maman Zuzu's help, climbed in, then opened the front door from the inside.

The house had the appearance of a temporary dwelling, like a bunker. Even the second-hand furniture seemed makeshift. In the living room, the bookshelves were composed of boards and bricks. There were some mismatched rattan chairs and a table. A red light reflected off a plastic curtain and made the space resemble the interior of a bar. Then they came to a dark kitchen deepened by the red light. The smell of frying oil erected an invisible wall in the air. Barney poured them three glasses of wine.

Maman Zuzu ran a hand over her hair and asked, "What news do you have, Nuri-jun?"

"What news?"

"What about all this noise we hear from Iran? Is it true that everything is topsy-turvy?"

"What noise?"

"Eh, you don't seem to know anything. They say there will be a revolution. You yourself said gunshots are heard in the streets." She laughed and took a sip of wine. "They say each week a million people demonstrate in the streets. Apparently, the shah is going to leave the country, and a thousand things like that. . . . "

Barney narrowed his eyes, put two fingers parallel to each other in front of his nose, and pretended to fire a gun, "Bang, bang, bang."

If Nuri didn't laugh, Barney might take offense. "There are always rumors like this in Iran, but nothing ever happens. Everything is the same as when you left."

He had a sip of wine and took the presents he had brought from his knapsack. He searched for something to say, but he came up with nothing. It was as if a light had turned off inside him. He put Maman Zuzu's presents on the table: a samovar, a copper platter, and tea glasses in silver holders. Then he clumsily presented an inkpot and a hand-painted box to Barney, apologizing for their inadequacy. Maman Zuzu and Barney thanked him enthusiastically, as if they had long wished for such precious gifts. That was it. They had nothing left to say to each other. Fortunately, Maman Zuzu caught on. She said in Persian, "May God kill me, how late it is! Maman, you must be exhausted." In English, she told Barney that Nuri was tired and had better go to bed. Barney stretched his legs, put his feet on the coffee table, and played with the stem of his wine glass. He threw a private glance at Maman Zuzu. She asked, "What do you want to tell me?"

Barney sat up straight and said, "I wish you could sleep peacefully for a few hours like Nuri."

Maman Zuzu smiled at Nuri, "Do you understand what he's saying? I can't sleep at night. It bothers Barney." She continued in Persian, "I keep telling him, 'What's it to you? You go to sleep. I'll sit in the living room and read.' He doesn't listen. He keeps worrying about me."

Nuri took his suitcase and knapsack. The minute they went down to the basement, he recalled Ladan's funny face on the night she had recited the dreaded poem "Golden Litter" by M. G. Shabkhiz—a poem she had recited so many times that Nuri couldn't forget it. She had stretched out every word and heaved deep sighs, speaking as if her voice came from the depths of a cave.

> On the throne of the sun
> I travel
> My golden litter chased by the wind.
> May my prayer be lavishly blessed by the pure morning chill.
> I speak of pain.
> And now, I
> And this stormy pond
> And now, my course this tar-beset formidable tide
> Every moment surges to the marble throne of moonlight . . .

He could hear Maman Zuzu's breathing and feel the warmth of her body near him. When their gazes met, she smiled, reassuring him that this night would pass. Tomorrow they would talk more openly, and maybe they would be less cautious with each other. She switched on the overhead light and busied herself with the bedsheets. Then she shut the blinds and put a glass of water by his bed—exactly like the years in the Shahreza Street apartment when she had always been fidgety and looked out the window, as if anticipating someone's arrival. She mumbled, "You have to forgive all this. This is not the Dezashibi house; otherwise, I would have received you much better." She laughed, "What formal nonsense am I speaking? Don't tell yourself your mother has become all formal in America. If you do, I'll get even with you." She threw one of the pillows to Nuri, hugged the other one, and showed him how to put on a pillowcase. "By the way, now that you're in America, who's going to take over your room? I called Ladan yesterday. She says she prefers her own."

She patted the pillows on the bed. Nuri threw himself on the bed the way he used to in the Shahreza apartment, despite their five-year separation. "What should I know? This is good for me." He looked around the basement enthusiastically. "I like this place a lot. If only Ladan were here, then it would be perfect."

Maman Zuzu continued tidying the basement, but her frown indicated that she was listening to him. She seemed preoccupied. She said, "So you can speak to each other in your own language? Do you still say 'Mamakh' and 'creezy' like before?"

"'Craizy.'"

Maman Zuzu turned around and asked, "Nuri, why have you come here?"

Nuri was stunned. He pointed to himself. "Are you talking about me? Shouldn't I have come?"

Maman Zuzu put the back of her hand to her forehead. Then she bent to pick a feather from the floor and examined it closely. "Oh God! This cat of ours, this evil Meany, catches little sparrows, brings them to the basement, and leaves feathers everywhere. Do you know her name means 'mischievous'?" She shook the feather in Nuri's face. "This is America. You have to keep your wits about you."

She threw the feather in the wastebasket. Nuri sat up in bed and asked, "Did I do wrong to come here?"

"No, my dear. It's great that you came. I meant to say you should wait a few days to get used to it. To tell you the truth, our hands are a bit tied. Barney hasn't had a job for a while. With this economic crisis, I don't know how people make ends meet in America. Prices go up every day and make life more difficult for hand-to-mouth people like us. You can't find a job in this country. After this OPEC episode, you have to line up for gas every day. Most people are happy to clean floors in hamburger joints or wash dishes for meager wages. Poor Barney has been waiting a month for a contract to play guitar in a famous bar. I have to look after my own affairs and knock at this and that door to earn some money." With one hand on her hip, she paused. "Don't say anything to Mumzie and Grandpa. They don't understand anything. Anyway, when did they ever understand, that they should now? If you want to, tell them. It makes no difference to me." She paused again. "Don't imagine that I'm unhappy with my life here. Despite all its hardships, I prefer it to life in the Dezashibi house. I have absolutely no patience for those relatives. I want to live in a place of my own, even if it's small. I want to be in a house where I can come and go as I wish, with no one to nag me and ask me why I insulted His Majesty the Shah, why I embarrassed us in front of the relatives."

Fearful that Maman Zuzu might turn her anger toward him, Nuri sat still on the bed. Maman Zuzu slowly lifted her head, like a person who has just awakened from sleep, and said, "The day after tomorrow is Sunday. No, I'm wrong. I mean it's next Sunday that we have to take you to Saint Joseph's School. On the way, maybe we'll visit Lake George and Niagara Falls to give you a change before you begin school."

"Do I have to go to Saint Joseph's?"

"Why not?"

"I would like to stay with you a bit longer."

Maman Zuzu asked incredulously, "You want to stay here? Here?"

The stress she put on "here" surprised Nuri. He held his head high and said in a loud voice, "Yes. Right here. With you."

"That's enough. No need to put on an act. Keep these formalities for people such as Mumzie and Grandpa who like it."

"No, on your own life, I'm not just being formal." He threw his arms around her. "I would like to stay with you. I'll wash floors to make my own money and not be a burden to you."

Maman Zuzu showed no reaction. Perhaps her silence indicated her disapproval. She kissed Nuri's cheek. "No, Maman," she said. "You have to go to your school. If you don't study, you'll have to wash dishes for the rest of your life. Now, catch some sleep. At least these few days that you are with us, you have no worries. Tomorrow Barney will take you sightseeing in New York." She paused, "What do think of Barney? Do you like him?"

Nuri wanted to insist on staying in New York, but he nodded and asked, "Why shouldn't I like him?"

"All Americans are open like that. Poor Barney was very anxious at the airport. He kept asking, 'What if Nuri doesn't like me?' You don't know how kindhearted he is. He adores Iranians."

"Will you let me stay with you?"

Maman Zuzu patted Nuri's hair. "No, Maman. I would love for you to stay with us, but you shouldn't forget your studies. Enjoy these few days you are with us. You can come back for Christmas and Easter break and stay as long as you want." She kissed him again. "We're in the upstairs bedroom. If you need anything, give us a little shout, OK? Don't be embarrassed. Good night, Maman."

How gentle Maman Zuzu's movements were! She climbed the stairs as softly as a cat, reminding Nuri of the New Year's Day he and Ladan had moved to the Dezashibi house, when Madame had quietly left him alone in the reception hall and disappeared to the third floor.

For the first time, he felt overwhelmed with fatigue, yet he was unable to sleep. What he could not discuss with anyone was his strange longing— a longing that resulted from coming into contact with a new world. He was tempted to get out of bed and look around the basement: the red brick walls with mortar sticking out from between them, as if they had been hurriedly put together. Maybe he would find precious objects that would surprise him. He was excited. He got up and walked toward a row of metal shelves on which Maman Zuzu had placed vitamin bottles, liquid shoe polish, lightbulbs, and canned food—indicators of a harried life. Not like Madame's storage room, whose contents always reminded him of the slow progress of time in a European city. Around midnight, he used to get out of bed and walk around the storage room, remove Madame's china dolls from the glass cabinet, arrange them in a family scene, and watch them take on a life of their own. Then suddenly he would realize that dawn had broken.

The electric appliances, screwdrivers, saw, and drill that Barney had hung on the basement wall offered Nuri no possibility of daydreaming. These objects prevented any longing for lost time.

With a simple twist of a dial, he could overcome immense distances and speak to Soraya in her room in Amirabad. He went upstairs to where the red light was on. The room was so dim that he couldn't find the telephone. Even if he did, what good would it do? What permission did he have? He was weak with longing for Soraya. It was like an old pain focused on a specific spot.

He heard Maman Zuzu's voice from the kitchen. She was reading by a weak light. "Maman, do you need anything?"

Nuri felt like an imaginary creature walking on clouds. He tiptoed into the kitchen, sat in a chair facing Maman Zuzu, and put his palms on the table. "Maman, you are still awake?"

Maman Zuzu took a sip of hot milk and clasped her hair back. "What can I do? I can't fall asleep. I sleep for a half-hour, then I am wide awake. I have to read for a few hours before I can sleep again."

"You just sit here and read. Don't you think about anything?"

"Of course I think about things." She tilted her head and smiled. "Sometimes I think I am in Iran, driving with Papa Javad on the Chalus Road. Then I remember the accident, and I come to. Well, sort of. Sometimes I rub my hand over things, as if I am trying to find you and Ladan. I want to make sure you haven't been hurt in the accident." She asked, "Why are you awake?"

"I wanted to go to the bathroom."

"Go ahead. Don't worry."

After saying good night, he went to the bathroom and then returned to the basement. He curled on the bed and writhed like an injured animal, repeating Soraya's name under his breath. "Soraya-jun, my Sori-jun! Soraya Khanom-jun!"

The more he repeated Soraya's name, the more needy he felt. Around dawn, he remembered Princess Bertha, and for a while he stopped thinking about Soraya. He wondered about visiting Princess Bertha. Maybe he wouldn't let on to her that he knew about her past. He would take Siegfried's picture from his jacket and show it to her like a winning hand. No doubt she lived in one of Manhattan's older apartments. Its interior would probably be decorated in the 1920s style: silky curtains with ruffles, a green-velvet-topped desk displaying a pair of hunting binoculars, an English pipe holder, a globe, and a lamp with an ornate shade. He would wear a formal suit and introduce himself to Princess Bertha as a mysterious young man from the East. Princess Bertha would be wearing a lace dress and a black handkerchief with an ivory clasp. She would sit by a window and receive him like an arrogant Russian countess in mourning. He laughed at his own childish thoughts. He would not have allowed his imagination to run wild had he not needed to stop thinking about Soraya.

... 13 ...

The next day Barney took Nuri to the Rockefeller Center, the Metropolitan Museum, Staten Island, and the Statue of Liberty. The jostle of people on the subway left nothing but a blur in Nuri's mind. He felt as though he had walked against the wind with his eyes half-closed. His only vision of the city was of rows of steely skyscrapers, advancing along parallel lines and converging at an imperceptible distance, and of a tornado of flags, blinking lights, street performers, Red Cross volunteers, and street evangelists.

At home, he collapsed in a chair. Now Princess Bertha alone could bring him out of his daze. He had to come up with a plan to visit Princess Bertha. Despite his youth, he felt ridiculously old.

He gave an excuse to leave the house and then wandered in the streets, watching the crowds of shoppers. He wanted to find out where they lived, who their acquaintances were, what they talked about in private! Around noon, he became so powerfully hungry that he suddenly remembered Madame's raw meatballs. He walked into a small restaurant called Darcy. Inside, it looked like a Swiss chalet, with cozy little booths and pots of geranium and empty wine bottles adorning niches in the wall. At a table near him sat a couple in their sixties. When they talked, their mouths stretched as if filled with toffee. The woman explained to the man why two nights ago she had not let him into the house. "Bill, it was just a mistake. A simple misunderstanding. I am very frank. If I had something to say, I would have said it."

The man didn't reply, but sat nodding his head and slurping his soup.

The waitress put a bowl of fish in front of Nuri. It looked like *eshkaneh* floating in a watery green soup. Eating the fish was like chewing on plastic. Without finishing his meal, he settled his bill. He was not yet ready

294

to return home. Instead, he decided to go a supermarket. The store front was decorated with crates of oranges, apples, and pears. He looked in his wallet and guessed from the wad of five- and ten-dollar bills that he had about five hundred dollars. He bought a fillet of beef, a twenty-pound turkey, two chickens, and some fruit. At least for a few days, Maman Zuzu would not have to worry about her food expenses.

Maman Zuzu was stunned to see the plastic shopping bags in Nuri's hands. After a brief pause, she looked inside one of the bags. She frowned and asked him, "Why did you buy these?"

Nuri lied. "For Princess Bertha. It's not good to visit her empty-handed."

Had he had more time, he would have come up with a better explanation. Maman Zuzu looked him up and down with an aggrieved expression. "Princess Bertha doesn't touch a thing. What would she want with these? Why not take her a bouquet of flowers, a bottle of perfume, or a scarf?"

"I just didn't think."

"Please return these. I hope you bought them from the Maroni Supermarket. I know the owner. Maybe we can get a refund."

Nuri pursed his lips. "It doesn't matter. If they don't take them back, so what?"

"What do you mean?"

"We'll put them in the fridge and eat them ourselves."

Maman Zuzu looked inside the bags again. "You waste your money. You have barely arrived and already, like other Iranians, you think yourself an expert and imagine that you know America better than the Americans. If you want to buy something, why don't you ask me first?"

She talked as if America were her private property. She brushed her hair back agitatedly. She put the plastic bags inside the fridge. That night she made *ghormeh sabzi*, filling the house with its aroma. After dinner, she gave Nuri permission to phone Madame and Ladan. Ladan broke into tears right away. She called him "Mamakh, Mamakh," but she couldn't finish her sentence and passed the phone to Madame. Nuri listened intently, ignoring the faces Maman Zuzu and Barney were making. Barney raised his eyebrows, shut his eyes, and pretended to play a violin.

Maman Zuzu, who was washing dishes, pressed her face to her shoulder to stifle a laugh. Madame's voice was weak and hesitant, as if something bothered her. "How is Your Excellency? Are you enjoying America? Or is it so-so? Huh?"

"Your place is really empty. Maman made a delicious *ghormeh sabzi*, and what crusty *tahdig*, thick and crunchy. Your place is really empty. I've talked too long. It will be expensive. This simple little greeting has already cost seven dollars, I bet."

"Write about your trip. Tell me a little about your life with your *maman*. I hope you all are in complete possession of your health and will lead happy and successful lives for many years to come. Please believe me that I constantly think of you and pray for you. With Mr. Shariat's help, I am going to give a ritual food offering for Saint Abbas to ensure that you do not feel lonely there. Don't feel like a stranger. Yesterday I told Mr. Shariat, one should not compare Nuri to his peers. He will not allow himself to waste away in exile. My dear Sinbad, everywhere is the house of love, be it a mosque or paradise. Last night I was playing Schubert's *Fantasy* on the organ when I remembered my papa-*jan*'s last telephone call. I kept calling, "Papa, Papa," but he didn't answer. I didn't understand then that the absence of a reply from Papa-jan was itself an answer from beyond the world of appearances, a place from which no traveler has returned. Those days I was a simple, bold Austrian girl and measured everything by my own standards. Appreciate time, my dearrr. This too shall pass. Please extend your servant's greetings to everyone. I will call you soon."

When Madame hung up, Nuri felt he needed to go out. The kitchen seemed terribly confining to him. Maman Zuzu and Barney beckoned him excitedly to join them for a glass of wine. He sat quietly in front of them. Barney poured wine for him and Maman Zuzu. Maman Zuzu put a hand on Nuri's shoulder, indicative more of a friendship than of a maternal bond. She did not ask about his exchange with Madame. She talked about herself and her studies. She had received marks higher than the Americans. Nuri asked, "Where are we going tomorrow?"

"I don't know. Ask Barney. I have to work tomorrow."

She worked eight hours a day in the jewelry department of Macy's and seemed very happy with her job. She received a ten percent commission for anything she sold. In addition, she had many benefits—life insurance, medical insurance, and a pension that was the envy of the other Iranians. She snapped her fingers like Americans to indicate how clever she was. "These recently arrived Iranians can't believe it. They wonder how a person who has not yet received her certificate can have such a high-paying job."

◆ ◆ ◆ On the day of their departure for Saint Joseph's School, Nuri woke up excitedly at the crack of dawn. He packed his bags in a silence broken only by Maman Zuzu's humming. Maman Zuzu and Barney were supposed to spend a few nights with Nuri and take him to Niagara Falls. For some reason, on that day Nuri no longer thought about Soraya and Tehran, nor did he worry about going to Saint Joseph's School. He was putting his suitcase and backpack into the trunk when a woman wearing dark glasses walked up to the car. He recognized Princess Bertha immediately. Her corpulent body, fake auburn braids, and wobbly high-heeled shoes made it impossible to mistake her for a Russian countess, though. Close up, she seemed rather ordinary and could easily blend into any crowd. She opened the front passenger door and seated herself next to Barney, which meant that Nuri and Maman Zuzu had to sit in the back. Princess Bertha nodded to Nuri as if forcing herself to greet a nuisance of a newcomer. She grumbled in her thick German accent and asked why they were going to Saint Joseph's. She needed fresh air and had no desire to be cooped up in a musty old Catholic school.

Her ancestors were Polish Jews. Around the middle of the nineteenth century, they converted to Christianity in the vain hope of being left alone by the Russians. She didn't like Catholics. Every time a Catholic's name came up, she recalled the yellow walls and camphor candles of Saint Paul's Cathedral in Philadelphia and twisted her mouth in distaste. Nuri offered her encouraging smiles to engage her in conversation. When Barney stopped for gas, Princess Bertha asked Nuri to hold her arm and accompany her to the store for cigarettes. Afterwards they sat on a bench, and she said in her thick accent, "OK. Ask your question."

Nuri thought, How well this old lady reads my mind. He asked, "How do you know me?"

Princess Bertha lit a cigarette. "There is no need to know you. Ask your questions."

"From my childhood, I have thought of you as one of my relatives. I always knew we would meet one day and talk. Now I'm here, and so are you. You don't know how much I like to listen to your voice."

Princess Bertha drew on her cigarette and arched her eyebrows, "So you like it?"

"Yes."

"What do you like about it?"

"Madame said you are Russian."

"Madame? Which Madame? The one who runs a brothel?"

She threw back her head and laughed. Nuri smiled. "No, I meant Fräulein Frieda."

Princess Bertha pursed her lips and said, "Of course, she's right. I was born in Russia, in Odessa. It doesn't matter where, Moscow, Leningrad, what difference does it make? I love Russia. I love everything about it—its literature, music, and people—but I don't like its politics."

"Do you remember Fräulein Frieda?"

"I never forget my fans. My fans are my closest and best friends. They call me 'Linsky' or 'Linny.' But here in America they call me Lynn. Americans don't know how to pronounce foreign names. They give you an American name to feel closer to you. It makes no difference to me. I like all of them." She put her fingers to her lips and blew kisses in the direction of people standing around the gas station. When she noticed that Nuri was watching her every move, she shrugged. "I'm an emotional person and believe the heart is to be broken. What good is an unbroken heart? Do you like breaking someone's heart? Go ahead, break my heart. Like all Russians, I like violence and suffering. It's probably a disease. It's a kind of madness you inherit. In my veins flow the blood of Gypsies, Tartars, and Mongols." She thrust her hand at Nuri. "Feel my pulse. See how fast it is."

Nuri hesitantly put his finger on Princess Bertha's wrist and asked, "What year did you . . . "

Princess Bertha withdrew her hand and put a finger to her lips. "Shh . . . you're not supposed to ask about my birthday, OK?"

"OK."

"When the Bolsheviks took over, my sister-in-law stashed our fur coats in the space between two walls. For no good reason. Were she to return now, she wouldn't remember where she hid them."

"What about Fräulein Frieda Almstead?"

"Do you mean the one who calls me Linsky? Or the one who calls me Linny?"

"Your old friend. In Iran we call her Madame."

"The one who checks coats in restaurants?"

"No, no, no. A lady named Madame Frieda."

"Oh, that's an interesting question. I don't know how to answer it. My habit is to forget the past and focus on the present and the future." She pushed her glasses up her nose. "My husband died a long time ago. Most of my friends are dead. I sold my house in Vienna, and now no one remembers who Linsky was. Isn't that a shame? Last year I went to Vienna. I have a friend there who is a famous columnist by the name of Rhonberg. I phoned his office. Someone answered, and I said I wanted to talk to the editor in chief of the newspaper, meaning Rhonberg. He replied, 'I'm sorry, he's not in his office. I don't have permission to give out his home number.' I said, 'Maybe you'll remember my name. I am Linsky.' The poor man shouted, 'My God, I can't believe it. Yes, yes, yes.' And a bunch of stuff like that. He apologized to me and promised to tell Fritz to meet me at the Café Imperial that very night. I was already at the café when Fritz arrived. He sat next to me. All the waiters and busboys gathered around him to ask for his autograph. He smiled at them and asked, 'Do you know who this lady is?' They looked at me, but didn't recognize me. Fritz said, 'This is the famous Linsky.' They just stared at each other. I told Fritz, 'See how the world changes. As they say, out of sight, out of mind.' For these youngsters, there is no past. Kaput! We shouldn't waste our life on the past. Only the present and the future are important to me. Especially in America. The absolute sovereign in this young and dynamic country is the future."

Nuri took Siegfried von Friedhoff's picture from his wallet and gave it to Princess Bertha. She looked at the picture, then at Nuri, and said, "Is this a picture of you?"

"How can such an old picture be of me? This was taken more than forty years ago."

Princess Bertha examined the picture more closely. "Where did you get this?"

"Frieda Almstead is my grandmother. She asked me to give it to you."

Princess Bertha lowered her eyelids. Now she paid attention to nothing, not even Siegfried's picture. They heard Barney calling them. Princess Bertha put her hand on Nuri's shoulder and helped herself up. "Princess Bertha never forgets her fans." She asked Nuri to convey her greetings to Madame Frieda and thank her for the picture.

To what extent she had spoken truthfully Nuri could not ascertain. Maybe she was teasing him. He would have to find a more appropriate occasion to ask her his questions.

Barney was in a hurry to reach Saint Joseph's School. He kept urging them to return to the car.

They arrived at Saint Joseph's in time to attend the annual reception for new students at President O'Brien's house. Nuri was dressed and eager to leave, but Maman Zuzu was taking her time fixing her hair in front of the mirror. Then she put on a black paisley dress and high-heeled patent leather shoes, all the while grumbling that she would have preferred to wear a simple shirt, jeans, and sandals. She made Barney wear his gray suit and tie. He looked like a man in armor, pacing the floor. He turned off the bathroom light, arranged the shoes by the door, and took the room key from the table. Every few minutes he took a sip of coffee. His nerves were jangled because he hadn't slept the past few nights. Princess Bertha looked as if she were revolted by something she had touched. She wore a black- and white-striped blouse. The crease in her cream-colored pants could slice a melon. She put her fingertips gingerly on the wall and asked Maman Zuzu, "Where is your son? I have to ask him a question."

Maman Zuzu pointed to Nuri. "Don't you see him? He's standing in front of you."

Princess Bertha turned and said, "Nuri? Are you here?"

She looked more like the image Nuri had of her in Iran. Her auburn wig had sour-cherry highlights. She wore large glasses that covered half her face. Her subtle perfume connected Nuri to a damp and rainy space. He asked, "What did you want?"

Princess Bertha frowned. "Why don't you tell me anything about yourself? It seems you don't want me to know anything about you."

She was right. He didn't feel like talking to Princess Bertha now, but he couldn't shake her off. On the way to the reception and even half an hour into it, she held Nuri's arm and examined him with an inquisitive frown. She dragged Maman Zuzu, Barney, and Nuri from one corner to the other and introduced them to people she knew. When they came across President O'Brien, he threw his arms open and hugged Princess Bertha. "Bertha, Bertha, how wonderful to see you! Why didn't you tell me you were coming?" He held out his hand. "Welcome. Do you know how many years Bertha has been organizing benefit concerts for our needy students?"

He was a tall, bald man in his sixties. His mouth crooked to one side when he talked. He kept one hand in his pocket and nodded his head quickly, as if he were about to burst into laughter. Princess Bertha introduced Nuri and explained that he had just arrived from Iran and spoke English, although he was not yet familiar with American life. President O'Brien nodded his head a few times and put a finger on his chin. "Oh, Iran. I dream of going to your magical country, but in the present circumstances I don't think it would be wise to travel to Iran. Do you agree? We Americans know nothing about enchanting places such as Iran. I have met only one other Iranian student. His name . . . " He put his finger on his forehead and thought. "I don't remember his name, something like. . . . " He twisted his finger on his forehead. "I think his name was Ali Yavaran. Yes, Ali Yavaran. Did I pronounce it correctly? Do you know Ali Yavaran?" Nuri shook his head. "He's from an important Iranian family. Perhaps for you who are an Iranian, his behavior would have been perfectly normal, but for us Americans, lying in bed ten hours a day and puffing on cigarettes is strange. Ali grumbled about American food. He used to say American tomatoes had no taste. He had no appetite. He kept showing his thick, gray tongue to everyone. He asked for grapes, a kind of grape called 'ruby.' Is that right? Ruby grapes? Iranians use poetic and romantic names even for grapes—unlike Americans, who are only concerned with practical aspects of names. Americans say, 'seedless grapes, frying chicken.' These names are not romantic. OK. Had I been in Ali Yavaran's shoes, I too would have wanted to eat bread, cheese, and ruby grapes and write complaints to Iranian magazines in America about Americans' lack of respect for Iranian culture. Iranian antiques are displayed at the Metropolitan Museum as Islamic art. He always listened to a strange music that sounded like the howl of wounded jackals. I mean no offense. Americans understand nothing of Eastern music. But any time Ali heard Iranian music, tears rolled down his cheeks. I mean real tears. I would ask him why the music didn't bring tears to my eyes. He would say, 'You Americans prefer simpler forms of music meant to entertain. There are pieces of Iranian music that will make even camels cry. They are so moved that they even throw themselves into wells.'" He smiled and winked at Nuri. "Fortunately you and I are not camels, nor will our paths cross a desert in the near future. I bet even camels don't consider crying and drowning in wells to be fun." He looked into the distance. "Ali lasted only four months. His relatives came and took him back to Tehran on a stretcher." He put his hand on Nuri's shoulder. "I hope you enjoy this place. I've heard you are interested in gymnastics. We have plenty of exercise facilities. We hope you won't miss your country too much. With your permission, I should go now and offer my formal greeting."

He scratched the back of his neck and walked away.

He had barely taken a few steps when Maman Zuzu started cursing him in Persian. "He thinks he's talking to a bunch of villagers. A young man leaves his country and comes all alone to a third-rate school. He talks as if understanding Iranians is harder than understanding sheep. Americans don't know a thing. As soon as they mention Iranian music, they talk about camels crying. I don't know why I left New York to come stay in a rotten motel with a bed you can't even take a nap on." Like the other guests, they sat around a table. Maman Zuzu crumpled the cloth napkin in her hand and threw it on the table. She put her palm to her forehead and said, "My head is killing me. Does anyone have an aspirin?"

Barney took a package of aspirin from his pocket and said in English, "Why do you hurt yourself like this?"

"I'm sorry. It's fatigue. I have to pay more attention to myself. I don't know why I haven't been able to sleep a wink since Nuri-jun came from

Iran. I think it's because of excitement. I'm afraid I'll shut my eyes and reopen them to find it was all a dream."

Princess Bertha listened to Maman Zuzu quietly. She was also watching Nuri. She waited until Maman Zuzu calmed down. She asked Nuri, "Why did you leave your country?"

Nuri whispered, "If I had stayed, I would have been arrested."

He said this as a joke. But Princess Bertha's reaction was unexpected. Her eyes grew wide and she asked, "Oh, oh, why?"

Her surprise incited Nuri. "For political activities."

"Underground activities? If you said anything . . . " She held her knife at her throat and pretended to cut it. "No? Oh, what an exciting and terrifying revolution! For the Gypsies and Tartars, democracy is not important. They care only about blood, dust, and jealousy. Life or death. Everything or nothing. Am I not right?"

Nuri left the table, pretending to need to go to the washroom. He walked past young boys and girls in cowboy hats doing a square dance. The leader held a microphone in front of his mouth and shouted, "Do-si-do, one more time, Do-si-do." The boys wore western outfits, the girls puffy skirts and beribboned vests over bright shirts. They clapped and danced. The music was so loud that Nuri thought he was hearing a thousand-man army march. The boys and girls did a promenade. The man shouted, "Unwrap the diamond, percolate."

Nuri had an image of Ali Yavaran wandering the halls like a ghost and urging him to follow. He entered a hall with a winding staircase. Some of the guests, holding wine glasses, lined the staircase like statues.

Dum, dum, dum, dum.

Dum, dum, dum, dum.

He walked past etchings and oil paintings of frowning men dressed in capes. Some wore wigs, others had a ribbon of white hair encircling their head like Renaissance cardinals. There were old maps of cities such as Baltimore, Philadelphia, and Pittsburgh, but they didn't interest Nuri. He stood in front of a large painting of General Wolfe's final battle. It depicted foot soldiers, cavalry men in blue-and-white uniforms and triangular hats, smoking rifles, abandoned carriages, and a group of higher-ranking officers, white-haired men in robes, political representatives, and university professors all forming a circle around the general's body. Their poses were more appropriate for a scientific discussion.

The hall led to an old kitchen. Its open fireplace must have been at least two hundred years old. On the varnished wooden floor, one of the professors danced with an Indian student. With every turn, he closed his eyelids, and a smile spread across his face. He appeared drunkenly distant. Nuri took his carefree appearance as a green light. He continued walking through rooms filled with antique furniture, past walls lined with books so old that when he touched one of them, the gold-imprinted cover peeled like tree bark. He thought he was strangely alone and had lost his link to the rest of the world—a bizarre kind of loneliness that reminded him of another presence. When he turned around, he saw a very young blond girl in a white lace dress leaning against a palm in a brass pot. Her hair fell straight down the sides of her face and her blue-gray eyes made her look like someone who has just uncovered a secret. Behind her was an arched stained-glass window. The curling palm leaves reflected on the honey-colored floor as if on the surface of a spring.

He walked away and passed an amphitheater with sea blue wallpaper. The seats were arranged in semicircular rows. Then he entered a glassed-in patio that opened to a damp and green garden. He stepped outside and stood there watching the overcast sky, the moving clouds, and autumnal colors. Suddenly, as if struck by lightning, he realized that he was no longer in Iran. The insight shook him to the very core. He had stepped into an enchanted castle. Everything seemed to be taking place outside the realm of time and space. Even when he sensed someone's presence, he couldn't connect it to immediate reality. He walked toward the bell tower and climbed it. When he stuck his head out of an aperture, wind blew his hair to one side and puffed his thin shirt. Thunder and lightning, the howl of the wind, and the movement of heavy clouds absorbed his attention. He took ten minutes to descend the tower.

Twenty meters away from the entrance to the tower, the girl was waiting for him under a portal lit by a small bulb. He drifted toward the garden path, allowing her to keep up with him. One way or another he would figure out whether there was any connection between them. He sat on a garden bench. The girl stopped ten steps from the bench. She played with the stem of an unopened flower and looked at him challengingly. Nuri called out, "Hey." The girl swallowed. Nuri asked, "What is your name?"

She raised her eyebrows and said, "Amanda."

"How are you, Amanda?"

"OK." Then after a pause, "Thank you." She sat beside Nuri and said, "I like it here. How long have you been here?"

Nuri pronounced his words clearly, "I have just arrived."

Amanda asked, "Would you like to stay here?"

"Why not?"

Amanda smiled, "Really? Promise."

"I promise."

"You come from a beautiful place, right?" Nuri nodded in agreement. Amanda asked, "Probably people are rich in your country. What's the name of your country?"

"Iran."

"Oh, Iran. My daddy taught American literature at Pahlavi University in Shiraz a few years ago. Now he teaches English at Saint Joseph's. His name is Philip Brewster. Didn't you see him dancing in the kitchen with one of the students?"

"Yes, but I did not know he was your daddy. I am new to Saint Joseph's. I do not know anyone."

"Is Iran far away from here?"

"Oh, yes, very . . . "

"On the other side of the ocean, the land of a thousand and one nights? Do you know Sinbad the Sailor?"

"Yes."

She gestured. "Hold your spear like this to hunt whales." She imitated rowing an imaginary boat. "Be careful not to slip, or you'll fall into the sea. My mother and I once went to the seaside for our summer vacation. I was terrified of the water. My mother told me to float on a mat. Do you know what happened?"

"No."

"I went to sleep and fell into the sea." She bit her fingernail and fixed her gaze on him. "You probably have many lakes and seas in Iran. My

Daddy said the Caspian is the largest lake in the world and much more beautiful than lakes around here. I bet you would like to go back to Iran this very instant."

"Why not? How about you? Would you like to see Iran?"

Amanda said, "If I were you, I would have stayed in Iran. You'll get bored here."

"I haven't gotten bored yet."

"Do you like Americans?"

"Why shouldn't I?"

"How about cats? For example, one of those pretty Persian cats?"

"Yes."

"I have a cat. She has leukemia. She won't lick herself and won't eat. She's lost a lot of weight. We had to put her in a cat hospital."

"Why don't animals moan when they're sick? They just sit quietly in a corner."

"Poor things!" She waited. "If I die, would you like to take care of my cat?"

"Why should you die?"

"How should I know? Many people die. They sleep at night and don't wake up. Do you know what I'm really afraid of? I'm afraid of leaving my cat with you."

"Why?"

"Because most foreign students are poor. They'll do anything for money. If someone offers to buy my cat, what will you do?"

"I will tell him, 'Give me the money and take the cat.'"

He laughed. Amanda looked distraught. "For how many dollars?"

"It does not matter. There are plenty of cats."

"How mean you are."

She waved a languid good-bye and skipped away. Why did she get bored with Nuri? Why did she wander around all by herself? How free Americans were! How fearless!

He felt so listless that nothing affected him. He was lonely. He was far away not only from Iran, but also from himself. If Maman Zuzu hadn't showed up right then, he would have probably stayed put on the bench, watching the garden.

Maman Zuzu shouted, "Where have you been? Why don't you tell someone where you're going?" She threw annoyed glances at the copper statues of Peace, War, Death, and Time placed on marble stands in the four corners of the garden. The copper had turned green after the rain. "We've been looking for you for half an hour. We want to head back to the motel. Where have you been? Nuri-jun, you are no longer a child. I'm very tired. If I don't take a nap, you'll have to put me in a mental hospital and find another unfortunate person to worry about you. I haven't slept for three nights, and the three of you have put both feet in one shoe, insisting that we go to Niagara Falls. What's the big deal?"

"Maman, the Niagara Falls are famous all over the world."

"OK, but why shouldn't we go somewhere that is not famous and tells us something about American life? Every Iranian who comes to America has to visit the falls, the Empire State Building, Radio City Music Hall, and then tell us about them as if we haven't seen them a hundred times ourselves. Why doesn't anyone want to go to Harlem, Broadway shows, or authentic jazz performances? They know only how to buy one of these cardboard villas outside the city and brag about living like Hollywood stars. Construction companies have caught on. They build chintzy houses for Middle Easterners. They say, 'People from the Middle East have so much money that they don't know what to do with it. We'll show them.'"

When they got to their motel room, Maman Zuzu collapsed onto the bed. Nuri and Barney fell asleep too. When Nuri opened his eyes, he saw that Maman Zuzu had put a blanket over a lamp and was making peanut butter sandwiches for their trip. She wrapped the sandwiches in plastic and put them in a handbag. She collected dirty clothes strewn around the room and poured herself a cup of coffee. She sat by the window, lit a cigarette, and took more sips of her coffee. Just before dawn, she woke Barney up. She went next door in her nightgown to call Princess Bertha. She knocked so hard on the door that they could hear it in their room. She came back quickly and shouted in English, "Why doesn't Princess Bertha answer?"

"How should I know? Why this rush to leave so early? Stores are closed until ten, and nothing is happening in Niagara this early. Let her sleep."

"I would like to go to the Canadian side to do some shopping. Canada doesn't have a meat shortage like America. The stores open early. They don't charge tax on their liquor and cigarettes, and everything is cheaper than in America."

"We have lots of time. Let Princess Bertha sleep a bit longer."

"Maybe something has happened to her. She didn't answer when I knocked on her door."

Maman Zuzu hadn't finished her sentence when Princess Bertha walked in, wearing flannel pajamas and a pair of black velvet slippers. She rubbed her eyes and looked at them. "What's wrong? Why did you wake me up so early?"

Maman Zuzu turned around to give an answer, but as if addressing ignorant people, she shouted, "Because we're late. We have to get on our way."

"Why?"

Maman Zuzu said, "If we don't leave now, we'll have to pay for an extra day."

Princess Bertha raised her eyebrows and went back to her room. Nuri and Barney didn't look at each other. Maman Zuzu shouted, "Why are you just sitting there?"

They packed their bags and loaded them in the trunk. Then Barney's mood changed. He walked quietly to the motel office to settle their bill. When he came back, he leaned against a column in front of their room. He opened his wallet in front of Maman Zuzu and counted his remaining banknotes. Maman Zuzu blinked a few times. Barney's expression did not change. He put his wallet back in his pocket and headed toward the car. Maman Zuzu settled angrily behind the wheel and ordered Barney to sit beside her. Barney climbed in quickly before Princess Bertha had a chance to get in. Princess Bertha was stunned by Maman Zuzu's testiness. For a few minutes, she didn't know what to do. Then she settled in the back seat, barely disguising her anger. She patted the leather seatcover and, pursing her lips, asked Nuri in a maternal tone to sit next to her.

Nuri kept quiet and watched the green forests and the lakes emerging suddenly behind the trees. The winding road was as smooth as if it had been paved just yesterday. When they approached Niagara, the dusty leaves began to remind him of Damavand and Meygun. They drove through crowded streets filled with tourists and lined with shops, gas stations, and boutiques. They reached an amusement park that had a two-story mud hut and a balcony with a Mexican-style iron railing. In front of a ticket booth, a giant figure of a mustachioed Mexican kept blinking at the customers, pulling a revolver from his pocket, and exhaling smoke from his mouth. Nuri felt like visiting the spot, but one look at Maman Zuzu's face dissuaded him. It was just a few minutes past ten. A cold breeze snuck under his clothes. The sun slowly spread across the treetops and tempted him to curl up like a cat. He had seen Amanda's blue-gray eyes somewhere before. Why hadn't he asked for her telephone number? When he went back to Saint Joseph's, he could contact her.

When the falls came into view, the leaves sparkled under the sun. He compared this view with what he had imagined in Iran. He suddenly wanted to jump out of the car and run until he reached an arid field with a couple of poplars and a mud hut, a blue-tiled shrine, and a silvery river with a bed of small rocks like sparrow eggs. A place such as Meygun or Fasham whose green was a balm for thirsty nomads roaming the desert. Maman Zuzu drove around until she found a shady spot to park the car. She went to put money in the meter, but she couldn't find any coins in her wallet. She beckoned to Nuri. She took a cigarette from her purse and, with shaking fingers, placed it in the corner of her mouth. She fumbled in her purse for matches. Barney threw a box of matches out of the window, and she caught it. She spoke to Nuri while trying to light her cigarette. "Nuri-jun, how much money do you have on you? Do you have a couple of hundred dollars to lend me? When I get back to New York, I'll send you a money order."

Nuri quickly took his wallet from his pocket. As he counted his banknotes, Maman Zuzu stared at the crowd of tourists. She said, "I asked Barney to remind me to get some cash from the bank. He forgot because he is always smoking dope. He has no memory left. I told him, 'Now that we have paid for the gas and come all this way, why shouldn't we at least buy our groceries from the other side of the border?' Everything is cheaper in Canada these days."

Nuri counted two hundred dollars and handed the notes to Maman Zuzu. "If that's not enough, I can give you more. I won't have any expenses here. Why do I need money?"

Maman Zuzu didn't count the money. She folded the notes and put them in her purse.

"Thank you. Now you look around for half an hour while we go to the other side. We'll do our shopping and come right back."

"I'll come with you. Why should I stay here by myself?"

"You don't have a visa. They won't let you in. We'll be right back. Let's synchronize our watches. It's 10:23." Nuri glanced at his watch and nodded. "OK. We'll be back in an hour and a half. Dear, don't go far. Stay right here, and we'll be back."

She kissed him on the cheek and quickly got behind the wheel. Nuri didn't insist on joining them. Before coming to America, he had imagined that Maman Zuzu would forget herself as soon as she saw him and flutter about him like a butterfly. Now she was leaving him all alone in an unknown place to go shopping. Instead of being angry, Nuri felt ashamed, as if he had done something wrong. He sat on a bench and hugged himself. Maman Zuzu laughed at him, turned the wheel, and gunned the engine. The car took off, and Barney waved to Nuri. Princess Bertha stuck her head out the window to look at the rainbow over the falls and blew a kiss to Nuri. He suddenly felt abandoned.

On the other side of the street, there were restaurants and shops filled with knickknacks. He walked around, hoping to spot the amusement park. In a café, he ordered coffee and chocolate cake. Twenty minutes later he was back on the street, wondering how to pass the remaining time. He returned to the falls. Except for a few black men teasing each other under a pine tree, passing around a brown paper bag and laughing aloud, the street was deserted. He wandered around for hours after the others didn't show up when they were supposed to. Then he stretched out on the bench and shut his eyes. His muscles relaxed, and he slipped into a nap. When he opened his eyes, it was getting dark. Neon lights reflected halos on the street. He couldn't see the falls, but he could hear the rush of water. He grew fearful that he had missed their rendezvous. Perhaps Maman Zuzu, Barney, and Princess Bertha had driven back to Saint Joseph's and left him there. Nuri's big toes smarted. He took off his shoes and socks and saw that his toes had turned red. He rested his feet on the bench and looked at his watch. It was a few minutes past 10:30 P.M. The black men had disappeared. A policeman walked along the street, swinging his baton. Maybe Nuri should ask him for help, but he worried that the policeman might become suspicious of his accent. He put his socks and shoes back on and cut through the park to the lighted sidewalk. He stood on tiptoe and glanced toward the bench where Maman Zuzu had told him to wait. He walked by restaurants and bars filled with people. Then he reached quieter side streets where barefoot people in T-shirts drank beer on their front stoops. An old man with a cane limped past him. Nuri walked behind him for a while, but lost interest. He thought maybe Maman Zuzu, Barney, and Princess Bertha had come back and were looking for him. He walked toward the bench and spotted Princess Bertha first. Barney and Maman Zuzu could be heard laughing a few steps away. "Hurry up, or we'll be late."

Barney laughed. "Nuri is probably cursing us."

Maman Zuzu said in a more serious tone, "That's enough. I'm afraid my child is lost."

They appeared under the pine trees, each carrying a couple of large shopping bags and walking like pregnant women. Princess Bertha put her fingertip to Nuri's chin and said, "Nuri, I recognized you right away."

"Why are you so late?"

"Oh, Nuri-jun. There was an estate auction a hundred miles from here. Your mother needed a bunch of knickknacks she bought at a good price. But it's the weekend, and the roads are busy." She sank onto a bench. "Oh, how I would like a martini! When I first came here from Vienna, everybody drank martinis. I had an old friend in New York we called 'Eddy.' For him, drinking martinis was like gambling. When he drank one, he would mark the counter with his fingernail, meaning this could well be his last martini. I wish Eddy were here, and we could drink his last together."

Maman Zuzu put her shopping bags on the car roof and asked, "Why didn't you wait by the bench?"

She walked up to him in such a way that Nuri thought she was going to slap him. He pulled back and said, "You abandoned me, and now you're going to put the blame on me? I've been wandering alone for ten hours.

312 T A G H I   M O D A R R E S S I

I have blisters on my feet. I don't know anyone here. I didn't even know how to get back to Saint Joseph's."

Maman Zuzu appeared calm, but she was like a bomb about to detonate. He grew anxious and looked around for Barney. He was leaning against a lamppost, looking at Nuri from the corner of his eye as if apologizing for Maman Zuzu's bad temper. In such a situation, anything Nuri did would turn out badly. He took the shopping bags from the roof of the car. Maman Zuzu didn't unlock the door for him. She put a cigarette in the corner of her mouth and looked into the distance. Barney took a spare key from his pocket and opened the door for Nuri. He addressed Maman Zuzu softly. "Shall we go?"

Maman Zuzu paid no attention to him. She turned to Nuri, took her key from her purse, and said, "It's your turn to drive. I'm tired."

Nuri didn't have a driver's license, and driving at night on roads he didn't know with signs he didn't understand was sheer madness. But he had told Maman Zuzu that three months before leaving for America, he had obtained his international driver's license and had driven a sixteen-wheeler on the Karaj Road. Some of the best drivers in Tehran had insisted that he become a stunt driver for American films. No doubt these same lies were the reason Maman Zuzu was forcing him to drive.

Barney said, "Zuzu-jun, I don't think it's a good idea for Nuri to drive at night. He doesn't know these roads."

Maman Zuzu frowned and put the car key in Nuri's palm. "Until you taste danger, you won't learn to stand on your own two feet." She gestured to Nuri. "Show him your international driver's license to put a stop to his worrying."

Nuri said, "I left it in Tehran."

He threw a beseeching glance at Barney, hoping he would understand. Maman Zuzu shouted at Nuri, "If you were going to leave it in Tehran, why did you waste so much money on it?"

She threw her weight onto the front seat and exhaled a thick cloud of smoke. She sat there frowning until the engine started. She watched as Nuri put the car in gear, but Barney and Princess Bertha stared out the window. Maman Zuzu heaved a sigh and said, "Nuri-jun, may God be praised, how well you drive. It's a good thing you're not in Iran where they would find a thousand faults with your driving. Iranians know only how to point to people's faults. When Badri Khanom and Dr. Jannati came here on their last tour, I took them to Park Avenue. In the middle of all the beautiful stores, Badri Khanom would spot a beggar, bite her lip, and say, 'Zuzu-jun, may God kill me, didn't you say New York is beautiful? Why are there so many beggars and cripples here? Why do we see so many hooligans and drunks on every street corner? They follow us around like a bunch of crazies. In their entire life, they haven't seen a beautiful Eastern woman. What if one of them attacks me, what can I do?' A few years ago she had read in the paper that a black woman was hacked to death in front of her neighbors, and no one did anything."

Maman Zuzu squeezed Nuri's arm and heaved another sigh. "What kind of answer can I give this educated woman?"

Nuri said, "I don't know my way around here. I'm afraid the police might suspect something from my driving and stop us. When they find out I'm a foreigner, they'll fix me good."

"What a scaredy cat you have become! What will the police do to you?"

"For example, they may not take my word for it when I say I have left my driver's license in Tehran."

Maman Zuzu shrugged her shoulders. "No, my dear. The police here are not like Iranian police to bother a foreigner." She took a brown sweater from one of the shopping bags and showed it to Nuri. "How much do you think I paid for this?" Barney was about to say something, but Maman Zuzu put a finger to her lip. "Shh. I want to see what Nuri says."

"I don't know anything about prices."

"Well, say something."

"Ten dollars."

"Didn't I say we went to an auction? Did you forget? I bought this sweater, three silk blouses, and a beaded purse for four dollars. You haven't seen auctions around here. They talk so fast, as if they don't want you to catch the prices."

Barney made a sound with his tongue like a cork being popped. "She's right about that. Whatever the auctioneer said, your *maman* Zuzu raised her hand."

Maman Zuzu said to Barney, "Didn't I say I wouldn't be cheated? Show Nuri the Bible. They gave it to me for free. Nobody wanted it. See how thick it is. It weighs twenty kilos. They said it had been in that house for a hundred years. Exactly like our own old Korans passed from generation to generation in which they record birthdates and weddings."

Princess Bertha asked, "But you're a Muslim. Why would you want a Bible?"

"Because it's an antique. It's beautiful." She turned to Nuri and said, "I wish you had been there. Auctions here are amazing."

"I was going crazy by myself. If you hadn't come back, I wouldn't have known what to do with myself. How was I going to go back to Saint Joseph's?"

Maman Zuzu said in Persian, "On your own life, I told Barney a hundred times, let's go back. My poor child will worry. Barney would say, 'It's a shame. An auction like this happens only once every ten years.' Well, he's American. He doesn't understand."

Nuri answered in Persian. "Does an auction last ten hours?"

"No, no, Nuri-jun. If the roads weren't so packed, we would have made it back sooner. The restaurants near the border are very expensive. They charge seven or eight dollars for a measly sandwich. We got hungry. We drove a hundred miles to find a cheap restaurant. It was by a river. What a nice spot!" She said to Barney in English, "What did you do with Nuri's sandwich? Give it to him. I don't think he has had anything to eat since lunch."

Barney offered Nuri a wrapped sandwich. Nuri turned it down. Maman Zuzu leaned her head against the headrest and said, "You don't know how tired I am. I would love to rest my head here and sleep for a couple of hours. But I won't fall asleep. I say to myself, 'Why do you complain? Complaining is for those who are never satisfied.' I live in a country where I am free to express my own opinion. Nobody bosses me around. Sitting beside you right now is wonderful. I calm down when I listen to your voice. You drive really well, Nuri-jun, as if you have been driving in America for ten years." She took from a shopping bag a pair of woolen socks, two silver dishes, a cake cutter, and two lamps and examined them closely. "All this cost us eighteen dollars and fifty cents. That's nothing in America. If you give it to a beggar, he'll turn it down." She folded the socks and put them back in the bag. She could barely keep her eyes open. "I wish I could have a short nap."

"Why don't you shut your eyes and sleep a bit?"

"Me, sleep? How naïve you are! I'm always awake, worrying that something might happen to you. Do you believe me when I say I'm constantly thinking of you and Ladan?" She shut her eyes. "I have to have someone beside me to talk to me, sing, or tell me a story. Then, maybe I'll fall asleep. Now, why don't you whistle a bit, Nuri-jun? Do you still know how?"

"I don't know. I haven't practiced for a while."

"Whistle one of your nice tunes."

Nuri whistled the folk song "The Deer Hunt" and sang a few verses. "'I want to go to the mountain, on a deer hunt, where is my gun, Leili-jan, where is my gun?'"

Moonlight outlined Maman Zuzu's mouth, lips, and nose, and made her face look like an African mask.

♦ ♦ ♦ Instead of attending classes, Nuri spent his days on Ali Yavaran's old bed, staring at the images on the TV screen. He missed Ladan and the Dezashibi house. He was fed up with a world that demanded new things of him all day long. Focusing on the television screen cut him off from his surroundings and enabled him to think of cozy places with Persian rugs whose patterns emerged as if from under ashes. He called the Dezashibi house a few times and spoke to Madame. She asked him excitedly about his life in the boarding school, his friends, his progress in English. She wondered whether he had found a girlfriend by now and hoped that he no longer missed Iran. Nuri complained about being lonely and gave Madame such a dismal picture of life at the school that he made himself anxious. To atone for that, he talked about Professor Brewster's kindness and the fact that he had invited him to Thanksgiving dinner. Professor Brewster couldn't believe that a young Iranian could learn "Jingle Bells" so quickly. When he had lived in Shiraz, Professor Brewster had tried to learn Persian, but learning foreign languages was not easy for Americans. Nuri also told Madame about his new friends, Linda Cox and Salvador Sable, but he didn't mention Amanda. Madame might not understand.

Every afternoon Amanda came to his window at four. She would rest her chin on the window ledge and watch him. As soon as Nuri saw her heading toward his window, he would fix his gaze on the television to avoid talking to her. After a while, Amanda would get bored and leave.

On Monday of Thanksgiving week, she didn't show up. Nuri sat in front of the TV until five. It grew dark, and the church bells began to ring. The students headed toward the chapel. Nuri looked for Amanda, but found no sign of her. He began to worry. Perhaps she had been in a car accident or one of her relatives had died. Nuri joined the other students walking to the cafeteria. The cafeteria was not very busy. No one joined him at his table. He left to go back to his room and watch the evening news.

The next day there was still no sign of Amanda. If something had happened to her, he would have heard by now. This thought calmed him down. Then he worried that maybe some trick was being played on him. Was it possible that Amanda was deliberately staying away to make him anxious? At last, he had to admit defeat. He could not stop thinking about Amanda. He became obsessed with finding her. He dropped by the bookstore, post office, coffee shop, and other spots until he found her in the amphitheater. She was seated in a front-row seat. When she saw Nuri, she bit her fingernail and offered him a mischievous smile. She said, "Good thing you came."

"Were you waiting for me?"

"I knew you would come."

"How?"

"Do you know the story of the rabbit and the fox?"

"No."

"The fox asks the rabbit why he hides in his hole when he sees him. The rabbit says, 'If you don't want me to hide, you have to train me.' The fox asks, 'How?' The rabbit says, 'Come to my hole every day for a few minutes and let me get used to you. Then one day don't come at all. I'll miss you and come out of my hole to find you.'"

Amanda smiled and turned up her palms in a way that irritated Nuri. How could a little girl like her wrap him around her finger? He decided to go back to his room, but Amanda followed him. When they reached his door, Amanda said, "I know Iranians very well. They just want to go back to Iran."

"*You* know Iranians?"

Amanda said, "Iranians are jealous. Whenever someone praised America, Ali Yavaran spat on the ground and said, 'Americans don't know anything. They organized a coup in Iran. They milk other countries.' I would say, 'If Americans don't know anything, how could they organize a coup in a big country like Iran?'"

Nuri pouted and said, "Don't be so smart."

"Why do you get angry? I was just kidding." She took a prayer stone and beads from her pocket and asked, "Would you like these?"

"What for?"

"For your prayers. A couple of Iranians gave these to me. They get together by a lake on weekends and play backgammon." She followed him into his room. "You don't mind if I come in?" Nuri smiled but said nothing. "Are you sure?"

"Yes."

She gave Nuri the prayer stone and beads. He sniffed them and put them on the radiator. "Don't you have school?"

"Of course I do. But since last year when my brother, Michael, was killed in a car accident, my mother is terrified of being away from me."

"Oh, why?"

"My mother doesn't say anything, but when I talk about anybody, she starts crying. She says a sister shouldn't forget her brother so quickly. This year she's giving me lessons at home. On Sundays I have to go with her to the cemetery and place flowers on Michael's grave. We kneel by it and pray together. Even then she gets angry that Michael's friend Henry visits his grave alone and leaves flowers there. She says, 'Henry visits Michael's grave for his own sake.' He uproots the flowers my mother has planted around the grave. I say, 'What's it to me? I can't listen to stories of Michael's death for the rest of my life and live in his stead.' Were you in my place, could you do that?"

Amanda went over to the mirror where Nuri had put up his family pictures. She couldn't believe Nuri had so many relatives in Iran. She pointed to a picture showing Nuri swallowing a kebab skewer. She said, "What tricks you know!"

Nuri took a knife from the table and turned its blade toward her. "Do you want me to teach you how to swallow a knife?"

"A knife this big?"

"Yes. This big."

"You're kidding."

"I'm not kidding. Do you want me to swallow it or not?"

Amanda's eyes grew wide, and she backed away. "My mother is waiting for me. I have to go back. Will you let me go?"

"Why shouldn't I? You came here on your own, and you can leave whenever you want. But if you want me to swallow this knife, I'll show you."

Amanda suddenly ran away like a cartoon figure. Nuri laughed, but something didn't feel right. He threw the knife on the table. He put his face between his hands and watched the TV screen from between his fingers. Amanda could complain to her parents about him. On the screen appeared an image of millions of people demonstrating in the streets of Tehran. A sea of bearded men shouting angrily. They carried banners showing caricatures of Jimmy Carter and Menachem Begin as two-horned devils.

It was clear from the beginning that skipping class would land him in trouble, but he couldn't help it. He was worried about incomprehensible events taking place in Iran. The first few weeks he didn't go to class because of his fear of speaking English. He loitered around the cafeteria, the post office, and the bookstore. Then he got a job at United Parcel Service. He became adept at driving the truck and delivering packages to customers. He changed his manner and wore a beret like Che Guevara, a burgundy turtleneck, and boots he bought from an Israeli student. The boots had originally belonged to a Russian soldier by the name of Alexi Jordanof who had entered Hitler's bunker under German machine-gun fire and planted the Russian flag there.

At night, when he walked into the Purple Unicorn around 8:30, the other students cheered him and invited him to their tables. He would tell them about his antigovernment activities and the tortures he had endured in the Evin Prison as a result.

Driving a truck six hours a day, imitating the accent of an English lord, and having to deal with a bunch of malcontent American customers finally exhausted him. He quit doing any schoolwork. He hurried through everything to distract himself from his private concerns. In the mornings, he had a bitter taste in his mouth and felt terribly lonely. But he stayed in the Purple Unicorn until two in the morning listening to rock and roll music. He bought many tapes, ate whatever he desired, and went to bed and woke up any time he wanted. Only a few times did he go to class. After one of these occasions, he went to the cafeteria and sat at a corner table. A Filipino student, Salvador Sable, and a girl from Chicago, Linda Cox, asked to join him. Salvador was small, with a bony, hairless face and rabbit teeth. He was very curious about Iran. Linda Cox claimed to know two retired Iranian brothers named Badamchi. She worked in a restaurant they had opened called "Shokufeh." She asked Nuri in Persian, "How are you?"

Salvador asked why Iranians disliked such a nice and handsome king. If an Islamic government came to power, what would happen to the religious minorities? Nuri spoke about the violence of the secret police and the American coup against Mosaddeq's government. Had it been possible, he would have stayed in Iran and joined other Iranians in their fight. He was not afraid of being arrested, tortured, or killed. He pulled up his shirt and showed a mark Black Najmeh had left on his chest by applying a suction cup. Linda could not stand looking at wounds. She shut her eyes, but Salvador asked inquisitively, "That's a mark left by the secret police?"

"Of course."

He told them how the secret police had burned him with cigarette butts to make him reveal the name of his comrades. But he hadn't even frowned; he had just bitten his lips. "Torture is hard only in the beginning. After a few minutes, the skin goes numb. You have to control yourself and not be afraid of pain. Then nobody can hurt you. That's the secret police's weakness. They go crazy. They attack you like wild animals to hide their own defeat."

He said all this without a pause, not realizing that his fabrications were taking on a reality of their own.

Salvador took his guitar from its case, hugged it, and sang "When the Swallows Come Back to Capistrano" so movingly that the other students applauded. Nuri's only effort to attract Linda's attention was to bow to her jokingly before he left. He spread one hand across his chest and gave an exaggerated bow like characters in *Ali Baba and the Forty Thieves*. Linda bit her lower lip and smiled at Nuri.

It was dark when he came out of the cafeteria. A few students, looking like ghosts, walked toward the chapel. It was a month before Christmas, but the outside of the chapel was already decorated with lights. A candle burned under the statue of the Virgin Mary. The smell of melted wax reminded him of the old shrines in Iran. He sat in a pew and knelt like the others. Everyone rose suddenly and began singing a hymn. Nuri realized that he had made a mistake. He rose slowly and mouthed the words.

Fortunately, the service ended quickly. He left the chapel and saw Linda walking toward the dormitory. He didn't have much time, so he worked up the courage to invite her for pizza. But he regretted it immediately. Linda excused herself, saying she had to go back to the dorm. "Another night. I have to write a ten-page report by tomorrow."

Nuri shrugged and scraped his shoes on the brick path. "OK. No problem."

Linda clutched his arm. "Don't be hurt. I'm really sorry. How is tomorrow night?"

"Maybe you say no because I am Iranian."

"Don't be an ass. How is tomorrow night?"

Nuri couldn't calm down, feeling as if he had to prove his point and take Linda out that same night. "You mean you don't even have ten minutes now? We'll take no more than ten minutes."

He guzzled a beer at the pizzeria. Linda held her beer glass and looked at the other students sitting around them. The customers talked and laughed loudly. Nuri felt comforted by these sounds. He got excited and began talking about his adventures. His friendship knew no limits. He was willing to suffer for a companion like Buki Tahmasbi or Linda. To quote a famous Iranian poet, human beings are parts of the same entity. They are created from the same essence. "Iranians are so full of life that sometimes they forget the difference between enemies and friends. They become as excitable in friendship as in enmity. They'll kill to prove their friendship. As one poet says: 'O slain one, whom did you slay to be killed. Another will kill the person who killed you.' My English is not good. I don't know how to translate it."

Linda took a sip of her beer, put two dollars on the table, and rose. "I have to go back to the dorm."

"Another ten minutes?" Nuri tried to put the money in Linda's palm. "You have to take this back. This would be an insult in Iran."

Linda put on her coat and walked toward the door. Nuri took a ten-dollar bill out of his wallet and threw it on the table. He ran out after Linda. "Linda! Linda! Wait for me."

He could hear Linda giggling. He caught up with her and grabbed her hand. She did not protest and walked more slowly. Nuri put his hand on Linda's shoulder and kissed her on the cheek. "Linda, I'm happy. I like you very much."

Linda blinked a few times and said, "Thank you. You're very kind."

"I don't think you understood. I said I liked you. I didn't want to flatter you. I am in no way indebted to you. If I didn't deserve it, you wouldn't be so kind to me."

"Thank you."

"Do you like me?"

"Of course I do."

Linda disappeared inside the dorm.

The next day he was suddenly struck by fear. Maybe he had put Linda off. His head spun at this thought. How would he meet her gaze? Around dusk, he saw her coming out of the Administration Building with Salvador and an Indian girl named Joswinder. Maybe he could set things right with a joke. He walked by a row of trees and stepped in front of her. He gave a deep bow, hoping she would forgive him. Linda smiled and walked on. He returned dejectedly to his room. He lay on his bed and watched TV until news time. When he heard Amanda's footsteps, he pretended to be asleep. Through half-open eyes, he watched her place a plate of cream puffs and fried chicken on the windowsill. Mrs. Brewster must have made them herself. Amanda looked confident, as if she knew all aspects of Nuri's life. She obviously knew Nuri would be alone during the Christmas holidays.

He pretended to be surprised by the plate of food. He ate it quickly, looked out the window, and said, "Amanda, the fried chicken was excellent."

Amanda wore a playful smirk. She blurted out, "Are you happy?" Nuri nodded. Amanda asked, "Are you happy now that there has been a revolution in Iran, and they have taken Americans hostage?"

"What can I do?"

"You sit here alone and watch TV?"

"What should I do?"

"Don't you know anyone here?"

He started to say something, but Amanda left. On the screen, he saw the American hostages celebrating Christmas. A chador-clad young woman read a communiqué. If Maman Zuzu had any idea about his loneliness, she would have invited him to New York. He dialed Maman Zuzu's number. She recognized his voice immediately and asked, "Nuri, what are you doing alone on a Saturday night? Don't you know anyone to go out with?"

"I want to go back to Iran."

"Where?"

"Iran."

Maman Zuzu's pause meant she had taken him seriously. "Do the kids bother you there?"

"Where?"

"Saint Joseph's, I mean."

"Why should they bother me?"

"Because of the hostage crisis, the Americans are livid."

"What does that have to do with me? I haven't taken anyone hostage."

"They've fired a lot of people here. An Iranian was beaten so hard in the subway his brain hemorrhaged."

"Nothing like that has happened around here. I'm just worried about Mumzie."

"Has something happened?"

"She just had an operation and can't talk on the phone. Whenever I call, Badri Khanom answers and speaks very softly as if she doesn't want anyone to know I have called."

Maman Zuzu listened quietly for a while. Nuri asked, "You don't know anything?"

"No, I haven't heard anything."

"Maybe I should come to New York."

"Yes, Maman. Come as soon as possible."

"I'm coming."

He hung up.

... 14 ...

The night before he was supposed to go to New York, he left the Purple Unicorn late. Sporting his Che Guevara beret, he made faces he would normally make only in front of the mirror, but no one was there to see him.

He suddenly felt that he was being followed. Huge shadows appeared on the snow-covered ground. The figures seemed to be wearing the shoulder pads of the school football uniform, although the weather was too cold for that. They walked slowly, scraping their shoes on the gravel path, exclaiming "fucking ayatollah," "fucking Iranians." They seemed fearless, but not necessarily aggressive.

Nuri walked faster. There was a sudden frightening silence, like the quiet before a storm. Then ghostlike figures stepped in front of him. They wore skull caps and cloth masks with holes for the eyes. One of them, who was taller than the rest, staggered closer to Nuri. He pulled off Nuri's beret and placed it over his own cap. He stood on tiptoe, leaned his elbow on Nuri's shoulder, and looked him up and down. "Hello."

"Hello."

"Are you Iranian?"

"No. I'm Greek."

The masked man addressed his friends. "Did you hear? This motherfucker says he's Greek. His blond hair and blue eyes seem to back him up on that. Right?"

He raised his hand. Nuri thought he was about to be hit and ducked. Instead, the masked man scratched the back of his head. He seemed to be only teasing. Yet Nuri stood still, feeling an intensity in the air that made him anticipate an explosion. The man suddenly signaled to his friends, and they jumped Nuri like a pack of wild boars. They dealt him such hard blows that he almost passed out. He felt himself being dragged across the gravel. They abandoned him in front of the girls' dormitory and fled.

He knew he shouldn't give in to the pain. If he lost consciousness, he would freeze. For a few minutes, he fixed his gaze at the dormitory lights whose glimmer and warmth reminded him of the mesmerizing flames of a fireplace in a cozy room. He could hear the wind blowing through the trees. His fingers were numb. Grabbing a branch, he pulled himself up. A sudden surge of anger filled him with vigor. He stumbled to his room and collapsed onto his bed.

He was embarrassed about being beaten for being Iranian. Up till then, he hadn't imagined it possible for anyone to hate Iranians so much. He berated himself for mingling with American thugs. He didn't leave his room for two weeks after Christmas, knowing he would have to report to the school clinic and explain his black eye and bruised face. The day he decided to leave his room, he introduced himself as Norman or Normy from Sweden. He deliberately mentioned the hostage crisis and ranted against the Islamic government. He returned to his room exhausted.

He expected to be called to President O'Brien's office, and he didn't have to wait long. Three weeks after the Christmas holidays, the president's secretary phoned and made an appointment for him to meet with President O'Brien and Princess Bertha to go over his school report. As soon as he heard this, he felt a huge burden had been lifted. Now he was certain of being expelled from school.

He put on a frown when he walked into the office, implying he had no desire to be there. President O'Brien was seated behind his desk. He offered Princess Bertha a golden box of pebblelike chocolates. He held the box in front of Nuri. Nuri took one, but didn't eat it. The president smiled and said, "Don't be afraid. It's chocolate."

Then he placed his elbows on his desk, examined Nuri through his thick lenses, and pointed to a chair for him to sit in. He addressed Princess Bertha. "Big companies rarely help educational institutions. They donate money mostly to museums and art foundations because it makes more noise. Then we educators have to fight con artists trying to defraud foreign students. Foreigners are so gullible sometimes they make you angry. By 'foreigners,' I mean people from the Third World, not Europeans who are familiar with our culture. The con artists go only after people from the Third World. They show them free samples of cigarettes and alcohol and try to sell them life insurance. Do you understand? Life insurance to youngsters who haven't even turned twenty. They gave one of these boxes of chocolate to an Indian girl by the name of Joswinder . . . poor thing didn't know what to do with a bunch of pebbles. She asked me: 'Why do Americans eat pebbles instead of chocolate?'" He threw glances at Nuri's bruises, then turned his gaze to a picture of sailboats on the wall. "Norman, unfortunately your first-semester reports indicate that you hardly ever go to class. You're smart. Do you know where you're headed with these reports?" He pointed to the school gate.

Princess Bertha seemed to be unaware of Nuri's anger. She played with her pearl necklace, rearranged herself in her seat, and said, "This same thing happened to me in Vienna. My papa enrolled me in a lycée and entrusted me to a handsome teacher named Franz Heulick, who knew nothing but astronomy. Do you understand?" She winked at President O'Brien. "Just imagine. A sixteen-year-old girl in the hands of a romantic astronomer! Most of the time, instead of working on my language, algebra, and math lessons, we stared at the stars in the sky. I didn't know much, but I wasn't shy. Before the exams, I went to our principal and said, 'I'm not ready for the exams. What should I do?' The principal looked at my report and said, 'Your grades are all good. You can advance to the next form.'"

President O'Brien took off his glasses and rubbed the lenses with a red cloth. "Don't compare prewar Vienna with this place. At that time in Vienna, principals were little Hitlers themselves and could do anything. But I can't make any promises to Norman. If he doesn't do better than this, he'll have to leave the school."

Princess Bertha rose and kissed President O'Brien on the cheek. "Oh Henry, no one knows better than Easterners how to enjoy life. You should take a course in enjoying life. Don't be so serious." She kissed his other cheek. "If you had shaved properly today, I would have invited you to lunch."

She held Nuri's arm, and they left the office together.

This scene was repeated twice within the next few weeks. After each meeting, Nuri grew more stubborn and paid even less attention to his schoolwork. Just before the beginning of February, he received a letter from President O'Brien that looked no different from his previous ones, except that in the last paragraph he was informed that "in light of the above reports, the school has no choice but to expel you. Your accounts indicate that you owe the school two thousand dollars in back fees. We would be grateful if you could pay this sum before leaving the school. We wish you success in the future."

Nuri was happy and hoped to leave for New York as soon as possible. He could not stay in his room. He had to tell Salvador that he was leaving.

He couldn't find Salvador anywhere and so went back to his room. He longed for one of Amanda's plates of fried chicken, but Professor Brewster had sent Amanda to Austin to work as a sous-chef in her uncle's restaurant because a year away from Mrs. Brewster might be good for her. Then Nuri remembered Majid Khatami, an Iranian student he had met in a used-car lot. Majid had talked mostly about a girl named Bridget who was tall and athletic. Unfortunately, Bridget wanted to become a nun. Majid followed her around until he found her alone in an elevator. He begged her to change her mind and asked her to allow him to touch her breasts just once. He told her that if she granted him this one wish, she would be doing an enormous act of charity for a Third World Muslim.

"On your own life, Nuri-jun! Listen. Bridget didn't get upset. She knelt right there in that elevator and prayed for me."

Nuri's mouth hung open. Then he shouted, "Majid, what an animal you are!"

"What do you mean?"

"Don't you value anything?"

"Why should I worry? They're the ones who lead you on."

"How would you have felt if someone had done the same to your sister or your mother?"

"This is America. These same Americans staged a coup in Iran and stole our oil. Leave me alone."

"So you just think that you should do to Americans whatever you want? Does nothing matter to you?"

"Why do you think I left my country and came here? Just to sit in the corner of a room like you do?"

Nuri decided against finding Majid. Instead, he thought of Linda. She was always friendly when they ran into each other, but her arrogant look fueled a bizarre rage in him. Had he not been concerned about maintaining appearances, he would have flung a few Chaleh Maidun curses at her. He couldn't understand why Linda made him so angry, especially since she wasn't the type to say anything behind his back. He had only himself to blame. He had assumed initially that American girls would be delighted to meet a dreamy Eastern boy with a love of poetry.

Saturday morning Nuri found a note addressed to him on the message board. He immediately recognized Linda's handwriting. He ran excitedly into the bookstore and hid behind some bookshelves. He stood still to calm his nerves. He planted a kiss on the paper, but this struck him as childish. He read the note. It was short and direct like an office memo: "Nuri, can you come to the cafeteria around noon? I need your help with an important matter. Thank you, Linda."

Although a vague presentiment warned him against going, he left the bookstore and headed toward the cafeteria.

He entered the cafeteria at three minutes till noon. He was in turmoil. Linda was seated at a table in a far corner. She seemed to be writing a letter. Her bare legs were crossed, and she swung them under the table. She had grown up in Chicago and was used to the cold. She wore a white silk blouse under a black wool vest. He stood in front of her for a while, waiting for her to look up, but she continued writing her letter. He made a great deal of noise getting into the chair facing her. Linda seemed startled to see him. She jumped up and, instead of her usual greeting, hugged him. "How nice to see you, Nuri. I'm very happy you came. How about a cup of coffee? Would you like me to get you one?"

But Nuri wanted to get to the heart of the matter quickly. He held his head back and folded his arms across his chest. Linda tapped her pen on the table and said, "Thank you for coming." She left to buy them coffee and a Danish. "I'm giving a party tonight, and I'm going to make Persian food. I wanted to see if you could come." She looked at Nuri cautiously. When Nuri didn't answer, she asked, "Did you understand what I said?" Nuri didn't reply. Linda asked, "Didn't you understand?"

When he heard "didn't understand," especially from the mouth of an American, he was engulfed in rage. He had to show Linda. There was nothing in the world an Iranian could not understand. Instead, he said, "I can't come. I'm leaving for New York tomorrow, and I have to pack."

Linda looked dejected, "Why can't you take two hours out for a party?"

Nuri said to himself, "Oh really!" It didn't matter to Linda that he was leaving tomorrow or that they would probably never see each other again. She was thinking only of her party. Nuri asked, "Do I have to show you documents to prove I can't come to your party?"

Linda was taken aback. She was quiet for a moment. Then she sighed and said, "No. That's not the point. If you can't come, fine. If you don't mind, I would like to talk to you about something else, OK?" Nuri nodded. Linda leaned closer. "Do you remember Mr. Badamchi?"

"Mr. Mehdi Badamchi?"

"The owner of Shokufeh Restaurant. The tall one with white hair combed straight back."

"What does he want from me? Does he need car insurance? Or does he want to get green cards for his relatives?"

Linda shook her head. "No, no, no. You always try to guess what I'm going to say. He's in terrible shape. First, he said his blood pressure was high, he got headaches, and dreamed of his own death and a bunch of things like that that his brother, Mr. Hadi, and I didn't take seriously. Now Mr. Hadi keeps calling me and saying, 'Miss Linda, maybe there is something else.' I say, 'Like what?' He says the Americans are angry with Iranians, that they're threatening his brother."

"I don't think so."

"I don't think so either, but I'm stuck. I don't know how to set the Badamchis straight without hurting their feelings."

"Why don't you tell them what you just said?"

"Because both brothers now think I'm a CIA agent." Nuri couldn't help laughing. Linda waved a hand to stop him. "I'm not kidding. I worry that they might take out all their frustration on me. I don't understand their language."

"Do you know what has made them suspicious?"

"I think it's because I asked the editor of the school newspaper to pub-lish an extensive report about their restaurant. We thought with all these troubles between Americans and Iranians, this kind of cultural promo-tion would help the Badamchis. Any other restaurant owner would have paid to have such a report published. I don't know why the news made Mr. Mehdi go pale. He hid in the kitchen. When I called to him to come out, he wouldn't answer. He left through the back door, called his brother from the drugstore, and told him to throw the reporter and photographer out of the restaurant and to put a sign in the window announcing that the restaurant would be closed for forty days because of a death in the family. I just can't understand Mr. Mehdi's crazy behavior. Nuri, there's some-thing wrong, but I can't figure it out. Mr. Mehdi doesn't trust me anymore. The few words I said to him made things worse."

"What did you tell him?"

"I just said the report would make them famous and they would get more customers. Now they both think I'm a CIA agent. Mr. Mehdi shouted at me, 'Our restaurant is already famous. We don't need advertising.' I said, 'It's not more famous than McDonald's. Don't you see how much they advertise despite their fame?' I wish I hadn't said that. Mr. Hadi, who is usually the calm one, asked me to leave before he called the police. I told him, 'It'll be worse if you call the police.' He didn't understand at all. Imagine, these two brothers have left their country and managed to carve out a living here, and now a simple little misunderstanding might cause them to lose everything. Norman, you're Iranian and know them better than I do. Do something."

Linda's compassion made Nuri more stubborn, "What should I do?"

"Let's go to the restaurant. You can talk to them."

Nuri didn't want to go, but somehow he agreed. His first glance at the dark interior of the restaurant made him aware of his own inner weak-ness. The greasy walls, the smell of fried onions and rice, the second-hand fridge, and the unwashed aluminum bowls on the counter reminded him of the kitchen in the Dezashibi house. Mr. Mehdi was seated on a bed in a small cubbyhole at the rear of the kitchen. He seemed unaware of their presence. Mr. Hadi had difficulty adjusting to the idea of a blond and blue-eyed Iranian.

"How old is Your Honor?"

"I'm . . . twenty-two."

"You must have just come to America. We have been stuck here for eight years. May my child die, for the sake of this. . . . " He tore a piece off the *sangak* bread. "If I could, I would go back to Iran tomorrow. We lost our minds and decided to bring our children here for their education." He whispered to Nuri. "May this American education be cursed. American life has no order. No, our children have to grow up in our own culture. I promise you the minute I receive my ticket, I'll go back to Iran. These people are trained to work all the time. They are told the harder they work, the more money they will make. They have no more than two weeks' vacation a year. Then they want to send a reporter and photographer to make us work as hard as themselves. I keep saying, 'Father dear, we are happy with this little bit of money.' But they don't give up and want to print our picture in the newspaper. I bet they'll land us in court and rob us of everything we have."

Nuri's attention turned to Mr. Mehdi. He sat on the bed in a serge suit, hugging his knees and mumbling to himself. Some stones and pieces of scrap metal were arranged into a pattern next to an overflowing ashtray. A fly floated in a bowl of water. Nuri said, "Mr. Mehdi, hello. I hope I am not disturbing you."

"May I sacrifice myself for you. You are most welcome. I have been waiting for you for a long time. Ask my brother. He is my witness."

"What can I do for you?"

He took Nuri's hand and seated him on the bed. "Dear Agha, compatriot, may I sacrifice myself for you, we don't have to be shy with each other. Please help me. I am sick. Something is eating me from the inside. I don't know what it is. I have to go back to Iran. My cure is to go back there, nothing else. I keep telling this American girl, your friend Linda, 'You Americans are not familiar with such illnesses.' She just gives me advice. Can you believe it? I am old enough to be her father. I have worn out a few more shirts. She gives *me* advice."

"What can I do for you? Do you need money, a lawyer, or a plane ticket? I'll get whatever you need."

He shook his head. "No, dear Agha. Your servant can't just pick up his suitcases and go to Iran. First, I have to prove my ownership of this land." He put his finger on a specific point on the stone and metal diagram. "Yes, if my memory does not fail me, this is our place. Now after the revolution, they don't accept the old title deeds. I phoned the head of the Lands Title Office. A revolutionary guard grumbled, 'If we let you present your deeds, it's not because we owe you anything. No, it's because the Islamic Republic wants to do you a favor despite all your dirty dealings.'"

"I know someone influential in a revolutionary *comité*. I promise Mr. Shariat will arrange matters for you."

"Don't do anything to make more trouble. My brother and I are still locked in a dispute over our share of the land. My brother says we have to continue this line to here . . . "—he moved his finger from one stone to another, held his chin in his hand, and got lost in thought—" . . . Seyyed Rafi's public drinking spot used to be in this corner before they demolished it in the Pahlavi era."

Mr. Hadi pointed to another spot. "No, it used to be here."

Nuri waited for a while. The two brothers became so absorbed in their dispute that they forgot Nuri and Linda. Yet when Nuri wanted to leave, Mr. Mehdi grabbed his wrist. "Dear Agha, I am sick. Believe me, my illness is not ordinary. If you don't send me to Iran, I'll go crazy. Then you'll regret it, and regret is useless. . . . "

"Fine. I'll contact Tehran."

"Definitely contact Tehran and let me know as soon as possible."

Nuri felt as if something were stuck in his throat. When they reached the street, Linda took his arm. "What do you think?"

"Nothing. People like this give Iranians a bad name."

"Don't you feel sorry for them?"

"For them?"

Linda nodded but said nothing. She asked suddenly, "Will you come to my party tonight?"

"Where?"

He said this in such an aggressive tone that Linda was taken aback. She put her hand on Nuri's. "If you don't want to, it doesn't matter."

"You think people have nothing to do but wait for three months to be invited to a party?"

"Why do you shout like this?"

"Whenever you Americans see a foreigner, you think he needs money or he has to be taught the meaning of democracy."

"Norman, don't be angry. If you don't want to come to the party, we'll do something else."

Nuri pulled his hand out of hers. "What do you mean 'we'll do something else'?"

Linda hesitated. "Let's go to church on Sunday, OK?"

"Do you want me to kneel down and pray like you?"

"I'll do the praying. You just come along, OK?"

Nuri shouted, "I won't go to church."

"Why don't you suggest a place?"

"Why do we have to go anywhere at all?"

Linda lowered her head, ran her hand over his wool sweater, and said, "OK, we don't have to go anywhere. Just promise to take care of yourself."

"What's all this feeling sorry about?"

"Fine. If you want to leave, go ahead."

"Did you think I would stay here?"

Linda brought her face close to kiss him. Before realizing what he had done, he struck Linda's cheek so hard that his fingers left red marks on her face. Tears welled up in her eyes. She rubbed her cheek with an elegance Nuri had never seen in her and walked away.

He didn't have the courage to offer Linda a simple apology. He had given her the worst possible image of Iranians: a seemingly warm and sensitive person who is actually self-centered and doesn't respect anything but Iranian customs, ridicules other languages and cultures, roams the world with a bundle of his "everlasting culture" in search of that which can never be found, and brags about being Iranian.

Perhaps he should apologize to Linda. He went to her dorm. He heard Salvador's guitar from inside. The smell of food permeated the air. There could be any number of people inside her room, and he couldn't think of an excuse to go in.

He had to pack his bags and go to New York. Leaving without saying good-bye wouldn't change her impression of him, but in time she might remember him as a fairytale character not unlike Ali Yavaran.

He put his bags on the platform of the train station. The train would leave in a few minutes. The crisscrossing rails and the sounds echoing in the distance reminded him of long journeys. He thought of phoning Linda, but he saw Salvador waving to him from a distance. He ran toward him and opened his arms to hug him. "Salvador, what are you doing here?"

Salvador winked and said, "You can't run away. I'll find you wherever you go."

Nuri wanted to ask about Linda, but he squeezed Salvador's hand and asked, "Did you have fun last night?"

"As Iranians say, your place was empty. Did I say that right? Hah, hah, hah. You missed a good Persian dinner."

"A Persian dinner?"

Salvador put on a proud look and said, "I helped Linda."

According to him, Linda had soaked dried chives and fennel with Minute Rice, then steamed the mixture to make *sabzi polo*. Instead of fried fish, she had served canned tuna. He looked down and said, "It was delicious. We missed you."

The train was moving when Nuri boarded it. He could still hear Salvador's voice in his head. He put his bags up on the luggage rack and stared out the window at the snowy mountains. The pine trees occasionally piercing the cover of snow made the peaks look like a pot of *sabzi polo*.

◆ ◆ ◆ Madame's illness was the most pressing reason for Nuri's decision to return to Iran. In the two weeks since he had left Saint Joseph's, he had managed to talk to Madame only once. Her conversation had nothing to do with her state of health. It seemed as if she wanted to put her affairs in order. She asked the whereabouts of the earrings the Senator had given her on the occasion of the shah's coronation. Who had dared tear out the first two pages of her old album? Who was the third person in her wedding picture? What was her name?

Maman Zuzu's sudden mood changes were also responsible for Nuri's decision. On the surface, she was very warm toward Nuri. Whenever Barney and Princess Bertha talked about Saint Joseph's, Maman Zuzu defended him. She would say that no Iranian spoke English as fluently as Nuri. He sounded like an English lord. None of them dressed so meticulously or behaved so well. Every chance she had, she reminded Barney that they owed Nuri two hundred dollars. She would throw her arm around Nuri and kiss him on the cheek. "Don't worry. We'll give you the money before you go to Iran. You don't need it right now anyway."

"OK. There's no rush. I still have money."

"You devil, open your wallet. Let's see. I thought you had spent all your money."

One day Maman Zuzu came home looking agitated. She took off her raincoat and threw it on the radiator. She went into the kitchen and busied herself for an hour with dinner preparations. She grumbled to herself until Barney came home from his new job at a computer store. She asked him why he hadn't picked her up at Macy's. "I have to wait in the rain for forty-five minutes and get drenched so that you can wrap up a simple sale and do such a miserable job of it to risk losing the whole deal." Barney frowned. Maman Zuzu smiled suddenly and tickled him to make him laugh. "Isn't that right, honey?"

Barney took his feet off the table, threw a cursory glance at Maman Zuzu, and began reading the newspaper. Maman Zuzu shrugged and tiptoed into the kitchen, careful not to annoy Barney. Nuri followed her. She continued in Persian. "I have always stood on my own two feet. I don't expect anything from anyone. I'll be frank with you. I bought this wreck of a car with my own savings. Nuri-jun, I have given up on Barney's measly wages and make ends meet on my own salary. I am the kind of person who has to do everything on her own. It's not worth my while to lean on others." She wiped sweat from her forehead and grabbed Nuri's arm with a barely controlled excitement. "Don't tell your mumzie anything. I prefer this life with all its complications to living in the Dezashibi house." She was beginning to raise her voice, apparently no longer worried about disturbing Barney. "First of all, I came to America with my own money. After what happened to your father, I didn't ask anyone for help. I did everything myself. I will never go to Iran and live in the Dezashibi house, where I would have to take orders from that Mr. Shariat." She sighed, and a smile appeared on her face. "Do you believe that they have put Grandpa Senator under house arrest and handed everything over to Mr. Shariat. What can I say? Imagine. Mr. Shariat with his comical face."

Nuri said, "Had it not been for Mr. Shariat, they would probably have executed Grandpa by now."

Maman Zuzu nodded in agreement. "Once upon a time he wore strange clothes to impress Ladan. Have you heard that he has shed all that and goes to work in a turban and robe?" She suddenly dropped onto a kitchen stool. "Now Badri Khanom and Aunt Moluk answer the phone and speak in code. They say, 'Madame is not feeling well, but don't worry. We have brought a *seyyed* from Savjabblagh who is treating her with goat droppings and mouse piss. Thank God, now when she needs to go to the bathroom, she blinks to tell us to put a bedpan under her." She looked for a handkerchief. She asked, "What can one person do? How can she attend to a thousand problems? I don't have much trust in Mr. Shariat. I bet if Ladan doesn't marry him, he'll get even. He'll stop that little bit of help he gives Grandpa. He'll report him to the *comité* and throw him in jail."

"Maman, I'll buy my ticket tomorrow and go to Iran."

"You mean you'll leave just like that. How brave you are, Maman! It's difficult to go back to Iran these days. You might regret it."

"I'll regret it even more if I don't go. I'll berate myself for leaving them alone. Mumzie has done a lot for me. She has always kept an eye on me."

Maman Zuzu paused. "Nuri-jun, you are right. Someone has to look after Mumzie. I would feel better if you were there. Maybe I would be able to sleep a couple of hours a night. I can't sleep even ten minutes. As soon as I fall asleep, I dream of Papa Javad. I see the scene of the accident and ask myself what has happened. How can a wonderful person like him be killed for no reason? You have to ask those who think there is a reason for every event. Sometimes I tell myself, 'Maybe it was just an accident, and there is no other meaning behind it.' Then I wake up drenched in sweat, and I don't know where I am."

Nuri threw his arm around Maman Zuzu's neck and kissed her on the cheek. "I'll call Air France and see about a ticket for a week from now."

"Are you really sure? Won't you get bored and want to come back to New York? What if they throw you in jail or put you in front of a firing squad because of your blond hair and blue eyes? They might think you're a CIA agent returning to Iran to spy."

"Nothing like that will happen."

"I hope you're right. But call every day and tell me about yourself and Mumzie. In my opinion, you should bring her here for treatment. I'll do what I can to help."

Maman Zuzu looked like she had many years ago, although a bit darker and more wrinkled. She had an inquisitive gaze like those old-fashioned intellectuals. When she talked, traces of her lost youth returned to her face.

On the day of Nuri's departure, Barney was half an hour late. All the way to the airport, Maman Zuzu kept haranguing him. "You call yourself a driver?"

"What should I call myself?"

"The way you drive we won't get there before midnight. Nuri will miss his flight."

"I promise we'll get there an hour before the flight."

"Don't you see the traffic? Why don't you change lanes and pass this wreck?"

"There's no room to pass."

"Let me drive. I'll show you."

Nuri grew impatient and said, "I bet we'll get there on time. Let's enjoy these last minutes together."

Maman Zuzu frowned at Barney and fell silent.

They arrived at the airport forty minutes before his flight. There was no time for good-byes. Nuri went through security and waved to them. Barney had his arm around Maman Zuzu's waist. Together they walked toward the exit.

Nuri all of a sudden felt at peace. He saw himself as strangely prepared for any eventuality.

The ocean and the clouds drew his mind to his arrival in Iran. He thought about what he would say to the officials at the airport. He needed to collect his thoughts.

The last leg of the trip from Istanbul to Tehran made him feel even closer to home. Most of the passengers looked tired, offering boxes of cookies and treats to each other. Every now and then Nuri would smile with a sense of safety and proximity to home. The younger passengers would turn around and smile coyly at the others. Young women drew their chadors over their heads. A man in his forties, dressed in a nice Parisian suit, smiled at Nuri from across the aisle. When Nuri smiled back, the man told him, "If you want to avoid disasters, always choose an exit-row seat."

"Why?"

"It's easier to flee."

Nuri said, "The country seems to be in chaos."

The man bit his lip and looked away. "Nonsense. They spread all this poison for the benefit of those of you living outside Iran. Agha, two million Iranians have been martyred. We have stood up to superpowers like America. Agha, don't listen to rumors."

He folded his hands on his lap, leaned back, and shut his eyes.

It was so dark outside that Nuri could see only the outlines of the terminal building and the glimmer of lights surrounding it. As soon as the plane landed, he rose and looked out the window. He saw nothing but the headlights of motorcycles surrounding the plane as it taxied closer to the terminal. They formed a motorcade, as if meeting a VIP.

Stepping off the plane, he noticed a row of armed revolutionary guards. Nuri put on an innocent expression, descended the stairs, and boarded a minibus for the terminal. He sat by the door. When he reached the terminal, he hurried ahead of the other passengers. Large posters of ayatollahs and banners in Arabic adorned the walls. He looked for the man he had spoken to on the plane, but didn't find him.

His hands shook. He took more than ten minutes to fill out the customs forms, which he placed in front of a young officer with a goatee. The officer compared the passport photograph with Nuri's face. "Are you Iranian?" he asked. Nuri nodded nervously. The officer played with the tips of his mustache and raised his eyebrows as if he had come across a problem in Nuri's documents. Nuri scratched his head with a shaky hand and looked around. Then the officer smiled unexpectedly. Nuri thought for a moment that the man might be playing a game with him, but his suspicions were unfounded. The officer asked, "Should I stamp it?"

"Yes."

He stamped the passport and returned it to Nuri. "Welcome, compatriot."

Nuri was so dazed he almost forgot his bags. He felt so choked up that if Mr. Shariat had not arrived just then, he might well have broken into tears. It was hard to recognize Mr. Shariat. He had put on weight, regrown his beard, and substituted a robe and turban for his suit. He walked with an arrogant demeanor. When he reached Nuri, he whispered into his ear, "Look exhausted."

Nuri couldn't remember having ever been addressed by Mr. Shariat so commandingly. He drew back and asked, "Look what?"

"Exhausted."

It was hard to believe that Mr. Shariat had transformed himself so radically over the past year. He spoke to the revolutionary guards authoritatively and prevented them from inspecting Nuri's bags. The guards treated him with respect. Nuri followed him obediently. Mr. Shariat kept shouting, "Brother, step back! Let us through! I have to get this patient to the hospital quickly."

Nuri was not allowed to greet Ladan, Aunt Moluk, and Badri Khanom or to listen to Amiz Abbas, Amiz Hosein, and Shuri Khanom's teasing. A jaundiced yellow light enveloped the terminal, and the peeling plaster of the walls made it look like a sleeping village. This image hung on in Nuri's mind until they reached Tajrish. Even the headlights of the army jeeps didn't make it easy to recognize Dezashib. But when he saw the house, he came out of his daze. A breeze from the garden caressed his face and reminded him of spring. He wondered how many weeks there were till the new year! The stone pool lights were unlit, and no sounds came from the garden. Black Najmeh and Vaziri were waiting in front of the half-open garden gate. Grandpa Senator paced up and down in his pajamas. When Nuri jumped out of the jeep, the Senator ran toward him with open arms. He said, "Nuri? Is that you, Father? You finally came back to your own stable?"

He kissed him excitedly on both cheeks. Maybe Grandpa's behavior had been like this in the days when he had attended Fräulein Frieda and

Princess Bertha's performances with Amiz Abbas. He didn't seem concerned about his balding head. Hiding something in his fist, he took Nuri to the stone pool and opened it. In his palm sparkled a diamond ring. "This is yours. It was worn for forty-eight years by your great-grandmother."

He gestured to Nuri to take the ring from his palm. Nuri took it and hugged and kissed the Senator. He heard Mr. Shariat's footsteps. Mr. Shariat was bringing Nuri's bags into the garden. Badri Khanom held Amiz Abbas by the arm, and Ladan walked behind them. Then Dr. Jannati, Amiz Hosein, and Shuri Khanom entered the garden. There was no electricity. Only Black Najmeh's oil lamp burned in the kitchen. Nuri took all this as a sign from Madame. Something moved on the third-floor balcony. Nuri brought his head closer to the Senator and asked, "How is she feeling?"

The Senator twisted his lips, "Well, . . . "

"Should I go see her?"

"Of course. Go, but don't tire her too much. Her memory hasn't been good lately. Sometimes she doesn't recognize anyone."

"Why?"

He scratched the back of his neck. "Well, she is old. This Dr. Jannati knows even less than a cow. He says the tumor in Madame's bladder has spread to her brain. Do you remember how he killed his own son with his misdiagnosis? If he's right, she has only two months. No one asks why in that case they would hire people to teach her reading and writing again. Why are Iranians so stupid? Why don't they use their brains? Why do they make plans for a nonexistent future? What's it to me, anyway? Why should I bother myself so much? To hell with them. Let them do whatever they want." He started laughing. "Do you know Madame can't stand seeing me? Otherwise, I would come up with you." He whispered to Nuri, "Even if she did, I don't think my balding head and dentures would give her much of a thrill."

Nuri left the Senator and ran up the stairs. Even in the dark, the space seemed familiar to him, although smaller. It had the air of a clean and watered tomb. When he reached the third-floor balcony, the sky looked a brighter pinkish purple. Dressed in cotton pajamas, looking thin and bony, Madame stood holding onto an IV stand. One arm hung in a brace. Nuri wondered how to make her recognize him. If he said something, he might confuse her more. He stood still. Madame blinked, and the lights suddenly came on. "Nuri-jan, is that you?"

"Yes, Mumzie."

She reached out to hug Nuri, but stumbled. "I am glad you came, my dearrr. Whenever you catch a fish out of water, it is fresh. Did I say it right? Please correct me if I made a mistake. When you catch a fish, what do you do with it?" Nuri didn't answer. Madame continued, "My knowledge of Persian is shrinking by the day. But don't worry. Thanks to selfless and generous friends I'll learn it again." She spoke hurriedly, "How funny that I have forgotten Persian sayings and poems. May God give Badri Khanom a long life. Following the dictum of good thoughts, good deeds, and good words, she has brought me a teacher. This great teacher, this historically exceptional being—let me repeat, this historically exceptional man—is a treasure trove of Persian knowledge. He has helped me so much in learning sweet Persian that I don't know how to thank him."

"What's his name?"

"Have you forgotten Mr. Shariat? What a wonderful man! How generous! He has taught me all the Muslim rites, from fasting to ablutions to pilgrimage and making a will. Nuri-jan, I would like to die a Muslim and be buried as one. In death, Muslims attain true democracy, buried in a simple shroud without any adornments. But Christians, who talk so much about democracy, build monuments to the dead, place their statues with heavenward eyes on their tomb." She smirked. "Never mind. I don't have much faith in the possibility of learning in old age. An old person should be left in peace to end her days with dignity. It is said: Do not harm a seed-collecting ant, for he is alive, and life is precious. Did I say it right?" Nuri nodded in a daze, and Madame looked happy. "Yes. Bravo! I am grateful for your attention. How lonely I feel. How many terrible hours I have passed worrying about you! I wondered how you managed in America. Who made your food? Thank God, with Mr. Shariat's help, I put aside despondency and said to myself, 'He who gives teeth, gives bread. . . . '"

"Does Mr. Shariat teach you Islam?"

"Sometimes he stands over my bed and prays for me. That's all. Sometimes he sits in a chair beside me and cries softly. He rubs his hands together and asks, 'Madame, help me, what can I do? How can I make Ladan Khanom like me? What is the difference between me and westernized people like M. G. Shabkhiz that she doesn't want to marry me?'" She smiled bitterly. "It is most unfortunate. He rifled through Ladan's drawers and found her letters to Shabkhiz. He said they all are love letters. He read some of them to me and cried. I asked him to return the letters and never again enter her room without permission. Some Easterners don't seem to know any boundaries. If a door is shut to them, they don't just open it; they break it. In my opinion, they know loneliness only in pain and death. Never mind. . . . "

She threw an arm around Nuri's neck and kissed him on the cheek. Together they went into the study. "Oh, my dearrr, it's a pleasure to be with you. Tell me a little about your *maman* and your studies at Saint Joseph's. I know I won't be able to sleep from excitement tonight." She put a finger on his lips. "Quiet, Nuri-jan. Quiet. Appreciate the silence."

"Silence?"

"Listen to the silence. The evil of time is moving. May Satan be cursed . . . Shh . . . Do you hear it? Destruction, death, and darkness are on the way."

Nuri helped her sit in front of the Virgin of Solitude. He spoke to her softly, caressed her frizzy hair, and said, "You are a little weak and tired."

Madame ignored him, put the palms of her hands together, and mumbled:

The father will become suspicious of the son
The son will help his son
There will be no farmer, no Turk, no Mongol
Talk will turn to deeds
They will turn away from devotion and righteousness
Treasured will become evil and remorse . . .

She turned and looked at Nuri. She pointed to the floor. "Let us kneel down and pray together."

Nuri laughed. "Mumzie, it's two-thirty in the morning. Let's leave the prayer until tomorrow. Let's rest now."

Madame grabbed her IV stand and nodded. "You are right, my dearrr. It is much later than you think." She asked him to hand her the Koran. "It is said: You are the object of my desire, the Kaaba and the house of idolaters are but excuses. What difference does it make? I will pray with a Koran. You will kneel in front of the Virgin of Solitude in my stead. Our only difference is that Muslims pray together. In the West where I come from, you say your prayers in private. It's only in death that Muslims and Christians are left alone. Silence! Silence! Silence! It is said: 'There is a death that has no cure. How can I ask you to cure it?'"

"Mumzie, even if Mr. Shariat has taught you these things, you should not accept them all."

"I don't intend to argue with Your Majesty. I just want us to kneel down and pray together. What does praying have to do with Mr. Shariat?"

"Exactly. He was nobody until last year. Now he acts as if he owns the place. You shouldn't allow him to interfere in your affairs."

"It is said: 'I am the slave of him who is free of all belonging.' Did I say it right? A person my age gets along with anyone and can go wherever she likes. My journey might well take me to the other world, but like the Hafiz of Shiraz, I am not afraid of being a stranger." She pressed her Allah necklace between her fingers and began to pray. "In the name of God, the compassionate, the merciful . . . "

Nuri tried to help Madame out of her chair. "No, no, no, Mumzie. Let me take you to your own room. Sleep tonight. We'll pray tomorrow."

"My dearrr, please attend to my needs. You are young. The future is yours. It is necessary for you to pray. Ask God to protect you against the great Satan."

"I have just arrived. I'm tired. We'll have plenty of time tomorrow."

He helped her up, and she didn't resist. Her expression began to change. She acted as if she had suddenly discovered she was naked. She covered her chest with her hand. "Eh, Nuri, what am I doing here?"

"You are tired. I'll take you to your room."

"Did I speak nonsense? Did I embarrass myself? How was my Persian?"

"You said mostly Persian proverbs. You know more sayings than Deh-khoda himself."

Madame leaned on Nuri. "I owe this to Mr. Shariat."

Nuri helped her onto her brass bed. She crossed her hands on her chest and asked him to put a glass of water and two German books on her bedside table. Nuri switched off the overhead light, but left the reading lamp on. He kissed Madame's forehead. Madame grabbed his wrist. "Nuri."

"Yes, Mumzie."

"Don't leave me alone."

"Of course I won't."

"Promise."

"I promise."

"May God save Your Majesty."

Nuri tiptoed out of the room and left the door ajar.

. . . **15** . . .

Nuri began planning his return to America on his very first day back in Dezashib. He dreamed of Park Avenue, Saks Fifth Avenue's Christmas decorations, and the high domed ceiling of Grand Central Station. He quickly dismissed any urge to go to the Parand Pastry Shop or the Tahmasbis' apartment as silly preoccupations of his high school days. At night, the minute his head hit the pillow he would fall into deep sleep, not even pondering a visit to the storage room. He had no desire to chat with Ladan, Vaziri, or Black Najmeh. The relatives complained about high prices, long queues in front of stores, and people's testiness. The only changes Nuri perceived were the wilted leaves of the tropical plants and a sense of suffocation that gripped him in the middle of the streets.

The relatives' visits to Madame left the hall in disarray, empty teacups and overflowing ashtrays abandoned here and there. They grumbled that Madame's illness left them no energy. They would go to their own homes for their afternoon naps and return to the Dezashibi house in the evening, where they would sit in a circle outside Madame's bedroom and listen to Amiz Abbas's stories of Vienna and the passionate love between Agh'Ali and Fräulein Frieda. Even Aunt Moluk, who had kept her distance after Agha Javad's accident, was unusually sympathetic and spent the New Year holidays with them. Every night, after the relatives' departure, she would spread a chador outside Madame's bedroom door in order to be able to lend a hand to Ladan. When guests came to the door, she met them in the garden and greeted them pleasantly. She never mentioned Comrade Binesh. One day Vaziri brought news that Comrade Binesh had fled to Afghanistan, where he now taught Marxist Leninism in elementary schools. Aunt Moluk rose from the floor and, repeating "Ya Allah," went to the third floor. A few minutes later she could be heard practicing "What a Good Night, What a Dear Night" on her violin. When some guests arrived, she put her violin back in its case, came down to greet them, and led them politely to Madame's door. Amiz Abbas now spoke in a muffled voice more appropriate for mourning sessions.

Amidst all the comings and goings, Nuri thought mostly about Linda and her kindness. He had to return to Saint Joseph's. He wondered why he should settle for a miserable life in Tehran—a city caught in the turmoil of the revolution. Every day there were reports of shootings and arrests. He couldn't find Linda's telephone number. Instead, he called Maman Zuzu and held the receiver close to the window so that she could hear the gunshots from the Tajrish Bridge and the chants of "Death to America!" "Victory to the Islamic Republic!" and "Down with Israel!" Maman Zuzu said quietly, "Nuri! Nuri, wait. What's this crazy behavior? Why don't you talk about yourself?"

"What do you want me to say?"

"Well, tell me how you are."

"Fine. The same . . . " He paused and then added, "Did you hear that? They're shooting again."

"Father dear, I heard it. How many times do you have to tell me? Tell me something about Mumzie. Is she well?"

"I said she's fine. Everyone is here to see her. Amiz Abbas is retelling his memories of Vienna. But I . . . "

"Why doesn't Mumzie come to the phone to talk to me?"

"Sometimes she's asleep. Other times she doesn't feel like talking."

"Since when are you so reserved? Maybe something has happened and you don't want to tell me."

"Maman, I ask you this one thing: don't make a mountain out of a molehill. Nothing has happened here. Everything is safe and sound. But the streets . . . "

"Where is Ladan? Why doesn't she talk to me?"

"Because Shariat is still following her around. When Shariat's name comes up, her eyes grow wide, and she gets tongue-tied."

"Nuri-jun, I'm afraid that idiot will harm her."

"Shariat? He'll be laughing at his father's grave. We keep an eye on Ladan at all times."

"I worry he'll find her alone and hit her. We don't know what kind of parents raised him. I sense he is the violent type. Nuri-jun, promise by your father's spirit that the minute you see a bruise on your sister, you'll tell Grandpa. Why don't I buy a ticket this week and come there. What do you think? Can I come to Iran with an American passport?"

"Maman, why should you come all this way? Nothing is wrong here. I promise I won't let anyone touch Ladan."

"Nuri-jun, you don't know how much I want to be there. I'm afraid she'll be forced to marry that turbaned moron. May I sacrifice myself for your moonlike face, keep an eye on things. See how Shariat treats your sister."

"I promise Ladan can handle Shariat better than anyone else. But since you're so worried, I'll tell her to call you."

Nuri said this to appease Maman Zuzu. In reality, there was nothing any of them could do. Using the excuse of the possible confiscation of the Aghcheh land, the Senator had put Shariat in charge of his bank account. Even when Badri Khanom and Amiz Abbas asked him about their share of the land, he referred them to Shariat, who now played the humble servant to the hilt. Shariat had asked the local revolutionary guards to ensure that the Hezbollahis didn't bother the Senator and his family. When he found out that Nuri was discussing a trip to Cyprus with Ali the Mechanic, he waited outside the study until Nuri came out. He asked in a secretive tone if he could help him obtain a new passport. He locked his fat fingers together and lowered his eyelids, as if he were soothing an inner pain. He listened to Nuri attentively, leaned forward, and said in a paternal tone, "Consider the job done. No need to talk to a bunch of smugglers."

Little did he know that his readiness to serve irritated Nuri even more. He didn't want to owe Shariat anything, especially because of his eagerness to become a member of their family. The main problem was Ladan's own aloofness. She pretended constantly to be going to the office of the literary magazine *Shatt*, but actually hid somewhere in the house.

On the last Friday of Ordibehesht, Nuri found Ladan in the kitchen, preparing a tray of multivitamins and Monk's Syrup for Madame. She ignored Nuri. He knew that he had taken her by surprise. He tore off pieces of *taftun* bread, chewing them slowly and listening to her grumble to herself. She complained that she was losing her patience with Madame's bizarre behavior. Around ten every morning, Madame wandered into the hall and soiled her underwear. Then she would lock herself in her bedroom and prevent them from giving her a bath. Aunt Moluk would knock on her door to no avail. They could see through the keyhole that she was busy cutting her embroideries into pieces that she then hid in her old album. Only once had Ladan succeeded in entering her room. On that occasion, Madame had put her fists into her frizzy hair and demanded to know why Ladan had left her alone with a bunch of strangers such as Badri Khanom and Aunt Moluk.

Madame's footsteps could be heard. Ladan stopped talking and plugged in the kettle to make tea for her. Nuri asked, "How's Shariat behaving?"

Ladan looked at him suspiciously. "Mamakh, I was telling you about Mumzie, why do you mention Shariat's name?"

"I just wondered if he was still bothering you?"

"Do you take me for a child? Don't talk like this around the relatives. They'll spread rumors."

"Shariat has told everyone you're going to marry him."

Ladan's face turned red. Nuri continued. "I can't believe it. He's not your type. He's no good for you."

"I told Grandpa the same thing."

"What did Grandpa say?"

"He said, 'OK, Father dear, it's your own decision.' I hugged and kissed him so many times he said, 'Have you gone crazy? What are all these kisses for?'"

Shariat entered the first-floor hall, carrying plastic bags and ribboned boxes. He put the plastic bags in the pantry and took the boxes to the second floor. Ladan's expression became indifferent. This was not the first time Shariat had brought Ladan gifts. He had already presented her with numerous bottles of perfume, three gold bracelets, pastries decorated with pink flowers and green leaves, comforters and mattresses, cupboards, and a sewing machine. He would show up near noon in the Mostowfi Alley, walking in front of a man carrying a tray of gifts. He would wipe his forehead with a handkerchief and tell the man to take the gifts to Ladan's room. Ladan would sit quietly in her room, filing her nails, while the presents were piled in a corner.

Today she seemed to have lost her veneer of pretense. Maybe matters were becoming serious. She wouldn't tell Nuri anything for fear he might confront Shariat. Nuri was enraged. He climbed the stairs and ran into Shariat in the second-floor corridor. He was arranging the gifts meticulously outside Ladan's room and throwing admiring glances at them. He turned to Nuri and stared at him with a vacant gaze. He put his fist in front of his mouth and swallowed, making a burplike sound. He said, "Don't imagine that your blood is redder than anyone else's just because you have spent a few days in America. You asked me to contact the head of the passport office. I did it out of loyalty to your family. That was three weeks ago, but you haven't asked once where the plans for your trip to America stand." He narrowed his eyes, looking like an animal ready to pounce on his prey. "Why all this arrogance? Maybe you imagine we're still living under the rule of tyranny? This is an Islamic country, and everyone is entitled to respect." He pointed to the gift boxes. "Do you see these? They all were imported. They have been bought with dollars at an exchange rate of sixty tumans to a dollar. If you don't believe me, read the labels. I don't say anything because I have been treated generously in this house, but I know ways of settling accounts that I don't think you would like to hear. I don't want to say anything now, especially because this marriage is about to happen."

Nuri didn't understand how Ladan suddenly appeared there like a ghost. She asked anxiously what the argument was about.

Shariat lowered his head, walked past Ladan, and headed downstairs. Ladan forced a smile and said she would have to get to an important meeting at the *Shatt* office. She went into her room and shut the door.

Nuri left the house. Maybe he would go to the Tahmasbis' or look up old friends.

He ran into Naser Shahandeh in front of the Parand Pastry Shop. He was dressed in a short-sleeved shirt, navy blue–striped trousers, and polished shoes. He threw his arm around Nuri, planted a couple of big kisses on his cheeks, and invited him to coffee. Nuri asked about Buki, but Naser knew only that he had gone to the front. He had more news about Soraya. The most important was that she had married Mr. Shirzad and was expecting a child. Mr. Shirzad had bought the Colonel and Mrs. Tahmasbi a house in Khazar Shahr.

Nuri returned home feeling dejected. The organ had been brought down to the second floor. He saw Madame leaning on her cane on the third-floor landing. Nuri didn't want to talk to her now and went into his room. A few moments later he heard her slippers shuffling closer. The door opened and Madame's skeleton-like figure walked in. She sat in a chair facing Nuri and waited to catch her breath. She smiled weakly and asked, "How is Your Excellency?"

Nuri didn't answer, but instead asked, "Mumzie, what can I bring for you?"

Madame wrinkled her forehead and spoke mechanically. "Oh, I wish there were no death." She took a handkerchief from her bodice, breathed into it, and placed it on her heart. "My heart aches. I have to keep it warm."

"Why?"

"I don't know, my dearrr."

"I'll call Dr. Jannati." Madame shook her head. Nuri said, "Mumzie, tell me what is bothering you."

"To quote Mr. Shariat, after death one loses all control. The dead look enviously at what they have left behind and shout, 'Take me back to the world of the living and let me do good deeds.' But regret is useless. Their shouts cannot be heard. You can beg and cry, but you can't get the chick back from the cat."

"Has Shariat taught you these things?"

"No. He just prays for me. You promised you would pray with me too. Why didn't you honor your promise?"

"Because no one listens to my prayers. You pray for both of us."

"Oh, your servant always prays for you. I will continue to pray until with God's help you return to Saint Joseph's. You belong to America, and I belong here. Isn't it funny that I am an Easterner at heart and you a Westerner? Laugh. There is no shame in laughter. Then please take me back to my room so that I do not miss the story of the sacred ones. I forgot that Mr. Shariat would be starting now." She smiled and looked around the room.

"Oh, my dearrr, how beautiful is an Eastern soul in its neediness." She lifted her arm toward Nuri. "Do you know? Your servant is in every way ready to make room for others and leave for the other world."

"Mumzie, I would like to tell you something . . . "

"I didn't hear you. Please speak louder."

"I feel indebted to you. You have always protected and helped me. I don't know why you have never given up on me. Mumzie, knowing you makes me feel free, do you understand?"

"You are most kind. I hope that you make successful strides in the future and spend a life of happiness and pride in America. Do not worry about your servant."

They went to the third floor together. Shariat stood politely by the brass bed. He stared at the ceiling while Nuri helped Madame onto her bed. Then he began reciting the story of the blessed ones in Arabic.

Madame was so absorbed in Shariat's words that Nuri suddenly thought of scenes of mourning. He left the room. He had not gone far when Shariat ran out after him and gestured for him to come back. Nuri walked into the bedroom and saw Madame sitting tailor style on the bed. When he got closer to her, she grabbed his wrist and put seven gold Pahlavi coins in his palm. "Pray for me to get better. We'll take a trip to America together. Princess Bertha will come to greet us."

Nuri looked at the coins and asked, "What should I do with these?"

"Keep them, take them to America. . . . Mr. Shariat . . . "

Shariat, who was standing quietly by the door, said, "Your wish is my command."

"Have you told Nuri what a good shot the Senator used to be?"

Shariat said, "He used to tape a piece of paper over a metal ring and ask Vaziri to throw it to the rear of the garden. He would aim and shoot from the edge of the stone pool, always leaving a hole the size of a chickpea in the paper."

Madame lay down and shut her eyes. " . . . I have been waiting since last night for the emir to come to the bedside of this Shiite and recommend me to the other world. Your servant is ready."

Shariat held his agate ring in front of Madame's eyes. "It is related that Imam Mohammad Baqer believed staring at an agate ring and crying

for three days to be the best way to commemorate the innocence of Imam
Hosein." He stopped himself from crying. He recited:

Where is the eye that has not been moistened in grief for you?
Or the pocket that has not been torn in grief for you?
No one better than you has been entrusted to the earth . . .

He took a big handkerchief from his robe pocket, wiped his eyes, and
left the room.

Nuri didn't see Madame again until the morning that she came down
to the first-floor hall for breakfast. Ladan placed a breakfast tray in front of
her and asked Badri Khanom and Aunt Moluk to keep an eye on her.

Madame didn't touch her food, nor did she speak. When she tried to
stand up, she bumped against the wall and fell into her seat. Nuri ran to
help her. She hit Nuri's chest with her fist so hard that it took the wind out
of him. Badri Khanom shouted, "Vaziri, Vaziri, get the car. Madame is not
well. We have to take her to the hospital."

Aunt Moluk came into the hall and said, "Father dear, don't take her
from here. If you move her, it will all be over."

Nuri tried to help Madame out of her chair, but she stared at him suspiciously. Badri Khanom called, "Vaziri! Vaziri, have you stopped your ears?"

Vaziri answered, "What do you want? Why do you shout?"

"What are you waiting for? Hurry up and take Madame to the hospital! Don't you see how she is slipping through our hands?"

Shariat and Grandpa Senator burst into the hall. Madame did not
seem to recognize them. She said, "Bertha! Bertha! Bertha!"

She tried to move, but the Senator grabbed her wrist and said, "Frieda,
what's wrong with you?"

Madame melted into his arms and, pointing to the relatives, asked,
"Who are they? What do they want from me?"

The Senator comforted her. "They are our relatives. Don't you remember Badri Khanom? How about Moluk?"

"So why is the emir's place empty among them? Mr. Shariat tells me
not to fear the narrowness of the Sarat Bridge. They'll widen it for me like
the Karaj Highway so that I won't fall off. I don't know why I am so afraid
of heights." She looked around. "Isn't this my home?"

"Of course it is."

Madame cheered up. "Yes, my dearrr, this is my home. I like it very much." She nodded her head. "What a pleasant place it is! There is no God but God. . . . "

The Senator put his hand on Madame's shoulder. "Let's go to the hospital. The doctor will examine you, and we'll come right back. Then you can say your prayers, OK?"

"Ali-jun, you are a wonderful husband. I'll do as you say."

Nuri and the Senator helped her out to the hall. She took her red felt hat off the coatrack. She was about to put it on when her head hit the door frame, and the hat fell to the floor. The Senator commanded, "Frieda, be careful."

Her head fell back against the Senator's arm. Her jaw dropped slowly, and her mouth hung open. The Senator shouted, "Dear God, take her to the emergency room right away. Frieda is lost. Help me!"

Shariat ran over, took Madame in his arms, and carried her to the floor near the pantry. He put his head down by Madame's and cried. When Badri Khanom came in, he asked her to take the Senator away. Then he held a mirror in front of Madame's mouth. A few moments later he shook his head, put his hand inside Madame's mouth, and took out her dentures. He touched her Allah necklace, but did not take it off. He took off her gold bracelet and covered her with a white chador. He gave the dentures and the bracelet to Nuri and asked, "Where does she keep her loofah and soap?"

"Why?"

"We have to prepare her bath kit for the mortuary."

Nuri glanced at the Senator's stunned face. As Shariat repeated, "God is great," Badri Khanom and Aunt Moluk shrieked.

Before noon, a coffin was brought from the mosque. The relatives were sniffling in the garden, and the Senator could be heard crying in the first-floor hall. Shariat went into the garden and asked why the mosque had not given the relatives a chance to prepare themselves. He ran back to the hall and told the Senator, "Hajj-Agha, you go into the study and rest a bit. Leave everything to Nuri and me."

The Senator looked angry but said nothing. His face was red and splotchy. Shariat backed away and went to the verandah. Akhund

Shahsavari, the Friday prayer leader, walked ahead of the men carrying the coffin. He was tall, had a goatee, and wore a white turban. He kept saying, "Farideh, Farideh, Farideh." He asked Shariat, "Am I right, Hajji? Is the departed one's name Farideh?"

Shariat looked at the relatives and said softly, "No, Hajj-Agha, her name is Frieda Almstead."

"Oh! So she is a foreigner. Why didn't you tell us before we came all this way? My knees are no longer like a few years ago. My joints are killing me. I am not ungrateful, but what's the use of life like this? Imagine not being able to bend your knees even as much as a finger joint. I have to stop and rest every few steps."

Shariat said hurriedly, "Everyone in the neighborhood knows she is a foreigner. What does that have to do with taking her body to the mosque?"

"Hajj-Agha, I didn't expect you to say this. You want us to take a Christian corpse to a mosque? It's unclean, Hajj-Agha."

Shariat asked, "What do you mean it's unclean? Two years ago Madame became a Muslim in your own presence. She gave half of her belongings to Saint Ma'sumeh. Besides, isn't a Muslim corpse unclean? It still gets carried honorably to the mosque. A corpse is a corpse regardless of its religion."

Akhund Shahsavari lowered his head and said, "No, you did not understand your servant. We have our own customs and rituals that we must safeguard against foreign contamination. Call the Coroner's Office, ask them for the address of the Armenian cemetery, and take Madame Farideh there. I promise Madame Farideh's soul will be much happier. They have their own more elaborate rituals. This is the truth. I have seen with my own eyes how they sing over the corpse. It makes your hair stand on end. You imagine a chorus of angels is opening a path in heaven." As if awakening from a terrible dream, he blinked a few times.

The Senator shouted, "If you are not going to accept the corpse, fine. Why do you insult a respectable lady?"

The *akhund* shrugged and said, "Hajj-Agha, no one has insulted her. I just said that we don't have the right to take the corpse to the mosque. The permission has to be issued by the *comité*."

Shariat addressed the Senator, "Don't sully yourself unnecessarily. No need to argue. Ayatollah Musavi has promised to bury Madame beside the shrine of Saint Ma'sumeh in Qom. You rest a bit in your room, and I'll arrange for the trip to Qom."

The *akhund* said, "I don't think Ayatollah Musavi will give you permission." Turning to the relatives, he said, "Even if he does, Qom's soil does not accept foreigners."

The Senator asked, "Why not take her to our own private plot in Shabdol Azim?"

Shariat accompanied the *akhund* to the garden gate and returned to the hall. He seemed to have recovered his confidence. He told the Senator, "Let me tell you one word. There is a plan to level Shabdol Azim and run a road through it. No burials are allowed there anymore, not even private ones. Don't you see how the country has changed? They bury everyone in Behesht-e Zahra. Madame's blood is not redder than anyone else's. It'll be an honor if we can get permission to bury her there."

The Senator grumbled, "What honor is there in being stuck like a sardine in a grave next to a bunch of other people?"

"You don't want us to take Madame to Behesht-e Zahra? OK. But they won't let us bury her in the private plot. There's only one possibility left, and that's to take her to Qom. That's all." He said in a more gentle tone, "Please believe that I say this out of devotion to you and Madame. I contacted Ayatollah Musavi half an hour ago. He sent his greetings to you. He especially asked to thank you for the new wing of the Qom hospital that was built with Madame's generous donation. The people of Qom are not ungrateful. If they find out that you have buried Madame in Shabdol Azim, they'll be offended and raise hell."

The Senator asked Shariat to order *khoresht-e bademjan* and *qeymeh* for the mourners' lunch. Shariat mumbled, "As you say. But if you permit, we have also to think about the corpse. I mean no offense. What if we bury Madame in the shrine of Saint Ma'sumeh. What's wrong with such a beautiful and pure place?"

"The only thing wrong with it is that we have to beg and plead and may not even then get permission to bury her there."

Shariat blew his nose. "Let's get to Qom, you'll see how they will carry her body with their own hands. How many people do you know in this country who have renounced their own religion, spent forty years living in a strange country, and donated all their money to the bare-bottomed people of Qom? Huh? We have about an hour before the bus gets here. We'll put the coffin on the roof of the bus and take it to Qom with proper ritual and respect. You'll see how they will greet us."

The Senator seemed shattered. He held his head in his hands and looked toward Nuri, "What do you say?"

Shariat answered for Nuri. "Nothing. Ayatollah Musavi himself will say the prayer for the dead, and we'll bury her near the shrine."

"Eh, you are talking again?" The Senator asked Nuri, "Why don't you say anything?"

"It's your decision."

"You can't think of anything else?"

Nuri thought of Ali the Mechanic, whom he was supposed to meet tomorrow to talk about his plans to flee through Turkey, but he was afraid to mention the smuggler's name in front of the Senator. The phone began to ring. The Senator mumbled, "That will be Zuzu from America."

Aunt Moluk picked up the phone. All the relatives stared at her, which made her nervous. She stuttered, "Thank God . . . we are well. How is Mr. Barney? Please thank him for the cassettes. Many thanks. . . . How are you? Are you OK? Are you happy? Are you healthy? . . . Madame? . . . Well, all in all she is fine . . . We have to keep an eye on her. . . . " She put her palm on the receiver and looked at the Senator and Nuri. Their sad expressions made her turn to Badri Khanom. She said in a muffled voice, "She wants to speak to Madame. What should I tell her?"

"Tell her she's not feeling well. She can't come to the phone."

Aunt Moluk repeated this, then looked at Badri Khanom worriedly and said, "She says she has to talk to Madame herself. She wants us to take the phone to her room."

Badri Khanom thought things over and said, "Tell her she has a cold." She paused. "No, tell her that there was a draft last night, and she has become stiff as a board. She doesn't feel like talking to anyone."

Aunt Moluk relayed this to Maman Zuzu. She covered the receiver again and said, "She says, 'What nonsense! No one gets stiff as a board because of a draft. Besides, what need is there for her to move? Why don't you put the receiver to her ear?'"

Badri Khanom said, "What patience you have! Tell her it isn't like the old times when you could plug the phone in any room. Second, you have to feel up to talking on the phone. Madame isn't feeling well. She is in a coma. . . . "

She winked at Aunt Moluk and looked pleased with herself. Aunt Moluk threw hesitant glances at the other relatives. No one said anything. She spoke into the receiver and repeated Badri Khanom's words. She put her palm on the receiver and told Badri Khanom testily, "She asks how high her fever is."

Badri Khanom shrugged. This time the Senator said, "Father dear, what has made her think of Madame's temperature? Tell her, 'Madame is not an American doll that we should put a thermometer in her mouth every five minutes! How should we know what her temperature is?' Tell her not to worry. Madame's body is too cold for us to think about a fever."

Aunt Moluk was talking to Maman Zuzu, but suddenly stopped. From Aunt Moluk's dazed look, Nuri realized that Maman Zuzu had deduced Madame's death. Aunt Moluk passed the receiver to Nuri and began crying.

Nuri wanted to put the Senator on the phone, but one look dissuaded him. Maman Zuzu seemed to have accepted Madame's death. She cried for a few moments, but when Nuri began talking about Madame's burial arrangements, she stopped. He heard her blow her nose. She said that the only solution seemed to be to bury Madame in the Armenian cemetery.

By the time the bus arrived, the Senator had resigned himself to taking the body to Qom. He followed Amiz Abbas into the bus and sat in the rear. Nuri helped Shariat and three neighbors tie the coffin onto the luggage rack. He waited for everyone to board, counting to make sure no one had been left behind.

They drove through streets congested with cars, bicycles, and carts. Rusty wrecks lined the road all the way to Qom. In front of Ayatollah

Musavi's old house, a few armed revolutionary guards stood talking to one another. The bus had not yet come to a full stop when Shariat jumped down and ran to the guards. He whispered a few words to one of them. One guard examined Shariat closely, nodded his head, and led him into the house.

Not more than fifteen minutes later Shariat came out, his hands longer than his feet. He addressed the Senator, "In a word, Madame's burial is going to cost three hundred thousand tumans. The ayatollah says Mr. Namazi's sister paid five hundred thousand tumans for her brother's burial, although he had dedicated his life to charities in Qom. Because Madame has drunk the salty water of this country for forty years and became a Muslim, they will charge only three hundred thousand."

Badri Khanom began fanning herself. She shouted, "May your bodies be carried away by corpse washers, oh shameless ones! How quickly you forget Madame's donations of land and money! Fine. The Senator has three burial plots, each more beautiful than the other. Why should he pay three hundred thousand tumans to bury Madame in a godforsaken place far away from her relatives?"

Hajj Mohammad Taghi Jazaeri, the ayatollah's old representative, came up to the bus. "Please convey my greetings to the Senator." He was thin and wore a khaki suit and a collarless white shirt. Leaning on his cane, he climbed onto the bus. He ran his small black eyes over the passengers. When he spotted the Senator, he said, "In Islam, it is not forbidden to have money and property. There are different forms of corruption. Anyone might fall prey to Satan and waste the money that God has given him for the poor and the dispossessed. Human beings are allowed to make mistakes. But his Excellency the Senator is different from those who send their money to foreign bank accounts for personal use." He scowled at Badri Khanom because her chador had slipped from her head. Then he turned to the Senator again. "I offer my condolences to you and your entire family for the loss of Madame. I pray to God for health and long life for all of you. Believe me, we all are in mourning. Qom mourns. Iran mourns. If the laws permitted us, I would have issued the burial permission this very instant. I have the honor of being the ayatollah's representative, and in that capacity I am most ashamed to say that we cannot allow the departed one's burial in the shrine. Instead, I promise that for three hundred thousand tumans, we will find a delightful spot farther away from the shrine area."

Badri Khanom pulled up her chador and turned her back to him. "You are now riding your donkey and can be disrespectful to Madame's body, but this world too has an owner. There is someone up there who will ask you for an accounting and mete out to you what you deserve." She addressed Shariat. "What are you waiting for? Let's go."

The local residents were beginning to gather around the bus. One of the *bazaaris* asked, "Where are you going?"

Badri Khanom stuck her head out of the window and shouted, "Ask this agha who says we have to put three hundred thousand tumans in the palm of the ayatollah to get permission to bury a Muslim woman. Madame's body has been sitting for four hours, and no one will accept it. She donated everything she owned to Qomis. Now her husband has to pay out of his pocket to receive permission to bury her. What wonderful sense of honor you Qomis have!"

Shariat shouted, "I swear by Saint Abbas that no one has done as much for Qom as Madame!"

One of the *bazaaris* said, "We'll collect the money from the bazaar right now. We won't let you take the body from Qom. She is a blessing to Qom."

Badri Khanom said, "Even if you collect fifty million, we won't keep her here. You Qomis have no honor. You don't deserve it. You just know how to wrap two meters of cloth around someone's head, call him 'ayatollah,' and watch him ride herd on you. From now on you'll just have to dream of a selfless, honorable, pure, and dedicated woman like Madame."

They returned to Dezashib around eight in the evening. Drops of rain pelted the roof of the bus. Shariat was afraid that the water would seep into the coffin. Badri Khanom reassured him, "Cool rain is good for the corpse. It will prevent it from rotting."

The bus stopped in front of the mosque to leave the corpse there overnight. The mosque superintendent came out and looked at Shariat through narrowed eyes and said, "Hajj-Agha, do you know that the soil of the mosque does not accept a foreigner's corpse? It has been said: 'Two of a kind will fly together, a pigeon with a pigeon, a goose with a goose.' Take Madame where she belongs. Take her where her soul will not suffer. Let me go in before I catch my death in this wind."

Shariat sat beside the driver and quietly stared out the windshield.

They put the coffin on a rug near the verandah. Shariat took a wad of banknotes from the pocket of his robe, counted out some, and handed them to the bus driver. He stood in the rain until the driver left through the garden gate, then he took the Senator by the arm and led him up to the study.

After Shariat and the Senator went upstairs, Ladan sat tailor style beside Nuri in front of Madame's coffin. She made her skirt rustle to draw Nuri's attention. Ladan had always had modest ambitions. She didn't ask for much, nor did she go beyond certain self-imposed limits. Perhaps at that moment she felt more sorry for Nuri than for herself. Despite all this, Nuri had a sudden urge to tease her, to tell her that Madame's body could begin to move of its own accord. He wanted to talk to her in the secret language of their childhood.

♦ ♦ ♦ The next morning Nuri noticed a broken branch of the apple tree drooping to the edge of the stone pool. All night long he had heard murmurs he thought came from the relatives who had gathered in the house, but now the house seemed strangely quiet.

He went to the pantry, looked at himself in the glass door of a cabinet, and straightened his hair. There was no time to shave. He climbed the stairs to find the Senator. On his way, he ran into strangers rifling through drawers. Two people sat in front of the TV watching a video. He felt out of place.

He listened to the Senator's muffled voice on the telephone. Badri Khanom was issuing orders to Amiz Hosein and Dr. Jannati. "Call the Senator's relatives and friends and tell them to come here as soon as possible for the funeral." Amiz Abbas could be heard dictating the death announcement. Badri Khanom said, "Agha-jan, first let's find a way to bury the corpse. We can deal with the newspaper announcement later. We don't even know where we are going to bury her."

"Something has to be done anyway. If permission to bury is not issued soon, the corpse will begin to smell in this hot weather." Amiz Abbas paused. "Badri Khanom, had Madame herself been here, what would she have said? I remember once we were sitting in the Raso Bar. I don't know why I felt warm and was fanning myself. She put her hand on mine and said, 'Will you mind if I put my unclean hand on yours? It's cool.' I said, 'I would be honored, Fräulein Frieda. Why should you say such a thing? If Islam forbade the touch of unbelievers, it was to prevent Muslims from coming into contact with foreign microbes and bringing back a thousand diseases to the Arabs. But we live in a different world. With all these medical advances, no one pays any attention to such edicts.' She said, 'Amiz Abbas, I think it's preferable to be an untouchable than a stranger.'"

Shariat and Vaziri came back from yet another disappointing visit to the mosque. Badri Khanom washed her hands in the stone pool and addressed Amiz Abbas loudly enough for everyone to hear. "They waste their time with a bunch of brainless, uneducated, and strict believers. We have to do something about this smell."

She poured disinfectant from a plastic bottle into a watering can and gave it to Vaziri to sprinkle around the coffin. Nuri and Vaziri each took one end of the rug on which the coffin lay and carried it to the third floor. This worked like a magnet, drawing the relatives with it. The air conditioner on the third floor didn't work. The women in their black chadors sat on the landing like a bunch of ravens and argued about where to bury Madame. Were Iran a normal country like any other, a simple burial like this wouldn't have created such problems.

Around dusk, the third-floor balcony began to smell like the bottom of a pool after it has been drained. Aunt Moluk called the Coroner's Office, but no one answered. Shuri Khanom asked, "Is the coroner's an ordinary office? Dying doesn't follow a set schedule."

Food arrived. The relatives sat quietly in the dark dining room, but didn't touch the food. Nuri and Ladan sat in the first-floor hall and looked at the garden. Ladan rested her chin in her palm and said, "Mamakh, what should we do about the corpse?"

"I'll call Ali the Mechanic. Maybe he can help."

"Who's Ali the Mechanic?"

"The person who is going to smuggle me out of Iran."

Ladan grabbed his wrist. "You're leaving?"

Nuri blurted out, "Did you imagine I would stay here after Mumzie's gone?"

Ladan said nothing. Nuri could not stand her gaze. He rose and dialed Ali the Mechanic's number. Ali answered and listened to Nuri intently. He said in a compassionate tone that he would come in an ambulance just before daybreak. There was less chance of running into revolutionary guards that early in the morning. He asked Nuri to keep everything to himself and make sure no one else came along. If the revolutionary guards found out, Ali and Nuri would be executed.

Ladan couldn't believe that Nuri wouldn't take her to the Armenian cemetery for the burial. She begged, "Nuri-jun, I want to come with you. Please take me."

"I can't."

"Nuri-jun, how can you leave me in this house?" She began to cry.

Nuri put an arm around her and kissed her on the cheek. He picked three of Madame's red roses and threw them into the stone pool. He sat by the edge of the pool and watched them float on the water. "If I could, I would take you, but I have no choice. I have to follow Ali the Mechanic's orders."

Ladan walked toward the first-floor hall. Nuri followed her. She said, "Look, Nuri, I know what you're going to say, but I'm not the type to emigrate." She lowered her head. "If you go, your place will be empty in the house. It will become frightening for me. A handful of memories I have to change every day in order to keep myself alive." She opened her arms wide and hugged Nuri. She rested her cheek on his shoulder and said, "You are my good brother. You are my protector. Otherwise, I would not complain so much about your absence."

Nuri felt her tears on his shoulder.

. . . 16 . . .

When Nuri woke, it was still dark, but he had no idea what time it was. He decided to go up to Madame's room. Maybe she was merely pretending to be dead.

The coffin lay on the bed, and the room smelled of camphor and another horrible odor. He did not linger long.

He shaved, took a bath, and dressed, making an effort to return to normal life.

Shariat, who had been spending every night at the house, was nowhere in sight. Badri Khanom and Aunt Moluk had stayed to keep Ladan company. He remembered his conversation with Ladan, her pleading to be taken to the Armenian cemetery. Maybe she was afraid of being left alone with Shariat. She was probably in no mood to watch the relatives wandering from room to room, touching Madame's belongings and arguing about their right of ownership. He found no trace of Ladan and wondered where she was sleeping.

Ali the Mechanic was not due for another fifteen minutes, but Nuri waited by the garden door. He was anxious to take Madame's body to the Armenian cemetery and bury her according to her own wish under a tree whose blossoms would cover her grave like Omar Khayyam's. Madame had thought of Neyshabur as the quintessence of Iran and claimed that no other place drew her to Iran and Iranians as Omar Khayyam's city did.

Instead of the ambulance, he heard a horse. He opened the door slightly and saw an ordinary horse-drawn cart, covered with black tarpaulin. The driver seemed to be dozing in his seat. He wore a rain-soaked poncho. Only the dark circles around his mouth were visible under the wide brim of his black hat. Ali the Mechanic sat next to him. When he saw Nuri, he raised a hurricane lamp and asked, "Master, is that you?"

363

"Weren't you supposed to bring an ambulance?"

He jumped down, still holding the lamp. "Master, where could I find an ambulance at this time of night? I had to make a thousand promises in order to borrow this cart from the Armenian cemetery. You have been away and don't know how things are these days." He ran a hand over the horse's mane. "If I were you, I wouldn't have come back. What's happening here that you leave a nice place like that?" He shook his head and introduced Nuri to the driver. "Vahaness is at your service. He will do anything you ask. I am not kidding. On my mother's grave, he'll do anything you ask."

In the light of the hurricane lamp, the protuberances of Vahaness's cheeks made him look like a mummy. He had glazed blue eyes and narrow eyebrows, and a light brown stubble covered his face. Nuri nodded at him. "Thank you."

"He will take the corpse to the Armenian cemetery without anyone finding out and bothering you." Ali whispered, "I have to go back to Tehran. I can't come with you. If you run into revolutionary guards, don't say anything. Let Vahaness deal with them. This godforsaken rain doesn't end. It's washed everything away. I bet in two weeks the walls inside the houses will be soaked too." He handed the lamp to Nuri. "It's only an hour to Jajrud. If you don't hurry, you might run into revolutionary guards. Keep a few tumans in your pocket." He laughed halfheartedly. "The guards' hands have glue on them. Banknotes stick to them for good." He put his cheek against the horse's neck. "Let's go. Are you feeling OK? You will be OK? Are you sure?" Nuri nodded. "OK, where is the body?"

They brought the coffin down quietly from the third floor, pausing in the first-floor hall to catch their breath. Nuri felt like a body snatcher. He sensed Ladan near him. He asked in a hushed voice, "Is that you, Ladan?"

"Yes."

She was crying softly. He said, "Don't worry. The rest is easy. We'll take the body and come back before noon. Everything is under control."

Ladan squeezed Nuri's arm. "Mamakh, may I sacrifice myself for you." She paused. " . . . Nuri-jun, take me with you."

"I don't mind, but Ali the Mechanic won't let me."

Ali the Mechanic grumbled, "Master, we have no more than five minutes. I told you from the beginning that no one is to find out. Either we leave quietly in five minutes, or the deal is off."

Ladan didn't protest. She wiped her hands on her skirt, followed them, and watched them load the coffin onto the cart. Nuri turned to her and said, "I'll be back soon. Don't worry."

He climbed in and sat by the coffin near sacks of vegetables. The cart began to move, and Nuri saw Ladan's figure grow smaller and then disappear behind the trees in the alley.

It took them forty-five minutes to reach the open fields. The rain had finally stopped. The wheels creaked and wobbled. The Gardanak Pass and the dotted hills of Jajrud seemed far away. Except for two vultures circling overhead, there was no sign of life. If something happened to them, who would come to their rescue? Vahaness craned his neck and said a few words about the weather. Nuri stayed quiet, wanting to be left alone. Twenty minutes later Vahaness stopped the cart by the side of the road, jumped down, and dusted himself off. He looked at the rein mark on his palm and rubbed it against his pants. He asked, "Why don't you talk?"

"What should I say?"

"You should sit up front with me."

"What's wrong with where I'm sitting?"

Vahaness leaned his elbow on the cart and asked, "Are you afraid of me?"

"You?"

"I could cut your head off and no one would know." He laughed and gestured, "Come sit with me."

Nuri shrugged. Vahaness took Nuri's hesitation for a no and walked to the front. Nuri called, "When will we get there?"

"In half an hour, we will hand over the body to the archbishop. Do you know the archbishop, Hakup Keshishian?"

"No."

Vahaness tilted his head. "He likes pickled cucumbers and eggplants. He is a vegetarian." He imitated chewing on hay. "Like sheep." When Nuri said nothing, he continued. "He gets sick if you put meat in front of him. He says meat is good for wolves, not human beings. He makes a great arrak that burns all the way down to your stomach." He held up a plastic bottle. "This is not as good as Hakup Keshishian's arrak, but it will warm you. Would you like some? Help yourself."

He drank from the bottle, put the cap back on, and threw it to Nuri. Nuri caught it in midair. "Bravo!" He swung the whip above his head. They took off. "We have to go faster. You should sit beside me. What are you afraid of? Death? Like everything else in life, death has two faces. You can look at it two different ways. Do you know why people are afraid of dying? Because most of them want to see things from one angle only. They think when they die, life will have no meaning. Or when they are alive, they are completely separated from the dead. For me, dying is a kind of living." His cheeks were flushed, and his eyes glistened with a devilish delight. "You aren't afraid of me, right?"

"Didn't you say there is no fear in dying?"

"That's right, but you don't know where I'm taking you."

He stopped his cart in front of an old stone church. Two priests with tall hats like black chimneys came running to the cart. They held up the hems of their robes. Vahaness gestured toward the rear, and they unloaded the coffin.

Church bells punctuated the moment. Groups of Armenians arrived, wearing peasant clothes. They carried Madame's coffin to the altar and removed the lid. The organ played a sad tune. The semidark interior of the church was permeated with the smell of wax and incense. The weak lantern light made Madame's body resemble the Virgin of Solitude. Her hands were clasped around her Allah and the cross that had been placed on her chest. Her face was heavily made up, and she was dressed in black.

In the line of mourners walking in front of the casket, an old woman's lips began to move in a silent prayer. A young girl with braided hair tied in a ribbon placed a spray of sweetbriar in the coffin. The organ music rose up and carried Nuri to a space of inner loneliness. Through his tears, he stared at the mourners. The organ music became softer and reminded him of a verse Madame had taught him, "Remember the extinguished candle, remember!"

The only other funeral he had attended was with Madame in the Church of the Sacred Heart. He couldn't believe the peaceful look of the deceased, who was surrounded by dahlias and begonias. In that setting, death appeared beautiful, like an artificial flower. It was the opposite of the images Muslims had of the dead—skeletons, stripped of all adornment, rising from their graves on the Day of Judgment and staring into a scorching sun.

The relatives were probably gathered around the stone pool, awaiting his return. They would ask him in detail about the funeral. Nuri wanted to leave the church as quickly as possible, but instead of going home, he had an urge to visit Amirabad and the university. Not that he had any desire to see Buki or Soraya or anyone else. Even if he ran into them, he wouldn't have much to say. He wanted only to go to a familiar spot from his past.

He signed the memorial book and headed back to Tajrish.

♦ ♦ ♦ With Madame gone, he felt strangely distanced from daily life in the Dezashibi house. As in his earlier years, he had a desire to wander around. He would leave the house late at night and walk to the Tajrish Bridge. He quickly got used to the prayers that were broadcast on loudspeakers.

Like a devoted friend, Ali the Mechanic took care of all the necessary travel documents. He called Nuri every day or dropped by the house. He asked about Madame's past and promised to take Nuri back to the Armenian cemetery. "Master, don't tell anyone. If the revolutionary guards find out, they'll bulldoze the church and kill the priest and the archbishop. They don't respect priest or rabbi. They don't even fear God."

Nuri listened in a daze, silently consenting to keep the whereabouts of the cemetery a secret, but the relatives would not leave him alone. When he told them about Madame's funeral, their eyes grew wide. Badri Khanom remembered that years before the revolution she had seen an Armenian cemetery on the way to either the Imamzadeh Davoud or Meygun. If the names of cities and roads had not changed, she would have remembered the exact location. She would have hired a bus and taken everyone there. The others tried to locate the cemetery on an old map. When they didn't succeed, they turned their attention to Amiz Abbas's stories of Vienna. They regretted not having appreciated Madame enough when she was alive. Now they had to spend many years trying to find her grave.

As promised, one late afternoon Ali the Mechanic took Nuri on his motorcycle to the Armenian cemetery. Madame's grave was covered with damp brown dirt. No blossoms decorated it. Nuri took off his jacket and threw it over his shoulder. He had finally attained what he had always longed for. He felt deeply connected to Madame.

He remembered his trip to New York. Before entering the customs area of the Mehrabad Airport, he had felt thirsty. Shuri Khanom had given him a box of chocolates and a package of cotton candy and said, "Eat this now. Drinks are free on the plane. They'll give you whatever you want." At that very moment, Madame had walked through the revolving door. She wore a pink overcoat and held a white umbrella under her arm. She smiled and grabbed Nuri's hand so enthusiastically that the chocolates and cotton candy fell to the ground. Madame paid no attention. She brought her face closer to Nuri, and he kissed her. "Thank you, my dearrr. There is no time left for me to teach Your Excellency the secret of attaining anything your heart desires."

Nuri laughed and said, "Mumzie, I have got all my wishes right now."

"How easily Your Excellency sells his wishes!"

He hugged Madame and kissed her again. The Senator smiled and asked, "What's going on here? What's all this craziness?"

Madame seemed to be with him wherever he went.

The Senator appeared to be fine. The only change in his behavior was that he no longer went into the bedroom he had shared with Madame. He slept on the sofa in the study. Shariat would bring his food there and prevent visitors from disturbing him. When the Senator ran into Nuri in the corridor, he would say a few hurried words and return to the study. He would spend hours listening to the news on BBC and Radio Israel. He would cross his legs like Madame, hold her embroidery bag, and fondle it. Sometimes he would call Ladan, who always seemed to be in the storage room. She looked twenty years older, not because of the wrinkles that had appeared around her eyes, but rather because of the decisive manner in which she handled her encounters with Shariat. Shariat listened to her and responded to her orders with, "Absolutely. Absolutely."

When she ran into Nuri, she would smile and walk past him quickly. Only on certain occasions, when no one was around, she would stare at him, as if wanting to surmise his inner thoughts. Maman Zuzu was still worried that Shariat might be bothering her. She asked why Nuri didn't make arrangements to bring Ladan and the Senator to America.

He sat beside Madame's grave, hugging his knees. Once again he felt as if Madame were standing near him. Had it not been for Ali the Mechanic's voice, he would probably have remained in a daze. Ali the Mechanic said, "Master, let's go. It's getting dark."

Nuri got on the motorcycle. They said nothing to each other on the way back to the Dezashibi house.

◆ ◆ ◆ The day after his visit to the cemetery, Nuri saw Shariat dragging the brass bed into the third-floor corridor. Ladan came out of the storage room and called out Shariat's name.

Shariat did not respond. Nuri asked, "Ladan, why do you shout?"

Ladan said, "What do you mean? We have to clean these rooms. You just keep disappearing. This house is a mess. No one has swept here for a month." She walked closer to Nuri and said, "When did you come back last night?" She struck a pose that made her look like an older woman. "Is everything OK?"

"What do you mean?"

"Is her grave still there?"

She didn't mention Madame's name. Nuri replied. "Of course. Did you think it would have moved?"

"No, Mamakh. I just wanted to see if you found a respectable place for her."

Nuri nodded. "I bet next spring the Armenians will hold a memorial ceremony for her with all sorts of music, the kind Muslims don't know anything about."

"The way she wanted?"

"Exactly."

Nuri was not sure how much Madame would have liked the Armenian cemetery, especially after her conversion to Islam, but Ladan suddenly looked younger and kissed him on the cheek. "Thank you, Mamakh." She pulled back and asked, "Why is your face so hot? Do you have a fever?" Nuri didn't have a fever. Ladan said, "One day we'll go together to her grave, OK?"

"I won't do that. Why should we create trouble for ourselves?"

"What trouble?"

"If the revolutionary guards find out an Austrian woman was buried without legal permission, they'll bury us alive. . . . Imagine that Madame never existed and that you have only dreamed of the Armenian cemetery. Forget it."

Ladan wiped tears from her face. She said, "I know. I'll never mention it."

Badri Khanom's voice rose. "Nuri-jan, if you ask me, Madame became a Muslim to please you. She always did things for other people. Once, when we went to the bazaar, she took me through winding alleys to a house with a stinking garden pool. A decrepit, blind old woman lay by the pool. When she heard Madame's footsteps, she raised her head and said in a strange voice, 'Greetings.' I was stunned and asked Madame, 'Madame, why have we come here?' She bit her lip, indicating I should not talk. I saw with my own eyes how she took a wad of ten-tuman notes and put it under the old woman's mattress. Then we left. See, that's what you call a generous person. May God bless her soul. For her, money was like desert sand. It had no value. So what if she was a Christian? What's it to us? It's not as if they're putting us in her grave. On the Day of Judgment, she will have to account for her own deeds. In my opinion, she is worth more than a hundred of these people who call themselves Muslims."

Ladan asked Nuri quietly, "Mamakh, when are you leaving for New York?"

Nuri was surprised at how well she read his thoughts. "I don't know. One of these days. Do you want to come with me?" Ladan shook her head. Nuri asked, "What are you going to do?"

"I have a lot to do."

"You've always had a lot to do."

Ladan lowered her head. "It's OK. I'll keep busy. Everyone has to keep busy somehow."

"If I stay here myself, I'll rot. You have to accept that. I wish we could be in New York right now. In New York, you can be yourself. You probably think, 'Nuri is just inviting me along to make me happy.' You are wrong. We have always been together. The year I was in America, I saw myself as a traveler. I was always waiting to pack my bags and come back to be with you. But now that I am ready to leave again, I tell myself, 'If I leave, it'll be forever.' No point in coming back. A person who is attached only to the past is no longer free. He can't like anything else."

"Just look after yourself. I'll take care of Grandpa."

"I wish we could take Grandpa to New York."

Ladan shifted her weight and looked at Nuri, barely hiding her frustration. She said, "Don't think about it, Mamakh. It doesn't matter."

"You'll be lonely."

"I feel Mumzie is still here."

"I hope you're not going crazy."

"I don't know. In this house, you can never be alone."

Nuri had only one more matter to discuss with her, but it was too difficult to broach. He gathered from Ladan's expression that she could no longer deny the reality of Shariat's demands. She seemed to have resigned herself to her fate. They parted without exchanging another word.

In their later encounters, they talked only about domestic matters, the possibility (which Ladan disliked) of putting the Senator in an old-age home, and the division of the storage-room goods. Nuri didn't want to take anything to America. He would place his share in the basement.

One day he was surprised by a note Ladan left on his dresser.

"This afternoon an American girl named Linda called and left a message that if you do not register at Saint Joseph's within a week, you will not receive a scholarship."

Scholarship? He didn't remember having applied for one. Did they even give them out to foreigners, especially Iranians? He felt an irresistible urge to call Linda. At first, he thought that his delay in calling her was just an example of the procrastination that always plagued him before a journey. For instance, he had planned to get an international driver's license, but he kept telling himself he had plenty of time left, even though

Ali the Mechanic phoned him every day about his imminent departure. Nuri called Maman Zuzu. She grilled him about his travel plans. "Nuri, quit lying to me. I believe you're planning something dangerous."

Nuri shouted, "What do you know about my plans? Why do you doubt my word?"

"I don't doubt your word. I doubt you. I know you very well. I know you'll do something crazy." Nuri heaved a deep sigh, but it had no effect on Maman Zuzu. "Nuri!"

"Huh?"

"We are past formalities. Listen to me. If you take one step without my permission, I swear by the Prophet I will never talk to you again. A decent human being doesn't lie to his own mother." After a pause she asked, "Did you hear what I said?"

Nuri answered mechanically, "Yes, I heard."

"So why don't you say something? You know how much I hate silence."

Nuri swore that his trip to America was legal. All his documents were ready. He was waiting only for Ali the Mechanic to obtain his visa. Maman Zuzu didn't believe him. She lectured him about the terrible consequences of lying. How could he trust a smuggler like Ali the Mechanic? Ali could cut his throat in the middle of the desert. Nuri laughed. "Ali the Mechanic is closer than a friend to me. I have borrowed half of my trip expenses from him without even a signature. Both of us are coming to America."

"Does he want to come too?"

"It seems. But don't tell anyone. Keep it to yourself."

Maman Zuzu reprimanded Nuri for borrowing money from Ali the Mechanic. She didn't seem to want to hang up. She gave him the lowdown on life in New York. She complained about Princess Bertha, who could barely see now. Maman Zuzu had to chauffeur her around every day. Barney had pawned his old guitar, and if he didn't come up with enough money by the end of the month, he would lose it. It had rained nonstop for three days. She was worried about the two jasmine plants she had bought from Woolworth's for Nuri. She had placed them by his bed close to the window, hoping that with enough sunlight they would blossom by the time he arrived. But they kept losing leaves. On Mr. Beaver's advice, she had taken the plants out to the front steps. Now she regretted it because jasmines are from the same family as gardenias and magnolias and do not like too much moisture. She didn't know what she would do if the rain didn't stop soon. She should have left the plants by Nuri's bed. This had kept her awake most of the night. Even when she dozed off, she dreamed of the Shahreza apartment the time when it had rained so much that water seeped in from everywhere. She woke up with a crick in her neck. She was thinking of going to the drugstore to buy herself a neck brace, but she thought it might be too expensive. "Everything's terribly expensive in New York. You can't buy even a piece of frozen fish for five dollars."

Nuri finally excused himself and said good-bye.

He was to leave on a bus for Tabriz at ten that night. Ali the Mechanic would meet him at a place called Sholeh Zagh near the Turkish border. They would have no documents on them in case they were stopped by revolutionary guards. He needed to get in touch with Linda, but he worried about what he would say to her. Maybe he had better write something and read it to her. But that would be even worse. He picked up the receiver and mistakenly dialed the Shokufeh Restaurant. After the first ring, Linda herself answered, "Hello . . . "

"Linda!"

"Yes. Who is this?"

"Can't you guess?

"Oh, Nuri, is that you? I'm glad you called. Did you get my message?"

"Why do you think I'm calling you?"

"Where are you? Are you calling from Iran?"

"Yes. What did your message mean?"

It turned out that Linda had registered Nuri in Saint Joseph's and paid his fees. She didn't say why she had done this without asking him. She spoke in a playful tone, as if discussing a trivial matter. Nuri grew anxious and blurted out, "What if I can't get there?"

"Norman, it's no problem. The money is not an issue. If I hadn't registered you, you wouldn't have been eligible for a scholarship."

"Linda, why did you do this? You shouldn't have . . . "

Linda laughed and insisted that he give her his flight number and time of arrival. He had no idea if he would be able to cross the border, but Linda's voice gave him a renewed sense of confidence. Linda said a few words about the Badamchis. "He's in bad shape. He doesn't speak to anyone."

"Who?"

"Mr. Mehdi Badamchi. He doesn't want to see a psychiatrist. He says he'll talk only to Manijeh Khanom, his wife, but she's in Iran."

"Why doesn't he call her?"

"He says Manijeh Khanom has to come here. He thinks Hitler has arrested her and is going to send her to a concentration camp. Look, Nuri, he just came in. Do you want to talk to him? Maybe you can understand what's bothering him."

He didn't feel like talking to Mr. Mehdi. He promised to call her soon and tell her his flight number. Linda grew animated. "Hey. All right. 'Meet Me in St. Louis,' Norman."

He hung up and called Ali the Mechanic, but didn't find him at home. He went to his room. It felt emptier than before. A warm breeze ruffled the lace curtain. He took his Samsonite suitcase leaning against the wall, but thought he didn't need to pack a bag for his trip. When Madame's image came to his mind, it didn't make him sad. He saw her performing at the Café Imperial, her hands lifted above her tilted head, wearing a long sleeveless silk dress and bright white shoes.

Streetlights cast shadows of leaves on the walls. The house was very quiet. The silence made him suspicious. He left his room and went downstairs.

Shariat and the Senator stood in the hall near the verandah. Ladan was behind them. Then the kitchen door opened and Black Najmeh, Vaziri, and Puran came into the hall. The Senator wore a blue-striped shirt whose tail stuck out of his olive-colored trousers. He must have dressed in a hurry. He pretended to ignore them. Ladan, Black Najmeh, and Vaziri stood on tiptoe as if trying to warn him of something. The Senator told Nuri, "So, you have made up your mind and want to flee tonight."

Nuri threw a quick glance in Ladan's direction and said nonchalantly, "I'm fleeing?" The Senator nodded. Nuri asked, "Who said I'm fleeing?"

The Senator looked toward Shariat, who kept his eyes lowered. Then he turned back to Nuri and said, "It seems you don't take good care of yourself. You must always be on guard. You should be very grateful to Mr. Shariat." Astonished, Nuri stared at the Senator. The Senator continued. "Are you surprised? You didn't expect me to ask you to thank Mr. Shariat. It's too bad you don't know how much you owe him. You can't thank him enough, but I know 'thank you' doesn't exist in your vocabulary. Even when someone saves your life, you don't show any gratitude. Correct me if I am wrong."

"Grandpa, what do you mean? Whom should I thank?"

"Now go ahead and thank Mr. Shariat. Hurry up. Go on."

Nuri asked, "Why?"

The Senator raised his eyebrows and, turning toward the others, said, "He asks why! Did you hear?" He took an envelope from Shariat. "Nuri, who has prevented you from going abroad that you make arrangements with a bunch of smugglers? Most of these smugglers are enemies of the revolution. They take advantage of idiots like you to ruin this country. Fortunately, there are responsible people who keep an eye on everything. Had it not been for Mr. Shariat, Your Excellency would have been in the Evin Prison right now. Do you know what it means to be in the Evin Prison? Go ask those who know." He addressed Shariat deferentially. "We are most indebted. We owe our safety to you. May God pay you back." Shariat kept his gaze down. The Senator addressed Nuri again. "He had to see people at the *comité*, act as your guarantor to obtain a legal passport and exit visa for you." He leafed through the documents he had taken from the envelope.

Nuri thought of Ali the Mechanic and worried that something had happened to him. The word *smuggler* reeked of executions. He blurted out, "Did you say smuggler? Which smuggler?"

The Senator asked, "Where do you find these characters? If you want to go somewhere, why don't you go to someone who is trustworthy? Did I stop you?"

Nuri said, "Which characters are you talking about?"

The Senator answered, "My door has always been open to you. Even after Mumzie's death, when I have no energy for anything else, I am always ready to see you. Why do you treat your grandfather like a stranger?"

"Grandpa, please tell me the truth. What has happened to Ali the Mechanic? I swear to God he is blameless. He has not taken even one sannar from me. He has lent me money." He approached Shariat, who stood motionless like a statue. Nuri tugged his robe. "You have to do something. Ali the Mechanic has done nothing wrong."

The Senator intervened. "What's this? You still don't know how to thank a person who has your best interest at heart?"

Nuri shouted, "Where is Ali the Mechanic?"

The Senator answered in a authoritative tone. "What's it to you where he is? We don't have time to waste on such silly things. Thanks to Shariat's generosity, all your documents are ready. Until tomorrow night, you will not take one step without my permission. Your ticket, passport, and visa are all in my hands." He shook the documents in front of Nuri. "Tomorrow night, we will put you on the plane, and you will go straight to New York. That's all. Be careful, or you won't go anywhere."

The Senator walked away like a ghost. Nuri wanted to follow him, but his feet didn't move.

He was supposed to leave at ten-thirty at night on an Air France flight to Paris. He followed the Senator's orders to the letter. He felt Madame's absence. As he walked through the rooms, he would suddenly recall an image of Madame and feel a void inside him. He listened intently for any unexpected sounds. Anger incited him to protest, but he was afraid to jeopardize his trip to New York.

He shut his door and set about packing. He found no traces of the old mementos among the jumble of things scattered around. He thought about traveling alone, free of all constraints. Ladan opened the door and walked in as if drawn there against her will. She sat in the chair next to the cupboard and wiped her tears with a handkerchief. She folded her hands on her lap and focused her gaze on Nuri. He thought that maybe the moment he had long awaited had finally arrived: Ladan would tell him about Shariat. But her silence finally forced him to say something in a fake devil-may-care tone. "At last you'll be rid of me."

Ladan played with the handkerchief in her lap and spoke haltingly. "Mamakh, do you know what's happened to Ali the Mechanic?"

Nuri was frightened. "What do you mean? You know I don't know anything."

Ladan said more calmly, "I'm sure you know, but don't want to talk about it."

Nuri stopped packing and approached Ladan. "No, I don't know anything. If you know, why don't you tell me?"

"Didn't you read in the newspaper about Ali the Mechanic's arrest and the execution of some smugglers?"

Nuri was stunned. "How do you know Ali the Mechanic was among the ones who were executed?"

"From his name that was printed in the newspaper." She suddenly grew angry and rose to leave. "We no longer live in our own house. This isn't our place. Can you live under the same roof with people who denounce an innocent person to the revolutionary guards? I can't. If I have stayed here this long, it's because I had to take care of a few things before starting a new life for myself."

Nuri felt confused. Was she about to leave the Senator and Shariat? Did she intend to lead a clandestine life with M. G. Shabkhiz? Now nothing could bridge the gap between them.

The Senator hadn't told anyone to come see Nuri off. Even Ladan did not come to the airport.

◆ ◆ ◆ Nuri stood outside the Shokufeh Restaurant with Linda and other students, awaiting the arrival of the Fourth of July parade. Drums could be heard in the distance. He rose on tiptoe, hoping to spot Maman Zuzu and Barney. Once again they had gone across the border into Canada.

He didn't know how to deal with Linda's reserve. Not that Linda didn't go out of her way to help him. On his first day back, she had sat with him in the public library and filled out his Social Security application and medical insurance forms. But she spent most of her time in the language lab with a Czech student named Rene whose wardrobe consisted of clothes reminiscent of the Prohibition era—glittering shirts that slithered over his corpulent body. The few times they ran into each other, Rene ignored Nuri, but Linda greeted him pleasantly. Nuri found out that

Rene planned to take Linda to San Francisco, where she would work in the advertising agency his father managed. His father had sent them two tickets. The only problem was Rene's fear of flying. At the very thought of boarding the plane, he would dig his fingers into Linda's arm and, with bulging eyes, beg to postpone their flight.

Nuri once asked Linda directly, "Aren't you supposed to go to San Francisco with Rene?"

"Rene makes a lot of plans, but he never carries through, and I'm left sitting in my room staring at the walls."

"What about me? I'm here. We can go somewhere together."

"You? You are so lost in your own world that I sometimes wonder if you're still living in Iran."

"Why do you say that?"

"You don't talk about anything but Madame's burial and the Armenian cemetery."

"I haven't called Tehran once."

Linda didn't seem convinced.

Nuri shouted, "Eight days, do you know what I mean? Not one or two days. Eight days Ali the Mechanic and I walked barefoot, hungry, and thirsty through snow-covered mountain passes to get to Turkey."

"OK. Why do you get so excited?"

"The minute we crossed the border into Turkey, Ali the Mechanic started dancing. He kept shouting, 'This is Turkey. This is Turkey.' He couldn't believe we were finally out of Iran. It didn't take two hours before hunger and thirst got the better of him. He imagined he was aboard a ship with a cargo of dried apricots and figs. He listened to the wind and said, 'Master, do you hear the creaking of the cart?' I said, 'No.' He replied, 'Listen carefully. Do you hear it?' He lost a lot of weight. I carried him into a cave to keep him warm. I took off his shoes. The stench almost made me throw up. Gangrene had turned his toes black. Oh, what a stench! He grabbed my hand and said, 'Master, when do we reach New York?' Do you understand? In the middle of a snowstorm he asks me, 'When do we reach New York?' What a crazy world this is! Instead of crying, you feel like laughing. Something was on the tip of his tongue, but he could not say it. All of a sudden his eyes rolled up, and he died in my arms. Kaput. Finito."

Whom did he think he was fooling? Linda had met him at the airport a week ago. He hadn't looked like a person who had fled through mountain passes. Nevertheless, she didn't challenge him. She talked about the Badamchis, who continued to argue over their land.

"Norman, you're Iranian like the Badamchis. Why are you so different from them? They drop by my place unannounced. They insist on giving me wall calendars, transistor radios, flashlights, and even bottles of aspirin."

"There are all sorts of people in any country."

The crowd grew more excited as the parade approached. The Badamchis came out of the restaurant. The older brother, Mr. Mehdi, bowed to Nuri and said, "Your Excellency Hushiar, please give me the honor of offering you an *akbar mashti* ice cream."

Nuri said, "No, thank you. How are you feeling?"

Mr. Mehdi twisted his lips and said, "Not bad. It's not important. Have you come to watch the parade?"

"Yes. I have enrolled in Saint Joseph's again."

"Congratulations. I wish you success. But I have to say I regret having come here."

"Why?"

"I don't make enough money to bring my wife and kids here. People talk behind my back and say that I have a comfortable life, sleep on a feather bed, and don't give a thought to my wife and children. Maybe they're right. Between you and me, I haven't been a good husband."

"Really?"

"Yes. I have treated my wife badly. Sometimes I wouldn't go home for three nights, or I would bring my friends home unannounced. If she said one word, I would curse and make her shut up. I would shout, 'You whore, why did you look at that man?' I hit her a couple of times. I swear to God, every time I shut my eyes, I remember those scenes." He sighed. "Well, Mr. Hushiar, the past is the past. You can't change what's done. There's no point saying, 'I regret this, I regret that.'"

"This sort of thing happens in everyone's life. I am sure by now Manijeh Khanom has forgotten all that."

Mr. Mehdi said in a louder voice, "No husband has done as much for his family as I have for Manijeh and my children. Why did I get this restaurant going? Only for Manijeh so that if something happened to me, she wouldn't have to turn to others for help. I haven't denied her anything. I have given her presents on a silver platter, taken her to Europe, and bought her the best clothes. I'll be honest. I have also hurt her. You know in these twenty-five years she has never complained about me. Her sisters sit around and try in vain to make her say things behind my back. She doesn't let anyone say one bad word about me. If someone did, she would disembowel him like a lion."

Linda called from a distance, "Don't you want to see the parade?"

Nuri answered, "Yes."

"Hurry up, then, and take your place up front."

Mr. Mehdi dusted his pants and said, "These Americans know how to have fun."

Linda shouted, "Norman, why are you taking so long?"

He ran back to the sidewalk, put his arm around Linda, and kissed her.

Howard Jones, the mayor of Samt, walked in front of a Walt Disney float, pounding the pavement with a long brass key to the city. Behind him a dragon wriggled on the float. As soon as a group of students approached it, the dragon would spew fire out of his mouth and scatter them. The sound of firecrackers could be heard behind the trees, and then sparkles of orange, blue, and purple would dot the sky.

Linda grumbled. "Norman, it's getting late. I don't think Barney and Maman Zuzu will come back from Niagara."

"Let's wait a bit more."

He suddenly remembered Maman Zuzu the night before her flight to New York. She had crouched on the kitchen floor, scrubbing the pipes under the sink. When Nuri came into the kitchen, she stopped and beckoned to him. "Come here, Son. Let me see you, Agha."

She continued to smile, although she was still grieving for Papa Javad. She addressed Nuri like an adult, rose to her feet unsteadily, and bowed to him. Speaking like a street thug, she said, "I want to go to New York to be rid of you."

He heard her voice echo in his head. "Nuri-jun, may I sacrifice myself for you."

A telephone rang persistently in the distance. It had to be the public telephone three doors down from the Shokufeh Restaurant. He ran and picked up the receiver. No one answered. He said hurriedly, "Hello, hello, hello."

The silence persisted. A few moments later the person at the other end hung up, leaving him with a sweet lingering memory. It was as if he were saying good-bye to someone for the last time—a melancholic, but peaceful good-bye.

The students were laughing and singing together. He felt a dreamy sadness tinged with an excitement that made him want to sing his own song, albeit out of tune. Linda called, "Norman, we have to go home."

"Shouldn't we wait?"

"It's too late. Let's go to my place. I'll make *sabzi polo* and *mahi* for you."

The main building of Saint Joseph's School rose up before him with all the foreign majesty that had so absorbed his attention a year ago.